WHAT MY BODY REMEMBERS

Also by the author

WHAT
MY
BODY
REMEMBERS

Agnete Friis

Translated from the Danish by Lindy Falk van Rooyen

Published by Soho Press, Inc.
853 Broadway
New York, NY 10003

Library of Congress Cataloging-in-Publication Data

Friis, Agnete, author.
Van Rooyen, Lindy Falk, translator.
What My Body Remembers / Agnete Friis
translated from the Danish by Lindy Falk van Rooyen.
Other titles: Blitz. English

ISBN 978-1-61695-602-8
eISBN 978-1-61695-603-5

1. Murder—Denmark—Fiction. 2. Mothers and sons—Fiction.
3. Post-traumatic stress disorder—Patients—Fiction.
4. Psychological fiction. I. Title
PT8177.16.R55 B5513 2017 839.813'8—dc23 2016044298

Interior design by Janine Agro, Soho Press, Inc.

Printed in the United States of America

10 9 8 7 6 5 4 3 2 1

"Can't you get him to shut up at night?"

Rosa came to stand next to me on the gallery and took out a cigarette. Her hair was platinum blonde, if one were kind enough to ignore the ten-centimeter band of liver-pâté roots on top. Her skin was pink and chronically pocked, a skin condition from half a life of alcohol and too much sun. Her color combination reminded me of Neapolitan ice cream melting in the sun; chocolate, vanilla, and strawberry. The cheap stuff they dished up at Bakkegården when it was time for a party.

"He's got nightmares. He can't help it," I said flatly.

We'd had this conversation hundreds of times before, practically word for word, but Rosa had no sympathy for social aberrations of this kind. Her life—as I had come to know it in the two years we'd lived in the apartment next door—was little more than an endless row of repetitions. Morning coffee with the husband at eight, shopping at Netto at ten, rye bread with meat and raw onions at twelve. Then, two hours on the sofa with an indefinite number of Kodimagnyl and Valium swimming in her blood. Cake, coffee, and TV at three. Dinner with the husband at six. Some kind of fried meat, potatoes, and cooked vegetables. Then more TV, more coffee, and a stack of smokes. Washing was done Monday. Lotto Wednesday and Saturday.

"It's not normal for a child his age," she went on.

I was inclined to agree, but didn't say so out loud. Alex's nightmares were undiluted terror and, according to Doctor Erhardsen, most common amongst preschool kids. Alex was eleven, almost twelve.

"And what do you suggest I do about it?"

Rosa wrinkled her nose and looked away.

"He keeps us up, for Christ's sake. And Jens has to be fresh for work in the mornings." Her voice was tobacco-rough, no trace of a smile. "If your son were a dog, we would've had the super put him down."

Dry laughter.

The walls of our concrete apartment complex were thin as eggshells; after eleven, anything going on next door always felt like a blatant lack of consideration.

Rosa coughed, smacked her chest with a flat hand and sighed dramatically.

"Have you been to see Erhardsen about that?"

She nodded.

"It's the lungs. I've got to keep taking the pills."

"That's not what I meant," I said, clapping her on the shoulder. "I meant that thing you've got stuck up your ass. It's been there for quite a while."

"Shut the fuck up!"

She choked a smile, and I turned my back to fish a hand-rolled smoke out of my jeans pocket. I kept them in an old King's pack, so they smelled traitorously like the real thing, but tasted all wrong. When I needed nicotine, I had to smoke three of the hand-rolled before I could feel the same lull in my bones that a single King's could deliver. But it was still cheaper, and it was seldom that I smoked for the sake of the nicotine. The smokes were a habit; something to do with my hands, an excuse to stand on the gallery and look out over the other apartment blocks. We all need something to apply ourselves to. Even the apes at the zoo are made to pick sunflower seeds out of coconuts with a stick so they can sense the meaning of life. When we went to see the apes for Alex's seventh birthday, the zookeeper was kind enough to explain this to us. The habitual activity with the seeds makes the chimps happy, he said. They're also fond of smashing cardboard boxes, snapping twigs, and throwing shit at the other apes. Actually, I was envious of them. It seemed like a much more meaningful occupation than the kind of crap those idiots from Welfare had me doing.

The wind was blowing from the east today, bringing the smell of exhaust fumes and warm asphalt from the parking lot along with it. I leaned over the railing, just far enough to feel the pull of the deep drop.

"You've got to get him to stop screaming," Rosa mumbled behind me. "He's too old for all that."

"Okay," I said, without looking at her. "I love you too, Rosa."

I could hear her disappear into the apartment next door and lock the door behind her.

We were a fragile alliance, Alex and I; a freak and a skinny eleven-year-old boy. I was the only family he had, and he was mine, and although we'd spent the last eleven years in numerous apartments amidst various people on the dole or early pension with phobias about earth rays, allergies to electricity, and aches and pains in mysterious parts of the body, we still stuck out like pubic hair on the pussy of a porno star. I had no friends to speak of. In fact, there was only Rosa, and my friendship with her was, well . . . complicated.

Officially, Rosa had been diagnosed with a pelvic girdle disorder after the birth of an oversized diabetic boy some twenty-three years ago, when she had been declared unfit for work. Unofficially, it was an open secret that both Rosa and Jens had been permanently drunk up till about three years ago. The social authorities' forcible removal of their son, Michael, was one of the most spectacular stories in the history of our apartment block. Rosa had left the five-year-old Michael in the care of the dead-drunk Jens while she herself went grocery shopping: beer for the adults, rye bread, liver pâté, and milk for the boy. On her way back she was overtaken by the fire brigade, and by the time she got home, a small gathering of residents were standing on the tiles under their fifth floor window, where Michael was sitting watching the world go by, his feet dangling in thin air. The firemen managed to break down the front door before Rosa arrived on the scene with the keys, and afterward there was a screaming performance when Michael was brought down from the window and driven away. Jens had apparently slept through the whole thing, leaving Rosa to sob alone on the couch in a haze of alcohol.

For my own part, I had only known her sober, and she was one of the most respectable people I had ever met. She didn't smile very often, but she was honest. She did her best not to gossip about other people, which was as rare as life in space here in Ghost Town.

The heavens opened in the same second I caught sight of Alex. He came running through the crash of warm water with his arms stretched out wide, as if he were flying. The steam stood off his scraggly frame and his dark fringe clung to his forehead in jagged tufts.

I leaned out over the railing and whistled to get his attention. He smiled when he saw me and a moment later I could hear him rhythmically banging the banister, all the way up from the bottom of the staircase. He didn't like taking the lift on his own. He was afraid it would get stuck, or crash, and there was a permanent stench of piss from that shiny-black blotch in the corner. He was a sensitive child; his nerve endings were frayed. The child psychologist said it was something he'd inherited from me, but I don't buy it. When I see myself at age twelve, I see an angry forbidding girl, crew cut with small beady eyes.

Alex let his fingers run along the rails of the banister till he got right up next to me.

"Are you hungry?"

He nodded and we went into the kitchen, where I buttered a couple of slices of toast on the mottled kitchen counter. Presumably the surface had once resembled marble, but now it looked like what it was: worn, yellow plastic. I wiped the crumbs off the counter with a cloth, swearing under my breath. It smelled foul, stiff with dried porridge. The washing basket in the bedroom was overflowing and I desperately needed a twenty-kroner coin for the Laundromat.

"Do you want to go to the park with me?"

I put a hand on the back of his damp neck, but he pulled away from me. This was new.

"It's pouring," he said. "Can't we wait a while?"

"Nope, we can't. It's the perfect weather for collecting cans. We'll have the whole place to ourselves."

I went into the hallway and rummaged in the cupboard for my

raincoat and Alex's yellow windbreaker. It was too big, bought on sale. You could draw it tight round his face so only his olive-skinned nose poked out the front.

He shot a skeptical glance at the mirror.

"I hope we don't fucking bump into anyone we know."

"Don't swear."

"And I hope we get there before Sveske."

Sveske was a scavenger and can-collector and lived on the stairway opposite ours. He was a cute little tyke, as long as you didn't come on his turf—then all hell broke loose. The words that came out of his mouth were so filthy that even the bigger boys kept their distance when he lost his temper. Sveske usually collected the empty bottles and cans on the eastern side of the apartment block—and in the park, of course. But the park was fair game, a common expanse of grass—it was simply a question of first come, first serve.

We went down to the little stream together, each with our own plastic supermarket bag from Aldi. My flip-flops slipped on the wet grass and I had difficulty keeping up with Alex, who jogged on ahead, his hood still pulled down low. There was thunder in the clouds, and the rain was heavy and warm.

Splash.

Alex landed in a puddle right next to me, both feet planted close together, and muddy water splashed up over my legs.

"You little brat!"

Alex laughed, and ran, sprinting ahead for all he was worth in his flapping galoshes, but I caught up with him quickly and tackled him from behind, bringing us both down onto the muddy grass. I'd have to wash his clothes by hand, but as long as it didn't cost me any coins for the Laundromat machines, it was worth it. We were soaked, but he was grinning from ear to ear. He wrinkled his nose.

"There's got to be duck shit in the water," he said, pointing down to the stream, where the ground was marshy, clogged with the last couple of days' rain. Shiny water covered the lawn and a few clucking ducks waded about in the newly created biotope.

"Sissy."

I tore off one of his galoshes, got up, and swung it triumphantly over my head like an Olympic hammer thrower.

"Come and get it."

But Alex stayed where he was, his smile had disappeared. The transformation was so complete that at first, I thought he was joking.

"Stop it, Mom. You're acting like an idiot."

I followed his gaze and saw a flock of elder boys with school bags slung over their shoulders making their way over the grass in exaggerated slow motion. One of them cast a velociraptor-like glance in our direction without seeming to fix on anything in particular. Then they went along their way, cajoling each other in broken voices and high-pitched whoops.

I looked at Alex, who got up swiftly, half-turning away from me and pretended to study something important in the space between his feet.

"You can't just rip off my galoshes in the middle of the park," he said, angry tears choking his voice. "Now look what you did!"

He grabbed the boot and shoved his foot into it furiously. Then he picked up the Aldi-bag he'd lost in the tackle and steered straight for the nearest trash can and bench.

I remained standing for a moment to look after the group of boys, who were now on their way up the path to the concrete blocks, but I didn't recognize any of them. Or rather, I didn't think I did. The bigger kids from the complex all looked the same: enormous, tent-like hoodies with denim jeans and chunky shoes in winter. Huge T-shirts, shorts, and the same chunky shoes in summer.

Alex fished a beer can out of the garbage with two fingers as I waded through a puddle, following the gravel path to the next bench. Bingo. Two empty soda bottles and one mineral water. Just twenty minutes more, a trip to Hvidovre Square, and there would be enough coins for a cycle of washing at the Laundromat and two cupcakes from the bakery.

I waved my loot over my head, and Alex looked up and waved back. The gang of boys appeared to be forgotten, but he still pulled his yellow hood down over his eyes and turned his back when I tried to send him a smile. I recognized that look of shame; till now, we'd been a good team, Alex and I, but he was starting to look at me with a stranger's eyes. Not all the time, but more and more often, and eventually he'd desert me altogether. I could feel it, as I fed the empties into the automat outside the Netto store, and I could feel it afterward, when we went to the bakery. That measured glance, which saw me from the outside: Ella Nygaard, 28-year-old woman on the dole. Thin legs sticking out of a pair of denim shorts, feet stuck into a pair of pink flip-flops scavenged from the Red Cross's clothing container.

We walked home in silence.

In the foyer to our apartment block, I checked our mailbox.

The envelope was narrow, skimmed milk-white, and covered in postage stamps and markings. Tiny imprints of Buddha in orange overalls, elephants, and colorful flowers, all bunched together with my name and address.

The cupcakes fell out of my left hand and landed on the concrete floor with a soft thump. I could hear Alex pull up behind me, and I told myself that I could get through this, if I just concentrated on thinking logically, I could talk my body back to calm.

A faint buzzing sensation in my hands as I carefully refolded the letter and returned it to the envelop. I slipped it into a stack of advertisements. Carried the little package to the garbage shaft. There was a pain in the index and middle finger of my right hand. It was always the same pain that followed in the wake of the initial shuddering. I stretched out my arm and supported myself against the grey speckled wall. I tried to breathe deeply, into the pit of my stomach.

In and out. In and out.

It was a technique I had learned from Doctor Erhardsen that was supposed to dampen the fear. Not that it ever had. When the fear came, it washed through me like ice water, and the breathing exercises were no more than dams built of fine beach sand. Everything was destroyed and washed away. Breathe out. Breathe out.

I felt the familiar shuddering like a faint, inner hum. It felt very distinct, as if someone had stuck a vibrator in my chest and was slowly turning up the pitch. If I had made it up to our apartment, I might've been all right. The right dose of cheap vodka is a good trick to take the edge off just about anything: one glass filled to the brim, and then—if you have the patience—one more that's big enough to steady your hands.

"Mom?" Alex had picked up the bag of cupcakes from the floor. He was watching me intently. "Is it bad? Is it . . . ? Do you need to lie down?"

"I just need to get upstairs," I mumbled, but kept standing where I was. My legs were no longer cooperating.

Residents coming into the building were staring now as they passed. I tried to meet their gaze, but occasionally I had to kneel down to avoid losing my balance altogether. My arms and legs were shaking and soon the vibrator would reach full throttle. The world surged and closed in on me. Strangely enough, I rarely lost consciousness. On the contrary. My senses opened up, registering each and every painful, ugly detail. The filthy grooves between the tiles on the floor, the surface of the rough walls that looked like a contagious, greyish rash, the stench of the industrial detergent, the piss, and the wet concrete exploded in my forehead. I pitched over, taking a couple of kids' bicycles with me as I fell, then my hands crashed down after me.

It hurt. There would be grazes and bruises afterward. There almost always were.

In some skewed way, the cramps that followed reminded me of the time I gave birth to Alex; the sense of muscles moving me, rather than the reverse. My teeth scraped against one another and my body arched into a shuddering bridge. A separate, sudden jerk smashed my head down into the tiles. My head rang.

Alex was kneeling beside me. I could see him from the corner of my eye, but I couldn't turn towards him. His eyes were calm and dark as he carefully lifted my head onto his lap and stroked my forehead.

"Has someone called an ambulance?"

A man was bent over me, looking into my eyes. He was old as

Methuselah; he had bony shoulders and an enormous Adam's apple in his red, scabby-scaly neck. But his eyes were kindly, mild and brown. I tried to smile.

"Don't worry about a thing, Ella. We'll take care of everything, as usual," he said, pressing my cramped hand to his chest. "Rosa and I will take care of Alex till you get back."

"Close your eyes and touch your nose with your right index finger."

I did as I was told. I was used to being asked to behave like an idiot. In a moment he'd ask me to repeat the exercise with the left hand, and then he'd ask me stand on one leg, then look up and down, and sideways. The shaking had already stopped in the ambulance, but the staff outside the hospital had dutifully wheeled me into Emergency, which had sent me to Neurology, which had sent me to Psychiatry with all the other shaky people.

They didn't dare touch me at Neurology. MRIs cost a packet and all attempts to diagnose me with anything other than "uncontrollable shaking" had, till now, proved fruitless. I was checked for epilepsy and brain tumors and nervous diseases and life-threatening conditions, but there was nothing to be seen that the real doctors could hang their hats on. My brain persisted in depicting a fine, uniform grey mass on their screens. It practically beamed with vitality, as they said—not without a small measure of admiration. But this fine mass of grey matter obliged doctors to pronounce a psychiatric diagnosis, and the most awkward of its kind to boot: hysteria and neurosis. And after the charming environment of Neurology I found myself relegated to the worn linoleum floors, the heavy, brown curtains, and scratched tables of the waiting room in Psychiatry. I'd been there for two days, but this guy was the first doctor I'd spoken to.

"And now with the left hand . . ."

The doctor, a two-meter giant, sounded just as washed-out as I felt. He had, no doubt, skimmed my file with those little reading glasses of his.

"Panic attacks?" he asked, once we'd been through the gymnastic exercises. "You've had episodes of this kind before?"

I shrugged and traced a finger along one of the long, thin scars on the inside of my forearm. Something I almost always did—without thinking—when someone wanted to talk emotions. When I was a teenager, I'd had a predilection for decorating my body with razor blades. Before I was old enough to buy vodka, this had been a particularly effective way to tone down the fear. It had been years since I'd made my last cut.

"For once, we've got a free bed," he said. "You're welcome to spend another night here. Perhaps we ought to adjust your meds. New ones come onto the market all the time, and it is, after all . . ." He paused, turned to his computer and pushed his reading glasses up his nose. "It is, after all, a whole year since you've last been here."

I fought a sudden urge to be blatantly honest. I never took the antidepressants they prescribed. The meds did not work. They just made me soft in the head and unbearably tired. The fear sat in my bones—not in my head—and when I felt an attack coming on, it was the vodka and soap operas that made me feel better. The *Family on the Bridge* on TV3. *Gustav and Linse.* Or a documentary about people with weird diseases. But I couldn't admit this to a doctor—no matter how trustworthy he seemed. Doctors had a heightened duty to report to the authorities, and Welfare could scrap my social benefits if I refused treatment.

The great thing about having a so-called "organic anxiety syndrome" is that the potential range of treatment is never-ending. The people at Welfare started each and every conversation with a new, optimistic prognosis. My capacity for work could, in principle, have doubled in the interim. Had the frequency of attacks diminished? Not likely. But there was certainly cause for a fresh occupational initiative, a new offer for a subsidized job—or what about a newspaper delivery route? The possibilities appeared endless from the bottom of a trash can; there was plenty of blue sky to reach for.

"No, thanks," I said. "I just want to go home."

He nodded. "Is there someone we can call who could help out a little back home? You must be . . . physically exhausted."

He was right about that. I felt as if I'd run a marathon and my

T-shirt stank of sweat. It still bore signs of my tussle in the mud with Alex and I'd had to stuff the pair of baggy underpants the hospital had given me down so they didn't stick out of my tight denim shorts.

"I'll manage," I said, trying to sound flippant. "There's nothing wrong with my legs."

Self-irony suited people on the dole and psychiatric patients alike. Without it, we were not only crazy but devoid of charm, and then not even professional caregivers would touch us with a barge pole.

The doctor smiled despondently as he picked at the grey bristles on his chin. He tried to pin me down with his eyes.

"The particular kind of episodes you have are unusual," he said finally. "It's rare to see such extreme symptoms without some physical foundation. Do you have any idea what could trigger them?"

In a split second I heard the roar of the breakers, like thunder in the dark.

"A bad gene pool," I said. "Did you know that if you cross a kind and docile dog, a golden retriever, say, and a bat-shit-crazy pit bull, the whole genetic system short-circuits? When my parents got together, it was like a wolf fucking a sheep."

"That's not quite how it was phrased in the books on genetics I have read," the man said in a conciliatory tone. "Have you ever heard of PTSD?"

I shook my head, feeling an all-consuming craving for a smoke. I hadn't had a cigarette since early that morning; I'd managed to sneak out onto the lawn in front of the main entrance and power-puffed on a smoke before a guard came over and told me to get lost.

"They used to call it shell shock. During the First World War, a number of soldiers came back from the trenches with physical symptoms that couldn't be linked to any physical injury. They were blind, or lame, their muscles reacted in spastic movements . . . uncontrollable shaking. Like yours. Residual stress and fear from the trenches that flipped certain neurological switches. I'm a doctor, not a psychologist, but I'm not blind to the fact that sometimes it's a good idea to clear up a little in our past. Find out what has shaped us."

The breaking of waves again. The wind, the sharp smell of the ocean.

"I can't remember anything," I said.

"Unless you have a very unusual brain, that's a lie." His voice was laden with the authority that came from having passed judgment on idiots from behind his desk for the last thirty years. "All our experiences are stored somewhere in our brains and if the right buttons are pressed, a dark corner can be exposed to a sudden sharp light. Like the pop of a flash in a cellar. You can get help to find that button, Ella . . ."

"Thanks, but that won't be necessary. I know exactly what I am." I met his gaze. "The nurse said I could go now?"

I had a hand poised on the pack of smokes in my jacket pocket and he nodded without taking his eyes off me.

"Have you got money for a bus home?"

He held up a twenty-kroner coin between his thumb and index finger. I took it like a schoolgirl being sent into town by her mother, all the while neurotically calculating how many smokes the coin could buy me. When you're short of cash and have plenty of time, there's no need to take a bus. As I said, there was nothing wrong with my legs.

THE MOMENT ROSA opened the door I could see from her face that something was wrong. It was more red than usual and the too thinly-plucked eyebrows were drawn together in a frown above her water-blue eyes.

"Ella, I sent Jens to get you at Bispebjerg Hospital. At first we thought you'd been taken to Hvidovre. I called . . . " She ran her red hands through the brown-and-platinum-blonde hair. "Well, he'll probably come back, when he can't find you. They've been here to get Alex."

A cold fist grabbed my guts.

"Who . . . who came to get him?"

"Welfare, of course; that foster mother of his from West Butt-fuck Farm, followed on the heels by your social worker. They waltzed in here and gave Jens and me the beady eye, as if we were a couple of convicted pedophiles." Rosa looked at me as if I'd been personally responsible for the insult. "They told him to fetch a couple of his things from your place, and then they just left. Yesterday. We tried to get hold of you."

I cleared my throat. Picked at the smokes in my pocket.

"How did Alex react?"

"He was dead calm," said Rosa. "But he wasn't happy about it. That much was clear. He was white as a sheet, and his eyes looked all weird. They asked where you'd been taken, but I didn't know, for fuck's sake. And I was tired. The boy screamed all night, you know, the nightmares. I tried putting a cold cloth on his forehead. My mom used to do that . . . "

She trailed off. The Welfare people were her worst nightmare. They had been ever since the day they came and took her son. It was the way they looked at her, she once told me. Everything they knew. Personally, I had trouble believing that anyone at the welfare office still read Rosa's file. She'd been awarded her pension and could, in principle, take care of herself, until she clocked into the big welfare office of eternity. But of course it was there, her file. And all sorts of awful and shameful things were written in it.

"Okay." I breathed deeply and tried to smile at her. "It's probably just a misunderstanding. They probably just mixed up the weekends he's supposed to go out there."

Rosa looked at me with an inscrutable gaze. Her water-blue irises jerked on their blood-shot background; a legacy from a life as an alcoholic made it difficult for her to maintain eye contact with other people.

"Be careful what you say and do, Ella. You know what can happen once they've gotten wind of some crazy idea. Whatever you say is wrong. It gets used against you. They twist everything."

I didn't care for the note of comradeship in her voice. As if we were sworn compatriots. This was not the same as what happened with Michael. There was no comparison.

I spun round and went into my own apartment. I found a pair of jeans in the washing basket and grabbed a clean T-shirt. Then I packed a bag for Alex. He'd forgotten most of his things. His school books, his favorite T-shirt, and the only pair of jeans he had without holes at the knees were still lying on his bed. I had a painful lump in my throat, but Rosa came over and sat down on a chair at my kitchen table and this put a damper on my emotional outburst. We didn't have that kind of relationship, but for once, she offered me a cigarette in a silent gesture of solidarity. Rosa never stood on ceremony and she was pretty stingy, but she wasn't completely devoid of empathy.

"Has Jens come home with the car?"

She nodded.

"Can you give me a ride?"

She nodded again, jiggling a pair of car keys that she'd pulled out of her padded vest pocket.

"I'm ready when you are."

Jens and Rosa's car reeked of smoke and the little long-haired dog they'd adopted a few years after their son was taken away. It must be at least fifteen years old and it was so decrepit that every time it took a shit, a lump of pink colon pressed out of its anus and had to be stuffed back in with a rubber-gloved finger. I had never understood that kind of love for a pet, but once in a while, I took the dog for walks when Rosa's back was giving her trouble. It tripped round the block before ever so carefully selecting a corner by the garbage bins, where it would squat down and shit. This always took the dog the better half of eternity and I felt like a nurse at an old-age home every time my intervention with the gloved finger was required.

Rosa screwed up the volume on the radio. "Eye of the Tiger." Music from a carefree youth. I conjured up an image of a young, platinum-blonde Rosa with chubby cheeks and flawless skin, the ever-ready party girl, obligatory drink in hand. Perhaps she had dreamt of something other than a concrete apartment block on the outskirts of Copenhagen, but then again, maybe she didn't have the imagination for that. As it happened, she grew up in the apartment block across the road.

I flicked the butt of my cigarette out the window. The corn was still green, a silken gloss over the fields, and on any other day I might have enjoyed the ride. It was a thirty-two-mile drive out to Lisa and Tom's. The purpose of their farm was to let the children breathe plenty of fresh air, shovel rabbit shit, and go for rides on Icelandic ponies. Apparently there was broad consensus among social workers and pedagogic experts alike that the presence of farm animals had a therapeutic affect on the children of people on the dole. Clucking hens and fat-bellied pigs were the abracadabra that unlocked the volt of public funds, and organic soap-scrubbed Lisa and arch-fatherly Tom delivered the goods. Not to mention the convenient coincidence that the farm was located so far from anywhere that it was impossible to reach without a car, and this presumably suited both the Welfare authorities and the foster parents just fine. Ghosts like me didn't have the money for private transportation; as a rule, they didn't have the cash for a bus ticket either. I existed in the concrete block, I existed in my apartment and the social office, but on any other kind of turf I was a wandering spirit without body or voice.

I called up Kirsten.

"Ella!" Her voice was usually softened with maternal kindness, but now it had a sharp edge to it, I noted. "I'm glad you called. We tried calling you at the hospital, but you didn't pick up."

"Why have you taken him?"

"Ella, take it easy. He's with Tom and Lisa, of course. And he's doing just fine."

"But he was only supposed to go there next weekend . . . " I tried to keep my voice calm, but this was bad. Something was wrong. The social authorities didn't mix up dates. As a matter of course, a stay at the farm had to be arranged with Tom and Lisa in advance. They had been Alex's substitute family for a few years now in order to provide a measure of relief, but it wasn't clear who was to be relieved of whom.

After the Bakkegården Institute, I was allergic to pedagogic institutions, but Kirsten had made it very clear that the arrangement with Tom and Lisa was one of the many attractive programs the Welfare office had to offer that I couldn't refuse.

"Ella." Kirsten was breathing loudly on the other end of the line. "How are you feeling? You were hospitalized the day before yesterday. You must be tired. Don't you think it would be best for Alexander to stay with Tom and Lisa for a couple of days?"

I could see her before me. How she sat there, in her office, with her arms resting on the table in front of her and the heavy breasts pressed together into formidable cleavage in her flower-print summer dress.

Kirsten was the closest thing I had to a mother. She'd been my caseworker ever since I was released from Bakkegården on seventeen-year-old Bambi-legs, already five months gone in my pregnancy. It was her I turned to when I needed money for children's shoes and summer clothing. Kirsten was also the first and only visitor I had on the maternity ward after Alex was born. I remembered the scent of her hair in particular, because she bent down and kissed us both on the cheek. Lavender. It was always lavender.

"I'm sorry, Ella," she said. "But the flower farm called and asked us to tell you they're not interested. Too many days off sick."

I had been on a three-month apprenticeship on a flower farm in spring and the Welfare office had subsequently made a request that they consider permanent employment; urgently, if I knew Kirsten well. Three months bathed in the scent of flowers and potting soil. The names of the flowers still stuck: marigold, begonia, dahlia, and pansies. Asters and lilies. I had a flair for flowers; I could remember them all. They seemed to flutter into place in my head of their own accord, as I walked up and down the long rows, plucking wayward shoots and dead leaves. And I drank coffee with the others in a shed between the greenhouses. The men clutched their mugs with their broad, wrinkled fingers and laughed along softly when the women told stories about their children and grandchildren. It was a nice place.

"Ella?"

"Yes."

"The other thing I need to talk to you about is more serious." She waited for an answer. Probably for pedagogic reasons, but I didn't say anything. Let her hang in midair.

"We have decided to reevaluate your competence as a parent. You've been hospitalized in Psychiatric once again and your network is a little frayed at the edges."

"Do you mean Jens and Rosa?"

"Is there anyone else?"

"But there's nothing wrong with me," I said, a little too loudly. "It's not as if I'm hearing voices, or painting the walls in my own excrement. I'm completely normal. And I know that Alex misses me when—"

"In your application for early retirement the psychologist describes you as aggressive with a potential personality disorder. He believes that you are a victim of abuse. It can be hard to function as a parent when you have such serious problems yourself."

"I haven't been abused. The man is obsessed with sex."

"Ella . . . You know just as well as I do that I have to take these reports seriously."

"For Christ's sake, Kirsten. All he wanted to talk about was that blotch of ink. The Rorschach test. I said it looked like a dick with ears and he actually wrote it down. How can you take him seriously?"

"He's the psychologist we always use. He's reliable. And new reports have been filed."

"By whom?"

"You know perfectly well I'm not at liberty to say."

I swore under my breath. In our apartment complex everyone sold each other out. In an environment where everybody was living off social benefits, it was common practice to stab each other in the back if someone had blocked the machines on your washing day, or pissed against your front door. There was gossip about work on the black market, overnight visitors, violence against children, drug deals in the hallways. If Welfare didn't know something about you, it wasn't worth knowing.

"Kirsten . . . about those reports. I probably dropped a cigarette butt into somebody's balcony pot plant. You fucking know how it is."

I was so angry, I was close to tears, but tears weren't an option. As Rosa said, they held it against you. I didn't have the luxury of losing control. Breathe deeply.

"Can't you talk to them again?"

She sighed.

"Alex stays with Lisa and Tom until we've completed our re-evaluation."

By the time the call was over the telephone was burning hot in my hand. There was a shifting in my chest, but it was only once I was standing on the threshold of Tom and Lisa's house that I realized what it was.

Fear.

Not the well-known snake coiled below my heart, but a new, strange animal taking shape in the dark.

A life without Alex would be a life without me. He was the only one who saw me, and needed me. You don't exist if nobody knows you. You're destroyed. My breath quickened when I heard Lisa's steps approaching the door, and then it opened. "Ella! You should have called first."

This was a rule, I knew it well, and the reprimand stung.

"I just want to talk to him for a minute. We didn't get to say good-bye."

"He's in the forest with Tom collecting wood for the workshop. They won't be home for a while yet."

"Well then, in that case I—I mean we—will just wait."

I shot a sidelong glance at Rosa, who stood leaning against the car as she glared up at the house. She was only five foot two, but her attitude and stance, arms crossed in front of her chest, made her look like a bouncer outside Crazy Daisy's. She was mad as hell.

Lisa hesitated.

"Well, come on inside, then."

Rosa shook her head, but I followed Lisa into the worn family kitchen, where I'd only been a couple of times before. A two-year-old and two small schoolgirls were seated on bar stools at the counter. They were playing with lumps of Plasticine and stringing pearls on a waterproof tablecloth; all three of them had stretched leggings, tangled hair and shiny red cheeks. A couple of boys were play-fighting in the lounge with ninja words and strips of material wrapped round their foreheads. There was a pall of warm, wet diapers and freshly baked bread.

"So he'll be living here for a little while . . . perhaps even longer." Lisa smiled, hauled the piss-reeking toddler up onto her lap and started ripping the diaper off her.

The animal in my chest curled, digging in its claws, and I couldn't reply.

"He hasn't been coping very well with your illness either, Ella. He was very distressed when he arrived here yesterday. Seeing you like that . . . He needs some peace and quiet, don't you think? Some stability. And he gets on so well with Tom. Say, what's the situation with his dad?"

As if she didn't know. I saw Amir before me on the last day at Bakkegården; the big, intense eyes, a narrow, boyish face. After Bakkegården he was transferred to a locked juvenile institution, followed by various prisons around the country. I knew this, because the welfare office regularly reminded me in writing that he was unable to pay much child support.

"There isn't any real contact . . . "

"Coffee?"

Lisa boiled some water for a cup of instant coffee without waiting for a reply. She hadn't washed her hands after changing the sodden diaper that was left on one of the kitchen chairs. The toddler teetered about without her pants on, flashing her sharp little milk-teeth as she went.

I hunched over my mug and burnt my tongue on the scalding-hot coffee.

Lisa and Tom's home was an exotic environment to me. The wood burner and all those stuffed birds on display on the kitchen cabinets. Small antlers of roe deer mounted over the basket of chopped wood because Tom liked to hunt. Not to mention all those warm bodies intermingling in intimate formations. Lisa absently stroking the hair of a child with her right hand, gathering play-pearls on the plastic tablecloth with her left.

"You should know that Alex is very happy here," she said. "And in the long run, he can go to school with our very own Ask. There is plenty of room in his class. The boys have already talked about it."

I cleared my throat, tracing a finger along the pattern on the tablecloth. It was printed with enormous chickens of various races in a realistic scene with straw and eggs and corn.

"Shouldn't you wait for Welfare's recommendation before talking about all that?"

She looked up at me in surprise.

"I thought we were talking voluntary placement," she said. "Kirsten, for one, has made no mention of anything else."

"I don't know . . ." I looked up, and met her gaze for the first time. Standing there, her broad shoulders back, her large breasts thrust forward, she looked like a Nordic fertility goddess. "I'd prefer to keep him with me."

She looked at me intently, as if to satisfy herself that I meant what I said. Then she shook her head slowly.

"I know you only want what is best for him, Ella," she said. "You are his mother, and you love him. But it's just not possible when you're so unwell yourself. You can't keep leaving him with the neighbors."

"He likes Jens and Rosa," I said. This was the truth. Alex got along well with both of them, but off the cuff I couldn't come up with a single convincing reason why. "They play solitaire," I said. "And he takes the dog for walks, and I'm fine most of the time."

Lisa looked at me, her eyes shining with pity.

This should have been my cue to leave. Of all my failures, Alex was the one that hurt most, and the hardest one to own up to. But still I did not move, I remained seated, my hands wrapped round the hand-painted ceramic coffee cup.

The diaper-toddler had tripped over the leg of a chair and now started to howl; I fought an instinctive impulse to get up, get away from the sound. I had never been very good around crying babies, but Lisa simply strode round the table, picked up the butt-naked girl and deposited her on her hip. Her face softened somewhat.

"One of my friends told me about your father."

I stiffened.

"My friend comes from . . . Hanstholm, I think it is? I'm not very good at the geography of the region up there—though you surely must be. We were getting coffee, and she noticed your name on Alex's school bag: Ella Nygaard. The name isn't very common and then of course it had been big news in the media, she said. Her cousin was in your class."

Out on the lane I could see Alex walking side by side with Tom, who was pushing a wheelbarrow ahead of him. The sun shone from a beautiful, clear sky.

"It couldn't have been easy for you, Ella. There are so many things I understand better now. About you. About Alex."

The little girl was still yelling angrily, her head thrown back. I got up a little too quickly and the leg of the chair dug into the soft fir-tree floor. Lisa shot me a mildly reproving glance and came closer.

"What's important is that you don't let Alex be harmed by your situation as well, Ella."

A thought took shape in my mind.

"The new reports to Welfare," I said, without looking at her. "Was it you? You've told them something about me and Alex, haven't you?"

Lisa opened a cupboard and took out a chocolate cookie for the screaming infant. The little girl grabbed it, and smiled through her tears. The two school girls had long since found refuge in a more quiet corner of the house and the two boy-soldiers were running around yelling on the lawn outside. Silence crept into the kitchen.

"I never told Kirsten anything she didn't know already," said Lisa, looking at me with a dewy, sugar-sweet expression. "You don't have the strength for this, Ella. You never have. You're a damaged child. I know you want what's best for Alex, but he's not a happy boy when he's with you. He worries too much. When he's here, he sleeps like a log right through the night. No nightmares."

There are many disadvantages to growing up in foster families and juvenile institutions. You acquire a self-worth as ugly and shapeless as the clothing you get from the biannual shopping trips to Bilka Discount Store. On the other hand, you become intimately acquainted with rage. It would be fair to say that I developed an intimate relationship with mine at Bakkegården. I spat in teachers' faces, ripped plugs out of walls, and smashed my television on the ground. I stuck a fellow pupil's head down the girls' toilet and flushed. It was all part of that madness that Bakkegården was; a place where we clawed our way into the real world with hoarse voices and broken nails.

Since then I had mellowed. Everything was fine, as long as I was given some space and left in peace. Even in the presence of others, it took a lot to rile me, but Lisa was Chinese water torture; an eternity of soft, cool slaps in the face.

"He is *my* child," I said.

"Children don't belong *to* anyone. This is about what is best for Alex."

She smiled again in that slightly wistful manner that must be very effective with men. As if she had just said something deeply meaningful.

And you, I thought. This is also about what is best for you, Lisa. I had come across her kind before. Not in Bakkegården—heaven forbid. Girls like Lisa would never set foot in Bakkegården. No, from school. Lisa had been one of those solid, diligent girls whose charitable spirit was showered with the teacher's praise. Little-Lisa was sweet and clever, she comforted snot-nosed Peter and poor Rikke with her hopeless hearing aid; she was a trouper, swimming in healthy attention.

Alex and all the other humpbacked kids were big-Lisa's new social projects. Unhappy children she could nurse back to life while the social workers looked on, clapping their plump hands.

My pulse was throbbing in my neck. Had this been Bakkegården, she'd get her ass kicked till that self-satisfied smile was wiped off her face. All that quiet calm could be beaten out of her in less than ten minutes; it did something to people, being made a victim.

I lunged forward and grabbed hold of Lisa's long plait, pulling her head back so far that her neck bowed into a rigid arch. She lashed out at me, but her swings were weak and unfocused, most of her energy concentrated on keeping her balance. I reached for the sodden diaper and stuffed it into her pretty face and mouth. I let go just as swiftly, giving her a light shove, and she hit the floor, elbows first.

Everything happened so quickly. No time for concrete thought; the rage just exploded in my body. I turned on my heel and ran out the door to the yard.

"Alex!"

He and Tom were at the stables by now and the wheelbarrow was parked in the gravel, surrounded by howling ninja warriors. He looked up, smiled, and came running once he'd spotted us.

"We're leaving now."

I hurried over to the car and motioned to Rosa to get in.

"But I hadn't had my cocoa and cookies yet," said Alex, hesitating. "What are we doing?"

"We're just taking a drive. There're a couple of things we need to buy," I said, waving to Tom and giving him the broadest smile I could muster.

Alex could see it in my face, I think. The panic. He knew me. If he still had some doubts, he hid it well. He opened the door and got in the car.

"Drive," I said, but Rosa already had her foot on the gas, the wheels spun, eating into the gravel, and the car sprung forward. As we were driving back down the lane, Lisa appeared in the doorway, arms crossed over her chest, a furious expression on her face.

"Fuck," said Rosa.

As usual, I couldn't have agreed more.

"You're crazy. You do know that, don't you?"

Rosa was looking at me. She had a disturbing habit of trying to catch my eye when she wanted to say something important. Even if she was driving.

"You can't get rid of them, no matter where you go. They'll just send your file after you. That's how the system works. And now they've got it in for you."

I looked out of the window and didn't reply. I sincerely wished that Rosa would stop talking to me and concentrate on her driving. Granted, the cars were few and far between out here. But still. There were trees and stones and bends in the road, and only half an hour ago, she'd had to slam on the brakes for a herd of cows to cross the road with their ungainly, dangling udders and sad brown eyes. The June sun shone above, glittering in the blue sky, and Alex had fallen asleep on the back seat. It was piping hot. The air-conditioning had failed by the time we reached Roskilde Fjord, so now all four windows were rolled down, and the wind howled as soon as we drove any faster than fifty miles an hour.

Rosa lit a smoke and stole a glance in my direction, her bleached hair waving wildly.

"And what about all your shit in the apartment? What are you going to do with it?"

"You can take whatever you need," I said. "Welfare is welcome to the rest."

"But you don't have anything that anybody wants."

I shrugged. Tried to think about something else. Anything at all. The names of rapidly changing climate zones, the impact of the Gulf Stream on the dispersion of heat throughout the oceans of the world. The rate of rotation of the earth and its location in the solar system, the Coriolis effect that deflected eddies of current clockwise in the northern hemisphere, counterclockwise in the southern hemisphere.

"And why the hell does it absolutely have to be on the North Sea coast of Jutland?" Rosa went on. "I mean, it's fine living there in the summertime, but in winter, we're talking the ass-end of Denmark, with a capital A. Then there won't be a soul for miles—just wind and the stench of fish."

"I know someone up there," I said, reaching into my pocket. The letter was still there: a folded A-5 sheet of paper with checkered lines. Sent from a nursing home in Thisted almost two years ago; clearly my grandmother was not given to pathos.

"Like who?" grunted Rosa. "Nobody is dumb enough to live out there year-round. Is it that guy from Blockbuster Video? Niels? Has he gotten himself a job pimping porn to fishermen?"

"Shhh."

I shot a glance over my shoulder. Alex was on the backseat. He'd taken off his T-shirt and this had fortunately spared it from the twin red streaks of melted popsicle on his chest. Rosa had bought the popsicle for him at the gas station in Thisted. She'd also bought some supplies: cigarettes, coffee, soup, pasta, breakfast cereal, and preserves, and she'd withdrawn whatever cash she had left in her bank account. 752 kroner, to be exact.

The trees on the boundaries of the fields were gnarly and frail, bent towards the east. I closed my eyes and inhaled my new environment; the dusty cornfields, something tart and spicy, a wind borne over thousands of miles of sea. You couldn't smell the sea just yet, but the air already had a hint of something wild.

"It's a poor municipal district," I said. "It will take a long time before we pop up on someone's screen at Thisted social services. Their resources are limited."

"Are you sure this is a good idea? Are you sure you'll manage? You'll be all on your own, for Christ's sake. What if you have another fit? In the good ol' days, folk moved out to the country when their nerves were shot. Now it's the other way round."

I could feel her eyes on me, but I didn't open mine. Didn't answer. I needed to concentrate on keeping calm as my childhood filtered through. One picture in particular pressed to the fore. Or rather a strip of a picture, like one of those tattered film clips without sound, a little jerky with dark scratches on a red-gold background. Me, my body, a belly in a bathing suit, bare feet. I am running over the dunes; sand and cockleshells, bits of Styrofoam, crab's claws, seaweed, and that prickly lyme grass that leaves red itchy stripes on your feet and ankles. My mother's voice carried by the thundering, wild, wild wind. The sky above is white, bigger than the entire world.

I RECOGNIZED THE house at once, even though it was smaller, greyer than I had remembered. I would not have been able to recall its exact shape before, but once I was there, right in front of it, the image merged with a memory from the mire in my mind.

The springtime rains had cut deep furrows into the gravel path leading to the house and the dunes had filtered through the grey—not white—picket fence and hip rose bushes, but apart from that, everything was exactly the same as before.

Rosa bumped the Volvo over the sand, braking sharply in front of the low steps leading up to the house.

"Are you sure this is it?" she asked, looking skeptically at me. The GPS had long since given up.

"Positive," I said, opening the car door. I could hear the sea like a hushed rumble behind the grey-green dunes. I remembered not only the house, but all of it. The sky, the light, the smell, the sounds.

Alex shifted on the back seat, not quite awake yet. I stepped out of the car and walked over to the minuscule shed. The door was sagging on its hinges, the paint stripped down to the raw, weather-beaten planks. In the near darkness of the shed I felt my way along the wall till my fingertips found the baby dolls' chest. I opened the top drawer. The key still lay there, as it always had. It felt cold and rusty in the palm of my hand.

"The ass-end of the world," said Rosa, as she hauled our bags and bedding out of the trunk. "The owner has taken you for a ride. No one has lived here in years."

She had a point.

The house was a small, squat construction, its white-washed walls making it look like an animal that would gratefully sink to its knees had it not been held upright by force. The edge of the roof was only a few inches above my head and its outer dimensions were barely more than that of a doll's house. It had low walls with timbered windows and was built over an area that covered less floor space than my apartment in Hvidovre. The northern wall abutted an old stable that was literally hanging on its hinges. Someone had tried to reinforce it with a couple of thick rafters from the outside, but the masonry still gaped in several places.

Alex crawled out of the car, blinked into the bright light, and gazed through the grey-green haze of lyme grass. The wind was warm and dry and salty, and both the car and Alex seemed to be whirled in a waving, green sea below the fleeting sky. The dunes towered up around us, long-bearded and moss-grey with a bed of purple heather.

"Where are we?"

He was looking at me.

"This is our new house."

"It doesn't look very new to me." He turned once around himself. "There's fuck-all out here."

"Watch your language."

I trudged over to the front door and stuck the key in a lock that was rusty and unwilling, but finally it relented with a groaning oath of its own. I had to lean hard on the door to get it open, ducking instinctively on my way in so I didn't bang my head on the frame.

"It stinks in here. It stinks of old, dead people."

Alex pushed past me into the narrow entrance, demonstrably pinching his nose with one hand. He was right. The air was thick with dust and earth and mold and a hundred years' worth of stale cooking vapors. A cane, a pair of worn galoshes and a pair of black shoes in size dwarf were lined up under a naked row of hooks.

I edged a little further into the narrow entrance that separated the house from the old stable. The walls were covered in floral-print wallpaper, but apart from that, no one had bothered with the decor. The floor was grey concrete, uneven, and ice-cold, despite the bright sunshine outside. To the left, a cold pantry with shelves from floor to ceiling lined with an indescribable number of dusty jars and glass containers. Pickled cucumbers and cooked pears that looked like the fetuses of small animals conserved in glass jars in a natural history museum. An odor that was at once sweet and sour.

Leading off to the right, there was a narrow washing room that consisted of a scratched counter with a large sink under a single cold-water tap. There was no warm water. Neither in the kitchen nor in the house as a whole. Water for dishes had to be fetched from the bathroom that was located at the far end of the kitchen. The bathroom had turquoise tiles, a bathtub, and a sink. A dried strip of fly-paper dangled above the greasy stove.

I pulled the letter out of my pocket and studied the high, angular handwriting. There were instructions for turning on the heat in the bathroom and the electricity in the house. Everything still works, it said. She had someone who came by to see to the place once in a while.

In all the other rooms—including the kitchen—a grey threadbare wall-to-wall carpet spotted with large, greasy stains covered the floors. The sand had penetrated all the way into the lounge, crunching under your feet when you walked over the thin piling. The living room was located between the kitchen and an additional room that could possibly be fixed up for Alex. Two of the panes in the timbered windows were cracked, but that could be sorted with a little cardboard and a couple of garbage bags. I was pretty creative with that kind of thing. After ten years on the dole, I knew that wonders could be worked with duct tape and various odds and sods to be found on dumpsters. But just then, I had difficulty believing that we'd still be there when the winter came around.

"Up here!"

Alex had run ahead up the stairs to the first floor. Judging from the rhythmical squeak of springs, he'd apparently found a real bed to jump on, and Rosa reluctantly followed me upstairs to the first floor. Here there were two rooms with leaning walls covered in the same floral wallpaper as in the entrance and an attic storage room crouched under the bare ceiling. Mountains of old magazines were stuffed in between the roof and the crumbling plates of plaster. *Family Journal* and *Donald Duck*. An unwelcome and most inappropriate image of myself, aged six, lying on a mattress in one of the mirage-warm, dusty rooms, masturbating frenetically with a pillow wedged between my knees. My grandmother had insisted I take afternoon naps, but I was too old for that kind of thing and came up with my own way of passing the time.

"Did someone really live here once?" said Alex, jumping off the old bed. "It's not like a real house at all."

"Define 'real house,'" I said. "It's got walls and doors and windows and a roof. What more do you want?"

All at once he looked very unhappy, standing there with his arms hanging listlessly by his sides. He hadn't said much on the drive over, by turns sleeping or staring out of the window with a look on his face that made me wish I could put a glass to his skull, like kids put a glass against the wall to eavesdrop, and listen to his thoughts. Just like Hanne and I used to do at the Bakkegården Institute, when we were thirteen and wanted to hear if anybody was getting laid next door.

"It will grow on you," I said, trying to infuse a little girl-scout optimism into my voice. "A new school, new friends . . . And then there's the forest, and the sea . . ."

"There's fuck-all out here, Mom." He went back down the stairs and into the bathroom, slamming the door so hard behind him that the floor boards shook. When I came downstairs I could hear the running water through the closed door. He was washing his hands, I knew, and although the door blocked my view, I could picture him clearly. The lanky body bent over the sink, the slightly rounded shoulders, the dark, wispy fringe falling into his eyes. When he was through, he would get out his toothbrush. OCD, said the child psychologist. A number of things had gone wrong for Alex and me.

• • •

I EMPTIED THE dust and dead flies out of the kettle and washed a couple of plates in the sink in the washing room. I made some instant coffee for Rosa and me and some packet soup for Alex. The cups smelled like mold and dish soap even though I'd rinsed them thoroughly, and it felt like having a tea party at a plastic table in a doll's house that had been overrun by rain and spiders.

"You've got an admirer," said Rosa, nodding towards the window. At the end of the garage a thin, bent figure stood staring at us through the window. He looked haggard. His head was bare, his movements shaky and unsure. When he realized we were staring at him, he turned abruptly and walked down the gravel path, his walking stick swinging in his hand.

"Creepy," said Rosa. "You can still come back with me." She was warm and more ruddy-faced than usual after having carried our bags and the bedding up to the first floor.

"It's gonna be fine," I said. "We'll manage."

She shook her head, got up, and started gathering her smokes, lighter, and phone. She looked tired, but then she hadn't had the time to bring her pills. She'd made more than the average number of sacrifices that day.

We walked back to the car through the billowing grass.

"Yes, well, I guess this place also has its plus points," said Rosa, blinking rapidly. "And I'll bet there isn't a single foreigner in town."

Rosa had a thing about immigrants. The women took up too much space in the laundry room and they were arrogant as hell to boot. Especially the ones with the headscarves, she said.

"They say I'm a drunken old whore," she liked to gripe. "They don't say it in words. If they did, I'd sock it right back at them. No, they say it with their fucking headscarves. They say: we're better and prettier than you are. And the men are a bunch of chauvinists, the children are cockeyed, each and every one. Inbred. Nieces and nephews and uncles. And we are the ones who have to pay for their handicap."

Of course Rosa chose to ignore the fact that she herself never paid a cent for anything on behalf of anyone else and that, technically speaking, Alex himself was multiracial, the son of the Pakistani vanishing artist Amir; now you see him, now you don't. All this was lost on Rosa in context. With her habitual, self-assured lack of consistency, she had loved Alex fiercely from the moment she met him while still continuing to hate all other 'more Pakistani' Pakistanis with a passion. The same went for Social Democrats and all people working for the social welfare services.

"You can always call . . . " she said, rummaging for something in her pocket. An extra twenty-kroner coin. "Let us know how you are getting on."

"Yes, of course . . . thank you."

She shrugged, mumbled something under her breath and slammed the trunk shut. There wasn't much else to say. I watched the Volvo disappearing down the gravel road.

I pulled the letter from my grandmother out of my pocket again and stared at it. She was old now. At least ninety, if I remembered correctly, but I was sure somebody would have let me know if she'd died.

I know things have been hard for you because of what happened back then, but it is time you came back. Living without your past is like swimming on dry land, awkwardly, meaninglessly . . .

I refolded the letter and stood looking out over the dunes for a long time, trying to orient myself. The town and the harbor lay to the north, and, some place in between, was the house that used to belong to my parents. I could see the spine of the red roof and the chimney towering up over the hills of sand, and I knew that you could breach the distance in less than five minutes, if you cut through the dunes instead of taking the road.

I knew more than I had known two days previously, and I didn't like what I'd learned. Once, a long time ago, I made a conscious decision to move forward without ever looking back, and I stuck to it. The decision had worked for me, so I wondered what I was doing there at all. I read the last lines of the letter again:

Living without your past is like swimming on dry land, awkwardly, meaninglessly . . .

She stood by him. She had always stood by him.

HELGI, 1994

The day was bewitched.

He sensed it from the early hours of morning when he'd gotten out of bed to see the marten dragging the neighbor's cat away in its mouth. The fight to the death had been going on since dawn and he'd lain awake listening to the cat's screams coming in through the window in the roof. At first he'd thought it was just a couple of tomcats pursuing a female in heat, but the screams kept rising in pitch, finally becoming a deep, guttural gurgle that no living creature would ordinarily produce. As he stood at the kitchen window he saw the enormous grey tomcat's head bouncing heavily over the sand as the marten dragged it into the dunes. Scavenger devoured by scavenger. When two equally matched competitors go to battle, both parties risk losing their lives. A single rip of a fang could deliver the fatal blow, and nature doesn't go to such extremes unless it's a matter of sex or complete insanity.

And now it was raining. It had come out of nowhere, leaving the building site in a deserted chaos of flapping tarpaulin and ankle-deep puddles. The weather forecast had promised bright sunshine and blue, blue skies. But then it was May, after all.

He shot a glance at the prefabs and considered taking a coffee break with the boys. It couldn't fucking go on like this forever. And yet he lingered, staying put under the eaves, indecisive, feeling the cold creeping up his pant legs and in under his drenched overcoat.

"Excuse me?"

A woman was standing by the fence. She was armed with an umbrella and a pair of shiny, red galoshes.

"Excuse me?" she called again, and this time he was sure she was talking to him.

He left the relative safety of the eaves and bounded between the puddles as agilely as his age and bulky construction boots would allow. *Goddammit.* It was really pissing down now. He'd pulled his shoulders up around his ears, but still the rain filtered in under his collar in cold rivers.

"Yes?"

He'd made it to the fence unscathed and could now see the woman's face. Her eyes were dark blue, one slender hand was laced through the wire fence, her nails were long, and exquisitely painted; an exotic rarity in Thisted where the women cut practical figures both in their choice of clothing and their frame of mind. It couldn't be easy washing dishes with those claws.

"It's just that . . . " She squinted up at the dark sky, then leveled her eyes to meet his gaze. "I'm so sorry, I didn't mean to drag you out into the rain, but I'm looking for the art museum, you see, and it seems I've parked my car too far away. Is the museum close by, or would it be better to get my car and drive there?"

"The museum is on the corner of the next parallel road." He said, and pointed the way. "Are you going to see the Skagen painters?"

Rain water was pouring over his eyebrows, and he had to wipe it away with the back of his hand and blink rapidly in order to keep holding her gaze.

She laughed.

"Yes, I am. Have you been in to see them? Are they any good?"

He shook his head in answer to the first question. The thought of going to the exhibition had crossed his mind, it always did, whenever he saw one of the art museum's advertisements. He could just go in and see one of those exhibitions. Do something completely different from what he usually did. He'd done quite a lot of drawings when he was a young man, and for a while there, he'd even toyed with the idea of going to architecture school in Århus. That was before Anna, of course, but he could've been an architect. His grades had always been decent, and he was good at seeing the world in lines and colors. The sketches he'd once drawn were still stored someplace in the garage. The church from every imaginable angle. The fishing boats. Mostly buildings and objects, but there had been a portrait or two. The feeling of once having owned a corner of that world had, strangely enough, never left him, but it must be at least twenty years since he'd been to a museum, and he was an excellent carpenter after all.

"Thank you." She smiled and walked a few paces in the direction he had indicated. Her figure was exceptionally fine in that long, thin coat. Her hips swayed hypnotically from side to side. Her legs were bare in her galoshes, he noted. Fine, slender, suntanned limbs.

"Don't mention it."

The rain fell heavily between them.

"But . . . " She hesitated, half-turning towards him. "Perhaps you'd like to come along? It doesn't look like the rain is going stop any time soon."

He should have said no, he knew he should have said no, but the day was—and already had been—bewitched.

After Rosa had gone Alex and I followed the road into town.

Apart from an all-purpose grocery store, the town center consisted of no more than a bakery and a few kiosks selling German newspapers, candy, ice cream, and inflatable beach toys. The houses were low-slung and newly painted in ochre and Skagen-yellow tones, the front yards trimmed and well-kept. Most of the folk on the streets were tourists, elderly people wearing sun hats, short-sleeved shirts, and khaki shorts. And among these milled young, broad-shouldered surfers who, for the most part, hung out at the point, where the wind and current whipped up waves that broke in a foaming white inferno you could ride all the way in to the beach.

We sat down on the broad steps on the harbor front beside a group of dripping wet guys to watch the surfers engaging in their battle against the elements. The sun colored the sky pink over the horizon.

"What do you think a surfboard costs?" asked Alex.

"I think they're expensive."

He nodded, letting a handful of sand run through his fingers as he squinted into the sky.

"You can get one second-hand for a couple of thousand kroner."

One of the guys next to us smiled at Alex and rapped on his board. He'd zipped down his wetsuit, was resting his elbows on the warm cement surface. His fair chest was still wet with water and covered in goose bumps. His friends were talking to one another in Dutch and German.

"Okay, thanks."

Alex looked at me quizzically, but I simply sent the guy a wan smile, and looked away.

I was painfully aware of how old and worn-out I looked next to these younglings and their ten-thousand-kroner kit. I was 28 years old, and a mother, with everything that went along with that in the way of stretch marks and worn attributes. My shorts were too loose, bought at an H&M Family store on sale, my T-shirt had been washed at least a thousand times, too often with hand soap or dishwashing liquid, lending it an indefinable yellowish-grey-off-white hue.

My appearance wasn't usually something that bothered me. Appearances lay a long way down the list of my priorities, but in the company of such a large group of young men, I felt their eyes on me—and saw myself through theirs. I hadn't been with anybody for almost two years, and the she-wolf in me would gladly have murdered for just *one* lustful look from a man. Or, even better: a decent fuck on a regular basis with a guy who would brush the hair out of my face, kiss me deeply, and then preferably disappear immediately thereafter. Long-term relationships hadn't interested me since Amir.

"My name is Magnus," the guy said to Alex. "Do you think I could buy your big sister a beer?"

"No, you can't," I said, tying to smile politely, hoping he'd get the drift, but still understand that I appreciated the offer and the tad-too-thick compliment.

"Another time, maybe?"

"Maybe."

I looked away, hoping he'd leave, but I could feel his eyes on me for another long, awkward minute before he finally turned his attention back to his beer-drinking friends.

I got up and brushed the sand off my thighs, Alex reluctantly followed my lead. The surfers moved on, in all probability with the flock of young girls of about the same age in tow. They sat a little way off, the girls creaming their butter-smooth, filly legs in after-sun lotion. They looked barely twelve years old, yet already equipped with a woman's constant awareness of any attention zoomed in their direction. They cocked their heads to one side, laughed with their lip-gloss lips and shiny white teeth, scanning the turf for curious glances. Not a single twitch was left to chance.

One of them caught Alex's gaze, and held it till he looked away.

"Can we walk home along the water?" he asked.

"Not today."

"But it doesn't take any longer. We can take off our shoes and walk along the beach. Just like they do in films."

"It's too cold," I said. "It's very windy down on the beach. We'll do it tomorrow."

I couldn't tell him what was holding me back. I just needed some time before going down to the beach and the wild, whipping waves. I don't think I could've explained it to myself. I just couldn't go down there. Not yet.

"WELCOME TO KLITMØLLER."

The couple was staring at us, especially Alex, there was no smile.

We had eaten some porridge for dinner, discovered to our dismay that the television didn't work, and had gone into the dunes to watch the sunset, a flame-red sky in the background. The wind was warm, and we had come back to enjoy the benefit of a little shelter up against the house. I sat on the steps smoking and Alex was blowing a high-pitched tune through the blades of the broad-leafed couch grass he had picked in the dunes. A chorus of grasshoppers had tuned in as well, and perhaps this was why we only noticed the couple when they were standing right in front of us, staring. The woman was holding a hand-picked bunch of blue and white flowers in front of her chest—like an exorcist would wield a wooden cross.

I stubbed out my cigarette on the steps and hurriedly wiped my right hand on my shorts before offering it to the man; as he was the one who had stepped up to the plate. The man greeted me with a warm, dry hand that held mine no longer than absolutely necessary. The woman remained standing half-hidden behind her husband's broad back.

They looked like a solid couple. In their late forties, early fifties. The man was wearing jeans, brown sandals, and a white T-shirt with the logo of a machinery plant in some town I hadn't heard of. The woman was wearing comfy Ecco-shoes and a cobalt-blue T-shirt with a collar: Mr. and Mrs. Klitmøller.

"Good evening . . . "

I smiled at them both as the woman fussed with the ribbon bound around the flowers, taming a few imperceptibly wayward stalks in the bunch before finally presenting the flowers to me.

I took the bunch, and sniffed obediently. I didn't know what else to do—or say—for that matter. The flowers had no definable smell. White yarrows mixed with blue forget-me-nots.

"From our garden," she said. "Well, we just wanted to say hello. See who'd moved in next door."

She was very tan and weather-beaten in a way I imagined most people living on the North Sea coast must be. Given time, wind wears away the surface of a stone, so there was no telling what it could do to soft facial skin exposed to it every day. Her hair was a nice, even-colored dark brown, and utterly lifeless. I reckoned the color came from a tube of L'Oréal. A product I used myself when I was a teenager.

"Yes, well . . . that would be me."

"And this is your boy?"

The man nodded in the direction of Alex, who was sitting against the wall, sucking on a bottle of water. His silhouette was golden-black in the mild evening light and the fine Arabic bridge of his nose stood out majestically in profile. Their reluctance was palpable, and I returned it whole-heartedly.

"Have you rented the house from Agni?"

"This is my grandmother's house."

They exchanged looks.

"Then perhaps you're on . . . holiday?"

"We're only staying until . . . " I trailed off. Until the dust had settled at the Welfare office in Hvidovre . . . until the smell of warm piss had faded from Lisa's memory. No, I didn't know how long we'd be staying.

The man cast Alex another long, measured glance. The wife was already scraping her Ecco shoes against the cobblestones. She'd heard and seen enough, I imagined. Ella Nygaard had returned, Pakistani son in tow. Ella Nygaard, of all people. Who would have thought it, hey?

"And what will you be doing in Klitmøller?" The man—he still hadn't introduced himself—was asking through pursed lips.

"Nothing."

"What do you mean, nothing?"

"I don't work. I live off the dole. That is, just as long as my application for a state pension is still pending."

They would probably have been slightly less antagonistic had I lied and said that I was studying to become a teacher, but I wasn't in the mood for chitchat. Admitting that you're on the dole is an excellent conversation stopper, and now the man had a shoe trawling the gravel. The wife had laid a hand on the back of his neck, like you would grip the collar of a vicious dog.

"Well, naturally you're both very welcome to Klitmøller," she said, meeting my gaze fleetingly. "We are your closest neighbor, and here in Klitmøller we like to help one another out, it's such a small town. It's a wonderful place to live. Folk living here know how to treat one another. Our house is right over there."

She pointed to the roof of a red-brick house nestled in the row of dunes directly behind ours.

I nodded, and lit another smoke. Cupped the flame in my hand as I clicked my lighter.

"You should take care with fire in the dunes," said the man. "Not everything out here is sand."

His wife took his arm gently, and they commenced their retreat with cool smiles.

"Thanks for stopping by."

I gave them a smile, lifting two fingers in a half-cocked salute. I could handle Mr. and Mrs. Klitmøller. I could handle the whole fucking world.

ANNA, 1994

Ugly.

This was the first word that came to mind as Anna parked the car in the driveway and saw the gaping front door. The black hole in the wall looked like the entrance to a ghost house. The word came to her before she realized that the pane of the door was broken, before she looked for Helgi's car, before she registered that no lights were burning. She knew that nobody was home, and the door ought to have been closed against the rain and unseasonable storm.

She switched off the ignition and sat watching the house for a moment until she finally persuaded herself to get out.

"You have to go in there. The door wasn't closed properly. It blew open. That's all. No reason to panic, Anna."

Even the broken pane and the long, awl-like splinters of glass in the entrance could be explained; the door had been blown open, smashing it against the wall. The flurry whipped a few loose pages of paper over the floor as she carefully picked her way over the glass and closed the door behind her. The air was rushing through the frame.

"Hello? Helgi?"

Silence. Nothing but wind and darkness. In the kitchen, chairs knocked over. Jars of flour and pasta were shattered, their contents spread over the dinner table, smeared together with marmalade and marinated herring from the fridge.

Anna turned on the light and stood looking at the scene of destruction for a long time. Break-ins were not unusual in Klitmøller, but the summer houses were seldom targeted. And break-ins were rare after the high season, when the more rebellious teenagers in town couldn't run after the tourist girls any longer. Then all that frustrated teenage sexuality was channeled into drinking yourself into a stupor, and whatever desires couldn't be numbed by alcohol were sated by thievery and vandalism. But this was . . . unbelievably thorough. Anna picked her way to the range hood by the stove where some wise-guy had perched one of Ella's ragdolls. A message had been stuck to its belly with a safety pin.

JESUS IS COMING—LOOK BUSY.

The doll's painted pupils and curling eyelashes had been painstakingly scraped off.

Anna took down the doll and tossed it into the trash can, which, miraculously, had been left standing upright.

In the living room the telephone cables had been ripped out of the wall. The line was stone dead—but who should she call? Nothing much had been stolen, she noted. Just a CD-player and a couple of hundred kroner from the petty cash bowl in the kitchen. It was the extent of the destruction that upset her most. Books were ripped out of their shelves and a couple of white porcelain vases had been viciously shattered, their remains sprinkled like snow over the living room floor, as were the shredded pages of her photo albums from the bookcase.

The terrace door had been left wide open and the curtains waved eerily in the cold. She hurried to close the door to her pitiful garden, but stopped dead.

A wooden stake had been driven into the middle of the lawn.

At least this is what it looked like from where she stood. She blinked against the driving rain and went outside with a renewed sense of dread. Neither Ella nor Helgi would dream of hammering a stake into the lawn. It had been her garden ever since they had moved into the house. Not that she was particularly fond of that wind-swept patch of earth. Nothing could grow there. The apple tree she had planted fifteen years ago was no more than a dwarfed and crooked trunk covered in scab, and she had yet to see a single apple blossom bloom. The hedge, which was meant to offer some wind protection to the west, was frayed and sparse, and in her flower beds a couple of razed pansies with yellow leaves and split stalks shuddered in the wind. The only plants she'd managed to save were her potatoes and the sea hollies she'd rescued from the dunes—hardly a victory over Mother Nature.

The wooden stake was a good two yards long and thick as an arm. Fir-wood, if she wasn't completely mistaken. It still bore its scaly bark. Only the top part had been carefully sharpened with an ax or a large knife. A sticky, dark mass of blood and tufts of grey hair strutted from the light wood, and she recalled what Helgi had said about the neighbor's cat the day before. That it had been killed by a marten.

But that cat wasn't killed by a marten, Helgi. It was a band of teenage boys with too much time on their hands and too much alcohol in their systems. That's all. No hocus pocus. Plain and simple. Primitive human behavior.

And yet, an all too familiar Bible quotation flashed in her head:

. . . when the Lamb opened the fourth seal, I heard the voice of the fourth living creature say, 'Come!' I looked, and there before me was a pale horse! Its rider was named Death and Hades was following close behind him. They were given power over a fourth of the earth to kill by sword, famine, and plague, and by the wild beasts of the earth.

She clenched her jaw in grim determination and heaved the stake up out of the sandy ground. Ella was not to see the stake. Nor Helgi.

She didn't want to talk about it.

Neither about death nor what the stake meant. It was nobody's business but hers.

Whatever is written on my birth certificate is irrelevant. In my mind, I was born in the back yard of a villa in Aalborg, and the memory of the day I came into this world is one of the most vivid memories I have.

I am about eight years old, and my foster mother at the time is yelling at me from the bottom of that tree I've crawled up into. In my hand I'm still holding the stone I've used to smash her greenhouse. All the panes, all the way round. The roof I couldn't reach. A blessing, really, for had I shattered the roof as well, glass would have rained on my head. But things are bad enough as they are. I have a deep gash in my right upper arm, it's bleeding, and my foster mother, whose name I cannot remember, is screaming for me to come down at once. But I'm not listening. She's an evil cow, and she isn't my mother. I pitch a glob of spit through the leaves below, it splatters on her upturned face.

That was the summer I got the first cut on my arm, and it was also my first conscious memory after the "family tragedy," as Dr. Erhadsen poetically insisted on calling it. He had a tendency to embroider when reality became too concrete for him.

Whatever had given rise to my destruction of the greenhouse remains a mystery. There were snippets of a blue bathroom, floral tiles, a man going for a walk with a dog. But those memories could just as easily have stemmed from a later stage. I had been with seven foster families in five years. Nobody liked me, and, as a rule, the feeling was mutual. I knew I needed someone, but it wasn't Hanne, Lene, Bodil or Bentha—or whatever it was the bitches were called. Irrespective of who they sent me to, the result was always the same: I screamed and yelled, thrashed out at the adults, bit the children, if there were any.

I was a freak.

I knew this already, and I wasn't the only one who knew it. The rest of the world could see it as well. It had been written in the newspapers, and it was written in those piles of papers that followed me from foster family to foster family, followed me to the Bakkegården Institute—home sweet home—and finally, the web of welfare programs, flexi-jobs, sick leave, and the Guidance for Young Underprivileged Mothers. Everyone had always known. My father had blown my mother's brains out. At times, I was absolutely certain it was written in my face; the tainted mark of shame. This was definitely the case in Hvidovre, and the first day in Klitmøller was no different, even as Alex and I ran barefoot along the sandy paths among the dunes, the roar from the ocean looming larger and larger.

At the top of the final dune, Alex stopped and turned suddenly, staring out over the grey-blue hills of sand, eyes shining bright with glee.

"Fucking amazing," he said after a long while. "Is this where you come from?"

I nodded, something knotting in my chest. This was the first and only thing from my childhood I had ever shown Alex—and it was really beautiful. The sea was mine; it had rested in me like a deep, slow rush from a faraway place. And now the smooth, grey giant of a dune lay in front of me, untouched by the time that had come between us.

The sun beat down, and a couple of children ran wild like little savages along the shore, half-naked, white hair flying in the strong breeze. Alex was more reserved. He walked quietly on his own, collecting sea shells, mostly cockleshells and a few finely polished oyster shells. There were also a few bright-red crab claws with big jagged pincers, and bladder wrack that oozed a clear jelly when you squashed it between your fingers.

"Is there any amber to be found around here?"

Alex looked at me eagerly. The prospect of finding riches worth more than empty Coke cans was clearly exhilarating. I told him not to look between the stones, but higher up the beach, where the seaweed had gathered in a dark belt.

"Amber is relatively light," I explained, not knowing where this knowledge was coming from. "A bit like plastic, so it washes higher up on the beach than the stones. The best time to look is just after a storm."

A new text message from Kirsten bleeped in. The seventh since my flight from Lisa and Tom's Neverland.

WHERE ARE YOU? CALL ME SO WE CAN TALK.

I switched off my phone and watched Alex curiously combing through twisted mounds of murky seaweed.

Afterward he built a sand castle and dug channels and moats with his bare hands. I lay on the beach, flat on my back, staring up into the sky. You couldn't swim here, I knew instinctively—just as I seemed to know so much else about this place. Something had happened right here. A stump of memory came swimming towards me.

I had ignored a direct order and waded out into water over my knees. It is warm, the waves are unusually peaceful, of the kind that neither break nor foam on the top. You can actually see patches of the sand below, as well as a shoal of sticklebacks, and perhaps this is why I am distracted for a moment, my yellow pail has drifted beyond my reach. I think of calling for my father, but he is nowhere to be seen. Behind me the beach is deserted, the dunes a green mountain range. I take a few steps further out, then a few more, until finally I'm swimming a couple of strokes into the sea. It feels harmless, even though there is movement in the water, and I am lifted up from the bottom and dunked down again, the water momentarily splashing over my head. I reach out for the pail that has tilted on its side. I get two fingers under the red handle, reach down to put my feet down, and stand up.

But I can't.

Cold hands are pulling my feet out from under me. It's like trying to stand in a rushing river. Every time I try to put my feet down, they are swept out from under me, and I float further, out and away. But it's only when I turn to look back at the beach that I'm struck with terror. I have been swept so deep into the foaming water that my lonely sand castle is an insignificant dot, a long, long way away. People can die like this, and I know it.

It's so easy to die at sea. It happens every year on our beach. Germans and Dutchmen. Those who don't know this great grey sea, the ones who believe they can ride the monster.

I move my arms and legs again, try to work my way across the cold, rushing current, but I have to wait till the shore curves to sweep me closer to land, only then can I dig my hands and feet into the sandy, cockleshell seabed and crawl up onto the beach. The sand is ripped away from the soles of my feet. My hands and feet and knees are cut and bleeding, the blood is trickling down my shins in a thin, flame-red stream as I limp back to my sand castle.

Then I catch sight of my dad on top of a dune, but he's not looking in my direction. He's looking at something else. I call out to him, and he turns towards me, shading his eyes against the sun.

We walk home in silence, hand in hand, don't say anything to Mom. It's our little secret. But I'm tired of secrets.

I GOT UP a little too fast, and called to Alex. The feeling of stretching out a small, ice-cold hand to my father had made me nauseous. The memory was just as intrusive and unwelcome as a visit from one of those door-to-door Animal Rights fundraisers.

Alex came running towards me, his face alive with wonder. He had tossed his T-shirt, and his tendons trilled below the surface of his thin, boyish body. It wasn't often I caught a glimpse of him like that, released of a pre-teen child's critical and crippling view of himself, but every time it happened, I was stunned by the thought that all that beauty had come out of my own body. For my own part, I was thin, pale, and unglamorous. The only thing pretty about me was my hair. It was huge, a curly, dark-brown halo that looked like the work of a professional stylist at any given time of the day. You have to remember to appreciate the little things in life.

"Mom," he said. "The house is shit, but this is really neat. How long are we staying?"

I didn't reply.

We had reached the top of the last dune, and we could see down to the house, where a green sedan was parked. A guy was snooping around in the garden with a fat, black yapping dog following in his heels. He lifted the garage door and kicked at the foundation. I backed up, and sat down in a dip between the dunes. If we waited long enough, he would probably disappear again, whoever he was. But Alex had already acquired a sense of ownership.

"Shouldn't you ask him what he wants? It is our house, after all." His face was dark and wary. "What if he steals something?"

"Then he'd be sorely disappointed," I said, running a tuft of lyme grass through my fingers.

"Come on!" Alex peeked over the dunes. "He's still there. He's going into the garage."

He stuck his hands into the pockets of his shorts, just like he often did when one of my fits started building up.

"Fine," I said, and got up reluctantly, taking my cigarettes and lighter out of my back pocket in the same motion. "But you must know that we run the risk of pissing him off when he finds there's nothing to steal but my battered Nokia and your crusty lunch box. He might even shoot us. Thieves are designer-label freaks."

Alex tried to smile, but didn't succeed all too well, and he still had his hands in his pockets as we walked the last stretch to the house.

"Was there something in particular you wanted?"

The guy, who had now disappeared into the dark interior of the garage, popped up in the doorway and squinted at us through the sun, not otherwise looking especially suspect.

"Yes, excuse me," he said, coming out into the light on the yard. Smiling. "I thought I might as well take a look around while I waited . . ."

He was about my age, between twenty-five and thirty years old. Track-suit pants, sneakers, and a thin, long-sleeved sweater, an ear-ring in the left ear, and an infantile anchor tattooed on his neck. Probably a fisherman's son or a fisherman-wannabe who'd had a one-week holiday job on a fishing boat between the eighth and ninth grade. His hands weren't rough enough to have grappled with rope, fishing tackle, and salt-water for an extended period of time.

"Waited for what?"

The guy looked at me intensely for a moment, then his smile broke into a broad grin.

"You, it seems. Ella? Have you just arrived?"

"I got here yesterday," I said.

"I can tell it's you by the wild hair," said the guy, pulling a smoke from his pocket. "We went to school together, perhaps you remember? My name is Thomas."

"I can't remember anything," I snapped and made for the front door, steering Alex ahead of me with a firm hand between his shoulders.

I could feel the guy's eyes in my back as I paused next to his dog. It lay chewing on something half-rotten, lazily wagging its tail.

Thomas.

I couldn't remember him. Nothing. Faces from the past were pale shapeless moons against a black sky. I could have had friends. Perhaps I'd even missed them after the grown-ups packed me out of town. I couldn't remember if I had—all I knew was that I had no desire to find out one way or the other.

"Hey, wait up a minute."

He took several long strides after us. This guy Thomas was clearly not the type who could take a hint, and his broad west-Jutlandic accent irritated me just as much as his intrusive overfamiliarity. He spoke the language of my parents, and it made my skin crawl, my pulse throb.

"My dad asked me to let you know that he's interested in buying the house, if the old lady wants to sell. It's a large plot. And this is the last house that was built before the area became part of the conservancy; no neighbors in your back yard, and only one hundred yards to the sea." He whistled, and rubbed his thumb and forefinger together by dint of demonstrating the property's capital value. "The house has been empty for a few years now, but perhaps you're thinking of staying?"

I didn't answer. Kept my back turned to him.

"Have you talked to her? Your grandmother? Usually she doesn't let anyone come anywhere near the house. People say she's crazy. Either that or senile—or both."

I turned to face him, and saw that look in his eyes I knew so well. *Poor little girl.* I was someone who inspired the same response that neglected puppies and performing bears at a circus did.

"She has that old guy Bæk-Nielsen keeping an eye on the place. Perhaps you've seen him? He's the one who told my dad that you were here." He stubbed out his smoke in the sand.

I thought about the old man Rosa and I had seen before. Apparently my grandmother's supervisor had been spying on us.

"I haven't spoken to her in years," I said, quick-stepping to the door once more. "We don't have . . . We don't have that kind of relationship."

When I put the keys in the lock, it stuck, and I inwardly cursed the city-paranoia that now was costing me precious seconds. My pulse was hammering through my whole body, with every heartbeat the clamor rang louder in my ears. Thomas had come up next to me, and, seeing me fumble with the lock, put a hand over mine.

"Here, let me try," he said. "I think it could do with some oil. It's pretty rusty. I can come over and see to it some time, if you'd like."

He might as well have burnt me with an iron rod, so swiftly had I pulled my hand away, but he didn't seem to notice. Just pushed the door open, taking a ridiculous bow as he did so. I didn't invite him in.

"My mom still talks about what happened," he said. "And then you just disappeared. Puff. René still lives here, and Robert and Mette got married. They've got the bakery."

"I didn't disappear," I said. "I just moved away. And I can't remember anything. Isn't that what I just said, for Christ's sake? I don't have a clue who you are, okay? If you want to talk to my grandmother, do it yourself."

I pulled Alex with me through the door and closed it behind me, my pulse beating hard and fast in my neck. My fingers hurt, in fact, the whole hand ached, my entire body was vibrating, but I got to the small, rock-hard couch before the shaking took hold with a vengeance. I managed to ask Alex to go on upstairs. He could look through the old *Donald Duck* comics in the loft in the meantime. I was okay, I assured him. He nodded, and reluctantly left me alone in the dark of the living room.

Big boy. I vowed to get a bottle of vodka for next time.

HELGI, 1994

Sometimes he wondered how his life would have been if Anna had died in the bathtub that night. Like now, for instance, as she stood bent over the tub with strands of her hair wrapped around her neck.

His life would have been different, of course.

Perhaps he would've gone to Århus to study, just like he'd dreamt of doing once, and perhaps there he would have met a wild and adventurous young girl studying tropical medicine who would have dragged him along to Africa or India or Borneo. Or perhaps he would've become a seaman or an oil-rigger or a teacher in Odense with a cheerful woman rollicking in his double bed that they shared with four children in a townhouse with a garden. He had never thought of it before that day at the Art Museum, but now he thought of nothing else. In the prefabs on the site with the boys, when he put on his overalls, and especially when he went to bed with Anna, her soft contours in a white night-dress lying next to him. Her back always turned.

She smelled of peach shampoo and that fatty Nivea-cream she always rubbed into her skin after her bath.

Anna. The woman who'd promised to stand by her man till death did them part.

The only thing he could remember from their early years together was an all-encompassing lust—which was probably as much as one would expect of a seventeen-year-old boy getting his leg over for the first time. Anna had not been beautiful in the way of some of the other girls, but she was pretty and sweet and eager to please. Appetizing. He'd liked her, there was no doubt about that, and they seemed to have been brought together by an unthinking hand that put her at the bicycle shed with a punctured bicycle tire at the exact moment he happened to be standing there, one of the last boys making his way home after school. Of course he had a bicycle pump, and he politely offered to pump some air into her tires—to no avail—and they ended up pushing their bikes home together, they were headed the same way, after all. Talk turned to the party at Eva's house that night, and he suggested they go there together, but he had never intended to ask her out. He never gave it a thought, nor did he think anything later, when Anna, after far too many drinks, leaned towards him, her lips slightly apart, her eyes blank, black as the night and filled with the same longing he knew from his own lonely evenings in his bedroom at home.

It hadn't been love, he could see that now. Just teenage hunger.

He had been irrepressible and insatiable, and the admiration of the other boys—both those down at the harbor and his classmates from school—was huge and laden with envy. He was doing it; he was having sex with a girl, and Anna had been so warm and willing and smiling. Even in the shameful silence that followed as he pulled on his socks, shorts, and pants once more.

And then one day she was standing on his mother's doorstep in tears with a suitcase in her hand. She had run away from home, because she wanted to be with him, she said, but it probably had more to do with everything else. The abortion in Aalborg. And her parents. Her family's religion was sated in shame, and Anna was inconsolable.

He felt guilty. Because he was the one who had insisted they didn't need condoms if he pulled out just before he came against her soft belly or rocking breasts. But that hadn't worked—of course it hadn't—and things went badly wrong on more occasions than he cared to remember. He got the girl pregnant because of his unruly dick. Back then, he had thought that was why people got married. The pregnancy was a trick of fate, because more than twenty years were to pass before another child blossomed in Anna's womb.

"Would you like to have sauce with the potatoes or would you prefer a chunk of butter instead?"

She turned towards him inquiringly and smiled, keeping her

mouth closed as she did so. A habit she'd acquired after he'd made some remark about her breath. He couldn't bear having her close to him.

"Butter is just fine."

They ate baked cod with mustard and potatoes to the sound of Ella's running commentary. Her teacher had drawn an ape on the blackboard, she had grazed her leg in gym class and got a plaster on her knee, Christian had fallen off the swing and she had seen Louise down at the harbor. She filled every silence with the same precision that she used to color in dresses and crowns on the heads of princesses.

"Do you want to watch a film with me, Mom?" Ella stared at Anna with big, vacant eyes. "Maybe *Father of Four?*"

Anna smiled and gently touched a hand to Ella's hair. "Of course," she said. "Perhaps Dad would like to go for a walk in the meantime."

Again that sidelong glance, a quiet reproach that made his hands ball into fists. But yes, he did want to go for a walk. He needed some air, he needed . . . the warmth in his chest rushed down to his crotch. Perhaps she would come today. Perhaps she was already waiting for him. The lack of certainty was part of the game; the part that was driving him crazy.

He zipped up his thin jacket, walked down the road and ducked behind the dunes. It was still warm, but the wind had acquired a hint of autumn, the light was soft against the fading blue sky. The thunder at the horizon was carried in over the lyme grass, drowning out all other sound.

He left the low-slung villas behind him and turned into the sandy paths of the conservancy. Just about here. Sometimes she came walking towards him from the deserted, wild no-man's-land of the dunes, but usually she was already waiting for him.

And so it was today. She was sitting with her arms wrapped around her knees, looking over the water, her long, blonde hair flying in the wind. He slid down next to her and took her hand, and she looked up at him with smiling, dark blue eyes. It was always the same, like being sucked into an abyss; a feeling that everything made sense when their fingers entwined and closed instinctively. She leaned her head on his shoulder.

"Hey, you."

He buried his nose in her hair. How he had missed her. Oh God, she'd been gone for so long.

"I've been losing my mind," he mumbled. "You didn't come yesterday."

It wasn't a question. He had learned to accept that she came and went as she pleased, rarely telling him where she had been in the interim. He suspected that she was married. This would explain a lot—but not everything. Sometimes she would disappear for an entire, painful week, and he would masturbate compulsively in her absence, a lump of sorrow and longing wedged in his throat.

But now she was here.

"How are things at home?" she asked.

"We were at the school yesterday to hear Ella's recital," he said. "'Puff, the Magic Dragon.' She knew all five verses by heart."

"Clever girl." She smiled. "I know that song. We used to sing it when I was at school."

He pricked his ears. He collected the merest bits of information about her, whirled her back in time in his mind, back to a scene constructed of black-painted plywood in a high school hall. He could hear her singing.

"That can't be very long ago," he said, brushing a thumb over her chin. "You're still a child yourself."

She laughed.

"Most people would consider a thirty-three-year-old woman to be all grown up, you know."

She dug in her bag and took out a royal-blue box. When she opened it, a jack-in-the-box popped up and swayed on its springs.

"For Ella," she said. "I made it myself."

"Who should I say it's from?"

She shrugged. "I saw her down on the beach one day. I was waiting for you. She looked wild and happy, like a troll, so I . . . I just wanted her to have it."

He pushed the jack back into its box and put it down next to him in the sand. His eyes followed the line of her collarbone, the little chain with the golden pendant, further down her V-neck, where he could just see the curves of her beautiful breasts. He swallowed hard and let his hand follow the same route his eyes had taken. He freed one of her breasts from her bra so he could look at it more closely. The nipple was small and pink and hard long before he lowered his head and took it in his mouth. She shifted slightly under his touch, resting her head against his neck as he fondled her nipple with his tongue.

"I've missed you," she said. "I miss you all the time."

"Hmm . . . " He straightened up and pulled off her T-shirt. Opened her bra and reached for the other breast. She smelled of flowers, and something sour-salty that he now knew was her cunt.

There was sand everywhere, but she had showed him how it could be done, how she liked it, when they met in the dunes. She turned round onto all fours, and he felt under her skirt, shifted her panties to the side, and thrust deep inside her from behind. She sighed, and he pushed deeper still; both the technique and his perseverance had been perfected over the long summer months. But the last thrust, just before they came together, was always the same. That bond with the universe, a breathless collapse into each other's arms. Sand below and blue skies above, their fingers entwined.

This was right, and Anna was wrong. How could he have lived more than half a life without knowing what love was? He had watched countless love scenes in the cinema with Anna, but it was only now he understood what they were about. *Almost fifty years old and never been kissed*, that's how he'd felt the first time he took Christi's hand in his. The thought of being with Christi at some point in the future glowed like a mid-summer-night's ball on the beach—and died just as swiftly again.

Anna will die if I leave her.

It will kill her.

We woke to the sound of a dog barking in the yard.

Alex had crawled into bed next to me and fallen asleep once the cramps had died down. The sun had been up for hours, and the loft was cooking hot.

"There's someone outside," said Alex. He leaned over the side of the bed and fished a Donald Duck comic up from the floor. "You better go see who it is."

"Or I could just stay in bed."

I pulled the blanket up over my head, but outside the dog had switched to an insistent falsetto that was difficult to ignore. There was a knock at the door, three firm raps, and I tumbled out of bed, still groggy. The aftereffects of the fit lingered like a stiffness in muscle and limb as I dragged myself down the stairs and opened the door.

"Were you still sleeping?"

It was that guy again. Ex-classmate Thomas. I had no difficulty remembering either his name or his neo-pubescent get-up. The choice of the day was a hooded sweater and a steel-blue, serrated earring that looked like a nut sans bolt. I wasn't in the mood to reply and was pretty sure the question was rhetorical anyway. I was scantily dressed in my T-shirt and panties and peered at him and the world through millimeter-wide slits.

"It's ten-thirty in the morning," he said. "Haven't you got stuff to do?"

"Like what?" I held his gaze. Normal people, people with jobs and houses and cars and dogs and summer houses and holidays in Thailand, liked to think of my life was an interesting—almost exotic—affair, subject matter fit for anthropologists and psychiatrists alike.

He smiled. "Actually, I just wanted to know if you'd thought about . . . about selling the house. Whether you'd spoken to your grandmother?"

I shook my head.

"Why don't you and your dad get the old man to talk to her? You both know him, don't you? Bæk-Nielsen, right?"

"We've asked him, and he doesn't want to," said Thomas. "He reckons it's between you and your grandmother."

"Hmm . . . tough luck for you guys, huh?"

A flash from my confirmation ceremony. I couldn't recall having invited my grandmother, but she'd showed up anyway. Even back then she seemed to have one foot poised on the edge of the grave. She spoke Danish with a thick Icelandic accent, you could barely understand what she was saying, and between the roast pork and the ice cream, she gripped my elbow and went on and on about my father. About how sorry he was that I'd never answered his letters.

I fled, and went back to join in on the festivities. A whole row of teachers and advisors had donned their nicest party dresses; there was a telegram and two thousand kroner from social services. Not a dry eye in the house.

I hadn't answered her letters since.

"Perhaps it's tough luck for you too," said Thomas, watching me all the while. "It could be a good deal for you as well. Having your family around is usually a good thing."

"I just live here," I said. "Can't you get your dog to stop that?"

Thomas's black Labrador-runt was still hollering at the side wall abutting the old stable.

"Yes, I'm sorry about that." Thomas dug both hands into the pockets of his sweater. "I think you've got a marten in your loft. The dog's gone nuts."

"You don't say."

I smiled stiffly and tried to close the door, but he was too quick, just managing to jam a foot in the door.

"I also wanted to ask, if you . . . if the two of you maybe wanted to go down to the harbor for an ice cream. We could chat about old times, you know. It might be fun."

"No thanks. I'm just fine with things the way they are. Don't you have stuff to do yourself? You look like a fixed-day-job-followed-by-a-little-TV-in-the-evenings kinda guy. A guy who jerks off Wednesdays and Saturdays."

The last bit might have been unnecessary, but it felt like he was rubbing himself up against me on the dance floor, for Christ's sake. His penetrating chumminess called for an aggressive defense.

He glared at me. I could almost hear the cranking behind that thick skull of his. It had probably been his dad who'd come up with that ice-cream-down-at-the-harbor routine, and once that had crashed to the floor, he was completely blank.

"Or I could show you where your mother was shot," he said.

A gust of wind tore at his sweater and flapping track-suit pants, but his body was rooted to the ground. He just stood there, looking at me, his legs slightly bowed, his hands buried deep in his pockets. A flash of light at the edge of my mind; a pounding pain above the right eye, heated voices, an attic bathed in yellow light. It wasn't enough to push me over the edge, no spasms in my body, no foaming at the mouth, but enough to sharpen what I called my live eye. An eye for all that was naked and ugly in my immediate environment; the cracks in the stable wall, the flapping garbage bags over gaping windows, the sharp, yellow fiber-glass pushing through the ceiling. I leaned a hand against the doorframe.

"Why would I want to see that?"

He shrugged nonchalantly. His eyes weren't unfriendly, just curious—as if I were a fascinating case of perfect idiocy.

"I'm not sure," he said. "I guess I would want to know, if it had been me, who . . . If it had been my dad who'd blown my mother's head off just outside my doorstep. You could end up in that hollow in the dunes before you know it. Most of us locals avoid the place, but the German tourists often sunbathe there in the summer. They don't know any better, of course."

I breathed in deeply.

I'd never thought about where the whole episode took place. To my mind, it was merely an impenetrable and dark terrain—not an actual place. But that was before. I looked out over the dunes, wondering whether I would feel anything standing on the actual spot. A cold wind, a hint of terror hovering in the air. I was neither religious nor superstitious, but I had always given my childhood home a wide berth. Like the coward that I was.

I heard Alex rummaging around upstairs—he was probably getting dressed and going about his compulsively thorough hand-washing routine. Sometimes he only needed to do it three times to avoid death in a car crash, sometimes seven times; sometimes he didn't have to wash his hands at all. The magnitude of his fear swung in time with the frequency of my fits like an eerily precise pendulum.

"It's so long ago now that it doesn't matter anymore," I said. "But if it makes you happy to be the designated tour guide, then fine. Let's go."

WE WALKED THROUGH the lyme grass with the dog frisking around us.

"This entire area has now been placed under conservation," said Thomas. "You aren't allowed to build anything here, and you have to stay on the paths; if the lyme grass is trampled and disappears, everything would blow away." He smiled briefly. "Do you recognize any of it?"

I shrugged. "I recognize the scene. The landscape, the houses, the sounds and smells. But the actors and the story are missing."

He nodded, and we turned along a path that led in the direction of the sea.

"The body remembers those things, not the brain," he said. "I read about it once. Memory is a finicky little devil."

We had reached the top of a dune and could see the ocean. An enormous bird of prey hovered in the sky, its wings spread wide over the water. I followed its motion with my eyes. Suddenly, it tucked in its wings and plunged towards the sea. A white-tailed eagle. One more thing I knew without knowing how or why. Thomas cast a searching glance into the dunes.

"There," he said, pointing.

I stopped in my tracks. I felt like I needed to bring something.

You cannot come to the dead empty-handed; it felt like a lack of respect. My mother was buried in a graveyard somewhere in Northern Jutland, but I hadn't been there as an adult. My second foster mother dutifully drove me up there a couple of times, but I don't remember having felt anything in particular when I got there. At most, a gnawing irritation over my fretting foster mother; she had bought me a bunch of tulips on the drive over, and watched me from a distance, wringing her hands, as I laid them on the grave. She seemed to expect tears. I failed to deliver. I just stood there, staring at a gravestone. It was brown, brightly polished, and very ugly. When she'd had enough, we piled into the car and drove home again.

This was different. It struck a live chord in a way I'd never experienced before. It was here my mother had ceased to exist. The thought felt like a slow-motion explosion in my head, a gradual unfolding of something dark and mournful.

I bent down to a thorny bush, Burnet roses, and plucked a single flower. Burnet roses have glittering white petals and a sungold center. I remembered that once, a thousand years ago, I'd gathered bunches of these flowers and crushed their petals in a bowl to make perfume for my mother.

Then I followed Thomas down into the hollow. A hard gust of wind whirled sand around us, and I pinched my eyes closed. Fucking wind. I'd only been in Klitmøller two days, and it was already driving me insane.

"She lay here in the sand," said Thomas. "Do you remember the place?"

I tucked as much hair as possible behind my ears, and looked around.

This hollow between the dunes looked the same as all the others. Sand, lyme grass, thorny hip, and Burnet rose bushes. Nothing to see. No pools of blood, shattered teeth, congealed brain tissue, or splinters of skull.

"Why would I remember it?"

"You were here when it happened—or right after, at least," said Thomas. "My mom says you were covered in blood when the police finally found you out there." He was turned away from the sea. "You had fled into the plantation. You could have frozen to death. It was November, after all, and cold as hell. The whole town was out looking for you. I remember sitting up in my room, praying to God they'd find you in time."

I stared at him.

"That's a lie," I said. "Surely I would have remembered that. Something like that I would have remembered."

I sat on my haunches in the sand and dug a little dip for the Burnet rose so it wouldn't blow away, but even inside the hole, the wind tore at its frail petals.

"Believe whatever you want. But you can ask anyone in town, and they'll tell you the same." Thomas dug a pack of cigarettes out of his pocket and offered me one. I took it without meeting his gaze. We smoked in silence for a while.

"Do you remember that we were really good friends once, you and I?" he said.

"I don't remember anything."

I picked up a stick and started drawing in the sand. Anything, as long as I didn't have to look at him. I knew what he expected to see: grief, perhaps some inkling of sorrow, like when you hear a really sad story. Tears would make me human, but the truth was that I didn't feel a thing. Yes, I was angry with my father. But I was just as angry with my mother. For marrying the bastard. Women who marry psychopaths are hard to like. Especially if they are dumb enough to have the psycho's child.

I stared resolutely down into the sand till Thomas sat down next to me. He'd quit staring.

"You were wild," he said. "Like a boy or a troll. You could run faster than any of us, and you had the most amazing collection of sea urchins. Sea urchins and amber. Our parents let us comb the beach alone, even as kids, and you had eyes that picked up on everything. Once you found a lump of amber the size of a fist. Have you still got it?"

I had rifled through the contents of the suitcase that had accompanied me from foster family to foster family over the first couple of years. There was no amber inside. In fact, I had no idea what had happened to all our stuff. It must have been sold, or thrown away.

I shook my head.

"Well, we grew up with the North Sea, and we were clever enough to stay clear of the water. None of us would dream of going swimming in these waters. Only the tourists do."

"And what about you? How do you pass your time?"

I worked my stick deeper into the hole, piling dark, wet sand onto the sides.

"Plumbing," he said. "So let me know if you need to get your pipes done. I live in my parents' old house, if you remember where that is."

"No, I don't."

"Okay. Well, it's close to your parents' old house, so we're bound to bump into each other. So remember . . . free plumbing."

"Thanks."

"I didn't mean anything sexual."

"I know that."

I got up, brushed the sand off my legs, and bounded back up the dune. And stopped dead. Three quarters of the way up I had spotted a solitary, long-stemmed rose tangled in the lyme grass. I picked it up and turned it over in my hands. I reckoned that it was a couple of days old; the petals had originally been yellow, but now had the hue and consistency of coffee-stained paper. But it was the note tied to the stalk that made me freeze. It had been torn from a checkered pad of paper and there was a black cross drawn in the top right-hand corner. Below the cross, a single word:

Anna.

When I got back to the house Alex was standing by the garage, triumphantly waving a fishing rod in the air. He had already eaten his breakfast and decided to go on a scavenger hunt in the yard, starting with the stable and the garage, where he was sorting out a large pile of junk: the yard was now furnished with a set of rickety old garden chairs, an equally ugly, grey plastic garden table, a yellow handcart, a rack of empty bottles, and a woman's black bike with neither tires nor saddle. But there was no mistaking that it was the pile of rusty tackle, spoon-bait, and reel of fishing line that had captured his fancy most. His dark eyes were alive with glee.

"Where can you go fishing around here?"

"Down by the harbor," I said automatically. "You can fish from the pier or in the harbor itself."

"Do you want to come along?"

"I'll come down later."

He looked a little disappointed, but the thrill of finding the fishing gear wasn't that easily to kill. I helped him unwind the rusty pile of hooks and bait, and we finally managed to assemble the tackle, reel, and line onto the rod. For good measure, I armed him with a knife from the kitchen and a plastic bag to carry his bounty—should he be so lucky as to catch anything.

He disappeared, walking tall and barefooted over the dunes, and I waited till he was out of sight before laying the rose down on the garden table.

It shouldn't have surprised me that someone in Klitmøller still mourned the loss of my mother. Before she died out there, she must have had a life. Perhaps she'd had friends, or gone to choir practice, Italian classes, or whatever the hell it was you did to pass the time on the wind-blown evenings in Klitmøller. I just had a hard time believing that my mother had had that kind of life.

In the hardcover *Book of Childhood Memories* that my second foster mother had made for me—a couple of months before I smashed all the mirrors in her house—there were several pictures of my mother. The book had only traveled with me during the first couple of moves, and then disappeared, but I could remember the pictures clearly: fuzzy snapshots of a serious-looking woman with me sitting on her lap, my mother wandering down an anonymous road with me in tow. In all the pictures her shoulders were hunched around her ears like an old woman, her eyes avoiding the lens of the camera.

She looked like someone who was always alone, even in the company of others.

You always recognize your own affliction in other people.

I untied the note from the stalk and slipped it between two of my grandmother's thick books on the bookcase in the lounge. Afterward I went back outside, loaded the rack of empties onto the handcart and took them to the camping site for recycling. A return of almost fifty kroner. Enough for a packet of tobacco and two kilos of potatoes from the improvised grocery store next to Tourist Information. I considered swiping a roll of chocolate cookies for Alex, but felt the sting of a bad conscience when I saw the exhausted expression on the face of the woman behind the counter. Life as the owner of Klit-møller Camping—pearl of the northern North Sea coast—was clearly something that wore on both health and humor. Many things had been easier in the faceless Netto in Hvidovre.

We wished one another a *nice day!* with a smile.

I sat outside in the sun and rolled myself a couple of smokes. In fact, a drink would have been in order. I felt sufficiently calm without one, but when my hands weren't occupied with cigarette rolling, they tended to rap a rhythmical riot, now combing through my hair, now tapping on my thighs, now drawing glowing smoke-rings in the air. Thomas's words dug into my flesh.

I was there.

Had I seen her die?

I pulled out my phone and scrolled down my pathetic list of contacts till Kirsten's number came up. She picked up after a single ring.

"Ella, for God's sake. Klitmøller?"

"How did you know?"

"You've changed your address. That kind of thing doesn't get past us. Did you really think I'd just let it go and forget all about you?"

"Yes, that's exactly what I think you should do. I no longer live in your jurisdiction."

"Christ, Ella." Kirsten was breathing hard on the other end of the line. "I was seconds away from notifying the police and sending out a search party. I thought you were suicidal, that you were headed for Copenhagen harbor and taking Alex with you. You had just been released from Psych, for Christ's sake! What else should I think?! Luckily Rosa called and told me you'd gone up North before I had a chance to initiate an investigation. Every time you pull a stunt like this, it goes on your file. It isn't good for you, and it isn't good for Alex. And that business with Lisa . . . If she had pressed charges, you would have been finished for sure, Ella."

She held an artistic pause, breathed deeply, and I could hear her making her way down the long corridors of the governmental buildings of the social services offices in Hvidovre. Kirsten had always preferred to conduct her private client conversations in the bicycle shed.

"Are you all right?" she finally asked.

"Yes."

"And Alex?"

"He's fishing down at the harbor."

I could detect Kirsten's smile beaming down the satellite connection.

"Okay. So now that we've established that you're okay and that Alex has gone fishing, why are you calling? There's not much I can do for you from my end. As you so rightly pointed out, you are very much out of my jurisdiction."

"I want my files."

"Which files do you mean?"

"Everything. Everything on my childhood. The court case, the foster parents, Bakkegården—the whole damn lot. I want to see if there's anything written there about my mother."

Kirsten was silent for a while.

"Naturally you're entitled to see your files, Ella, but, quite frankly, I'm not comfortable with you reading those papers when you don't have a psychiatrist on standby. One who knows you. You're not exactly stable, emotionally. And I still think you should get Alex professional help. Your apartment is still available until the end of the month, and I'm sure that Lisa . . . "

"I want to see those files," I said flatly. "Just tell me what I need to do to get hold of them. I don't want to argue with you on this."

Another pause.

"Send me an official application, and I'll see what I can do. But I'm still worried about you."

"My case is no longer a matter for your concern. And we're fine. Really."

She was quiet for a bit.

"Ella," she finally said. "I've known you a long time, and I like you, although God knows you're hardly a model client. You're too bright and too angry to be caught up in the system. That has always been your problem, my girl. I think you should come home so we can work this out. Here, where we know you best."

Something softened in my chest. Kirsten had always had a power over me that stemmed from her deep voice, her round form, and her willingness to reach out and take me in her arms. Then and there I was glad she was no more than a voice on the end of a line.

"What will happen if I come back, Kirsten? I want you to be completely honest. As a friend to Alex and me. What will happen, Kirsten?"

A long silence. I knew she was at war with herself, and I knew what this meant. Kirsten was an excellent social worker, she'd been working for the department of social services for a hundred years. She wasn't the one who was trying to take Alex away from me, but she had seen enough to know if others were.

"Thank you," I said. "You have my new address. I'll look forward to hearing from you about those files."

Then I cut the connection.

Alex sat dipping his rod in the water at the far end of the pier when I got to the harbor.

The wind had picked up, and white foam was whipped into the air by the brutal meeting of sea and stone. When I slid down next to him, I saw that he'd actually had a bite. Something dark and wet lay in the plastic bag, the knife was smeared with blood and torn intestines.

"Three." He had to shout to be heard above the roar of the sea. "I've caught three flat fishes. One of the surfers killed the first one for me, but the other two I killed myself. We can eat them for dinner tonight."

I kissed him on the forehead. It was cold and salty.

"My big, strong huntsman," I said. "Beats collecting cans, huh?"

He laughed, and pointed towards the beach.

"That surfer guy from yesterday helped me. He said I could try his surfboard later. Can I?"

The long-haired wetsuit, Magnus, looked over in our direction and waved. I looked away. I told myself I had no illusions what the guy was after, and it had nothing to do with either Alex or the surfboard. I also told myself that I wasn't flattered.

"You go on ahead," I said. "I'll take care of our fish in the meantime."

Alex drew in his line, left the rod lying next to me, and bounded off to the beach. We hadn't spoken about leaving Hvidovre, or the spasms that had lasted deep into the night. The only remaining signs of the fit the night before lingered in my aching legs. I took the three fat fish out of the bag, slit their bellies, and cleaned out the black, congealed blood and insides with my index finger. I ran a hand along the sandpaper-rough surface of their skins and felt a wild, child-like joy spill from a spot just below my breastbone. Then I climbed down between the boulders and washed the fish in the waves. One more thing I knew how to do. My mother or father must have showed me how to clean fish. I hoped it was my mom.

Down at the beach the surfer guy had helped Alex up onto his surfboard and was literally showing him the motions. Alex had been kitted out with an orange life vest and they were standing knee-deep in the waves together. Alex clambered up onto the board on wobbly legs, then opted to kneel on the board instead. Even from a distance, I could see his smile, both exhilarated and awkward at once.

Klitmøller was as good as a holiday for him. If Kirsten's colleagues in Hvidovre managed to convince the welfare office in Thisted that I was unfit to be a mother, then at least Alex would have experienced this. He had seen the sea. The closest we had ever come to a holiday was taking the bus to Amager Strand while the sun melted the rest of the city of Copenhagen.

The surfer-guy waved at me, and I waved back. I had returned the fish to the plastic bag and was climbing my way up onto the pier when my eyes leveled on a pair of well-worn, brown leather shoes. I looked up to meet the gaze of the man I had seen on the road outside our house on our first day in Klitmøller. He was a lot older than I had first assumed—he looked at least eighty years old. His shiny scalp was covered in liver spots, he was skeleton-thin, but the broad hands and shoulders gave me the impression of someone that once had been a big man.

He smiled down at me.

"Ella?"

I scampered up onto the pier and nodded in his direction, just once.

"My name is Bæk-Nielsen. I'm looking after your grandmother's house. Perhaps you saw me the other day?"

I shook my head, very slightly. It had always been a strategy of mine to tell other people as little as possible. When your most intimate secrets are pooled in a database that is shared with ten thousand government-appointed caregivers you tend to fiddle with those precious few details you had to yourself.

"Your grandmother has asked me to drive you—you and your son—to Thisted. She would like to see you both."

I felt an ice-cold jab in my stomach. She had no business in contacting us. She was sick and senile and dying. She was already half dead fifteen years ago, for Christ's sake.

"Thanks, but no thanks," I said. "I'm not interested in reviving the acquaintance."

"You're living in her house."

He practically had to shout to be heard over the howling wind. His broad beige trouser legs fluttered against his knuckle-thin thighs; he hardly amounted to any kind of physical threat. And I could just take off if I had to. I glanced over my shoulder at Alex and the surfer. They were still standing knee-deep in the waves, maneuvering the rocking surfboard.

"I didn't realize this obliged me to talk to her. This wasn't stipulated in her letter, and quite frankly, I don't feel like listening to her shit."

The old man raised his eyebrows, but stood his ground.

"As you may know, your grandmother believes your father is innocent."

I shrugged. "If that's what she wants to believe, it's fine by me. She's his mother. I'd probably feel the same should Alex blow his girlfriend's brains out one day. A mother's love is blind."

"She believes you might know something that could help him."

I had trouble suppressing a sudden, inappropriate urge to laugh. The rumors about my grandmother's insanity weren't exaggerated.

"The man was convicted. He has served his sentence. I fail to understand how I could be of any use to him now. And even if I could . . . why would I want to help my mother's murderer?"

Bæk-Nielsen followed my gaze towards the beach and Alex, who was still frolicking in the waves.

"I'm not sure I believe your father is innocent," he said kindly. "But there may be some good in this for you. You've never had a family, so you don't know what you're missing. Family isn't love. That's nothing but sentimental blubber. Family is an extension of your own body. Many youngsters believe they can live without the bonds they are born with, but for most of us, these bonds are the only ties we have in the universe. This you will realize when you're older, but right now,

I am here as your grandmother's friend. Not yours. She has lost everyone who has ever meant anything to her, and now she would like to see you. And your son."

Out in the breakers Alex had managed to stay standing on the board for a brief moment, long enough for him to feel the surge of the sea and lift his arms high in triumphant glee.

"She's unhappy," I said. "I can understand that. But I can't help her. Tell her I'm not interested."

Bæk-Nielsen looked like he wanted to hit me, but he couldn't force me to come. And we both knew it. I shrugged, tried to swallow the painful lump in my throat. Then I picked up the fishing rod, walked past him, and left him standing on the wind-blown pier. My hands had already started to shake, and it was only a question of time before the remainder of my body followed suit.

It was time to leave.

I WAS OUT of breath and weak in the knees by the time I reached Alex and surfer-Magnus. The surfing lesson was over, and Alex was sitting in the sand, frozen stiff in his wet jeans. His lips were blue and his teeth were chattering, even though Magnus had wrapped a towel over his shoulders. A big-breasted girl in a bikini was woven into the luxurious terry cloth of his towel.

"We're leaving," I said.

"But Magnus said I could have another go once I've warmed up," protested Alex.

"I'm sorry," I said. "But we have to get our dinner into the fridge, don't we? Otherwise it will spoil."

Alex bought my excuse. Anxious about his loot, he sprang to his feet, as did Magnus, who had exchanged his wet-suit for a pair of large, floral-print boxer shorts.

"I'll walk you guys home." He smiled and passed me a can of beer that he'd already opened. It wasn't vodka, but better than nothing. I took a gulp and stole a glance at the pier. The old man was nowhere to be seen.

WE WALKED ALONG the beach with the fishing rod and a

six-pack that Magnus had hooked on the last digit of his index finger. I was relieved to hear that he wasn't from Klitmøller, he came from Aalborg, and was hardly likely to have been born when infamy came my way. He was harmless, almost soothing in all his boyish ignorance, his words devoid of depth. The conversation floated as easily as newspapers on the wind and waves.

Magnus liked techno and had a dog named Dirk that his parents took care of while he was away. He'd been surfing in Australia, and one day, he was going to move down there, live on Bondi Beach and go surfing every day, earning money on the stock market while everyone else was asleep—if he wasn't eaten by a great white shark first, that is. Hah, hah.

I let him talk. Talk suited me just fine.

"I also like skiing and motor-bikes," he said. "What do you like doing, Ella?"

He caught my gaze, and held it till I felt that well-known lurch in my belly. I was drinking fast—I had downed the first beer and was well on my way with my second by the time Alex had run on ahead to have a warm bath and get his fish safely stowed in the fridge.

"Would you like to sit in the dunes for a while?" I said.

Magnus looked at me with a smile that was supremely self-confident, bordering on the arrogant. This was exactly how I liked my men. I knew his type. He could get all the women he wanted, but he was a bit lazy, and preferred the easy conquest, the imperfect girls, so he could get in fast and leave just as swiftly. Girls like me, for example. I had no illusions about marriage and a white picket fence. I never had.

We walked into the dunes where we wouldn't be visible from the beach. I drank one more beer before he leaned over and kissed me, long and deep. Exactly as I had hoped. Then he pulled off my T-shirt and ran his fingertips down the thin scars along the insides of my arms.

"Where did you get these?" he asked.

I shrugged. "I was a fucked-up teenager."

"And now . . . ?"

"Now I'm a fucked-up adult."

My tongue traced along his collarbone and continued down till I found a nipple. It tasted of the sea. I had one hand inside his floral-print boxer shorts as he lovingly took care of my lower body. His rings were cold, but he was good with his hands. Very, very good. I wasn't his first true love, that was for sure.

Afterward we had a last beer each; we were sitting leaning up against one another. His hands played in my hair.

"I think I'll be off, now," he said quietly. "Will I see you again?"

I mumbled a "maybe" that I hoped was sufficiently vague to prevent him from making plans for the next day. I liked taking my liberties in so far as I had any to take.

"You know where you can find me," he said. "Alex is welcome to come by and surf, anytime."

I watched him as he strolled barefooted along the beach. A handsome young man, who would certainly never end up living on Bondi Beach. He would get married to a nice girl who worked in a bank, fixed her hair, got her nails done and her chassis waxed. The kind of girl you could show off to both your friends and your family with pride. They would buy a nice, prefabricated house on the outskirts of Aalborg. I wasn't bitter. And my body had finally found some peace.

I closed my eyes and let the sand run through my fingers. It was cold sitting there on my own, now that the clouds were blocking out the sun.

A flash of myself in shorts and red sandals with white flowers on the straps. I'm watching two people woven into each other. A man and a woman. They are fully clothed, but their clothes are rumpled, they are heaving, pressing their bodies against each other in rhythmic movements. The woman's long hair is covering the man's face, and they don't notice me, even though I'm standing relatively close by, watching. Seeing them gives me the same feeling I get in my belly when I watch a fight at school. Fear, mixed with a heat that spreads from my chest all the way down between my legs. Then the woman turns her face towards me. It is contorted, as if she were in terrible pain.

I back up, tumble down the side of the dune, and run back to the boy who is waiting for me on the shore.

"Did you see it?" he says with a crooked smile. He knew. "Did you see them? They were doing it in the dunes."

We were woken, hot and thirsty, by the burning rays of sun slanting in through the roof window.

Alex had woken me twice in the dead of night, bolting upright in bed, screaming, sweat pouring down his face. His nightmares had always been terrifying, but the torments of the night before had been particularly bad, even for him. The kind where he screamed in pain and terror at invisible beings that threatened to tear out his flesh.

But by morning all was forgotten.

The heat and the light from the window reminded me of the dancing patterns of light that Tommy from Bakkegården used to beam onto ants, beetles, and human eyes with his magnifying glass. I rolled out of the beam of light, bouncing both Alex and me out of the bed as I did so. He laughed.

I forced myself to stand under the cold stream of water in the shower for five minutes before we ate breakfast and walked into town. Or rather, I walked. Alex danced ahead, still wearing the same jeans shorts he'd been wearing for the last week. I had already tossed a pile of underwear and a chunk of flaking hand soap into the archaic washing machine in the kitchen. Washing powder was one of the first things I would have to get hold of somehow.

I needed money. Soon. The money I had borrowed from Rosa would only last for a couple of weeks, if that, and then only if I was very careful what I spent it on *and* found some kind of supplementary income in the interim. Of course we could collect empty cans in Klitmøller, there were plenty of tourists, and where there were tourists, beer was consumed. But I hadn't staked out the hunting grounds yet and I had no idea who else would claim the territory.

The grocery store was small and dark compared to the neon-lit

Netto I was used to from Hvidovre and there was only one other customer gliding along the aisles as we came in: a middle-aged woman with henna-colored hair and tinkling bracelets on her liver-spotted arms. I collected a tray of frozen chicken on sale, rice, tomatoes, and half a gallon of milk, and while Alex was distracted by a display of brightly-colored beach toys and fishing nets I managed to smuggle half a liter of vodka and packet of chewing gum in under my sweater. The store owner himself was commandeering a boy in the storeroom out back and Henna-hair was nowhere to be seen.

I had stolen before.

Mincemeat and coffee and toilet cleaner from Netto, Lego blocks from the slap-provokingly garish Toys "R" Us, and mobile phone covers from Fona Electronics. Usually it happened towards the end of the month, when I was broke, but sometimes I did it because I felt like it. Doctor Erhardsen would say it was because I was angry. He would probably be right. The hideous advertisements called for it. Across the board, they were tritely inviting, styled in well-composed scenes of perfect people in perfect worlds; a pseudoscience that relies on Photoshop and the manipulation of our senses, and it worked with everyone—including me: the flat-broke-weirdo consumer that belonged in the shabby, low-performance consumer bracket that the advertising industry habitually ignored. But the world pissed on me, so I pissed on the world. That was my moral, if I had one. But the grocery store owner could be a problem in the long term. I didn't want to know the people I stole from.

Afterward we went down to the beach to watch the surfers at the pier. Alex went down onto the beach to skim stones, exactly as he used to do on the duck pond in Hvidovre Park. A long, beautiful, throw that skimmed just above the surface of the water, the stone bouncing several times before it disappeared into the waves. He was so engrossed in his skimming that I saw the woman before he did. It was the henna-haired woman from the grocery store. The faux radiance of her red hair preceded her long before she stopped to stand directly in front of Alex. She bent down and picked up a stone, handing it to him with same solemnity as the Pale Faces once offered the American Indian shiny beads and blankets on the prairie.

Alex accepted the stone shyly, smiled and nodded as he said something in reply. He stepped back a couple of paces and skimmed the stone over the waves. It bounced over the surface several times, then disappeared. I couldn't see her face, but I knew that the woman was smiling. Then she turned, looked at me and waved. Her long red hair flew wildly in the wind.

"I WOULD VERY much like to make a sketch of Alex. He's a beautiful boy."

The woman, who had introduced herself as Barbara, nodded in the direction of the parking lot.

"And what would that cost me?"

I didn't mean to be unfriendly. That's just the way I tended to come across. And in my experience, it was wise to be on your guard when someone started saying nice things about your children. Alex *was* a beautiful boy, but it was rare for people to mention it without wanting something from me.

"Nothing." She flashed a smile with beautiful, film-star white teeth that didn't fit the rest of the picture. "I only charge the German tourists. This sketch would be for my own work."

"So you sketch?"

"Yes, I have my own studio just outside town. Perhaps the two of you would like to come over . . . It would only take half an hour to make a sketch, and perhaps take a few pictures. I'd be happy to pay the young man a hundred kroner for his time."

It was not as if we had better things to do, Alex and I. The long summer days stretched in a blank row before us, at least until a caseworker from Thisted Welfare Office had registered me in their system and started sending me window-enveloped letters with threats of job placement initiatives and pep-talks at the local job center. It would take time. There was a change of address to attend to and a transfer of files and papers. And, even armed with an artillery of files, Welfare would be obliged to send one of their own, probably overly-exerted, caseworkers to talk to me personally so he or she could file an independent evaluation of the case—and that at the beginning of the summer holidays to boot.

So yes, we did have the time. It was Barbara herself I had a problem with. There was something at once aggressive and insecure in the way she had approached us. She was definitely some kind of social outcast, her artist existence a thin veneer for her pathetic life on the fringe of respectable society.

But Alex was game. Barbara's compliment had won ground with a boy's pre-teen vanity. But it was more than that. Alex liked to draw as well. He had won a couple of art contests at school. It was mostly ninja warriors and skeletons armed with shields and a large arsenal of knives, swords, and fatal weaponry, but he was clearly keen to see what Barbara had done herself. Not to mention the hundred kroner—a sizable fortune that Alex rarely chanced upon for so little effort. His hopeful gaze rested heavily upon me.

"Sure." I forced myself to smile at Henna-hair. "It seems he'd like that very much."

"Yay!"

The woman clapped her hands affectedly like a teenager in a Disney movie and we followed in the wake of her flowing robes to the beaten-up van in the parking lot. The sliding door was open wide and there was a sign propped up against the wheel. *Die schönsten Urlaub Souvenirs wird gezeichnet. 150 kr.* A couple of laminated portraits in A-5-format were stacked next to the sign. I threw a disparaging glance at the drawings. They looked like those sentimental sketches you find in *Good Housekeeping*, albeit an amateur rendition. Children with large, expressionless eyes, hair that looked as if it had been glued into place. The shadows were grey and smudged at the edges. The noses were asymmetrical, the lips over pronounced. There were also a couple of aquarelle landscapes of the sea and beach and fir trees and houses in mint green, yellow, and beige. In the back of the van a flea-bitten German shepherd looked on with weary, amiable eyes as Henna-hair packed up her things.

"Did you draw all of these?" Clearly impressed, Alex nodded at yet another stack of laminated works in the back of the van.

"Yes. Shall we go? It's just down the road . . . " Henna-hair flashed her chalk-white teeth once more and motioned vaguely in the direction of the highway. "You could always stay for lunch, if you like. It would be fun. I have a wonderful little place."

Free grub, I thought. At least that was something. My mood lifted a few degrees.

"JUST DOWN THE road" proved to be an understatement.

We sped past the WELCOME TO KLITMØLLER sign and drove on for several miles without her showing any inclination of slowing down. On the contrary. The landscape flattened out into meadows and plantations of thin, sickly looking pine trees.

"Are you on holiday or do you have your own place in town?"

Our new best friend, Barbara, was smoking with her left hand nonchalantly resting on the rolled down window.

"We moved here a couple of days ago," said Alex. "We have a house in town."

"Marvelous." She tucked a wayward strand of hair behind her ear. "This is a wonderful place to live . . . Isn't the nature fantastic? It's so peaceful. And you come from Copenhagen, I hear."

"Hvidovre." Alex was squinting at the landscape rushing by. "Will we be there soon?"

She nodded, pointing towards a barely visible gap between the pine trees. "I'm just over there."

The van bumped down a sandy road in the middle of a plantation and stopped in front of a house that resembled my grandmother's to a T: crumbling and dilapidated, consisting of three ramshackle buildings. Several stray cats raced up to meet us, rubbing themselves up against the warm tires of the car. To the west of the house, in what once must have been an herb garden, there was a junk yard of three rusty cars with grass and sapling trees growing through their bodywork.

Barbara followed my gaze.

"They belong to my landlord," she said. "The house is great, but he's a lunatic. I'm only staying here till I find something else. But come inside, come inside."

She collected her shopping bags and led the way into the low-ceilinged kitchen.

"If you have something that needs to be kept cool, you can put it in the fridge," she said, pointing to the crouching monstrosity standing in the middle of the room. The extension wires were yellowed by age, and when I opened the lid, I was met with the sour whiff of decomposition. I found space for my milk cartons and chicken inside, banged shut the lid, and followed Alex and the woman into the lounge.

"The light is good over here," she said, motioning to Alex that he should stand in front of a man-sized, battered easel. Apparently she'd opted for doing a pencil sketch in a larger format than the drawings we'd seen in her van.

"Now if you'd just take off as much of your clothing as you feel comfortable with," she went on. Alex looked less at ease now. He'd probably envisioned something more in the style of the polo-shirted portraits of children he'd seen in the van. He glanced nervously at me.

"It's up to you, Alex," I said. "We can just go home, if you'd prefer."

He shrugged awkwardly, tossed his T-shirt on the floor, and sat himself down in profile as Barbara had instructed him to. The sun was streaming in through the window and cast a warm glow over his body, the black hair and hooked nose giving him the air and aspect of an upstart Greek god. Barbara got to work.

"Can you make a living on this?" I asked, looking around me. The coffee table at the opposite end of the lounge was overflowing with portraits, half-drawn sketches, cigarette ash, and dust.

"Umm . . ." Her hands were moving in rapid strokes behind the easel. "It's probably more a question of living for than making a living from it. I make a little money in town and sometimes customers send me photos to copy in response to an advertisement I have in the local paper. For parties and grandparents, you know. But I only charge a hundred and fifty kroner for a picture and they take a long time to do."

I nodded. I didn't know anything about art, but I noted that assembling arms, legs, and torso in some kind of orderly fashion made Barbara pull strained—bordering on pained—faces.

"Of course I would prefer to work on my own drawings," she said. "Landscapes. And portraits like these. I've had a couple of exhibitions at Hanstholm library . . . but people aren't very interested in original art. They would rather have a print of Monet hanging over the sofa, you know? Seen from that point of view, we live in a poor country."

I suppressed a yawn. Barbara reminded me of my neighbors back in Hvidovre. There was a diffuse indictment of the entire world just below the surface of her words. *I never get my just rewards.* I would bet my next bottle of vodka that, at best, she had two paying customers per month, black market, of course, and that the remainder of her income consisted of a lousy pension from a social office that didn't know what else to do with her.

I had a sudden urge to get the hell out of there, gratis lunch or not. I got up abruptly. Half an hour had long since passed, especially if you included the drive in the calculation.

"I think we'd better be going . . . "

Henna-hair narrowed her eyes and bit into her lip with those all-too-white teeth of hers. She had a grotesque amount of make-up on her face. A thick layer of foundation gave her complexion the same color and texture as clay. Her lips were just as fire-red as her hair.

"Already? I was just getting started. Well then, I'll just take a picture."

She took out her mobile phone, and, squatting on her haunches, took a picture of Alex from a frog perspective.

"I work better from pictures anyway," she said. "But won't you have a drink while I make us a bite to eat?"

"I don't drink."

"Is that so?" She walked over to a yellowed pinewood cupboard and took out a nearly full bottle of vodka and two glasses. "And I thought we had something in common, you and I. Free spirits. There aren't too many of us around here."

I froze. There was a code underlying her words. An aggressive one.

"Alex, why don't you go outside and play with the cats for a moment?"

He hesitated, trying to catch my eye, but I simply nodded and looked away, so he put on his T-shirt and went outside.

"What are you talking about?" I was having trouble hiding my annoyance. Under ordinary circumstances, this would have been my cue to leave, but the fishwife had driven us out to the middle of bloody nowhere and . . . and Alex had earned his fee. She owed us one hundred kroner.

Barbara handed me a glass of vodka that I hesitantly accepted.

"I saw you," she said. "At the store. I saw what you did. We've got the same taste in liquor, you and I. No need to worry, you won't hear any recriminations from me. I know what it's like not having money for the basic essentials. Believe me. But it's either incredibly brave or incredibly stupid to steal from the one and only store in town. You risk complete social exclusion. If someone had seen you . . . "

I shrugged.

Social exclusion is a blessing if you're not interested in talking to anyone, but I doubted very much that Henna-hair had a feel for the finer nuances of life in this regard. And I had Alex to think of.

"What I'm trying to say is: I like you," she said, tying her long, red hair in a loose knot in the nape of her neck. Her long, false nails scraped against her dry scalp. "You're different."

I nipped at my glass. The liquor burnt pleasantly down my throat, but couldn't quell the sensation of something crawling over my skin.

"You don't know me at all."

"But I know who you are," said the fishwife. "Everyone in town is watching you. Poverty is embarrassing, and your story is . . . infested. It's not easy moving to a place like Klitmøller. I came here myself from Århus five years ago. The houses are cheaper, but it's a closed community. You are either in or you're out, and right now, you're out, just like me. C'mon, Ella, stay for lunch. The drawing is not nearly done yet."

WE ATE HARD-BOILED eggs, sundried tomatoes, shrimp, and rye bread for lunch and sunbathed in tired garden chairs in the yard. I could feel I was getting sunburned on my nose, but after the second glass of vodka I didn't give a shit. Barbara got her German shepherd, Lupo, to shake hands with his paw and roll over in the sand, making Alex laugh, a Faxe Kondi soda clutched in one hand.

We drove home in almost complete silence, Barbara with a fresh smoke hanging out the window, intermittently gazing into the setting sun. She had written her mobile number on the back of a bus timetable to Thisted and given Alex the hundred kroner she owed him.

"Great place," she said, when she dropped us off in the yard in front of my grandmother's house. "Like I said: the nature is fantastic; it's good for the soul. Call if you need anything. You know where I live."

ANNA, 1994

Ring . . . ring.

Anna looked up at the clock even though it wasn't necessary. It was seven o'clock, just like yesterday, and the day before. Whoever was calling her, was as regular as clockwork.

Anna dried her hands in her apron and slowly approached the phone. Ella was up in her room and Helgi wasn't home yet. She lifted the receiver and listened to the faint rush on the other end of the line.

"Anna?"

The voice was soft, her name sounded more like a sigh than a word, but she gripped the receiver firmly. Today she would say something.

"Leave us alone," she said. "I don't have anything to do with you—any of you—anymore."

There was nothing but silence on the line, silence and a rapid intake of breath that sounded like suppressed laughter. Anna tried to imagine Birgit as she had been when she was twenty years old and Anna's world, as she knew it, came apart at the seams. Her sister, perfect as always, sitting at the dinner table with her fiancé, Torben. They were holding hands—above the table, of course, never below. Every now and again Torben caressed Birgit's hand. They were talking about the house they wanted to buy just outside Thisted. Talk of that house was endless; the floors were to be sanded and oiled-treated, the attic renovated for later, when the children were born. Their enthusiasm and faith in the future was impressive, especially considering the immanent destruction of the world, and the fifteen-year-old Anna sat writhing uncomfortably in her seat. Wanted to protest and deny their obvious deceit. Neither of them actually believed what was said in church. Not really. For if they did, they wouldn't be talking about houses and children and holidays in Austria—not to mention the color of their couch; if the world was really on the brink of destruction, they wouldn't care what color that couch should be. They would just take a seat, wait for the horror, and go mad in the process.

But Anna didn't say anything. Just sat there, dead still, picking at her potato salad while Birgit's eyes weighed heavily upon her. It was a cold, contemptuous, and triumphant gaze. Birgit had known all along that she would get everything right and that Anna would get everything wrong. And Anna could feel an all too familiar chill through the receiver.

It was summertime, but at any moment the meteor could hit the earth and suck all oxygen from the universe; in a moment, everything and everyone could be gone. Anna clenched her fists, tried to block the surge of childhood fears. She didn't believe any of it. Not anymore.

"Just die."

The person on the other end of the line sounded angry and impatient, she thought. The voice was slurred, reaching out to her through a layer of thick, glittering silk. Then the line went dead.

She stretched her limbs, kneaded her muscles in an attempt to expel the unease from her body, but the barb had stuck, propelling her into motion. She went up the stairs to the first floor, where she could hear Ella listening to music in her room at the end of the corridor. *The Animals of Hillbilly Wood*, "The Mouse That Sang for Mikkel the Fox,", and Ella was humming the tune. Anna knew Ella would be lying on the floor, drawing, her pencils spread out in a fan about her. Right now, she was caught up in her princesses and horses. It helped to think of Ella's drawings; something so completely ordinary, something to remind her that she didn't have to feel so alone.

Up here she wouldn't hear the phone if it rang again.

Anna turned into the bathroom and closed the door behind her. Helgi's overalls were dumped on the floor. They smelled of wind and sawdust and metal, only faintly of Helgi himself. A comforting smell, which never changed.

She emptied his trouser pockets.

The usual tidbits. A couple of receipts from a diner in Thisted, a few loose twenty-kroner coins, his favorite pencil-stub. But in one of his back pockets she found a brochure for an art exhibition in Thisted. *The Light of Skagen*. The brochure was doubled over twice in the middle, its glazed paper surface worn so thin that she had difficulty unfolding and reading it at all. The exhibition had been running since the middle of May; there had been a single painting by Hammershøi, one by Anna Ancher, and a selection of correspondence between the artists from the Skagen Period.

Helgi slammed the front door behind him in the entrance and Anna hurriedly refolded the brochure in a wash of scattered panic, suddenly feeling as if she'd been snooping around in his things.

"Anna!"

He called up the staircase, and as she opened the door she smelled the pall of charred sauce downstairs. Helgi was banging with the pots on the stove, whistling under his breath.

He was happy when she wasn't nearby, she couldn't help but notice. Much happier than he had been in years. He played with Ella more wildly than ever, threw her up in the air, swung her round till they were both dizzy and his legs got all wobbly. He was also better looking physically. He'd lost some weight and bought new shirts, jeans in a stylish cut, and a pile of boxer shorts.

Around her, he was silent and morose, and he hadn't touched her in months. Not even to put his arms around her in bed, half asleep—this much he had always done.

He was going to leave her. He had already left her. The certainty punched her like a blow to the stomach. She had been a fool for too long.

AT NIGHT SHE dreamt she was standing in an annihilated village by the sea. There were other people milling around her, a small group that had survived by fishing and collecting saplings they had found in the slowly rotting fields.

But something evil was near.

This they could tell from the dead animals being washed onto shore; enormous sperm whales and turtles shrunken into their shells. Evil was lurking somewhere out there, where the water met the end of sky. But there was more. When they ventured deeper inland all sound disappeared, and darkness fell. A pale, doll-like girl appeared out of the dark. The doll dug her long, needle-like nails into Anna's chest. Anna knew who the child was, and she knew what to do. Gathering her strength, Anna pushed the girl down into the ground, finally kissing her porcelain-white forehead.

"You're an angel," Anna whispered, and the child closed her black eyes, and let go.

"Ella Nygaard?"

The man standing outside in the pouring rain was from social services. I knew exactly who he was before he opened his mouth to say his name: He was in his mid-to-late-forties with an extended academic education behind him; he'd been a teacher before he became a social worker, specializing in juveniles or drug-addicted prostitutes when he was younger, but now that he had the Family & Kids, he'd settled down behind a desk in a job with regular hours; he trained the little leaguers on Wednesdays and Saturdays with a still discreet but increasingly visible tummy perched above his one-time muscular legs.

And he had illusions about knowing how to handle people. How to handle me. He was a horse whisperer with a master's degree in the Socially Unfit. I could feel it in his confident handshake, his steady gaze. He already had plenty of information about me; all he needed was a personal impression, then he'd be set to type a report on his computer and send his recommendation to the social services committee.

"My name is Henning, and I work for Thisted Social Services. May I come in?"

"What happens if I say no?"

He didn't as much as blink.

"If you say no, I'll come back another day with a piece of paper and a colleague. According to the Social Welfare Office in Hvidovre, there seems to be cause for concern about you and your son, and I'm here to find out if that's true."

"Come inside."

Henning from Thisted had to duck to avoid hitting his head on the doorframe. He continued hunchbacked into the kitchen from there, carefully surveying his surroundings along the way.

"Coffee?" I nodded towards the cups standing in a row on a shelf just next to the stove.

"Yes, thank you."

He offered me an almost sincere smile, perched himself on the edge of a kitchen chair, and followed my movements with his eyes as I went to fetch water from the tap in the bathroom.

"I understand that the house belongs to your grandmother?"

"Yes."

"And you live here free of charge?"

"For the time being."

"Yes. That certainly must be a great help, considering your current financial situation," he said. "I guess one can live with the odd cosmetic defect."

He shuddered, his eyes taking in the browned blisters on the walls and cupboard doors that were thick and bulging with several layers of paint, most recently, a pale, curry yellow. When I failed to comment, he hauled his shoulder bag up onto his lap and took out a pen and notepad.

"You should know," he said, "that we at Thisted Social Office follow a very conservative policy with respect to the placement of children outside of the immediate family. We always exhaust *all* other avenues first. Family planning, support within the original home, assistance and support from the family's own social network . . . Do you know anyone around here? I know you have a history in Klitmøller, but . . . ?"

I didn't answer, just put the cup down in front of him on the counter and fetched some milk from the fridge.

"The reason I'm asking is . . . yes, well, to put it bluntly, we take the whole context into consideration. And we would hate for Alex to be left without support, if you were under considerable psychological strain yourself. It isn't healthy for a child. And where is the young man, if I may ask?"

"He's gone fishing," I said drily.

"In this weather?"

I nodded. The rain hadn't deterred Alex. In fact, he had been out fishing every single day since he found the fishing rod. His determination had already been rewarded with several plaice and a handful of cod. At the end of the third fishing day, he sold his catch to some tourists down at the harbor and came home with two steaks and a ready-made packet of béarnaise sauce from the store in exchange. The next day, he collected cans on the beach as well as going fishing and came home with lunch *and* two chocolate pastries in textbook hunter-gatherer style.

"Healthy boy. But do take care of him now, won't you?"

Henning wrapped his knuckles demonstrably on the counter, took a single sip from his coffee cup, and got up with a relieved smile on his face. The worst part was over. The client had been sufficiently amenable throughout the interview. There had been no screaming and yelling, no slamming of doors. All that remained were a few quiet hours at the computer. He was almost at the door when he turned round and faced me.

"I knew your father, you know," he said gravely. "He was a carpenter, as you know, and I did a couple of odd jobs for him when I was a young man. A nice guy. And a fair boss."

I froze with my cup in my hand. Dared not as much as look at him.

"It's a real tragedy, such things," he said. "So sad when people can't take leave of one another in a proper fashion. And the court case. I understand that most people felt he should have been given a suspended sentence . . . It couldn't have been easy for you, I imagine. Do you still have contact? I heard he moved to Thailand at some stage?"

"That may very well be. We don't really keep in touch . . . "

For some reason I played along, took great pains to match his polite, conversational tone, as if what he was saying had something to do with me—or him, for that matter. But still, something rankled.

"What do you mean he should have been given a suspended sentence?"

Henning was looking at me evenly. Perhaps his grand illusions about knowing people were not altogether illusory after all. At the very least, he must have seen something in my eyes that made him soften his tone that now became more singsong, more pronounced in its West-Jutlandic ring.

"I'm sorry," he said. "I thought you knew all about the court case, but of course it was . . . you were away. In my opinion, he was not accountable for his actions when he did it. He was beside himself in court. Very distraught. But he was standing with that bloody gun in his hand when the police arrived on the scene."

He lifted his arm, but it stopped in midair.

"Ella, we will make sure that you and Alex get all the help you need. Call me if there's anything I can do. We'll be drawing up an Activity Plan for you very soon. You know the drill, don't you?"

His hand brushed mine as he walked out the front door, and for a second, I wondered whether I would always be doomed to feel that yearning to have someone say my name, put their arms around me, without having been paid to do it first.

THE SHAKING STRUCK as I closed the door behind him. It hit me so suddenly, so violently, that I didn't get a chance to reach for the bottle of vodka. I fell to my knees at the kitchen counter, raking kitchen towels and newspapers down on top of me.

Black and white dots were darting before my eyes, the stench of rotten seaweed and blood in my nostrils. I got as far as thinking that this was new, interesting even, that my super-senses had failed me this time around, that this time they just left me floating in a soup of images torn from memories and dreams instead.

"Here, Mom, let me help you to the couch."

Alex must have come back, because he was bending over me, trying to catch my attention as he frantically pulled on my arm.

The smell got stronger. In front of me, black shadows gliding in and out of an impenetrable fog. I screamed for my mom until I was hoarse. The next glimmer of light I saw was Alex, standing right over me, but he wasn't alone. Barbara's face loomed up behind his, framed in a halo of hair that was so red I had to close my eyes again. Just for a little while. I didn't register that I'd been dragged to the couch and laid on my side so I could breathe freely. All I knew was that I had stopped shaking. And that I was terribly, terribly tired.

"Tell me about it."

Barbara was sitting in an armchair with her legs pulled up under her, a glass of vodka balanced on the arm rest. I had slept through most of the day and the better half of the night. Barbara had taken care of dinner for Alex. Rye bread and liver pâté. The same thing she'd fed me on the couch. My legs had refused to carry me anywhere.

"Tell you about what?" I stared at my nails. They were chipped and dirty. Barbara had the long, square kind that clicked against her glass.

She sighed, and narrowed her eyes. The near dark deepened the red of her hair and the wrinkles under her eyes had become black craters.

"I can't help you, if you don't talk to me."

I studied the holes in my socks. I had absolutely no intention of telling her anything. I had already said too much. The shock of the fit, the long sleep, and the vodka had loosened my tongue, but now I had to pull myself together. I leaned back in my chair and took a sip. It was my fourth glass of vodka, which was bordering on the excessive, but still on the safe side of the worst hangovers. The floor dipped under me, I was afloat in a rocking boat—and I liked it. Even the soreness in my muscles felt comfortable and warm when tempered by the right amount of alcohol. It was three o'clock in the morning, and up in my bed, Alex was sleeping like a stone.

"I can't recall having asked you for your help," I said. I could hear the words tripping over my tongue. I couldn't feel my lips.

"Alex called me," said Barbara. "Not an ambulance or the police or the fire brigade. He called *me*. Why do you suppose that is?"

"Your number is jotted down on a piece of paper on the kitchen counter."

"He called me because you're both on shit row if Welfare gets wind of your panic attacks. That's what he told me, and right now, I'm the only person you know in Klitmøller. Isn't that right?"

Barbara's words were equally slurred, and she refilled her glass. I was glad I wasn't the only one who was drunk.

"I'm guessing that all that in there . . . " she pointed a finger at my head and smiled her chalk-white smile. "All that going haywire in there has got something to do with your mom and dad. I've heard some talk in town about your childhood."

"What have you heard?" I said, trying to sound lighthearted; I thought about feathers, and smoke, I imagined being in one of those shithouse-sized hot air balloons that you sometimes saw floating over Damhus Lake in fine weather. I meditated on the state of weightlessness.

"I took a course in hypnosis once." She smiled weakly.

Of course you did, I thought. Barbara was a classic example of those forlorn souls who were staunch believers in deep breathing techniques, healing crystals, and reincarnation. It was always women. They bathed themselves in soap fabricated from the departed souls of flowers collected in the northern mountains of Norway, and their gurus were always men, whom they worshipped with the same abandon as teenage girls idolized their boy bands. I wasn't a fan of self-delusion on that kind of scale. On the other hand, my homegrown solution of a bottle of vodka above the sink and Alex dabbing my brow with a wet cloth was hardly sustainable in the long run.

"Perhaps the shaking would go away if you remembered what happened that night," she said. "Perhaps you would be . . . free."

I curled myself into a ball on the chair and closed my eyes. If Barbara's powers of psychoanalysis were comparable with her artistic prowess, I was in trouble. Her drawings were awful, but the most disturbing thing about them was the complete lack of self-awareness looming large behind her vigorous pencil strokes. Somewhere in her mind, she actually believed that she could make a living from her art one day.

But she could have a point about the childhood memories. Doctor Erhardsen and the majority of my psychologists had said something similar. But there was a reason why my brain denied me access to that part of my life. It was looking out for me. And what if remembering it all just made me more fucked up than I was? I was already balancing on the tip of total destruction, as Alex would say.

"I want go to sleep," I said. "I'll have to ask you to leave now."

Barbara lurched to her feet, took a woolen blanket off the arm rest, and spread it over me.

"I can't drive anywhere right now," she said. "I've had too much to drink. I'll find a place to sleep."

I could hear her pottering about in the kitchen as she hummed a Billie Holiday song. "Gloomy Sunday." Her voice strained until it became hoarse and cooing and smoky. She knew the lyrics by heart. But she was off-key, and the song sounded like an antiphonal dirge from a bygone, forsaken world.

"Can't you remember anything at all from that night?" she called to me from the kitchen. "It was November, right? So it must have been very cold and windy. What were you doing out in the dunes?"

"I don't know," I mumbled.

I tried to focus on one of my grandmother's pictures, which was mounted on the wall next to the window: a black-and-white print of an old painting that depicted a rowing boat in a foaming inferno of water, further out to sea, a glimpse of the stern of a ship at the horizon.

A rescue boat goes out to sea was inscribed below, and all at once, I knew that this was how my grandfather and my father's brother had died. At sea. My grandfather had been a fisherman, I recalled, and he had fished up my grandmother in Iceland. That was the story I had been told.

"You really can't remember a thing?"

Barbara was back. She leaned in over me, I could feel her alcohol breath on my face. The exhaustion made her look haggard, her teeth shone even more unnaturally white in her baggy-eyed face.

"No," I said, and closed my eyes.

• • •

WHEN I WOKE up again, I was still lying on the couch with the woolen blanket draped over me. The house was silent as the grave, even though the sun had already climbed high over the dunes, high enough to fill the living room with a thick and dusty grey light.

The aftereffects of my short, nightmarish sleep lingered in my bones as I crawled up the staircase to the first floor bedroom.

Alex was still sleeping. He was lying on his back and the quilt had slipped down to expose his frail, tan chest. His arms rested by his sides on the sheet, his palms turned upwards, like springtime flowers in bud.

Next to him lay Barbara. Like Alex, she was lying on her back, but she was fully clothed, and her arms were crossed over her chest like a corpse. Her fingers, the long red nails, adorned her collarbones like the wings of a parrot.

"Barbara!"

I whispered hoarsely in her ear, terrified that Alex would wake up and find her lying beside him; he would hate that just as much as I did. The nausea that curled in my stomach since leaving the couch intensified; water gathered in my mouth.

She turned her head and looked at me. Her face was pale, softer without all that make-up. But she looked younger. Stronger. Like a vampire after a solid meal.

I THREW UP in the toilet as Barbara busied herself in the kitchen and laid the table with cereal, sugar, and milk. The stinking porridge poured out of my throat in generous quantities, consisting mostly of vodka-flavored chunks of rye bread.

Barbara put a glass of water and a cup of scalding hot coffee on the plastic tablecloth in front of me. She reeked of hangover, that particular blend of formaldehyde and formic acid, sleep, and sweat, and my nausea gelled with the intense displeasure I felt in her physical presence. It was a familiar feeling of restlessness, a compulsion to get up and leave the house. I lowered my head, trying to breathe through my mouth.

"I'm going to stay for a couple of days," said Barbara. "I'll just fetch some bedding, and my drawings. You can't take care of him on your own right now."

There it was again. The brush of an angel's wing. A human being reaching out to me, even though I was so difficult to love. And all I could think about was getting the hell away from there. Once, I bit Foster Mother Number Three in the arm. The bite was so deep it needed stitches; her arm was yellow and blue for several weeks thereafter. If I remembered correctly, the woman had tried to stroke me on the head. Her two well-balanced daughters called me the Pit Bull until I was reassigned a couple of months later.

"I'm not very good at all that living together business. I've tried it before." I said between clenched teeth.

"And you are good at living alone?"

She put both her hands on my shoulders and looked me straight in the eye. Her face was so close to mine there was no place else to look.

"Come now, Ella," she said. "For your own sake—and Alex's. At some point you are going to have to accept help from somebody."

I tore myself away, but nodded. Just once.

"I'm going down to the harbor to fish with Alex a little later today. And then we'll see."

HELGI, 1994

"Why here? What are we doing here?"

He could hear that his tone was harsher than he had intended, but it had been bloody difficult to get away from the site, and she had called the office so many times that some of his colleagues had started giving him looks.

But Christi didn't seem to notice. She just laughed her girlish laugh, snuggled in under his arm, and pulled him along into the graveyard.

"I'm tired of the dunes," she said. "And I'm tired of the wind. I just want to hold your hand in a place that has flowers and shelter and sunshine."

He had to jog to keep up with her, and all at once he felt ridiculous in his clomping construction boots and beige overalls. A plodding and very grown man prancing about like a teenager with his much younger girlfriend in a graveyard. It was undignified, and utterly intolerable. He tried to slow her down.

"Christi, wait . . . "

She stopped short, and kissed him. Stuck the tip of her little pink tongue between his teeth and bit him on the lip. First softly, and then so hard that he flinched and tasted blood.

"Ouch, bloody hell!"

He pushed her a little away from him instinctively, but just a little. He wanted her. He always did. Even though her behavior was becoming more and more strange.

"The first kiss was for coming," she said. "And the second for being in such a foul mood."

"I was at work when you called," he said with a sigh. "It's really hard to find an excuse to leave a building site when you're the one who is supposed to be in charge. And then driving all the way out here . . . "

He looked around. The church was perched on a lonely hilltop without a trace of a town anywhere near, and he had taken two wrong turns before finding the church on the hill.

She shrugged. "I missed you, and there's something important I want to show you."

She took his hand again and threaded her fingers in his as they walked. The graveyard was thick with the smell of flowers, like in a flower shop. Everything was in bloom. Even the heather that was planted haphazardly along the stone wall presented itself in its most beautiful, dusty lilac splendor.

"I come here as often as I can," she said. "You're always saying you don't know enough about me. But now you know this."

"And you have . . . family here?"

He swept an arm over the graveyard, taking in the rows of gravestones, suddenly feeling a violent, unfathomable tenderness for her. It felt larger, different than the kind of tenderness he felt for Ella, and it had no semblance to anything he had ever felt for Anna. It felt like a need to fold his body around her, to protect her from evil, sorrow, and death. At night he dreamt of single-handedly warding off an army of furious men; then he folded her into his arms, plunged deep into her soft, inviting cunt, and this was exactly the way it should be between a man and a woman.

It was a ridiculous thought, he knew this perfectly well. He was a middle-aged man—not a warrior.

"Here we are." She had stopped in front of an unknown grave. "This is where I come to think about my boys," she said. "They were four and five years old, when it happened."

He frowned. It hadn't crossed his mind that Christi could be the mother of two children, nor that she could have suffered such a loss. That her children were dead. She had never mentioned it, and now she did so with the same matter-of-factness as if she were talking about a misplaced purse. His immediate impulse was sympathy, followed hotly by a grotesque jealousy. That she'd had a life before him, that she'd kept this life from him, that he would never be a part of it. He tried to pull himself together.

"Was it an . . . accident?"

She bent down and gathered a handful of small stones in her hand, slowly let them seep through her fingers. A thin layer of dust remained on the surface of her long nails.

"My father got in a car accident. They were sitting on the back seat. They were gone in an instant. But, it's irrelevant how I lost them. The damage done is the same. First they were ripped out of my body, then they were ripped out of my soul. I had this done when it happened."

She pulled her flowing skirt up high enough for him to see the lower part of her inner thigh and that tattoo he had caressed hundreds of times: two thin matchstick-boys holding hands.

"Touch me," she said, and it struck him that there was something extreme in her need to transform sorrow into sexual desire. It seemed as if it could never be wild or risky enough. Once she even called to him from the dunes when he was on the beach with Ella. When he reached her, he could see that she'd been crying, but she refused to tell him what was wrong. Just pulled him down on top of her with one hand while unbuttoning his pants with the other. Despite the fact that there were other people on the dunes, and despite the fact that Ella was alone on the beach. He had pulled himself free, and the whole episode couldn't have taken more than a few minutes, but when he got back to the beach, Ella was standing alone on the shore, shaking, and there were deep cuts on her hands and knees. Things could have ended badly that day. Christi scared him. And what was worse: he scared himself when he was with her.

"Not here," he whispered, carefully pulling her skirt back into place. "We're in a graveyard, sweetheart."

She narrowed her eyes and focused on a point in the sky just above the crown of hanging birches. Then she strode up to the church and opened the heavy grey door to the transept. He followed after with a deep sense of having done something absolutely unforgivable.

As yet, they had not seen each other without having sex. Not even the first time at the museum. She had touched him ever so lightly on the hip as they looked at the painting by Laurits Tuxen entitled *Naked Woman Sunbathing in the Dunes in Skagen*. Her touch was like talking without having to say a word. Afterward she jerked him off in the car till he came.

Christi walked to the front of the church and sat down in the front pew. He slipped onto the bench next to her.

"I come here every week," she said. "I sit here in the church and think about my boys. Every week. For at least two hours every time. I know each and every curl on the altarpiece up there. Each and every word . . ."

Were those tears in her eyes? Her face was bathed in colored beams of light from the mosaic window above them, her eyes were mere dark shadows, but there was a wavering in her voice that made him think of Anna, just before she started crying.

He sat dead still.

He felt mute and lamed, just like he always did when a woman bared black holes eating at her soul. He could build houses and garages and brick walls. He was a rock, as Anna liked to say. But a rock defined itself by being strong, calm, and silent in the whirl of a woman's ever-tilting sea of emotions. Anything other than that he neither could nor wanted to provide, and a spiritual or religious life was just as hopelessly unfathomable to him as a woman's intricately tangled feelings of loss and sorrow and love.

"So, you're . . . into all this?"

He tried to keep his voice light, sweeping a hand in the direction of the altar. Could not even pretend to understand any of it.

"In a way." She brushed a tear off her cheek with a trembling finger. "This is where I think about the family I once had. If you believe in God, then you believe it's Him who took my sons away, so I talk to Him about everything that has happened. Try to understand it."

He looked up at the figure of Jesus over the altar. His head lolled to one side, a stream of caked blood protruding from his crown and hands. This guy had definitely seen better days, and he looked the way Helgi felt. Wretched.

"Have you ever wondered whether it's even necessary to understand everything that happens to us?" he said gently. "I don't think there is a master plan for anything. We just live here on this earth, and we have to try to make the best of what we've got, right?"

The corners of her mouth were strained. She was definitely on the verge of tears now.

"I don't know . . . " She shook her head and sniffed a little. "I don't believe in God, but I do believe in justice, and somebody has to pay for me losing my boys. I have to be able to hate someone! Otherwise I'll fall to pieces, Helgi."

He put an awkward arm around her shoulders and wondered whether he should try saying something, or whether he should just let her talk herself calm—just like Ella could when she was feeling sad. But he needed to get back to the building site soon. Being in the church and the story about the dead children had made him restless.

"Why did you bring me here?"

She shifted a little closer and leaned against him.

"I never thought I would ever want to have a child again. But I do now. I want to have a child . . . with you. Before it's too late."

He stiffened. What she had just said was the most touching—and absurd—suggestion he had ever heard.

"Say something," she breathed against his neck.

"You're too young for me," he mumbled, realizing that he was saying this more for his own benefit. It was so hard not to follow the impulse she had planted in him. The thought of the two of them together, in a white house with big windows and a view over the never-ending meadows. Their double bed was broad and the bedcovers were just as blindingly white as the walls and the furniture, and between them lay a small, plump baby. Their child. A son. He had always wanted a son. The image inspired a vision of the future that transformed into a whole new life in which he was twenty years younger—and could start everything over.

There was space for Ella in that house. She would have her own room, and she would grow to love Christi and the little boy. Anna, on the other hand, was dead, or, at the very least, out of the picture. Perhaps she had found another man.

He shook his head and looked at Christi.

"It's not possible."

"I'm not too young for you," she said, nipping him playfully on the neck. "I've got an old soul, haven't you noticed? I've lived a thousand years just to meet you. I love you."

"And I love you . . . " He gently brushed the long hair away from her face. "I don't know what to say. It's not that easy when you're already married, when you have a child with someone else. And there are things about Anna that you don't know. She's fragile. It will destroy her if I leave her."

"Just say yes." Her voice had taken on a pleading tone now, and for a moment he thought that she had started crying again. It was only once he felt her tugging at his belt, saw her sliding down onto her knees in front of him, that he realized what she was doing.

"Now? Here?"

His cock swelled under her practiced hands, and in a torment of lust and horror he watched her eagerly working mouth.

A door slammed, hushed voices could be heard coming from the port outside, and this is what finally made him pull himself free.

"Not here," he said in despair. "Have you gone insane? We are in a church, by your children's . . . " He zipped up his pants and fastened his belt, watched her kneeling on the floor, her head still bent down.

"Don't call me that," she spat under her breath.

"What?"

"Don't call me insane." She looked up at him with blank eyes, and he felt wretched, immediately contrite. How could he have spoken to her so harshly?

"I'm sorry."

He took her hands in his and helped her to her feet.

"We can go to your car," she said. "We could drive out to the forest."

He shook his head. "I don't want to, Christi. I need to think. But I'd be happy to drive you home."

"There's no need. Thank you."

She turned round and walked away from him. Perhaps she expected him to follow, or perhaps she really wanted to be alone. He was reminded how little he understood about women. How he had always gotten it wrong.

"So long," she called, and, without turning round, lifted a hand in an ambiguous salute.

Barbara dragged a mattress into the room downstairs with the broken panes and put a basket in the kitchen for Lupo. "Just until you're feeling better," as she put it.

It was obvious that Alex didn't like her. Far too many middle-aged or aging women, advisers and psychologists, had already raked through his soft psyche; they had picked, prodded, and poked, searching for traumas, signs of abuse and developmental disorders. He kept Barbara at arm's length and dodged her awkward embraces. On the other hand, it was patently clear that he was a lot more relaxed now that there was an adult in the house who could take care of me.

A semblance of calm fell about the house.

Alex fished or strolled along the beach with Lupo following at his heels, and together they looked for amber and beautifully shaped cockleshells. Barbara provided more than just new-age spiritual healing and fresh supplies of vodka in the fridge for the evenings; when she wasn't working on her drawings, we cleared up the living room, and we dragged my grandmother's old couch and chairs out onto the windy lawn, where we beat the dust out of them till they smelled of nothing but sun and sea. We stripped the old carpet off the living room floor, and, to my absolute delight, we found beautiful, untreated wooden planks below that I scrubbed with a thick solution of suds. Afterward we rewarded ourselves with fresh rye bread, liver pâté, and pickled beetroot. There had been some money from Thisted social services, and the sum total of my fortune in the bank peaked at 1,183 good Danish kroner. I felt rich.

But the best thing about Barbara's arrival was her old CD-player, which she ceremoniously handed over to Alex. He and I went to the public library together to borrow books and CDs. Now we had Bob

Marley, Coldplay, and a whole stack of recordings of Billie Holiday and Fitzgerald, and the jazz music, replete with accompanying scratches and hollow recordings, blared in the background as we worked, played cards, or just chilled in the yard with plastic garden furniture, smokes, and blue, blue windswept skies above.

I had seen Magnus a couple more times since that day in the dunes. The first time he came by in his car, and we did it in a parking lot up near Hanstholm. Another time, he smuggled me into the summer house he was sharing with Dutch surfers and the increased available space gave him ample opportunity to prove that he was more than competent with his tongue as well as his hands. We pretty much didn't talk at all, but I liked him. Young men were bound to be arrogant idiots, but often revealed small cracks and human vulnerabilities in their souls. Like the story about a scar on his knee, the fleeting caresses on the back of my hand in the car on the way home, the open expression on his face when he came, that revealed that his happiness, at least briefly, lay caught up in another person. In me.

After the third time, I had to remind myself to stop before I began kidding myself that all these little things amounted to love.

"WHO IS HE?"

It was raining, and Barbara and I had been trapped in the house for several hours. I was reading one of my grandmother's books, a crime story with yellowed pages and a thin plot. Barbara was drawing at the kitchen table with all the lights switched on. I followed her gaze and caught sight of Bæk-Nielsen's emaciated figure on the road. He stood hunchbacked in the rain, staring at the house, but made no motions to approach.

"Bæk-Nielsen," I said curtly. "He's been looking after the house for my grandmother."

"And why is he standing out there on the road?"

Barbara's pencil had poised in midair over her sheet of paper. The drawing she was doing didn't resemble the big-eyed children from the photographs, but appeared to be an "elaboration"—as she called it—of a mural called *The Jaws of Hell*. A picture of the original was spread out on the table before her. It depicted a devil ramming a burning torch up a woman's body while a second grinning devil caught the woman's vomit in a bowl. Barbara's version had a deeper perspective, and the figures were more rounded out, more realistic. The woman's mouth was open, and her tongue stuck out between grotesquely large teeth. The devil with the torch was overweight, almost flabby, with horns sticking through a red baseball cap. He looked like a guy you could run into on the street in Hvidovre.

"He probably just wants to see how we are getting on," I said.

Barbara narrowed her eyes. "I assume he's in regular contact with your grandmother?"

I shrugged, and got up to boil some more water for coffee. Alex had gone down to the beach with Lupo, and I missed his company. Barbara had been following me like a shadow for days.

"I'm going outside to get rid of him," she said, abruptly getting up. "You don't need people peeking in your windows."

I stood by the window and watched her determined march across the yard. The wind drove the rain horizontally into her body, and she hunched her shoulders against it. When she reached the old man, she straightened up and stood before him with her arms crossed over her chest, her wet hair flying in the wind. She said something that made him shake his head. Then he pointed a half-crooked finger at the house and threw his arms out to the sides. His thin, dark-blue windbreaker was soaked black with rain, his sharp eyes blank behind his steaming glasses. I felt sorry for him. Barbara was not a tall woman, but what she lacked in centimeters she made up for in vitality. She was younger than Bæk-Nielsen, and she was stronger. Next to her, he looked like a stooping scarecrow that would be carried away on the very next gust of wind. The old witch of Thisted must have her claws dug particularly deep into him if he was prepared to chase after me in this kind of rain.

Barbara delivered what looked like her final volley of verbal attack, before turning her back on the frail shape and striding back to the door, her wet red hair clinging to her cheeks and forehead.

"Good Lord," she said, walking past me into the bathroom, our designated smoking room when it was raining. I heard her opening the window, the click of her lighter. By the time I came into the bathroom as well she was leaning on the window sill, watching her smoke rings shatter in the rain. I sat down on the toilet seat and fished out my own pack of home-rolled smokes.

"What did he say?"

Barbara turned her head and watched me through half-closed eyes. "That your grandmother would very much like to see you," she said. "I thought she was dead. And I thought you said you didn't have any contact with anyone out here."

"I don't."

"She's your grandmother. You're living in her house."

"That's got fuck-all to do with it," I said. "She doesn't know me, she never has. It wasn't me she chose. She wants me to forgive my father. That's all she ever wrote in her letters."

My throat closed painfully, producing an involuntary croak as I spoke. My father shot my mother. Her brains were splattered all over my galoshes. Given half a chance, I would have scraped his marrow from my bones and drained his blood from my body; when I was about sixteen and the suspicion dawned on me that my nose bore some resemblance with his, I made sure it got broken in two places the next time that witch Mathilde picked a fight with me. The stupid bitch got reassigned to a different institution and I got an aristocratic crook in the bridge of my nose. Win-win.

Barbara was blowing more smoke rings out the window. "Have you ever talked to your grandmother about it?"

"No."

"What about your mother?" she said. "Does she have any family?"

"I think they were very religious," I said, thinking of the missing *Book of Childhood Memories* again. It contained only two pictures of my grandparents on my mother's side. One of them sitting in an anonymous-looking backyard of a villa drinking coffee under a parasol, and another of the two of them flanking the four-year-old Anna, each holding a hand in theirs. "They cut all ties with her when she met my father. I know this, because the Welfare Office tried to place me with her sister after . . . after it happened. That's what I was told at Bakkegården, anyway, when I asked about my family. The sister didn't want anything to do with me."

"You've never had anyone to look after you," said Barbara. As usual, she was wearing a thick layer of make-up, and the dark-blue eyes were emphasized with black eyeliner and shadow. "My father died when I was two years old, and Mom drank like a hole in the ground. I had to take care of myself. I was the one who did the shopping. I was the one who got up and made breakfast and sandwiches for school. I was the one who went to the charity shop to buy second-hand coats and skirts for both of us. My mother lay on the couch all day long, stinking of booze. No one has ever been there for me."

"And what about after? Do you have any family now?"

She nodded emphatically. "Two grown sons. They're just a little older than you are." She went into the kitchen and produced a drawing of two freckled boys sitting next to each other with big grins on their faces. The boy that looked like the elder of the two had an arm resting on his little brother's shoulders. "Christian and Peter," she said. The teeth were drawn in grotesque proportions, the gums were far too pronounced.

"They both live in Copenhagen with their girlfriends now. But they come and visit me once in a while."

"What about their father?"

I had difficulty imagining Barbara in a conventional mother-father-and-two-children scenario. To begin with, she was the kind of woman men loved to hate. That demonstrably casual Bohemian look combined with the tinge of megalomania inherent in calling her hopelessly banal drawings art was, quite frankly, terrifying, and would probably tame the majority of erections. Not to mention the added madness of the river of vodka and the chain-smoking deep into the night.

"He died of cancer six years ago," she said. "After he died, I moved down here to draw. It was something I needed to do. There had been so much stress in my former way of life . . . "

She started working on her devil again. There was a grating

sound every time the long, squared-off nails scraped over the sheet of paper. Sometimes she moistened the tip of her finger with her tongue and rubbed a little in what I presumed were meant to be smudges of grey cloud. In some places the paper was worn through, disintegrating into fine, wet balls.

But when Barbara wasn't busy drawing big-eyed children, something extraordinary happened. I had become aware of this a couple of days before, when she was bent over a picture of hovering spirits in flowing robes: the lines still ran together in grotesque and distorted forms, but suddenly it seemed to make sense; the ugliness matched the motif, like when the devil really was the devil himself, even as he looked like a butt-ugly portrait by an amateur.

"I think you should stay away from your grandmother," said Barbara. "Let me help you instead. I can help you remember enough to let you forget—and move on. You have fought for so long ... you have been so alone. Let me be there to kiss your boo-boos."

"I'm not sure I want to remember." My voice was thick with the self-pity that suddenly surged in my chest.

Barbara undid her hairclip, clasped it between her teeth, and ran her fingers through her hair before tying her locks into a fresh knot in the nape of her neck. Not once did she take her eyes off mine.

"Sweet, darling, wonderful Ella," she said. "Nothing can stay buried forever. Memories work their way out of the body just like splinters do. It can be a relief to have somebody standing by with tweezers and a little alcohol. It will be an entirely sterile operation. Aren't you even a little bit curious?"

She winked at me, and I dropped my gaze.

Barbara made me intensely uncomfortable in the same way the nurses had done in the hospital when I had Alex. They kept on digging in their needles, trying to hit one of my dried-out arteries. It was that same familiar nausea, that violent urge to jerk my arm away.

"I can remember ... a little," I said cautiously. "I saw my father with the gun. He was yelling. I started to run, I think ... ."

"Nothing else? Nothing before or after?"

I shook my head. "No, and I think that is more than enough. I probably saw my mother with her head blown off, for fuck's sake, Barbara!"

It was the first time I had used her name, and the intimacy this implied magnified my acute discomfort. Barbara put down her pencil and put her hand over mine in the same way that Kirsten used to do. The long, shiny nail of her index finger traced along my wrist and gently circled one of my pink scars.

I jerked my hand away as if she'd burnt me.

The insult shone in her eyes.

"I'm sorry," I mumbled. "It's an old war injury. I have some difficulty with physical contact. A social phobia. One among many."

It was a half-truth. There was a particular kind of physical contact I had no problem with at all. Magnus, for example, could touch my scars, but I had a suspicion that lust could obliterate all phobias in a single blow. If something similar came on the market in pill form the entire psychiatric profession would go bust.

Barbara nodded and bit her lip. Still hurt.

"I'll try the hypnosis," I said. "I can't very well get more fucked-up than I am already."

WORMS.

Fat naked worms wrapped around each other as they slid over the bottom of the tin can that Alex had put them in.

That was the first thing I started thinking about: worms. The next thing I thought was that I didn't want to do this. I hadn't wanted to do it at all, but it sounded like an okay idea once I'd had something to drink and Barbara had set about drawing the curtains and getting me settled on the floor. But then I was just scared, and at the same time I had an irrepressible urge to laugh.

Worms.

I was lying on the floor upstairs in the loft, but I could see myself from above, lying prostrate on the checkered quilt, like an angel that had crashed to the ground. Barbara had lit several candles and placed them in a circle around me, but the whole scene still looked creepy.

My head was an opened can of preserves and a cluster of dark, red worms were spilling over the sides. Their pointy, black-blue heads worked themselves in and out of each other.

I snorted a laugh.

"You have to relax your muscles completely."

Barbara's voice had a faint echo to it, and I could see her moving around me. She bent down and picked up my right arm, which immediately thudded back onto the ground. Then she did the same with the left arm, carefully moved my head from side to side. I felt the movement like a rerun of what I had just seen. First I felt my head falling to one side, and a long time thereafter, I saw the same thing happen. It was the middle of the night and Alex was asleep. Dear, darling Alex.

I snorted again.

"Are you ready?"

Barbara's gaze flooded my field of vision, even though I was lying with my nose to the floor. She must be hovering in the air with me—but I was the one, who had swallowed the pill. The world was a magical place, I could no longer feel my arms and legs.

"I'm ready," I said, and grinned.

"It is dark outside," said Barbara. "It's raining, and you are seven years old. How do you feel?"

"Just fine, thanks."

My words were slurred. I could hear it myself, and laughed again.

"What did you get for your birthday?"

"A new bicycle."

I saw the bicycle standing on the gravel drive in front of me. It was purple, with white tires. Brand new, no training wheels.

"Who gave you the bicycle?"

"It's a gift from my mom and dad. Dad bought it, he brought it home with him after work. Mom wrapped it in tinsel paper and ribbons. She smiled when she gave it to me. She said I was the best little girl in the world."

"Do you like your dad?"

"Wait . . ."

I frowned. Something was wrong.

"Wait . . . " I said again. "I'm not feeling so well anymore. Can I come home now?"

I wanted to turn away from my dad and the bike. He was standing with his hand on the handlebars, staring down at me. My movements were slow and heavy, as if submerged in water. It took all my strength to turn my head.

"Try sitting up, sweetheart!"

My mom was sitting next to me. Very gently, she helped me to sit up. Her white hair brushed my naked arms. She gave me a glass of water, and an orange pill. I had already had one, but that was a long time ago. She put the glass to my lips.

"Take this," said Mom. "It will make you feel better."

The water was clear and clean, it quenched my thirst.

"Careful," I whispered. "He's out there, and I can't . . . protect you."

ANNA, 1994

Where will you be when the world starts to burn . . . ?

Anna stood petrified to the spot, staring at the words typed onto the card she was holding in her hand. She had found it in an envelope stuck under the windshield wipers of her car. Any and all hopes that this was some kind of mistake—that the card was meant for someone else, left on the wrong windshield—were dashed when she saw her name clearly printed on the front.

For Anna. It was one of those floral-print cards that you could buy for ten kroner at a Fakta supermarket. Yellow roses. Her father's favorite. And the words were her father's, an echo from their living room whenever she had dared to step out of line.

Where will you be when the world starts to burn, Anna? Will you be standing among the living or the dead?

It was three in the afternoon and the sun was bright and warm after eight hours under the neon lights of the fish factory. But the cold lingered in her fingers; they were stiff and clumsy, making it difficult to fumble the card into her bag. She wouldn't dream of simply throwing it away. If somebody saw it, saw her name written on the card, they would know the message was meant for her, that she had been caught in some unforgivable shameful act. She had to destroy it, get rid of it, later, when there was no risk of being seen.

Anna opened the car door and slid into the driver's seat. Tried to breathe calmly, looked up and out over the wind-blown parking lot. Other workers were leaving the factory now, either alone or in small groups. Little bow-necked Ellen scurried over the asphalt like a mouse fearing a hawk hovering overhead. And a little farther off the mainstays emerged: the routine floor-workers who reigned supreme over the other girls on the factory floor. They lived next door to one another, gave one another lifts to work; their children played together, and on the weekends their husbands watched soccer games together and stood around the barbecue drinking beer. It was a community she had never been able to find her way into, even though she'd made her own tentative attempts to do so over the years. On her fortieth birthday she had invited her neighbors to a barbecue. She had rented a tent, served white wine and homemade potato salad. Everybody came, and went home again. And nothing changed. She was alone.

Anna put the car in gear and turned onto the country road along the coastline leading to Klitmøller. The sun was shining in a pale blue sky, but the wind had turned, and the waves breaking on the beach sent a mist of shattered grey pearls into the air. Soon the roaring autumn storms would rage along the coast.

She wiped away her tears with the back of her hand, swore, and then cursed herself for doing so.

There was no reason to panic. All she had to do was think rationally, not let her feelings run wild. She was an adult human being, and she had to think of Ella. And Helgi. The life they had built together. It was only a card after all. Just words.

Helgi was already home. His car was parked in the drive. Ella's schoolbag lay abandoned in a corner at the entrance. He had fetched her from daycare and bought the groceries for dinner. The card was burning in Anna's handbag, but she knew that she couldn't show it to Helgi. It was meant for her.

No one can protect you from the wrath of God.

The rasped inner voice was calm and polite, muted.

Anna went into the kitchen. Helgi was sitting at the small kitchen table with his back turned. He was reading the newspaper. His shoulders were broad and so familiar to her. There had been a time when she knew those shoulders could bear whatever she laid there. She reached out and brushed a hand over them.

"Hi."

He did not look at her, didn't even turn around. It had been like this for some time now—stress at work, he'd said, but apart from that, he didn't say anything at all. She wanted to hold him in her arms, but he didn't look like something you could hold onto. He looked like steel and stone.

"I'm going for a walk," he said. His voice like rust.

"Again? But you've already been out for a walk today." Ella had appeared in the doorway, she stood there shaking those massive curls of hers. "Shall I come with you? Shall we go fishing? Last week you promised we could go fishing."

"Not today, Ella."

He tried to smile, but his mouth was little more than a line. Then he turned and went into the entrance, the car keys jangling in his hand.

He is leaving you. You left God for him, and now you are being punished. There is no love stronger than the love of God.

"Mom? Should we do something together?"

Ella's small face was tipped up to Anna's, bearing all the courage a little girl could muster. Rejection hurt, this Anna knew. She also knew that she had to go to her daughter now.

Anna's smile seemed reassuring and real.

"Let's sit on the couch together for a while," she said. "We could play cards, if you like."

Ella's face brightened up briefly, but after the first hand, she flung the cards at the wall and kicked the coffee table.

"Dad promised we could go fishing."

Her small blue lips were curled into a pout, demanding an answer, but Anna merely cleared away their game. Neither one of them said anything, and a little later, Ella jumped up, went into the foyer, thrust her feet into her galoshes, and darted out the door for Thomas's house. She and the boy had been inseparable all summer. Her little back cut defiantly through the wind as she disappeared down the drive. It was autumn, and it was already getting dark.

Anna wandered from room to room, lighting candles in the dark windowsills as she went—in the kitchen, the living room, even in the washing room. Then she went back into the living room and looked up Lea's telephone number in her address book.

Lea would calm her down. Lea had always had a calming effect on Anna when she started to panic. She too had left the church, but she understood the terror of Judgment Day, the depths of this fear, and she had found a place where it couldn't reach her anymore. Anna knew that when she heard about the card, she would laugh her hoarse smoker's laugh and swear all Anna's problems away. Tobacco was the only crutch Lea still clung to after her last rehabilitation. Tobacco and a little hash. That is, as far as Anna knew. It had been such a long time since they had spoken. Years, even.

Anna punched in the number and waited. Heard nothing but a mechanical beep. Busy. She called up again, taking extra pains to punch in the number correctly. The same aggressive, mechanical beep. Still no answer.

The restless dread returned. It seemed forever stored in her body, logged into her bones from a time when her father took her on his knee in the evenings and read the Proverbs to her.

The righteous—men of integrity—will live in this land of ours. But God will snatch wicked men from the land and pull sinners out of it, like plants from the ground.

Anna took the card out of her jacket pocket and held it over a candle. A weak, bluish flame caught, curled, and smoldered the card's edges as she carefully turned it over. She let the final embers fizzle out in the sink.

When I opened my eyes my body was shaking.

Barbara and Alex had managed to drag me upstairs to the bed on the first floor. My cramping arms and legs were wrapped in quilts and duvets so I wouldn't bang myself black and blue on the bedstead. There was a stench of vomit that I knew at once was coming from me. Stomach acid still burned in my nose and throat.

Alex stood at the foot of the bed in the grey light of dawn, staring wide-eyed at me.

"Can you hear me, Mom? Should I call an ambulance?"

I shook my head, trying to smile through clenched teeth. I wanted to avoid talking, if I could. I knew that if I tried, only grunts and gasps would come, no words.

Barbara appeared behind Alex. She laid a cold, wet cloth on my forehead.

"Now," she said, "we are all going to take *one* thing at a time." She was looking at Alex and me, but the words were probably more for her own benefit. She did not look well. The night before had left her looking deathly pale. The thick black eyeliner was smudged into dark blotches that extended down to her cheekbones, and when she stroked my hand, I could feel that hers was shaking.

"What a night . . . You were out of it for over four hours."

My back billowed and bucked as another spasm ran through my body. I could remember almost nothing from the night before. All I remembered was drinking a single glass of vodka with Barbara and taking an orange pill. I had asked her what it was, and Barbara had said 'angel dust'. For the hypnosis, she'd explained. *Angel dust can set trapped memories free, make them easier to catch, draw them into the light . . .*

There had been candles, the wonderful sensation of floating, and my purple bicycle below a matte-grey, saturated November sky . . . Fear flushed through me. Somebody was after me and I couldn't defend myself as long as I was lying on the bed, shaking like a pig on its way to market. Barbara dipped the cloth into the bowl of water again and put it on my fire-hot forehead.

"There's no need to be afraid," she said soothingly. "The chemicals will be in your system for a couple of hours yet and you might feel a little spaced out for a while, but I'll be here for you and Alex. Don't worry, Ella. I've got everything under control. I'm going to make breakfast for us now. Toast with baked beans . . . And then later we can talk."

My body started to relax. The spasms in my muscles eased gradually and finally died out altogether so I could slowly turn onto my side and curl into a ball. Alex crawled up onto the bed beside me and blew on my neck, my forehead, my cheeks—any and all parts of my body he could reach. It was a game we had played when he was little: If he bumped his knee, I blew on his knee, if he cried over a dead bird in the park, I blew on his soul; we had agreed that the soul was tucked in somewhere just above the heart, so, as a rule, I blew a little all over, just to be sure.

"I've never seen you like this before," he said, nodding at the stinking bowl of vomit on the floor. "I don't like it."

"No."

The muscles in my arms, legs, and stomach ached like hell, but I managed to reach out and run a hand through his dark hair, leaving a glittering, red aura along its path over his head.

"I will get better soon," I said. "I will try to get better, Alex. Okay? But there are so many things over here that I can't . . . figure out."

I could feel that I was dangerously close to crying, and I wasn't someone who cried. Crying wasn't part of my emotional make-up. In fact, I couldn't remember the last time it happened, apart from that time I found a puppy on the road whose hind legs had been run over. I must have been about thirteen years old at the time.

I knew that I shouldn't let my eleven-year-old boy comfort me, but I didn't have the strength to send him away, and then the tears came—with the same vengeance as the vomit had done. My pillow was soaked in tears and snot and blood from my lacerated tongue. Alex stayed put.

"Is it because of what happened with your mom and dad? Because you're mad at your dad for . . . for what he did?"

He sat on the bed staring at the quilt, picking at the floral-print flowers.

"Who told you?"

"Thomas."

"Thomas?"

"Yes, I bump into him a lot when I'm down on the beach with Lupo. His dog's name is Freddie. He says you used to be friends."

"Oh. Is that what he says?"

I pictured Thomas with his hooded sweater and his black dog. Of course. Not that I was surprised. Sooner or later Alex would have run into some idiot who felt obliged to mouth off about my past, and Thomas certainly had his own reasons for doing so. There was the house and the property and his father and the fucking subdivision of the plot to think of; the sooner we got packing, the sooner he could get his hands on the house.

"What else have you guys been talking about?"

"I told him that I've started surfing . . . "

I rolled onto my back. My head and forehead ached after my fit of tears. When I brought my hands into my field of vision they left dark shadows in the air. They drew intricate patterns above my head.

"I'm sorry you didn't have a mom and a dad when you were little," said Alex. "That must have been hard."

"YOU JUST SCREAMED," said Barbara. "I don't think you're receptive to hypnosis."

"No shit."

I rested my head in my shaking hands. I was feeling much better. Or rather, I felt nothing over and above aching muscles and a subtle vibration in my entire body. No relief, no revelation. Barbara hadn't had a clue what she was doing, and it shouldn't have surprised me. Still, I felt cheated.

"How are you feeling?"

"Like hell," I said.

Barbara, who had had a bath and donned her mask, smiled weakly in reply. There was a smear of leftover bean sauce at the corner of her mouth, and it was this spot I chose to focus on now. If I looked her in the eye, I was afraid I might explode. I could feel the anger like a physical itch crawling over my body. It could have been some residual effect of the little orange pills, but the chemical anger I felt was augmented by a bedrock of anger from long before the pink elephants came a-marching in the middle of the night. I felt . . . betrayed. I still couldn't remember what had happened in the dunes and the fit I'd had—was still having—was the worst I had ever experienced.

"It will get better in a couple of hours. You can sleep it off. And off course I will take care of Alex in the meantime."

"He's gone to the beach with Lupo. Or down to the harbor. And I can't get any bloody sleep. There are ants crawling all over my body!"

I went to the kitchen cupboard and yanked it open. No vodka. Of course there wasn't. We had finished the last bottle the night before. There was no beer in the fridge either.

"Ella, you need to lie down and try to get some rest until it's over."

Barbara got up from her chair and put her arms around me. She smelled of lilies and baked bean sauce. Her grip was surprisingly firm, and I wanted to stay where I was. In fact, I wished she would take a seat on the couch so I could crawl onto her lap and cry my heart out. But I jerked free and lashed out at her instead.

"Don't touch me."

"Ella, you need to relax . . . " She was looking hurt again. As if none of this was her fault.

I went into the entrance, slipped my feet into my flip-flops, and walked out the door. The sky fluttered over me in blue-and-white. The whole world seemed to be trembling now that my own body had stopped.

"Ella!"

I left her standing on the steps, and headed into town.

ANNA, 1994

Someone had written on the church wall. Graffiti, like in any city of the world at any given time. *Pinis* spelt with two Is instead of an E and illustrated with a drawing that resembled the despondent head of a sheep more than anything else.

Apart from that, the church building looked just the same as it always had: a low-slung, yellow-brick building with a municipal-grey parking lot in front and a row of beech trees flanking the wall. Anna remembered the smell of fresh paint and raw wood from when she was a little girl, a glimpse of herself dancing hand in hand with her mom over the asphalt on the way to Sunday school. She always wore a dress on Sundays. Red, white, or sky blue. That day it was lilac with a satin ribbon; her sister's was sun gold with white flowers and an elastic band that emphasized her slender waist.

Now other children were coming to church. Anna had been sitting in the car across the road, watching them arrive. Small children as well as awkward teenagers with howling-red jeans, checkered shirts, dreadlocks, and forlorn looks on their pimply faces. And, of course, the aged.

Anna knew there was no point in looking for her mother, but couldn't help doing so. Her mother had died of cancer five years before. The lawyer hadn't mentioned any details, simply notified her in writing that her father would remain living in the family home, and that no inheritance had accrued to date. No mention of a funeral or a wake. Not even the chance to lay a flower on the grave of the unknown before her mother disappeared into the ground.

Anna's hands left damp handprints on the raw plastic of the steering wheel, but the sweat evaporated quickly in the heat.

Despite its pale and colorless sheen behind white clouds, the sun cut straight through the windscreen, making Anna sweat under her washed-out T-shirt, which was cold and damp after her hour-long vigil in the parking lot.

She remembered once sitting behind those church walls, cross-legged on the carpet, drawing with Birgit beside her. It could have been yesterday. That's how it felt. In Anna's drawing, the millennial kingdom was drawn in peach, mint green, pink, and blue. Birgit was five years older than her, and very, very clever. In Birgit's picture, the damned sinners were drawn in the throes of death; intestines oozed out of sliced bellies, the arms and legs had been ripped off, their torsos stripped bare. The people always had surprised looks on their faces, were fully conscious till the last drop of blood seeped from their dismembered bodies.

Anna could see her now.

She was absolutely certain it was her, even though it had been twenty years since she'd seen Birgit. Even in a crowd, Birgit was the first person to catch her eye. Strange how blood ties seemed to have an almost supernatural strength, irrespective of every effort made to sever them.

As if Birgit could sense Anna's presence, she hesitated, remained standing by her car, turning her head to scan the parking lot. She was alone. Perhaps her husband was ill, or maybe he'd taken his own car to church that day. Anna wouldn't have recognized him. Or the children. They must be in high school by now, moved on with their lives.

Anna got out of the car and strode across the parking lot on unwilling legs. She saw Birgit stiffen, her car keys clutched in her hand, as soon as caught sight of Anna. She turned her back demonstrably on her sister, opened the car door, and got into the driver's seat, the roar of the engine coinciding with that moment Anna put her hand on the roof and leaned down to gaze through the reflections on the driver's window.

"Birgit!"

The car started to roll backwards; Birgit was no longer the young girl who thrived on drama and outbursts of emotion.

"Birgit, I need to talk to you."

Anna leaned over the hood, trying to catch her sister's eye through the windshield instead, and finally the car stopped, trapped at an awkward angle between Anna and two parked cars on either side. The sisters stared at each other through the blue-toned pane, tears clouding Anna's vision. But the very last thing she wanted to do was cry. Tears had never impressed Birgit, in fact, they just made her all the more pig-headed, as Anna recalled so well from sibling fisticuffs; trapped under Birgit, who sat on top of her, nailing her arms to the ground with her knees.

Birgit cast a glance in the rear- and side-view mirrors. People were gathering in the parking lot to make their way home. A family of four edged past them to get into the next car over, giving Birgit a penetrating glare as they drove off. Anna didn't know them, but was certain they knew exactly what filthy hole she'd crawled out of: she was Birgit's fallen sister, the shameful scourge of the family. That kind of thing was never forgotten.

"Leave us alone!"

Anna spoke loud enough for Birgit to hear it through the windshield, and for the first time, she met her gaze through the driver's window. Her eyes were small, and it struck Anna that Birgit had become an uncanny copy of their mother, exactly as Anna remembered her last; if you put the two of them together, you wouldn't have been able to tell them apart. Anna stood her ground.

"I'll report you to the police, Birgit," she said, banging on the window. "You have to leave us alone."

Birgit rolled down the window slowly.

"I always knew you'd go insane one day," she said. "I don't want to talk to you. Whatever your problems may be, I'm sure you can figure them out with the help of your support group."

Anna's courage faltered. For some reason, she had expected that Birgit would try justifying herself before resorting to a full frontal attack.

"How's it going with your friend?" Birgit pressed on. "How *is* Lea these days? I heard the two of you had a little argument."

The final whip hurt the most, and Anna recoiled. Took a step back.

"No mother deserves what the church put her through."

Birgit shrugged. "No mother ought to behave the way she has behaved. You know that just as well as I do. You both got what you deserved."

Anna regained her balance, straightened up, as if she had been dealt a physical blow.

"You have to leave me alone. All of you," she said. "Stay away from me and my family. Or I'll contact the police. I won't be harassed by any of you anymore."

Birgit smiled sweetly—a person could believe she was perfectly calm if it weren't for the clenching and unclenching of her fists on the steering wheel, making the thin, golden bangles on her wrists chiming gently in response.

"Go away, Anna," she said. "Nobody is afraid of you, believe me. You have always been a pathetic, attention-seeking human being, and that is exactly what the police will see, if you talk to them. No more, no less."

"Leave us alone!"

Anna felt defeated. And this was exactly how she had felt when they were children when Birgit had laughed at her, simply turned her back in the middle of an argument. But Anna had said what she had come to say, so she spun on her heel and crossed the parking lot once more, her shaking hands buried deep in her jeans pockets. Behind her, she heard her sister rev the engine and drive away. Anna didn't turn to watch her go. Just kept walking to her car and climbed into the driver's seat, leaving the door wide open. The cold October wind blew through her drenched T-shirt, cooling her hot cheeks.

There was a time when Anna would have fallen apart after such a meeting. She remembered the feeling of scorched skin, exposed and defenseless bones against the onslaught of the world. The car seat grazed her hands and arms, her clothes cut into her abdomen, but she did not bolt, and she did not panic. She was an adult now. They couldn't harm her anymore.

There were too many customers in the shop for me to move around freely. Tourists, each and every one. The weather called for bathing suits hastily covered by towels. Children were nagging for ice creams from the freezer and their parents were giving in. There was beach sand on the floor and the door was open so the warm air could drift unhindered down the aisles.

I rummaged in my pockets and found 35 kroner in change. That was good, just the right sum for an alibi-buy—two cans of beer—and a small bottle of spirits could be slipped into my bag on the way out—whatever was on offer. It didn't have to be vodka, just something with a decent kick to knock me out till Barbara's angel dust had worked its way out of my system. But I had to focus. Everything was vibrating slightly. I was an ant on a guitar string.

I navigated a course through a group of kids gathered by the freezer and headed for the pallets stacked with beers in the corner. I took two of the strongest kind I could find: Royal Danish Elephant Ale. It tasted like piss, but the alcohol-percentage would do me nicely. Piled next to the beers, the store owner had helpfully arranged two rows of fifty-ounce bottles of whiskey on discount. I turned my back on the nearest row and eased one of the bottles into my bag. No problem. Luckily there was nothing wrong with my balance. I'd made it half way over to the check-out queue before I collided with a tower of jam jars, accidently knocking a couple onto the floor. None of them shattered, though, and I carefully put the stragglers back into place. Everything proceeded just fine from there on, and when I finally reached the front of the check-out queue, I even managed to produce one of my sweetest smiles for the wholesome, elderly man sitting behind the till as I put the two cans of beer down in front of him.

"Will there be anything else?" The smile didn't reach his eyes, I noticed.

"No, thanks."

"Are you enjoying your holidays here with us?"

"Sure . . . you know." I threw my arms out to the side, heard the clank of the bottle of whiskey against something hard in my bag. "The nature out here is fantastic . . . it's good for the soul."

Suddenly I realized that nobody was talking anymore. And people were staring. Even the children froze with their arms in midair. They didn't stop staring, either, their eyes getting bigger and bigger. One guy whispered something to his pal, but I didn't catch what he said. My head was filled with a distant humming.

"Howzit!"

I gave the two boys a stiff-lipped smile and added a juvenile thumbs-up for good measure. The two boys ducked their heads in unison. The store owner looked equally embarrassed.

"Hope to see you again soon," he said gravely. I walked out into the sunshine, down the path, and onto the beach. I wanted Magnus; if you can't fuck when you're high when else are you going to fuck?

I looked at my watch. It was barely nine in the morning. It would be several hours before Magnus and his friends would get out of bed and zip into their superman outfits. I wasn't sure if I could remember where the surfers' summer house was. I squinted into the sun and peered to my left and right. There were summer houses all around me. And they all looked the same.

"Ella."

A hand was laid ever so gently on my shoulder. I jerked and swung round and identified the hand as belonging to Bæk-Nielsen. That aging skeleton had actually been able to sneak up on me without the rattling of his bones giving him away. I shook his hand off me and took a stumbling step back.

"What the hell . . . ?"

The grey eyes in his weather-beaten face never budged from mine and for a moment I wondered whether I'd underestimated both his stamina and his strength of purpose.

"The store owner sent me after you," said Bæk-Nielsen calmly. "He says you're stealing from him. We need to talk."

I shot a look in the direction of the store and saw the owner and his plump wife arranging the wares in front of their shop, intermittently casting surreptitious glances in our direction. This time I had been too stoned to do a decent job.

"I'll pay for your whiskey later," said Bæk-Nielsen. "But right now, we are going to see your grandmother. Or he'll call the police, and Ella . . . this won't do you any good. You're under the influence, and that's the first thing the authorities will record when they file their report."

My file. The white paper mountain describing Ella Nygaard down to the very last dot.

I remained standing where I was, my arms hanging loosely by my sides.

"But I don't want to talk to her," I said through clenched teeth.

A disdainful snort escaped from the frail man's body.

"We're leaving. Now." He turned round and made for his car. The wind tugged at his grey-brown tweed jacket. Despite the warm morning sun, his body looked like it was made of frozen bones.

THERE WAS A goldfish tank in the foyer of my grandmother's nursing home, but apart from that there was nothing exotic about the place. The long corridors smelled unmistakably of an institutionalized hospital, even though the windows and terrace doors were thrown wide open onto evergreen lawns.

The home was called the Rose Garden. Of course it was. Everyone loves the idea of old folks reclining in white-washed cane wicker chairs scattered among bushes of lilac lilies, roses, and color-radiant butterflies. There weren't any roses in the Rose Garden either. The home looked identical to the nursing home in Tåstrup near Solvang, where I had gritted my teeth through a three-month-long apprenticeship when I was twenty-two. The building was a modern cement block perched upon a grass-green landscape of lawns and cobblestoned paths. The meticulous and constant washing with alcohol and anti-bacterial soap couldn't quite camouflage the pall of corporeal excretions and slightly too seldom bathed bodies. In the sunlit patches of the long, bleak corridors imploded figures slumped in their wheelchairs as they stared out of the windows or down at their feet. It was a garden of wart-riddled, hairy, and crumpled creatures. Still as statues. The world around me was still trembling faintly.

Bæk-Nielsen followed my gaze.

"I've applied for a room here myself," he said. "It's not so bad. I know quite a few people here."

"Like my grandmother?"

"She's an old friend. The kind of friend you would happily walk to the ends of the earth for. Don't be alarmed when you see her."

"I'm not afraid of little old ladies," I said.

"No, but of getting old, perhaps," said Bæk-Nielsen. "Old age is not a pretty sight."

He had stopped in front of a door. *Agni Sigurdadottir Nygaard* was inscribed on the nameplate.

"She took back her Icelandic maiden name a couple of years ago," he said. "If she could have, she would have swum her way back to the volcanoes and hot-water springs. Now she has to make do with gravel and chalk. I guess she reckons it's too late to make a run for it."

He knocked on the door and went in without waiting for an answer. I followed suit hesitantly, and was immediately confronted by the sight of a small, bird-like figure sitting in a wheelchair by the window.

My grandmother.

There was almost nothing left of her. The body was as frail and slight as that of a six-year-old child, the eyes were small, sunk deep into her skull. It seemed as if every ounce that once had filled her being now had shriveled and gone. When I last saw her at my confirmation party, there had been a thin sheen of jet-black hair covering her skull, but now she was completely bald. She resembled neither man nor woman.

"Ella. You came."

I stood in the middle of the room, looking at her. Bæk-Nielsen had disappeared, closing the door behind him. We were alone.

"Sit down." One miniature hand pointed towards a small black armchair.

"I'd rather stand." I fished my bottle of whiskey from my bag and screwed off the cap. "I won't be staying long."

She nodded. "You look exactly the same, Ella. And yet, you are so changed."

I raised the bottle of whiskey in a mock salute, tried to smile. "I've become such a big girl, I know. Children grow."

The irony she chose to ignore.

"I'll come to the point," she said. "I believe your father is innocent. Yes, I am his mother, and I know that mothers don't always see clearly, as I'm sure you know too. We have to believe and hope for the best."

I took a sip from my whiskey bottle and peered at the old woman through the pleasant, red-tinted haze that had slid over my eyes like a veil.

"The Danish legal system never errs," I said. "I've seen the stats: Our police force is not corrupt; our judges are not on the payroll; they have no interest beyond uncovering the truth."

"Did you know that your mother tried to commit suicide when she was a girl? She moved in with Helgi and me after a horrible abortion. Her parents were very religious, and they didn't take it well at all, so she left. For a long time, things went well for them. Helgi and Anna were happy. They got on with their lives, got married. But just before they moved into their own house, Helgi found her in the bathtub at our house, full of pills, her wrists badly cut up. The cuts were made in a hopelessly haphazard fashion. Your mother wasn't made for blood and knives, but the pills could have killed her if your father hadn't found her in time. He saved her life back then. But nobody mentioned any of this during the trial. Nobody was called to testify about the way Helgi had looked after you both for many years."

"Even selfless, heroic acts don't give you the right to blow another person's head off," I said. "How long are you intending on keeping me here?"

I glanced pointedly at my watch. Bæk-Nielsen had forced me to come, but there was a limit as to how long they could insist upon my company. I could just leave. I knew the drugs would work themselves out of my system over the next couple of hours. And once they had, whatever Bæk-Nielsen and the store owner cooked up between them would be one person's word against another's.

"Your father blamed himself for your mother's death; he still does in all his letters. But he didn't kill her." She paused. Brought a shaking hand to her mouth, ran her fingers along her lips. "He pleaded his innocence in court, but he never talked to me, and he never defended himself. He didn't even want a lawyer."

"There is nothing in this world I care about less than what my father has to say about my mother's death," I said. All at once the whiskey left a foul taste in my mouth. I put it down on the coffee table in front of me.

"Here." The old woman took a stack of folded papers from the windowsill. "This is a transcript of the interrogation you were subjected to after they found you in the plantation."

I took the papers from her without looking at them. Shook my head. "Where did you get this?"

"You stayed with me the first couple of weeks after the murder. That was before they decided I was too old to look after a child," she said. "I asked for access to all reports, and I made some copies. Read it, and tell me what you think."

"Why?"

The old woman made a sound somewhere between a grunt and a sigh. "When your time is up, you want to know everything. All the loose ends have to be tied up. Not doing so would be . . . unbearable. And I want to know how and why I lost my son. The two people I lost at sea are gone, but my son is still alive. If you can't do it for your father, then do it for an old woman. And your mother."

I picked up my whiskey, took another swig, and unfolded the papers carefully. They had been read so many times that the paper was worn thin along the folding lines and already on the first page entire passages were underlined in fat red ink.

Interviewer: Ella . . . Thanks for coming to talk to me. How are you feeling?

Ella Nygaard: . . . (a shrug).

Interviewer: What we need to talk about today isn't very pleasant. We need to talk about what happened two days ago in the dunes. About your mom and dad.

Ella Nygaard: Yes.

Interviewer: Can you tell me what happened that night?

Ella Nygaard: My mom was shot.

Interviewer: Were you there, Ella? Did you see your father shoot your mother?

Ella Nygaard: No.

Interviewer: Did you see your father with the gun in his hand?

Ella Nygaard: No. But he hit her. He hit her again and again . . . He hit me on the head.

Interviewer: So you didn't see who shot your mother?

Ella Nygaard: (Crying) She was dead. She wasn't moving.

Interviewer: Perhaps you misunderstood what you saw, Ella. Perhaps you saw your dad with the gun.

Ella Nygaard: Maybe . . . He was shouting at me . . . I was scared.

The interrogation seems to have ended there, and a psychologist had scribbled some notes in the margin: *At best, confused. Testimony inconclusive.*

"Your father was not convicted on the basis of your testimony. It had to be disregarded, because you kept contradicting yourself. And you are his child, his daughter, after all. But there was so much other evidence weighing against him: The fingerprints on the gun were his. He had the gun slung over his shoulder when the police arrived . . . but Helgi was an experienced hunter . . . He would always pick up a gun that was lying on the ground. And he was beside himself, because you were missing . . . and then there was Anna."

I imagined my grandmother rubbing her hands against her bony thighs.

"In the final version of your testimony, you place the gun in your father's hands. You say that you saw him pull the trigger. What really happened?"

"I have no idea."

"Surely the correct sequence of events was fresh in your mind during the first hearing? The same questions are repeated in the second, third, and fourth interrogation, so it's more than likely that you learned to provide the answers the interviewer wanted to hear. Children are clever like that, and you were one of the brightest. Quick as silver lightning."

My rising discomfort spread like a rash over my skin.

"My father murdered my mother. I don't have anything else to say on the subject. Can I go now?"

She nodded at the papers in my hand. "It also says that your father hit you."

A sudden flash. A pinprick at the back of my head. A hand raised over my mother's pale, indistinct face. I felt a wave of rebellion swell. I wondered just how far my grandmother would go to clear her son's name. Whether she was prepared to brand the child I once was as a liar. I was seven years old, and seven-year-olds don't lie. The split brow that bore three stitches did not lie; the scar cutting through my eyebrow was still there. I saw the seven-year-old Ella sitting on a doctor's bench, blood matted in her curly hair, no mother to hold her hand as the doctor worked with needle and thread.

The thought of her kindled the pain in my chest.

"Yes," I said. "I think he hit me."

"Hitting your child wouldn't have been so unusual in those days," said my grandmother. "Where I come from, many parents hit their children back then. I don't even think it was against the law in Denmark. But Helgi never hit you. Ever. I certainly never saw him lay a finger on you. You were a strong, happy child, Ella. Wild as witches. No one could hit you. You couldn't be broken. Not by Helgi, in any case."

I shrugged. If that was her preferred interpretation of reality, it was just fine by me. It was not my job to change her mind on her

WHAT MY BODY REMEMBERS

deathbed. As far as I was concerned, people could go to their graves believing whatever they wished—including my grandmother. But my mother was dead. And my scar was real.

"There is one more thing . . . "

There was no end to this old woman. Her gaze rested heavily on me from under those bushy eyebrows of hers, and I marveled at how vigorously hair can grow on your face when you're old even as it deserts all other regions of the body.

"Helgi was not himself the last couple of months before it happened. I've seen it happen before. Cupid's arrow can prove to be particularly poisonous when it impales the heart of a man so late in his life; so much life has already been lived, time is suddenly scarce . . . a man in love can be very inconsiderate, but that doesn't necessarily make him a murderer."

"He was fucking somebody else?"

My grandmother's gaze didn't flinch a millimeter. "Hopefully you're only this foul-mouthed when you're drunk."

"Hope is lily-green." I shrugged again. It was news to me that my father had had an affair—but not surprising, when you thought about it. A marriage that ended in murder would necessarily have a couple of twists in the tail. But the fact that he was the one who'd been fucking around didn't exactly weigh in his favor.

"Many men are unfaithful," said my grandmother. Almost as if she had read my thoughts. "But this rarely drives them to murder. As a rule, the murder of a wife usually presupposes that *she* had been unfaithful, not him. And Helgi had always been a good man. He loved your mother and he took good care of her."

"Maybe he got tired of her. Depressed people can be such a bore." She ignored my remark.

"While he was in prison, he asked me to look up a woman at an address in Holstebro. He didn't know her real name, he said. But she possibly went by the name of Christi. I never found her. I believe this woman knows what happened to Anna. Perhaps she was even the one who shot her. An act of passion, maybe."

"I'm leaving now," I said, screwing the cap back onto my bottle of whiskey and slipping it into my bag. I tried not to meet her gaze.

"He's doing well, Helgi. Apart from the fact that he misses you, of course. He's started his own business in Thailand. Building houses. He has six employees now, he says, and a big house with a swimming pool. He's always been an excellent carpenter, after all. Perhaps you could give him a call one day. I've got his number right here."

She thrust a piece of paper at me. I let her sit there, her arm hanging limp in midair. I didn't move a muscle.

Just the thought of that number on a piece of paper made me sick. It wasn't just the fact that the numbers made him more real, but the fact that he and I were only separated by a row of digits. I could punch them into my phone by mistake or succumb to temptation, late one night, after drink number seven. The mere thought of it was enough to make my brain implode.

My grandmother could see the horror in my face.

"I also know where he lives." She let her arm drop into her lap. "I have his address. You could write a letter, if a call is too . . . expensive. He would very much like to talk to you."

I turned on my heel and walked out the door. Didn't look back. There were seventeen miles between Thisted and Klitmøller, and I didn't have any money, but, as I said: there was nothing wrong with my legs.

HELGI, 1994

Christi had changed. It was hard to say exactly when he'd first noticed, but something mournful had come into her expression when they made love. When she came it sounded more like a wail than a moan of pleasure.

Rain and the persistent autumn storms had driven them into an empty summer house near Hanstholm. It wasn't ideal. He knew the owner, Tommy, was divorced, and sometimes they drank a beer together after work. Tommy had gone to Greece for four weeks to drink ouzo and dance at the Athenian nightclubs. There had been talk about a lady down there, and he knew where Tommy kept his key.

"Your friend ought to wash the floor in the bathroom once in a while. It stinks of stale piss."

Christi appeared in the bedroom doorway. Her pretty nose was wrinkled in disgust, making her look all the more adorable—if this were possible at all.

"Nobody told him to expect female company while he was away. Men thrive in an environment smelling of their own urine. The more pungent the better. It keeps the competition off their turf."

He laughed, but Christi didn't. She didn't even look at him. She was concentrating on putting one foot in front of the other on the soft, fir-wood floor. As if walking on a tightrope. She was naked, and her long blond hair fell forward over her shoulders, covering her beautiful, beautiful breasts. He leaned back against the bedstead, threading his fingers behind his head, and watched her with an overwhelming tenderness burning in his chest.

She was perfect.

Her breasts swayed with every move she made, but it was her narrow waist, her navel, and that line from the tip of her hips down to the blonde pubic hair that moved everything inside of him. The perfect sample of a woman in Classical portraiture. Hips, waist, shoulders; thighs, breasts, cunt, which he knew was still wet and warm from before. The thought filled him with a primitive and exquisite pleasure.

She crawled in under the blankets with him, brushed over his penis with one leg as she did so, and curled up against his body. Skin against skin.

"How are things back home?"

The question was innocent enough. Her eyes were bright, showing no more than a natural curiosity.

"Hmm . . . the same as usual. We work and eat and sleep."

This was not entirely true. He was worried about Anna. She seemed more and more upset of late, and she wasn't sleeping, didn't say anything. And he didn't dare ask.

"And what about Ella? How is Ella?"

Christi was nibbling on his ear, and he flinched slightly.

"Wild as a wicked troll . . . "

He smiled at the thought of Ella. All the questions she kept asking right now. Whether it was possible to have an octopus sewed onto your stomach, and what would be worse: drowning, death by old age, or being swallowed by quicksand? He couldn't answer all her questions, but he had showed her how to clean the fish they had caught together from the pier. She was still a little clumsy with a knife, but she had the will to learn, and a keen curiosity was the most important attribute a child could have.

"I wish she were mine," said Christi. "I feel like I know her already. I know what she likes to read, I know which songs she likes listening to when she goes to bed . . . " Christi pulled him closer and looked deep into his eyes. "I wish we had ten more trolls just like her. I miss it. And I miss you."

He sighed. There were things he missed as well. He missed the carefree lightness of their initial meetings in the dunes. He missed the rush of joy that had carried him through the spring and summer. And in a strange, contradictory way, he also missed his relationship to Anna as it had been before Christi. That intimacy that, despite everything, still lay in the fact that they were faithful to each other in the midst of the grey their marriage had become.

"You will have your own family one day," he said, even as the though tormented him with a maddening jealousy.

"With you?"

"With someone. You are a beautiful young woman, Christi. You have your whole life ahead of you."

"I want you and Ella," she said. Her pelvis was moving against his—not without effect—and he had long since forgotten what they were talking about when she starting alternately licking and sucking on his nipple.

"I can't see you again till you're done with your wife," she whispered in his ear. "It hurts too much. Can't you understand that? I want all of you."

"Hmm . . ."

"Your wife is strong. She's a grown woman who can take responsibility for her own life. Doesn't she deserve better than being with a man who doesn't love her? If it were me, I would want to know the truth, so I could find someone, who really loved me."

"You are not Anna."

He pushed her away slightly, turned to face her, and thrust deep inside her. Kissed her mouth, her neck.

"You don't know her at all."

"She's using you."

She rolled away, leaving him exposed next to her, his rapidly diminishing erection resting against his thigh. She wanted to talk again, Christi. This happened more and more of late.

"What do you mean? How could she be using me?"

"You're not sleeping together anymore, are you? You don't love each other in that way. She keeps you because you have a lovely house together, and a chic sofa, and a beautiful child. The whole setup is so unimaginably dull, and you're not even getting any sex in return. Is that how you want to live the rest of your life, just because she's too ugly and too dull to find another man? She's nuts, isn't she? All that bloody religion."

She snorted with a glint of evil shining in her eyes, he noted, as she thrust her beautiful breasts under his nose. It was the younger, more beautiful woman's smile in anticipation of victory; the most desirable woman wins. The rules of the game were older than our modern civilization, and yet he felt the need to protect Anna from her attack.

"I don't want to talk about her, Christi."

"What would like to talk about, then?"

He closed his eyes, indulging in an echo of their first conversations in the dunes. All the things he had asked her while their fingers were locked together.

Favorite color? Yellow.

Favorite city? Paris.

Favorite musician? She'd laughed. *Elvis, of course. Who else?*

In the beginning they had talked about how Poul Henningsen worked with light and reflection. They had talked about traveling to Sydney to see the Opera House. Now it struck him how little they both knew about architecture.

THEY GOT DRESSED in silence and she went into the bathroom, locking the door behind her. He went into the kitchen and sat down at the kitchen table. That sharp look in her eyes when she talked about Anna still bothered him. Christi didn't know her. She had no right to poke around in Anna's mind. Call her crazy.

His hand rested on Christi's bag, which was slung over the chair next to his. The bag was open, and he could see the shape of her wallet. He lifted it out of her bag and opened it, carefully listening for sounds coming from the bathroom door. But the contents were a disappointment.

There were no identity documents. No cards. Only a couple of coins and notes, and a fuzzy photo of two boys, aged about three and four, playing in a sand-pit. A few slips from the gas station, receipts from a supermarket in Holstebro. He riffled through the slips of paper quickly, not knowing what he was looking for. Anything that could give him some foundation of proof, some balance of substance between everything she knew about him and the nothingness he knew about her.

He could hear the sound of water running in the bathroom. There was also a slip from the postman for the failed delivery of package for a Christi Johansen at Aurikelvej 18, Holstebro. He stuck the delivery slip into his back pocket, zipped up her wallet, and managed to drop it back into her bag a split second before she appeared in the doorway. Her face was arranged in neutral folds, but he could see that she'd been crying.

They drove back up the sandy road in silence. It was only once they reached the bus stop that she turned and put a hand on his thigh.

"You're not going to leave her, are you?"

He took a deep breath. Did not dare look her in the eye.

"No . . . not right now. It's not possible." Her lips narrowed, and he imagined he could see something of the girl slide from her face, and an older woman came to the fore. A woman the world had taken a few chunks out of. He was about to take it back, say he was sorry, but of course it was impossible. He had dreaded this moment for such a long time, and now that it had come, there was no point in prolonging the agony.

"Christi," he said. "We need to stop this. It's not working."

She looked at him vacantly. The tears of a woman. He remembered that only a month ago, he had promised to make her happy. During the last couple of weeks he had imagined what this moment would be like, let himself feel the pain in small doses. He had imagined a life without Christi stretching before him like a gold-and-grey landscape of trivialities, the days slowly passing by as he got older and older. Ella would move out in eleven years' time—and never come back. He and Anna would sit alone in the house, work for a few more years. They would buy a new kitchen, a new sofa, move into a nursing home, and die. The panic fluttered in his chest.

"I thought you loved me," she said.

The words hit him like a bludgeon to his stomach. Again he fought the urge to take her in his arms, say he didn't mean it, that of course they would see each other again.

"And I thought you understood me. It's not that I don't love you.

But I'm married, for heaven's sake, and Anna and I have been together for such a long time. We have a child. And it's . . . complicated. I thought that this was understood between us."

He tried to imbue his voice with indignant severity, but it crashed to the ground heavily. He just shook his head.

"I don't understand anything at all," she said. Her voice had become harder. "Why did you come with me to the museum that day at all, if you knew that you were never going to leave your wife?"

"Christi . . . if things had been different . . . I guess I also believed in it, in us, at least some of the time. If Anna didn't exist, there would be nothing in this world, I would rather do. Please don't be angry with me, sweetheart . . . I can't bear it."

She bit into the soft flesh of her bottom lip. Exactly how she had bitten him. A little habit she undoubtedly knew he found irresistible. "I need some time to think. You are . . . "

She stopped there, just before saying it: *a disappointment, not what I had hoped for*. And he felt . . . erased. Not once in their five-month-long dream together had she said anything other than how wonderful he was. She had whispered it in his ear when she came, and afterward, when they lay staring up into the sky. She had said that she loved him.

He felt a fresh wave of panic.

Initially, her secrets lent him a sense of freedom, as if their relationship was hovering above it all, suspended in the universe. But now . . . He knew nothing about her, and if he changed his mind . . . where would he even begin to look for her? He remembered all the sleepless nights he'd spent wondering whether she was alive or dead—or perhaps had just forgotten him.

"Give me a telephone number," he said, resting a hand on her arm. "I would like to call and make sure you're all right."

There was a twitch at the corner of her mouth, like a person becoming aware of the stench coming from a bucket of vomit. Then she opened her bag, rummaged inside, and hurriedly scrawled a number onto the back of an old receipt. He watched her strained expression, imagined a telephone in the hall of a house on

Aurikelvej 18 in Holstebro—a yellow-brick house from the 1970s, a flat roof, ivy growing up a low gable, perhaps a husband tinkering with a car in the carport. He felt a rush of insane jealousy burning wild and hot in his chest, but he let go of her arm.

She opened the car door and stepped out into the autumn rain. He remained in his seat. A slightly overweight, going-on-fifty man in a knitted sweater with a safety belt drawn over his slightly-too-big belly. The wipers swept over the windscreen. *Swish, swash.*

Before, when he had tried to imagine old age, he'd thought it would feel like a gradual loss of the ability to dream. A sixty-year-old could achieve less than a man in his thirties—such were the realities of life. But he would never have imagined that it would be possible to put a time and date to the day the world engulfed him, and all opportunities ceased to exist.

It was 2:30 on the afternoon of October 15, 1994.

"Food?"

I was lying on the sofa, staring up at the dirty, ash-grey ceiling with its fat cracks in the cement and spider webs in the corners. Barbara had already placed a glass of water in front of me on the coffee table. She put a cool hand on my forehead. Her bangles clashed in my eardrums. Indeed, everything about Barbara was loud. Her hair—newly-dyed in the interim—her eyebrows painted in brown earth tones, and her necklace of polished wooden pearls that rattled like an irate snake.

But I was no longer high.

The walk from Thisted to Klitmøller had burnt off the last of the chemical reserves in my system. The only thing I felt by the time I got home was a profound exhaustion in my bones. I was too tired to eat.

"No, thanks."

Barbara nodded, sat down in the easy chair in the corner, and tucked her thin brown legs in under her. Her feet looked like the claws of a crow. Two thin, tattooed snakes entwined around each other on her right ankle.

"Where were you?"

"I went for a walk."

"You've been gone for almost five hours."

I didn't budge. The visit to my grandmother's wasn't something I could put into words just yet, and I was still furious. Because Bæk-Nielsen had forced me to talk to her. But mostly because I kept thinking about what she'd said. About my father. That he claimed he was innocent. It wasn't as if I felt I owed him any loyalty—there was nothing to be loyal to—but that his treachery ran so deep ... I had always thought he would have the decency to admit his guilt.

"Would you like me to sing for you?"

I turned my head to meet Barbara's radiant gaze.

"You're nuts," I mumbled. "Why are you doing all this for me?"

"I guess because I like you," she said. "A clever man once told me that we don't always choose the people we have in our lives. Sometimes life, or circumstances, can bring us together, and sometimes we are deliberately chosen by others—and I have chosen you, sweetheart."

Her singing voice was off-key and smoky, and the tones became twisted on their way out of her brain and into the world via her vocal cords. Her song sounded like an echo from a different world. *Peace reigns in country and town . . .*

I closed my eyes, felt a ripple run through my body. I was no longer lying on my grandmother's sofa, I was in my own room, the attic walls were painted golden yellow, a poster of *Emil from Lönneberga* was stuck on the wall above my bed. My mother was bent over me, I could smell her. A mixture of soap and something honey-sweet on her breath.

I remembered her. I remembered her, and the sleep that followed in the wake of her memory was deep, and peaceful.

WHEN I WOKE up again it was getting dark, and there was a knocking at the door. Barbara was nowhere to be seen, but Lupo growled softly at the entrance as I walked down the stairs to open the door.

It was Thomas.

A hooded sweater and long pants—homage to the grey skies above. Just behind him stood Alex, looking like he wished he were any place other than right there. He had two brown paper bags clutched in his hands.

"Burgers and fries," said Thomas. "We bought some dinner at the grill bar on our way home."

"We?"

I caught Alex's eye, but he simply shrugged and slipped past me into the kitchen.

"Yes, I bumped into your son down at the harbor. He was collecting cans, you know . . . "

Thomas peered at me, dodged through the open door himself, and strode into the kitchen with Lupo hot on his heels.

"I don't mean to intrude," he said, "but people are starting to talk about you and your son's err . . . activities."

"What's wrong with collecting cans?"

I had followed Thomas into the kitchen and stood watching as the two boys ripped open the brown paper bags and tucked into their grub. Alex wasn't used to junk food, so he was certainly easy to tempt on that score. The puppy-dog look from before had disappeared just as swiftly as the oily fries and ketchup were disappearing down his gullet now. There must have been at least three hundred kroner's worth of food spread over the kitchen table.

"Nothing was wrong with it before. But things have changed. You seem to have become unpopular with the store owner," said Thomas, looking at me with a steady gaze.

"How much do I owe you?"

Thomas, who had just sunk his teeth into his burger, raised a conciliatory hand.

"Nothing," he said. "It's on me. You can buy the next round."

He knew I was broke, of course. I assumed that's what everybody in town was talking about. That, and the stealing.

"Thanks," I said. "I'll pay you back next month."

The kitchen suddenly seemed very small, and neither of us said anything else before Alex had finished his fries and gone upstairs. The sound of a faint bass beat filtered down to us through the cracked plaster of the ceiling.

"What I'm trying to ask, Ella, is whether you need any help," said Thomas. "If you're okay."

I shrugged. "Poverty stinks. Most people think it's contagious. Like lice, and the flu, and herpes. I guess it's not such a good idea to parade your symptoms in public, but I can't do anything about it. We need whatever extra cash we can scrape in on the side."

"Alex is starting school in less than three weeks." Thomas crumpled the burger wrappings and paper napkins together in one hand. "He's emptying garbage bins as fast as the other children can fill them. I don't know how things work in Hvidovre, but out here, that could become a problem."

"Maybe we'll move," I said. "I don't think this is the right place for us after all. It was only meant to be temporary anyway."

Thomas stared at me in surprise. "How so?"

"We needed to get away from Hvidovre."

"And now you need to get away from Klitmøller?"

His gaze shone with mock innocence, and I chose to ignore the implications underlying his question. "You're quick on the uptake, T. You've been pretty lucky with that brain of yours."

He got up without looking at me, petted Lupo affectionately on the neck. "Hmm, I'd better be going."

"Yes, I'll see you around."

"One more thing. About your parents." Thomas was standing half-turned in the doorway, still, without looking at me.

"Yes?"

"Did you know that your mother was a Jehovah's Witness?"

"Yes."

That was a lie. I knew that my mother's family had been very religious, but my beautiful *Book of Childhood Memories* had made no mention of Jehovah's Witnesses or the particular sect my mother's family had belonged to. Barring the optimistic and spaced-out religious types who occasionally roamed the apartment blocks in Hvidovre in the hope of roping in forlorn souls, I knew nothing about that kind of thing.

"And did you know that your mother had obtained a restraining order against her own sister and father? Apparently they harassed her after she left their church. They called her at all times of the day and night. On several occasions her father lit flame torches in your backyard, he planted wooden stakes right outside your parents' house; their congregation believed that Jesus was executed on a stake, not a cross. Apparently he was a real nutcase, her father."

"Where did you get this information?"

"You'd be surprised how much folklore there is in a closed tribal community like ours. Nobody can remember who saw what and when, but everyone knows the stories," he said. "Once you have ripped a hole in the web, all the spiders that were trapped inside come crawling out."

HELGI, 1994

He pulled the trigger as soon as he registered movement amongst the trees, but the shot was premature. The buck bolted in a twisted leap and crashed through the undergrowth in a stumbling, inelegant flight. It was hit, but only in the rump, and it would take some time to round it up.

He cracked the rifle, slung it over his shoulder, and made his way along the line of trees that flanked the plantation. There was blood on the forest bed. Not a lot of blood, but enough to create a trail of dark red dots on the carpet of dry pine needles. He bent down and pressed a finger into one of the murky smudges. The blood was warm to the touch, and all around him the forest breathed a haze of early winter. It felt good, and necessary; made it possible to breathe after Christi had gone.

Two weeks had passed since she'd stepped out of his car, and now she was nowhere to be found. When he sat down in the dunes in their usual meeting place, there was nothing but cold wind, sand, and the shredded sky above.

More than once he imagined that he had seen her. Between two containers on a building site, behind a shelf at the store, a shadow outside the window, on a street in Thisted. He ran after a woman on the road, but when he caught up with her and put a hand on her shoulder, it was a stranger's face that greeted him in return. Another time, he drove to Holstebro and parked across the street of the house on Aurikelvej. It was a small, ugly bungalow with a red-brick façade. The curtains were closed, and there had been no signs of life in the two hours that passed while he was parked there, but she was probably . . . at work, or visiting her mother—if she had one. He felt as if he knew her, knew her innermost being, but in fact he knew so desperately little about her. Once she'd told him that she worked in the field of cultural relations, whatever that was. Parents or siblings she never mentioned. There had always been more important things to talk about. A book she had read. A photography exhibition in Århus. Ex-boyfriends she never mentioned either, although there must have been at least one significant partner, the father of the boys she had lost. But the house showed no signs of a man's presence, and if there had been one, he was of one of the useless sort; the gutters were coming undone and the window frames were rotten, and he returned to Klitmøller with a renewed sense of relief coupled with a deeper desperation in his bones.

He was the kind of man that knew how to look after his own. He was a rock. You could harness him to a plough and he would turn up the soil of an entire meadow in the space of an afternoon. He could build things with his bare hands, and when he stood in front of the bathroom mirror, the bulges on his upper arms and the muscles that played under his skin when he flicked his wrists were testimony of his immense physical strength. But none of it could help him now. He was falling apart, and it was all because of her.

Her and Anna.

The two unhappy women who needed him—each in their own way. But he was just one human being with just one soul.

Anna was going to pieces too. It was as if they glided past each other much more frequently than they had before. On those rare occasions that he had tried to hold her, she was unable to soften in his embrace—or he was unable to open his arms to receive her. They repelled each other like two negative poles of a magnet.

He knew that she had tried to regain contact with an old friend. A woman she had met in a support group for people who had been expelled from their church. Anna and the woman had fallen out over something a number of years previously, and he had never met her, but apparently she was a rehabilitated drug addict, and this only added to his unease. It seemed as though Anna was moving even further away from him now that he was finally ready to come back.

He clenched his jaw. He'd already shot a couple of squawking pheasants earlier that day. Every shot had eased the tension in his muscles. The buck was meant for the butcher.

He could hear the animal's haphazard flight through the undergrowth and he followed after it patiently. There was no need for haste, there were plenty of daylight hours left, and there was nothing to hurry home for. Above him and beyond the tops of the dense fir trees a cold autumn rain was raging, but the raindrops never reached him. And then he spotted the buck. It was lying on its side, panting, its head lifted to the sky. The worst of the animal's panic had dissipated along with the drainage of blood, and for a while he stood watching it from a distance. It was a fine roebuck. Not one of the young bulls. In several places its coat bore dark patterned patches, presumably from deathly duels over the females in the herd. Warm clouds of breath rose from its flared nostrils.

He crept closer through the brush. He would prefer to shoot at close range, but he didn't want to scare the buck any more than he'd done already, nor did he wish to look him in the eye. Not today.

He lifted the rifle to his shoulder, and pulled the trigger. The animal shuddered and the shot resonated briefly in the air. A couple of pheasants were startled higher into the trees, and then the forest was completely still.

He went over to the buck and lifted its antlers. The flesh was torn on the edge of its jaw, the eyes dull against the shimmer of light. He bent down, gripped the forelegs in his hands, and slung the animal over his shoulder. Then he forced his way back through the scattered undergrowth.

The car was parked where he had left it, but when he opened the boot to spread out a few black garbage bags in the back, something seemed out of place. The cold had a hint of perfume in the air that disappeared the very instant he tried to capture it.

Christi.

He glanced rapidly over his shoulder, but there was nothing to be seen among the dense fir trees. Out in the clearing the cold rain poured down over him, and he flipped the hood of his sweater up over his head. He flung the dead animal into the trunk together with his rifle, opened door on the driver's side, and stumbled back.

There was a tiny doll sitting up against the grey upholstery. Not a baby doll, but a ragdoll with yellow threads of curly hair. Next to the doll lay an oblong white plastic tube that he first mistook for a thermometer, but after closer inspection he identified it for what it was: a pregnancy test. On countless occasions Anna had used a more primitive form of the tests over the span of years she'd tried to conceive before Ella was born. Sometimes, when she'd been particularly desperate, she had done three tests on the same day. The white strips of paper lay scattered on the edge of the bathtub, on the sink, on the tile floor, each displaying its own, solitary purple stripe.

He carefully lifted the doll and sat down with the tube in his hand. Two purple stripes were visible in the display.

The test was positive.

From her perch on the passenger seat the doll stared at him with embroidered, light-blue eyes.

Kirsten had arranged to have my case files sent to me within two weeks of my request—a not insignificant feat considering just how much paper was involved: two cardboard boxes filled with several hard-backed files and a stack of stapled reports.

I knew there would be a lot. I had, after all, been interviewed by a number of psychologists, doctors, social workers, and counselors over the years, the kind of people who took notes on everything and afterward wrote reports to social services and Welfare authorities and asked others to consider their prognoses.

Even so, I was surprised. I was only twenty-eight years old, and by ordinary standards, an insignificant human being. That I had been deemed worthy of such thorough documentation was overwhelming.

Lying on top of the files in the first box was a handwritten note from Kirsten.

Dearest Ella, I hope you are okay. Call me if you need to talk.

I crumpled the note in the palm of my hand and sent her a mental note of well wishes. *Thanks, but no thanks.* I paged through the first couple of files and came across one of my psychiatric evaluations from Bakkegården.

Ella Nygaard, 14 years old. Has several self-inflicted lesions on her arms, all stemming from preceding three months of observation. When asked to motivate her actions, the patient claims the cuts were "necessary" but is otherwise aggressive and/or unresponsive to therapy. On two occasions last week, the patient threw kitchen knives, glasses, and forks at staff on the ward. On the whole, the patient responds to her external environment with violence and communication is difficult. Recommend observation re: possible deficits in attention, motor control and/or personality disorders . . . Recommend a course of anti-depressants . . . recommend isolation in the interests of safety . . . recommend long-term behavioral therapy once the medication has taken effect . . . has a close relationship to Amir. NB: Advise on prevention and/or abstention from all sexual activity.

I put the report back into the box with a sense of having read a letter that hadn't been addressed to me.

I met Amir when I was thirteen. At that time, he was a mere waif of a boy, a year younger than I was, and already saddled with several convictions for assault. He robbed other boys of their brand-name jackets and extra change. He didn't earn any points for originality on that score, but he was a vain little devil, and his signature trait was breaking his victims' pinky finger. He did it every time. Something to do with a jujitsu trick he'd learned from a cousin in Avedøre, if I remembered correctly.

Amir was up to his frail neck in well-worn clichés. A chain-smoker that spewed cuss words like *you filthy whore*, *homo*, *shit-faced Dane*, and *I'll fuck your mother*. He wore a thick gold chain around his neck and he only assaulted nice Danish boys, the smooth and well-bred kind with perfect manners, big teeth, slicked hair, and expensive, designer clothing. Amir liked to point them out to me when we went shopping with the teachers from Bak-kegården.

"That guy over there," he'd say. "He's a real mama's boy. He'd piss in his pants if you asked him for a hundred kroner. The pretty boys never fight back, do they? They just take what's coming to them and piss themselves. Just like the family pet does when you break into their master's house. The dumb dog licks your hand, begs to be petted, and whines when you split. That guy would suck my dick if I asked him to."

Even if Amir was at pains to live up to every macho cliché in the book, it was his fear of the dark that eventually brought us together. He used to sneak into my bed when he'd had a nightmare. And I let him. He was a late bloomer. Small and weedy, and hairless till he turned fourteen—we didn't touch each other in that way until nearly two years later, when the force of nature finally took over.

Despite the youth counselor's repeated warnings and big-pal conversations, within three months after Amir's fourteenth birthday we had had sex on every horizontal and vertical surface at Bakkegården and its immediate environs. We were both alone, and neither of us had any family, so I guess it wasn't surprising that we fled into each others' arms. Nor was it surprising that I got pregnant. Strangely enough, the risk of this happening had never occurred to me. I was, after all, a crossbreed produced by the mating of two forlorn individuals—a victim and a murderer—in inelegant harmony.

I wrestled the cardboard boxes into the living room. Luckily Barbara had gone to Thisted to buy some supplies for her drawings, so I could lug the boxes upstairs unnoticed, and dragged them into the attic room for a later perusal. Bakkegården was familiar territory. It was what came before that I was interested in: the time that stretched back from that day I was born in a greenhouse in a foster family's backyard in Aalborg.

I WENT DOWN to the beach to look for Alex.

He was sitting at the edge of the water with Lupo and a boy I hadn't seen before. Alex was drawing in the sand with a stick, laughing at something the other boy said. Then they got up and strolled barefooted down the beach towards the pier, Lupo trotting in their heels. Alex's sandals dangled casually from the crook of his finger and every now and then one of the boys would bend down, pick up a stone, and send it flying over the surface of the waves, as if they had never done anything but be on the beach together.

"Anders Mikkelsen."

A person had come up next to me. It was Thomas, of course. He nodded in the direction of the boys.

"Anders is good company. Not to worry. There aren't any ghetto boys within miles from here."

"I'm not worried."

"The worst thing kids can come up with out here is the kind of game we used to play together."

I sneaked a glance at him. He was too thin for my liking. In fact, he was a lot thinner than one ought to be as a Jutlander living on the North Sea coast. In Hvidovre, he would have blended in nicely, but you'd think that the combination of fresh ocean air, gravy potatoes, and homemade rhubarb tart with extra cream would foster a more vigorous specimen of a man. But no, his cheeks were hollow and he had an odd, perfectly round, shiny scar between the tendons on his neck.

"And what game would that be, exactly?" I asked.

He smiled crookedly. "As I said, you were a very energetic child with a healthy curiosity for the physical activity practiced by . . . err . . . between the sexes."

I recalled the image that had sprung to mind as I stepped into my grandmother's loft for the first time, me manically masturbating in the dusty heat, a pillow clenched between my knees. I blushed.

"Don't worry," said Thomas. He kicked at a pile of tattered rope at his feet. "We didn't do anything like that. But we used to spy on people doing it in the dunes. It was foolproof. When the sun was shining, the dunes were crawling with lusty teenagers—and still are, for that matter. All we had to do was follow the couples who separated themselves from the group and headed away from the paths, deeper into the dunes. We were good at it. We waited, only crawling closer once they were so engrossed in each other that they were beyond noticing anything else. It's just like trout and salmon in spawning season, you know, when they lay their eggs. They tumble round each other just under the surface, and before they know it, you can wade right up to them, simply fish them out of the water with your bare hands."

I thought of my exploits with Magnus and hoped that the youth of Klitmøller preferred to stay indoors and get their kicks at their computer screens instead. My status as a thief had already been made public.

"You can't remember anything at all, can you?"

His eyes were crooked and kind when he smiled, and something dislodged in my chest, like small pebbles sliding down a bank. His smile reminded me of that tickling sensation you get when a yellow snail slithers over your hand. Ladybugs and fine green stalks of dandelion. My friend, Thomas.

Some things were coming back slowly. I hesitated. "Nothing that makes any sense. I'm not even sure it's anything that actually happened."

"What about this?" He said, sticking a hand into the pouch of his sweater. "I found it when I was cleaning up the loft recently . . . My parents live in Spain for the better part of the year. The plan is that the house will be mine one day. The house and all the junk that goes with it."

He handed the piece of paper to me, and I took it. Two words in a child's scrawl, half the letters inverted.

i swayr

I stared at the words intently, but nothing came to mind.

"Did I write it?"

He shook his head. "You forced me to write it down that summer before you left Klitmøller. It was the summer we . . . you know, had our little spying hobby, and our first summer together that I can remember clearly. I missed you terribly after you disappeared."

"Why did I ask you to do that?"

He paused. Whatever he'd planned to do or say before, he was clearly having second thoughts. I shrugged and headed for the sea. I'd never had the patience for artistic pauses. I'd spent too much time with too many social workers meticulously schooled in the art of communication. Artistic pauses were my cue to beat it. I rarely needed to hear what followed thereafter.

"Ella, wait!"

He jogged to catch up with me.

"I'm not sure whether I should tell you. And it's none of my business, but . . . "

I was standing at the edge of the water, letting the waves wash over my bare feet. On the other side of the ocean was England, and a little farther off, on the other side of the world, was America. I had never seen that world.

"During your father's trial the case attracted a lot of coverage in the media. People still talk about it. You know how it is—nothing much happens out here."

"And?" I wished he would wrap up his act soon so I could get back to the house. Barbara had taken pity on me and stocked up on vodka from the store.

"And your father initially testified that your mother may have committed suicide, because he had fallen in love with someone else. But when the police arrived on the scene, he was standing there with the hunting rifle in his hands. There was blood on his clothing . . . "

The water foamed over my feet and pulled the sand away around their contours. My legs were golden brown and streaked with salt. It was comforting yet disconcerting to feel like I was standing at the edge of the European continent with the wind in my hair. There was still time to find another town in Jutland to live before Alex went back to school after summer break. There were plenty of cheap houses in remote rural towns. It didn't have to be Klitmøller—with or without free lodgings.

"We saw her, Ella! We saw the woman your father mentioned in the trial. We saw them together on the beach. And afterward you got me to write the note. I had to swear that I would never tell anyone we had seen your father with another woman in the dunes. I was six years old when you left. I didn't know about the court case back then. I spent my time playing soccer and yanking out loose teeth, for Christ's sake. But you're back now . . . Aren't you even a little bit curious? Don't you want to know why everything became so fucked up in your life?"

I met his gaze. It struck me that Thomas was the only person I knew, apart from my grandmother, who had known me as a child.

"You're right," I snapped. "It's none of your fucking business."

I could hear how angry I sounded, but I gave myself credit for not walking away. We stood facing each other like two cowboys in a Western, Thomas with his thumbs stuck into the pockets of his jeans.

"When I look at you, Ella, I can see how badly things have gone for the girl I once knew," he said. "The girl you once were is still in there. I recognized her in you the moment I saw you, but when anybody tries to talk to you, you turn your back on them. Literally. That boy of yours must have been miraculously conceived when you either were too drunk or too high to fend another person off."

"Again," I said, my voice shaking, "why should you care?"

"It hurts to just stand by and watch, Ella," he said. "You were different when I knew you before. And I'm an optimistic soul. I believe things will get better, if you do your best to put the past right. I don't think you've ever made an effort with anything in your life."

"I do my best every single day."

"To do what, exactly? Why did you come back?"

Again those crooked, kindly eyes, the smile I couldn't parry. Especially because a part of me knew he was right. Of course I could tell him that I had fled from Hvidovre without any money, that I had nowhere else in the world to go. That would be the truth. But it wasn't the whole truth.

I guess I had brought Alex back to Klitmøller with the same compulsive confidence as an elephant mother herding her calf over hundreds of miles of desert-torn savanna to the watering hole of her youth. Before the murder, I had lived a life here. Perhaps I had even been happy.

"I'm trying to get better," I said, realizing the truth of my words the moment they were spoken. This was why I had left, and this was why I had asked Kirsten to send me the files. Because I needed to know what happened to me.

My childhood home looked the same as I had remembered in flashes.

A redbrick façade. A front garden with a patchy lawn, scoured by relentless salty gusts. The new owners had abandoned what was once a spacious lawn behind the house. Heather and tumbling roses crept all the way up the walls, their path broken by two wind-blown flowerbeds and a rusty swing. A plastic scooter was parked in the drive and a Disney princess ball had rolled in under the hedge, but other than that, there were no signs of life. The garage was empty.

I shot a glance at the neighbor's blank windows, then strode up to the front door. I slowly reached out to touch the door knocker. It was cast in bronze, in the shape of a lion's head that I remembered from a different angle—the feeling of standing on tip-toe to reach the knocker, the low metallic thud it produced—if I tried hard enough. There was no fear bottled in the sound. No inner tremor. Not yet.

I walked around the house, staying close to the walls. I could see names and hearts carved into the brick surface at a child's eye level. I traced my fingers along the grooves till I was at back of the house. *I like Tom* and *Annette* and *Anne-Mette* came up repeatedly. Perhaps the names of girls who had lived there after me. Children living a carefree life in the room I had left behind. They had counted the same knots in the wooden ceiling, climbed into the same bathtub with salt and sand matted in their hair. Perhaps they went on to study at the Gymnasium or enrolled in the University in Århus to study biology or English Literature. But I was looking for something that belonged to me, some sign that I had been there also, and finally I found it, etched into the wall near the terrace sliding door.

Ella. 7 years old.

I sat on my haunches and stared at the lines cut into the dark brick. Of course I had known that the house existed, that it was only a couple of hundred yards from my grandmother's house, but all at once, I could see her. Me. A girl. My house. I had lived here with my parents, with my mother.

Something warm pierced my chest—it felt like a crack peeling open. A faint vibration from the core of my body. I pulled out my flask of vodka and gulped down three mouthfuls. A donation from Barbara's ample depot. The alcohol burned a hot trail down my throat, spreading calm into my muscles along the way. I stood up and carefully tested the terrace door. It wasn't locked.

I hadn't planned on breaking into the house. It seemed natural to open the door and slip inside the semi-darkness. My body remembered the place. It seemed to recognize the way the light fell through the living room windows, the creak in the wainscoting, the particular odor of the air that had penetrated the walls, that part of the house that would remain the same irrespective of who was living there.

I sat down on the couch in the corner of the narrow living room. Fragments of scenes played before me, voices from the depths of consciousness bubbled to the surface. Our couch had stood in the same corner. The lamp and the coffee table also seemed familiar. When I looked at the door that I instinctively knew led to the kitchen, I imagined I could see a figure, my mother, appearing there to ask me a question.

More vodka.

I leaned back and closed my eyes. Red shadows flickered on the insides of my eyelids, and then the images I had seen a thousand times in my dreams came to the surface. The pictures that crowded my nightmares in the dark.

My father raising his hand and hitting my mother in the face. She doesn't defend herself. Doesn't even look up. The faces are indistinct, but I know they belong to my mom and dad, and the fear keeps rising like water in a bathtub. A wild, wild fear that makes me scream, hammer against my dad's back. And then the pain at the back of my head, the blood is flowing from my eye-brow, and it just won't stop.

I took another sip of vodka, got to my feet, and climbed the stairs. Once again I had that strange feeling that my legs knew the way before my brain could register my location. The curve of the stair-way, the door to the left that led to my parents' bedroom, the door to the right that led to the bathroom—I let myself be sucked in, and then I was standing on the same blue bathroom tiles I had studied at close range as a child, balancing precariously on the edge of the toilet seat. I remembered my own smell, my bare feet, the distance to the toilet paper on the wall was much too great; you could lose your balance and tip over at any moment if you weren't careful.

I knew it now, this is where he had hit me, where he had hit us. And as I tried to focus on the tile where the blood had trickled to the floor, an absurd thought intruded: an image of me making colored dripping candles there instead. There was nothing on the tiles, of course. The floor must have been washed a thousand times since.

It was hot in the bathroom. The sun came streaming through thin white curtains that had once been floral-print. I bent over the sink and let cold water run over my hands, splashed it onto my face and forehead. I went out onto the passageway once more and stared at the door at the opposite end. As a child I must have walked down this passage many times in the dark; woken by a bad dream, crawling into bed with my parents, simply going to the toilet. And in the mornings, I must have padded along the fir-tree floors on soft, bare little feet. The smell of wood, soap, and suds from my child-hood penetrated my mind and I remembered a nightdress I used to wear. It was pink with little flowers on it and a white ribbon running down the front.

My feet carried me towards my bedroom door, twenty-one years had passed since I'd tiptoed down that passage in the dark, looking in vain for my mom and dad in their bedroom. Time wound backwards. I became younger and younger with every step to my old bedroom, and I thought I could hear voices—a ruckus coming from my parents' bedroom.

Get out. A woman's voice rises up out of the dark, sharply cutting through time. *What are you doing?* If there is an answer, it's too soft for me to hear. More palaver and noise. Things being smashed against the wall—now the noise is coming from the living room downstairs. I sit down at the top of the stairs, terrified, my pink nightdress glowing ever so slightly in the dark. There is something evil in the house. I can feel it all the way down to the tips of my toes. Something that wants to hurt my mother.

Ouch, ouch . . . stop. Leave me alone . . . A woman crying.

I jerked myself away from the past and took another swig of vodka. With my free hand, I carefully opened the door in front of me and stopped short, my feet rooted to the ground.

The bed stood where it had before, built in under one of the slanted walls. In front of the window there was a white-washed table and on the floor a girl sat cross-legged, staring up at me.

"Oh, I'm sorry . . ." I took a step backwards and lifted both hands in a gesture that I hoped was universally understood sign language for non-threatening behavior. The girl didn't reply. She must have been about eight years old. Old enough to be home alone, and to know a strange woman shouldn't be in their house. She had dark ponytails, high cheekbones, and a determined line about the contours of her mouth. She was not afraid.

"I'm sorry," I said again, backing up even more. "I'm looking for your mom, but I guess she's not home?"

The girl shook her head. "She'll be back in half an hour. She's at work."

Shit, shit, shit. I nodded and turned to go. Whatever I managed to say would only make matters worse. If I got the hell out of there, the girl might forget all about me. Eight-year-old girls can be forgetful. Show them a lip gloss or a pink plastic pony, and the rest of the world disappears. Unfortunately, I had neither on me just then.

"I'm gonna go now," I said, smiling. "Perhaps I'll pop in again later."

The girl fixed her calm, brown-eyed stare on me. "Wait. What's your name?"

I didn't answer, tried to smile again, and made for the door. I could hear that the girl had stood, that she was following me on almost silent stockinged feet.

"You're welcome to wait," she said. "I know how to make coffee."

"No, thanks, that's really kind of you, but . . . I'm actually in a bit of a hurry."

I started moving down the stairs but realized that I had taken a little too much onboard this time. Everything was pitching under me and I had to hold onto the banister in order to navigate a straight course through a rocking universe.

It was so damn hot. Fucking Thomas. The whole escapade was ridiculous, I'd been doing just fine without his help. I had survived both my childhood and my youth, and one day, I would have survived my adult years without having known the details about what my father had done or why.

"My mom will be home any minute now."

The girl jumped down and planted herself at the foot of stairs, perched one hand on her hip and twirled a pony-tail with the other.

"I really gotta go . . ." I tried to skirt past the girl without touching her, but this was proving to be difficult.

"I could get you a glass of juice instead, if you like."

Again that steady, insistent gaze from a little grown-up. I was trapped. The vodka was no longer enough; I could feel the internal tremor penetrating my ribcage, up and outwards.

There is a man, it must be my father, standing in the dark in the living room with a telephone in his hand. He looks angry, but the words coming out of his mouth are kind and loving.

Of course we will be together. I'll leave Anna. My love . . . please don't . . .

The cut on my eye has stopped bleeding, but the back of my head is pounding. I am thirsty, but I don't want anything to drink. I am afraid of him now; I must not fall asleep.

"Water?"

The child was standing in front of me with a glass in her hand that she thrust in front of my face. If she could have, she would have poured the water directly down my throat, exactly as she liked to do with her dolls, no doubt.

I took the water and drank, still standing with one hand on the banister.

"I think it's the heat," said the girl pragmatically. "You have to remember to drink enough water when it's so hot."

I gently reached out a hand and touched one of her long, smooth ponytails. She didn't look like me, but she was the girl who was sleeping in my bed. An absurd homesickness took hold of me; my body knew its shape, and recoiled.

"I have to go now," I said. "But thanks for the water. You're an angel."

"Not really," said the girl, smiling for the first time. Proudly. She waved as I limped down the road, hoping that nobody had seen me.

"What are we looking for?"

Magnus was holding his joint out the driver's seat window. He had been dragging his heels ever since I called him that morning. There were rules for the kind of relationship we had, and I had broken them. The fact that he was willing to use his athletic tongue between my legs didn't mean he would be willing to do me any other favors; he wasn't my boyfriend. I knew this well enough, but he had a car, and his company wasn't nearly as demanding as Thomas's or Barbara's would have been. Having him tag along was the closest I could come to doing this the way I preferred: alone.

"Number twenty-two Forest Road."

He snorted. "There isn't a single tree within miles from here."

He was right about that. The town and its immediate surroundings were everything but picturesque. The main road leading into the center of town was flanked by claustrophobically narrow sidewalks and low-slung houses painted in screaming colors. The range of shops included a hairdresser, a suntanning salon, a bakery, and a grocery store that was dumped in the middle of a deserted parking lot.

I was struggling to make sense of Magnus's GPS.

"You have to take a right at the next crossing. Then take the fourth road on your left."

"Are you going to tell me what this is about? Is there something you need me to do for you?"

He wedged his joint between his lips, slipped a hand between my thighs, and starting working his long, strong fingers. I got his hand off me and pulled away. Magnus had parked in front of a yellow-brick house on Forest Road.

"No, and no."

He sighed dramatically, took a final puff on his joint, and flicked it onto the sidewalk.

"Perfect surfing weather today," he said, squinting up at the sky. "And here we are, fifty miles inland. How long did you say this was going to take?"

I shrugged. My body felt relaxed for once. The internal trembling had abated as soon as I had lifted the first file of my case history out of its box that morning:

> Girl, 8 years old. Till now, well-adjusted. Has been institutionalized with a view to finding permanent foster care after a recent family tragedy . . . registered mental illness in the family.

Apart from the notes made by the social worker, there were two private letters: one from my grandmother requesting custody of me, and one from my aunt renouncing all contact.

> . . . I was sorry to learn of the circumstances befalling my sister's daughter, but as we have not had contact with either the girl or her mother for several years we are unable to offer her a home in familiar, secure surroundings. Furthermore, taking in the girl would be directly opposed to the wishes of my sister, and this we have chosen to respect . . . Birgit Højer.

THE ONLY BIRGIT Højer close to Thisted was the woman living on Forest Road in this town with no forest.

The house itself was an anonymous, yellow-brick building with lilacs and rhododendrons in the garden and brown patches on the lawn. It was located at the end of a blind alley and beyond it lay open, newly-harvested meadows. The door onto the roofed porch stood open and in its shade I could see a glimpse of a hammock and a table covered with a plastic floral-print tablecloth.

Magnus took out two fresh joints out of the glove compartment and offered me one with a quirked eyebrow. I shook my head. I was stone cold sober for a change, and glad of it.

"Wait here."

Magnus cast one more rueful glance at the blue skies above and another at his watch. "Can you wrap this up in half an hour? Then I can still get a session in this afternoon."

I slammed the door of the van behind me, my mouth suddenly bone dry, and walked up to the garden gate. One of those awful miniature dogs was barking hysterically in the yard next door. It was spurting energetically up and down the other side of the hedge, looking for an imaginary hole to scoot through. There was still time to turn back. If my mother had felt the need to get a restraining order against her own sister, there probably wasn't a lot of sense in my looking her up at all; she must have hated my mother.

"Hallo? Can I help you?"

An elderly woman had appeared on the porch. She stood peering at me, one hand shading her eyes against the sun.

I took a step back involuntarily, suddenly aware of the fact that I was dressed in a T-shirt and flip-flops and now desperately wished I'd thought to change. And my hair reeked of Magnus's joint.

"I'm looking for Birgit Højer."

"Yes, I'm Birgit Højer." She stepped off the porch and came towards me purposefully. Not in a gesture of congeniality, but more like I imagine a goalie would meet the rush of a striker in the penalty area. She stopped in front of me and braced her arms across her chest. No trace of a smile about either the eyes or lips. Just grim determination.

"My name is Ella Nygaard, and I am . . . "

"I know very well who you are. You look like your mother."

We stood staring at each other in silence for a while. If my aunt also resembled my mother, I failed to see how. She was old, probably well over seventy, and neatly dressed in a pink short-sleeved shirt, white Bermudas, and sandals with a moderate heel. Her thin white hair was pulled severely back into a knot at the nape of her neck, mercilessly exposing the hard lines of her face. If there had ever been anything soft about it, time and life had shorn it off; only bare cheekbones, eye sockets, and the jawbone remained.

"I'm ill," she said, as if reading my thoughts. "So if you could keep it brief."

I shot a glance over her shoulder. My aunt had put a jug of ice-water on the table under the shaded porch. There wasn't a breath of wind on the sundrenched lawn.

"I wanted to know if you could tell me a something about my mother."

It was the soft approach I had prepared. Not a word about restraining orders and harassment. No mention of brain tissue splattered on galoshes.

"What would you like to know?"

"I thought perhaps you could tell me what she was like as a child."

My aunt shook her head. "She liked to attract attention to herself. Always wore pretty dresses and pearls, that kind of thing."

The last comment was delivered with a tight smile, and I guessed that Birgit Højer had never attracted attention to herself. Not even at an age that usually calls for princess dresses and diamond tiaras. The two sisters didn't have any physical likeness either, as far as I could tell. In the photographs I had seen of my mother she seemed like a shy, gentle woman. Her body was frail, slightly bow-necked, as if constantly warding off the world. Birgit, on the other hand, carried herself tall and rigid as a pillar.

"You and your family are Jehovah's Witnesses . . . "

The woman standing in front of me didn't reply, casting an impatient look over my shoulder instead. "Is that your . . . friend . . . over there?"

Magnus had gotten out of the van and was pacing back and forth on the sidewalk. He towered up over the hedge, lost in his own world and the music on his iPhone. His long blond locks had been gathered into a ponytail; his second, loosely rolled joint was dangling from the corner of his mouth.

"I'm really sorry about what happened to you and Anna. About all of it. I wish I had been able to do something for you both before it was too late. But you have to understand . . . " She squinted into the sun. "Anna had always had something ugly inside her, so in a way, it didn't surprise us that she died the way she did. Already as a little girl . . . seeing her do up her face like that . . . it was grotesque.

She used to paint her lips bright red with a brush, her eyelids light blue."

The corners of my aunt's mouth curled in unmitigated disgust.

"And then later, she met him. Your father. We knew he wasn't the first boy she'd had in that way, but he was the first one who was dumb enough to let her move in. My parents were heartbroken."

I touched a hand to the heart-shaped amber pendant I always wore around my neck. I wished I could put my arms around my mother; the little girl who liked to paint her eyelids light blue, her lips a dramatic shade of red. I would have told her she was just fine the way she was. My aunt turned on her heel and made for the house.

"You and your father harassed her," I said quietly. "You persecuted her when she moved in with my grandmother. Why?"

My aunt turned and looked at me long and hard.

"We tried to save her—till there was nothing left to save. The police called it harassment, but it was merely a loving reminder that her family was still there for her, that she could come back to us, if she wished. For a long time, we hoped that we could be reunited after her death. In spite of everything. What your mother said about us was all lies. The evil upon her was too great. It happens. We couldn't save her, but if she had stayed with us, she would still be alive today."

"If she had stayed with you, I would never have been born."

My aunt nodded, and smiled faintly. Clearly she wasn't deaf to the conversation's sharp undertones. "It's purely hypothetical, Ella. You shouldn't take that kind of speculation personally. Sometimes one has to take a theoretical stance to life. Imagine, for instance, what is lost by choosing one road instead of another. How different one's life could have been. Anna could have been happy with us."

"I'm trying to figure out what happened . . ."

I no longer knew what I wanted from her. She had known my mother, but it was hard to believe that my aunt had ever seen my mother for who she was. Everything my aunt saw was clouded by moral and religious interpretation. Not to mention persistent anger over being deserted. Drops of sweat had collected on the surface of her perfectly pale foundation, and her hands were clasped so tightly together that you would think she was fighting back a suicidal impulse.

"Ella." She turned and came up to me abruptly, opened her arms, and pulled me close with unexpected feeling. "I am really sorry about what happened to the two of you. You mustn't believe anything else. It hurts so terribly much. We are flesh and blood after all."

My aunt was luxuriously perfumed, but below the pall of expensive perfume was her own body odor. Summer sweat and something sharp, like that of an animal, a smell that brought flashes of my mother's face along with it; their bodies had the same odor, the characteristic scent of my herd. I saw my mother bent over me as I lay in my bed.

Then the two faces glided apart once more.

"She had a friend," my aunt said into my hair. "I know this, because her friend also fell out with the church. And there was gossip. The friend came from the Faroe Isles originally. Lea Poulsen was her name. She married into our congregation shortly after your mother left the church. She and her husband had two boys together, but they split up, and Lea got mixed up with drugs. Narcotics. Your mother and Lea were seen together a couple of times—they met each other in a support group for fallen members of the congregation."

An elderly man had appeared in the doorway on the porch behind her. He hadn't taken the trouble to greet me. My aunt let go of me and seemed to be making a determined effort to shake me off, as if I were an unwelcome burst of rain.

"I would invite you in," she said. "But I'm not feeling very well today."

I nodded, and smiled. She had given me what I'd come for after all.

"Farewell, Ella. It was good to meet you."

The man behind her stood completely still. He just stared at me and his comely wife till she finally turned her back and walked away.

ANNA, 1994

"Anna!"

Cool hands were laid over her eyes, pulling her backwards. A mouth against her neck. Soft lips and warm breath.

Anna spun round and threw her arms around her neck.

Lea. At last.

They walked north along the beach, hand in hand. The tourists had long since gone home and they had the beach to themselves. The wind whipped the water onto the shore, the sky was gigantic. Far, far at sea, a container vessel lay like a stone on the horizon. They walked for a while before either one of them spoke.

"I've missed you."

Anna shot Lea a sidelong glance. She rarely said that kind of thing. Not to Helgi, not even to Ella, but the whiskey from that morning had dulled her nerves and made her speak more freely. Say the truth.

Lea smiled. "Have you?"

Lea looked a lot better than she remembered. If it hadn't been for that voice, Anna would not have recognized her. She had bleached her hair and gained a healthy deal of weight. Her hips were fuller, her breasts heavier, and that characteristic restlessness underlying each and every movement had disappeared along with the drugs. It suited her.

Lea had always been beautiful, thought Anna. Even in her most pained and emaciated version, she had always been a beautiful woman. The dark-blue eyes, the classic profile, the heavy, dramatic jewelry, and the long black robes that somehow transformed her aura of frailty and misery into a sophisticated fashion sense. But she had obviously recovered, and her cheeks were a glowing crimson in the icy wind, her blond hair flying. It had been five years since she'd seen her, but miraculously, Lea had become a younger-looking woman than she was before.

"They've started doing it again."

Anna studied her worn galoshes. Just saying the words out loud sent a bolt of fear through her.

"Who? Your family?" Lea was watching her closely.

Anna nodded. "My sister—or my father. Or . . . I don't know."

Anna looked at her hands. They were red from the cold and the eczema that now had spread to the rest of her body.

"It's been such a long time since I've thought about all the warnings we were given. But they've all come back. I will be punished for . . . for being with Helgi. For deserting my family . . . and God. I know it's insane. Sometimes I feel insane. During the daylight hours it's still okay, but at night it just doesn't stop. There are so many of those signs we were instructed to look out for, the wars, the natural catastrophes. At three in the morning, I really feel as though God is sitting out there somewhere, watching the earth through a magnifying glass, ready to strike down dead those of us who haven't lived a life of obedience. If it were just me . . . but what about Ella? I keep thinking about all the terrible things that will happen to her before we die. It's the first thing I think about when I wake up in the morning, and the last thing I think before I fall asleep. I feel like I'm living in a burning building. Do you know what I mean, Lea?"

It was a relief to say it to someone. Pour out the madness in all its naked horror, even though she knew it was a tub that would fill to the brim just as easily again.

Lea regarded her with those intense, dark-blue eyes of hers. "Of course I do, Anna. What you learn in your childhood remains on your mind. Dark discolorations—like brown patches on a sheet, right? But they're just feelings, Anna. It's not real. In many ways, you have always been the stronger of the two of us. You left the church of your own accord; I was kicked out. I was stoned and drunk for years. You have wrestled this devil before—and won."

Anna laughed. She couldn't believe that anyone could think of her as being strong right now, or at all. "I'm not strong," she said.

"Something broke when I left my parents' home. I know very well that our . . . that their reality is twisted. My head knows this. But my body believes every word. It remembers everything. Sometimes I wish that I had stayed. At least then I would have had the comfort of the church."

They had reached the harbor and walked along the row of small fishing boats that had been pulled up onto land and covered with dark tarpaulin for the winter months. An icy mist of rain blew in over the deserted buildings. A handful of men in blue overalls were packing crates of fish at the warehouse. Several freshly caught eels were writhing in a bucket of stinking ammonia.

"What's that?"

Lea had stopped to watch the sprawling eels. They were half-covered by a foaming slime, their eyes open, blind, jaws repeatedly opening and closing. The stench from the bucket burned in the nose. Lea's eyes shone in the shaft of light from the warehouse.

"An eel's private hell," said Anna. "They put them into the ammonia while they're still alive so the slime will ooze out of their bodies. Gruesome."

Lea squinted against the stinging vapor, then reached out to touch one of the slithery eels, almost as an afterthought. "Human beings do many gruesome things," she said softly.

She took a moist napkin out of her bag and meticulously rubbed the sticky fish-slime off her hands and beautifully painted fingernails.

"I survived. I have found something to live for, and it's wonderful, Anna. I can see myself being with someone again. Having children. And a job. Who would have believed it?"

"I get these sent to me." Anna took a photograph out of her pocket and gave it to Lea. "Just when I think I've managed to forget, I get another one of these."

It was a color photograph of Anna in a bikini when she was young. She is walking hand in hand with Helgi on the beach, her shoulders are a little red, but she's laughing, her head is resting on Helgi's shoulder. It was their first summer together after she'd left the church. Her breasts and pelvis had been cut out of the picture, and on the back someone had written a message in fat, red capital letters, WHORES END UP IN HELL, followed by a citation from the Bible:

The stars in the sky fell to the earth . . .

"I don't even know where they get the pictures from. This photo is thirty-two years old. It comes from one of my photo albums; they've been in my house, Lea. Why are they doing this?"

"It's all bullshit, Anna."

Lea gripped her shoulders firmly, turned Anna round to face her, looked deep into her eyes. "There will be no Judgment Day, Anna. Certainly not the kind the church claims there will be. It may very well be that the world, as we know it, will disappear one day. But there will be no shining-white figure swooping in to save a chosen few. None of us are destined for special attention. We are all going to die, just like everybody else—of cancer or a heart attack, or a fall from an eighth-floor window. This is how it has always been, Anna. And this is what you have to learn to live with. Life can be hard enough as it is, but the church is just a scam operation that tries to make money out of getting us to believe something else. Forget it, Anna. Think about something else. Think about your daughter. Your garden. Your roses and your lilies."

"They're dying on me out here," said Anna. "Nothing can survive this wind. And something is not right with Helgi. He hasn't been himself lately."

Lea smiled. "All marriages go through rough times once in a while. Don't take it so hard."

Anna felt the tears burning in her eyes. "He's all the family I have, Lea. Without him, I would be completely alone. I don't want to be like . . . " she interrupted herself.

"Like me?"

"You know what I mean."

"Yes, I know exactly what you mean." Lea smiled and spun around, her arms stretched wide. "Freedom is nothing to be sniffed at, Anna. You should try it—at least once in your lifetime. It's as good as sex and drugs."

"Hmm." Anna laughed. "If damnation were a matter of degrees,

I've still got a few rungs on the ladder to spare. And that suits me just fine."

"Of course you have." Lea pursed her lips and looked out to sea. "You have always been a better and stronger person than I. I don't believe in God and damnation. I believe in pills and alcohol. And you know where that got me. I would have been dead if you hadn't found me and brought me back to the land of the living."

Lea smiled and put an arm around her. Pulled Anna close.

"How did you find me this time round? It's been such a long time since we've spoken, and I've got a new number. An unlisted one. There are people I cannot associate with anymore."

"Don't be angry with me . . . "

"Why should I be angry?"

Lea took her hands in hers, brought them up to her lips. Her cheeks were burning hot. "I went to see Tobias. He gave me the most recent number he had for you."

"Where?"

"At the school."

"How did he look?"

"Beautiful, Lea. Both your sons are beautiful."

Lea suddenly let go of Anna, as if she'd been stabbed with a knife. She picked up a stone and flung it into the foaming sea.

"They never call," she said. "They've never called. Not once."

WALKING BACK TO the beach Lea held Anna's arm below the elbow, as if they were two little old ladies going for a stroll in the gardens of a nursing home. The touch of her fingers was a long sought-after sign of affection.

"Thank you for coming, Lea."

"You would have done the same for me . . . "

"So you've forgiven me for what happened?"

"I can't even remember what happened, Anna. I was as high as a kite, remember." Lea laughed. "You did what you thought was right for both me and my boys. I know that now. I'm not the fucked-up junkie I used to be."

"I would still like to hear you say it."

"Say what?"

"That you forgive me."

Anna wretched and bent over. She hadn't been eating properly, and her stomach cramped in protest. Stomach acid was eating its way through its own lining.

Lea smiled and turned to face Anna. Then she took a small plastic bag out of her pocket. "They were not easy to get hold of, but I still have a couple of contacts."

"Will they work?"

"Yes, they will. You'll lose your mind if you don't get any sleep. You need sleep so you can think, so you can get back on your feet again. Everybody needs sleep."

Alex was sitting in our back yard trying to untangle a fishing line. His gaze was intense, his face locked like a fist.

He didn't notice me standing in the driveway watching him. In the three weeks since our arrival in Klitmøller, the city boy had been replaced by a barefoot fisherman. Sandals simply got in the way; they filled with sand when you went on the beach, and this is where he was most of the time, either with Lupo or his fishing tackle over his shoulder. He had stopped wearing his T-shirt—to spare his clothes, he said. The muscles and tendons of his arms and shoulders played under his skin as he worked.

Up on the road, Magnus revved the engine of his car and drove off. We had listened to music on the way home and I jerked him off in a parking lot. It never got any more passionate than that and I doubted that I would be hearing from him again.

"It's really cool you've got a son," he'd remarked. "Were you one of those chicks who just couldn't wait? Like in *The Young Mothers*?"

"Alex was an accident. There was nothing in the world I wanted less than a child."

Exit Magnus with the beautiful locks of hair.

Alex looked up and smiled when he saw me. "Take a look, Mom."

He pointed to a blue plastic bucket standing on the drive. It was filled with sand.

"What is it?"

"Lugworms." He smiled broadly. "Thomas showed me how to dig them up with a spade. There are a couple of brush worms as well."

He dug a hand into the sand and pulled out a finger-fat worm. Its body was covered in red hairs and it wriggled furiously between his thumb and forefinger when he held it up under my nose.

I grinned, knocking the worm out of his hand, and it fell onto the ground between us. There was a long red stripe along the ridge of its slimy body. Its blood supply line. You have to avoid this line when you attach the worm to the hook, or it will die and float motionless in the water. I could hear my father's voice; see his rough fingers on the thin membrane of the worm as he slipped the hook in, twisting it around and up against the counter hooks; careful and gentle as an angel to avoid bursting its body.

"Did you know that those worms can bite really hard?"

Alex nodded. "They're really gross, but I can sell them up at the camping site. Ten for thirty kroner. It's better than collecting cans."

"What about Barbara?" I shot a sidelong glance at the house. "Has she come back yet?"

Alex nodded without looking up, absorbed in untangling the fishing line once more. "She's painting in her room. It looks like shit, if you ask me. Is she moving in? Nobody has said anything to me about her moving in."

"Of course she's not moving in."

"I'LL PAINT OVER it again in a couple of weeks. But I wanted to give it a try. It's going to be just marvelous, don't you think?"

I glared at the bare walls for a moment before turning to face Barbara. She was wearing a pair of three-quarter Bermuda shorts, splattered with white paint, and a loose-fitting man's shirt, drawing broad strokes over the floral wallpaper with a roller as she spoke, exhilarated.

"You could've asked first. This isn't your house. It's not even mine."

"I'm here to help you, Ella. But I need to work or I'll go stark raving mad. It's a must, and besides, nobody can raise any objections to white-washed walls. Not even Bæk-Nielsen. It's classic, for Christ's sake. There's something to drink in the fridge, if you want some."

"No thanks."

Barbara shot me a glance as she dipped the roller into the tray and continued painting with hissing strokes. She was painting the last wall in her room; she'd been very industrious while I was away.

"Come now," she said, slightly out of breath. "It will be great. Take a look at some of the sketches lying over there."

I glanced at the stack she had spread over the floor in a corner. They looked like murals depicting a religious motif. Priests and bishops and dukes in a raging tower of flames, their arms reaching for the sky, the Devil fucking a witch in one corner, a malicious grin on his face, and angels with rigid wings and golden trumpets.

"Are you creating the nave of a church?"

"I think of it more as a back-drop," she said. "I like the idea of having all this around me when I sleep."

"You could've done it at your place."

She had taken up the roller again, and her back was turned once more. "The light is better here."

Something unsaid quivered in the hazy dust between us. I gave Barbara's mural with its clumsy Bible motifs another look. It was probably never intended to be either tasteful or beautiful, but in her hands, the pictures became grotesque—just like everything else she touched. Perhaps it wasn't just because she was a lousy artist. Perhaps something in her vision consistently twisted reality.

"Do you believe in all this stuff? The Bible?"

"No." She turned to face me, smiled her chalk-white smile. "I don't believe in any of it. I believe in neither heaven nor hell, and I have always done as I pleased when it came to sex and alcohol. But I really like the paintings. They're beautiful. And they portray the world as it is. Not in heaven or hell, but as things really are—here, on Earth. We have all been thoroughly done over by this fellow, for instance."

She pointed to a furious devil hunched over a farmer's wife. His cock was enormous and furnished with several prickly counter hooks along the shaft.

"Love hurts."

"My mother was a Jehovah's Witness," I said, mostly to change the subject. "Do you know anything about them?"

"Yes, I do." Barbara laughed. "They believe that the Day of Judgment is on our doorstep and that only a select few—those belonging to their church—will be granted access to heaven when that day comes. It's quite an arrogant point of view, but I guess we all get caught up in our own beliefs."

"Judgment Day." I followed the contours of a sketch with my hand. Traced a finger along the flames of hell. "I guess all religions believe in some kind of judgment day."

Barbara had started working with her roller again, covering the wall with long, determined strokes.

"All religions and the rest of us. Global warming, overpopulation, the loss of phosphates in industrial farming. The world is going to hell. The difference between the Jehovah's Witnesses and the rest of us is that we don't expect a savior to show up and rescue a select few—or any of us, for that matter. All we can do is prepare to die when the seas begin to boil. Fortunately, till then, we've got one another. Where have you been? Have you been talking to your grandmother?" She laughed again, but a sharp edge had crept into her voice. She sounded angry.

"Yes. I spoke to her a couple of days ago. She says my father is innocent. That someone else shot my mother. Or perhaps she shot herself. And she told me that my mother tried to commit suicide soon after she married my father."

"Does it matter what your grandmother says?" Barbara was watching me intently now. "I thought you had decided to let things be. You know what happened. You saw your father with the gun, didn't you?"

I shook my head. "I've started remembering. Nothing from that night, but bits of my father. He taught me how to fish. And my mother . . . I visited my aunt today. My mother had a friend. Someone who'd been excluded from the church—like she was. I think I should try to find this woman."

"You should have spoken to me first," said Barbara. "All Jehovah's Witnesses are liars. Her whole life your aunt has been lectured that everything beyond the walls of the church belongs to the Devil; she doesn't feel obliged to tell you the truth. I'm not saying this to upset you. But you need to know the truth. The truth about them."

I traced a finger along my scars. The skin was pink, satin smooth; it didn't feel as if the skin belonged to me. I missed Rosa. She had never been especially affectionate, but she was always the same, and she knew how to keep her distance when I needed some space. With Barbara there was always an angle. She expected the same obedience from me as a mother would expect from her daughter.

"I want you to move out," I said quietly. "I'm okay now."

"Are you?"

Barbara put down the roller and came over to me. She had been an attractive woman once—that much was clear. She was tall, her large breasts inviting, and without all that make-up I could see a glint of the intensity she must have radiated when she had a lover or an enemy in her sights.

"Are you really okay, Ella? You're completely alone in the world, and nobody loves or takes care of you. That surfer guy isn't here to stay, is he? Your phone never rings. Nobody from your previous life misses you, and half the time you're lying on the floor, shaking uncontrollably. Does that sound like somebody who's okay?"

She was so close to me that I could feel her red-wine breath on my face. She must have been on the sauce for a while; it was not just her breath, the alcohol was oozing from her pores.

My body prepared for battle. I had fought all my life. It's exactly like riding a bike. The body never forgets. All the blows it has taken, all those it has delivered, are stored in the cells. You don't have to think, just listen to the beat, and follow the rhythm.

"You have to leave," I said.

She laughed. And for the second time that day, a woman opened her arms and pulled me close. "I'm going to be the first person you cannot scare away, Ella," she said. "I will look after you."

I stood stiff, rigid as a pole, although I instinctively wanted to kick free of her nauseating stench. Red wine and oily hair. In the absence of sexual attraction, physical contact had always been anathema to me.

"I want you to move out," I whispered again. But I remained standing where I was. I was good at fighting, but not much else.

"I'm staying here for as long as you need me," said Barbara against the skin of my neck. "I'm not going anywhere."

I called Rosa in the middle of the night. Alex had woken me with one of his nightmares. It was the second attack he'd had since our arrival in Klitmøller.

He sat up in bed and screamed and screamed. The nightmare was wordless, they always were. He never told me what they were about. Never saw me at all, just struck out at invisible enemies with that unfathomable fear in his eyes. Finally he lay down on his side, his body steaming. His hair was soaked in sweat and water from the wet cloth I had used to dab his forehead. I couldn't tell if it helped, the cloth. I just had to do something. Anything. Chimpanzees and sunflower seeds. We all need to feel useful.

"Hey, it's me."

Rosa fumbled with a phone somewhere in Hvidovre. "Ella? Do you know what time it is?"

I looked at the display on my phone: 1:30. "Alex woke me."

"No need to make that a problem for the rest of us as well."

Jens grunted in the background, I could hear Rosa getting out of bed and going into the living room. A door being closed.

"What's up?"

"I think maybe it was a mistake."

"What was?"

"Everything. Coming up here. Keeping Alex. What if I ruin him?"

Silence.

I lit a cigarette and blew the smoke towards the open window in the roof of the loft. My first memory of the room had surfaced with the image of my erotic experiments on the mattress, but now I remembered something else. It was here that my grandmother had read Icelandic fairytales to me. The soft, rolling syllables rose and fell as I stared at the torn floral tapestry. More fucking flowers.

"Ella. You know I'll come and fetch you if things get really bad.

But, to be honest . . . " She hesitated. Rosa seldom hesitated, but it could have something to do with the fact that it was 0-shit-hundred in the morning. "There is nothing for you here, Ella. Welfare is ready to dig their claws into both of you the minute you stick your noses across their district line. What you did won't be forgotten in a hurry. And there's something else . . . "

Again an unnaturally long pause, the heaving of breath. If I didn't know better, I'd think she was either crying or throwing up.

"What is it?"

"Jens has started drinking again . . . It's not bad, not like before. It's only happened a couple of times that he's become . . . that he's come home with . . . but it's bad enough. I know the drill, right? I know where we're headed. He's going to lose his job. He's going to come home and put his beers on the table, and I know I'm going to drink them. I might have to move out. I've thought about you a lot the last couple of days, and I'm so happy that you and Alex aren't here. That the two of you are together on the other side of the world."

I closed my eyes. *Jens*. It felt like receiving news of a death in the family.

"In many ways being here is just like living in Hvidovre, Rosa. We're just digging up lugworms instead of collecting cans. And there aren't nearly as many stores where you can nick your booze. It's quite a challenge."

Rosa grunted. "Do you have anyone you can talk to? Neighbors? A local lover boy? Knowing you, you've probably bagged a line of guys already." Hoarse laughter.

I ignored the jibe. "There's this artist woman that's moved in. A hippie-freak living off some or other social pension. She's definitely not living off her art." I thought of telling her about my revulsion for Barbara, but it was too complicated.

"You've always been good at keeping folk at a safe distance," she said. "This—and the booze—have saved your life. So . . . should I come and get you or not?"

I paused. Got up and looked out of the window. The sea was a continuous roar behind the dunes, but I'd gotten used to it; I tried to tune into the frequency of the waves, pulled hard on the last drag of my smoke, and finally flicked it out the window.

"Would you do me a favor, Rosa?"

"If I can."

"Your son works for the municipal office in Copenhagen. In the IT department, right?"

"Yes . . . Michael is good with computers."

Rosa was always on guard as soon as Michael was mentioned. He was the god that seldom graced the cement hell of Hvidovre, and when he did show, Rosa hushed up the entire block and served salad with the meal, by turns mum as a church mouse or all atwitter. I guessed that if you didn't do good by your son in the early years, you never know which visit will be his last.

"Do you think he could find a person for me in the system? A woman called Lea Poulsen. She's from the Farøe Isles originally and she lived in Thisted in the middle of the nineties."

"I can ask him."

"And stay away from Jens's beers, Rosa. It takes an awful long time to kill yourself like that."

AFTERWARD I LAY watching my son in the grey hours of morning.

I hadn't had anything to drink for three days, but the shaking had not resurfaced. Kirsten and the other caseworkers at Hvidovre headquarters would have clapped their small hands and declared a complete recovery and 100% fitness for work.

My own prognosis was more conservative. I felt like a landmine excavator who had just begun to clear the topsoil of an area being combed for landmines. Even with patience and a steady hand, things could still go badly wrong. And I had neither of the two.

Henning from Welfare showed up sooner than I had expected.

It was pissing rain and I saw him flip up his collar before he got out of his car and strode across the yard. I wondered whether he had seen me watching at the window and whether I still had time to bolt the door. Barbara's empty bottles of red wine were piling up in the pantry and two days' dishwashing crowded the sink in the washing room. Social workers didn't care for rows of empty wine bottles, but they cared even less for uncooperative clients. People with attitude problems lost their kids.

So I opened the door. Of course I opened the door. I may have been an awkward, recalcitrant client who was devoid of shame, but basically, I was a good girl who did as she was told.

"Hey, Ella . . . " He turned and waved briskly into the sheet of rain. He'd brought a woman along, I now noticed, a dainty dolly-girl, about my age, the kind of she-being that carries her entire feminine frailty on a pair of high heels, even out in the field.

The doll picked her way over the brick driveway with delightful, ladylike charm. Thin legs, knocked knees, agile ankles. Her hair was brushed into cascading waves that were kept in place by a pair of sunglasses; the lip gloss was peach. I ought to introduce her to Magnus, I thought.

"Ella!" Henning turned towards me again, and smiled broadly. "I've taken the liberty of bringing Agnete with me today. She's doing her practical training with us at Thisted and will be looking over my shoulder today."

I replied by failing to reply. Doctor Erhardsen had also taken the liberty of inviting medical students to sit in on consultations when I was pregnant with Alex. As a rule, they entered the room when I already had my feet in the stirrups, my underwear and leggings lying crumpled in a heap on the floor.

I stepped aside for my guests, and the pretty Agnete feverishly raked a hand of slender fingers through her mane. Raindrops dotted her sunglasses like pearls.

"So, Ella . . . " Henning grinned and rubbed his hands together gleefully, his shoulders up around his ears, as if my kitchen was the coziest place he'd been in years. "It's been a while since I was here last. How are the two of you getting on? Is Alex getting any bites on his line?"

Agnete smiled and cocked her head.

"Yes . . . it's . . . Tea or coffee?"

I went into the washing room and rearranged a stack of crusty plates so I could fill the kettle with water, could see the scene with their eyes. The grey linoleum counter was pocked with holes and curling up at the corners around the sink revealing rotten brown patches under the plastic.

"Do you have any herbal tea?" Agnete was perched on the end of a kitchen chair, surveying her surroundings with interest.

"No."

"Oh . . . well . . . then I'll have whatever you've got."

I took one of Barbara's tins of diuretic tea from the cupboard, dropped a tea bag into a cup, and served it to Agnete with the most accommodating smile I could muster. Henning preferred instant coffee. This I knew already.

"And where is Alex? He's probably sitting in front of the TV on a day like this." Henning craned his neck in the direction of the living room door.

"The TV is broken."

"What a shame." He pulled a face. "Then again, on a hot summer evening it can be blessing not to be glued to the box."

"Yeah?"

"Yes, I believe that in America many parents are making a concerted effort to wean their kids off all forms of electronic media. Television, computers, iPad, iPod . . . whatever it is they're called these days . . . it's the latest pedagogic initiative."

"I would buy a new one if I could afford it," I said. Agnete bared her white teeth and tilted her head once more. In my experience that chimpanzee grin appeared on a social worker's face whenever the awkward issue of money came up; there were extremely sensitive municipal budgets to take into consideration, one had to factor in the aged and the youth of the nation, and all those diligent taxpayers who weren't keen to finance a television for people on the dole. She was a quick study, our Agnete.

"Perhaps you should try quitting the smokes," Henning suggested with a disarming smile.

"Would you like to talk to him?"

"Very much."

I went to the foot of the staircase and called up to Alex. A faint rummaging upstairs, followed by a score of jazz when he finally opened the door. Billie Holiday's drawl drifted down the stairs. Soon afterward Alex appeared.

"Hi, Alex my friend! It's nice to meet you."

The pitch of Henning's voice had risen by at least an octave, two flat palms raised in a salute to my son. I cringed. Body language could be just as false as spoken words if you mastered the nuances. And that Henning did.

Alex nodded uncertainly.

"Agnete and I are from the social services office in Thisted," said Henning. "We would like to know how you and your mom . . . how you are getting on, that is, how you are spending your time . . . "

"Why?" Alex didn't bite. He strolled past our guests at the kitchen table and made for the counter where he fixed himself some cereal in a floral-print ceramic bowl.

"Because it's our job," said Henning. "It's up to people like us to make sure that kids like you are doing okay. Are you looking forward to going back to school?"

Alex shrugged. He remained standing by the counter, shoveling the cereal into his mouth. "I'm doing just fine," he said. "Other than the fact that the TV is broken."

"You're not missing Hvidovre? You had a foster family over there . . . Lisa and Tom . . . "

Alex shook his head and kept wolfing down his cereal. "I'm fine."

Agnete laughed nervously. "A young man who doesn't have

anything to complain about," she chirped. "It's not very often you meet one of those."

Alex ignored her, finished his food, and went back upstairs. Billie's voice was smothered behind the door once more.

"And you've got a boyfriend?"

I looked up at Henning in surprise. They worked significantly faster in Thisted than I had given them credit for.

"What do you mean?"

"You were seen with a handsome young man in a van. Kissing," said Agnete, and blinked.

"Lucky you."

I sent a mental note of thanks to Mr. and Mrs. Klitmøller, who had been gawking the last time Magnus came to pick me up. Apparently they'd invested in the latest edition of the Welfare Act as soon as it became clear that two exemplars of white trash had moved in next door. I'd bet they'd been reading passages out loud to each other in the sofa in the evenings. People on the dole paid dearly for fooling around in public.

"We are not dating."

"What do you do together then?"

Henning was still smiling, but the smile had become a little stiff. This was one of the more difficult exercises in the book; a skillful balance on the client's personal boundaries had to be maintained. Just as Henning needed to know for sure whether a client's hemorrhoid condition indeed ruled out the performance of a desk job, he needed to know whether I was fucking this guy or not, and if so, when, and how often. There was no reason for social services to take care of me if I had a sugar daddy who was performing this service quite adequately already.

"We do nothing together."

"Forgive me, Ella, but you know very well that we are obliged to investigate circumstances that could impact your capacity to provide for your son as a single parent. If it becomes apparent that this man is spending the night on a regular basis, then perhaps he should be the one providing for you and your son."

"He's a student, and he lives in Aalborg . . . "

Henning smiled, and nodded. Scribbled down some notes on his pad.

"And he is not my boyfriend! He has never spent the night—not even once! Not that it's any of your fucking business."

"Ella!" Henning raised his hands in an apologetic gesture and smiled disarmingly. "The other matter we wanted to talk to you about concerns information we have received that you are no longer living here on your own."

"I live with Alex."

"So there isn't another woman staying with you?"

"That's temporary. She's just visiting . . ."

I wasn't sure how to explain Barbara's presence without having to mention the panic attacks.

"Can we take a look around?"

As if on command, Henning and Agnete rose in unison and went into the living room without waiting for an answer. Their eyes scanned my grandmother's shelves, the dusty dining room table, and the gilt-framed pictures on the walls. *A Rescue Boat Goes Out to Sea.* The furniture that Barbara had cleared out of the room next door stood in the middle of the room like some barricade from the French Revolution. Over in one corner the rain had leaked through the ceiling. Large drops gathered on the plaster, which had become too wet, too heavy to support the water, and was now dripping into the washing bucket I had ready on the floor below.

I could hear Barbara's humming from the next room as she worked on her well-endowed Satan.

The two guests from Welfare followed the sound, their cocked heads curiously yet cautiously preceding them, Henning even took the trouble to knock symbolically on the doorframe before stepping over the threshold.

Barbara stopped humming the moment she saw them. The smile slipped from her face, leaving it dough-like, expressionless, as she took Henning's outstretched hand in hers. Just behind him, Agnete had spotted the first of the penis-paintings on the opposite wall. In the absence of other seventh-grade girls, she tried in vain to hide snorts of laughter behind her hand.

"Good heavens. Someone has been hard at work in here." Henning smiled, motioning towards the sketches on the walls. A witch riding on a broom with flames coming out of her ass was almost life-size, her face almost on eye level with ours.

"Historical murals," said Barbara as she looked Agnete over. The aura of red wine was less penetrating today, but still unmistakable.

"Excuse me, but I don't believe we've been introduced. Henning Jensen from Thisted Social Services, and this is Miss Agnete Sær-mark, who is currently in training with us. We just came by to check on Ella and Alex. To make sure that they have settled in nicely."

"Of course." Barbara seemed out of sorts. Distracted. And it wasn't just the red wine. Henning and Agnete's presence made her otherwise steady gaze falter.

"And you are . . . "

"Barbara."

"And how do the two of you know each other, Barbara . . . ?"

"I'm an old friend of the family."

"Really? I wasn't aware of the fact that Ella's family had any friends." Henning looked genuinely interested. Curious. Helpful. He was a man who had mastered the entire catalog of verbal and nonverbal expression. I made a mental note that I would never be able to trust him. He was an exceptionally good liar. But he couldn't fool Barbara.

"I know Ella. What else do you need to know?"

"A little more about you, perhaps," said Henning now in a more measured tone. "Like whether you can confirm what Ella's neighbors have observed: that you have moved in here with Ella and Alex. The reason we need to know this for sure is that the social office in Thisted is responsible for Alex's well-being, and therefore we need to know the circumstances surrounding his immediate domestic environment."

"I don't live here," said Barbara, turning her back on them. "I'm just here for a couple of days to help Ella get settled."

"That's very kind of you."

"Yes."

"Pardon me, but I didn't catch your surname."

"Jacobsen."

"And do you have any family of your own, Ms. Jacobsen?"

"I have two sons in Copenhagen. They're both grown now. Over thirty."

"How wonderful!" Agnete was practically cooing now, probably at the thought of two grown men in the city. All decked out in shiny Armani suits, Gucci sunglasses, and jobs in the financial sector. Pretty young women were so predictable.

Henning rapped his knuckles on the doorframe once more. "We're just going to take a last look around, and then we'll be off. It was good to see you, Ella. I'm glad to see that you are getting on just fine . . ." He backed out the room, forcing Agnete into retreat behind him. Her knees buckled as she tripped over the threshold, sniggered, and apologized behind the same hand with which she'd shared the joke about the huge penis on the wall. I felt about a hundred years older than her and a great deal smarter, but she and Henning were the ones who would be filing the relevant forms. They were the ones who would write the notes that determined how my behavior should be interpreted; whether I was fit and worthy, could be trusted; whether I was in a position to nurture Alex's happiness and further development.

As soon as they had closed the door behind them, I went back to Barbara's room. She was still working with her back turned, drawing lines with a black brush, stepping back occasionally, readjusting here and there, touching up the contours. Outside, the rain hammered against the windows, the light was grey.

"You lied," I said.

She laughed softly. "About what?"

"About your name. It isn't Jacobsen. I saw it on the postbox back at your place. It's Jensen."

"Jacobsen, Jensen. Both completely irrelevant names. Whether they hear the one name or the other is not important."

I didn't answer. I opened the window wide instead and lit a smoke. The wind slammed the rain against my face.

"You're not mad, are you?" I could feel her eyes in my back. "Ella. We're in this together. They don't need to know everything. And besides, it's in your favor that there's more than one adult here to look after Alex."

"You're drunk," I said.

"So I drink a little red wine," she said. "Plenty of artists do, it helps them see the world in color—and you drink yourself, my girl. If I were called to testify in a case brought against you for the forcible removal of your son, I would be obliged to reveal this information. And I'm so awfully bad at lying about important matters, Ella. You know this perfectly well. So you be grateful I managed to get rid of them as quickly as I did."

Beyond the dunes the sky was blue-grey with heavy rains. All the birds had flown. My unease had returned.

HELGI, 1994

A child. Another child.

Helgi muttered to himself as the flat and colorless fields swept by. He hammered a hand against the steering wheel, furious. He had tried calling Christi at least ten times, and every time he got the same result. A high-pitched tone followed by an automated message that the number didn't exist. He refused to believe it, but had to admit that he had always known. That Christi's secrecy ran deeper than that sexual tension sparked by the constant uncertainty underlying their relationship. She was playing with him. And now his child was stowed in her uterus, along for the ride.

A child could never be kept secret from Anna.

His relationship with Christi had been a challenge from an organizational perspective alone. All those extra working hours on the building site, the walks in the dunes, the quick showers. Anna could still have her doubts, but her body reacted with a blind and unrelenting certainty. Somewhere in her mind she already knew he was having an affair, even if the fact itself had not yet surfaced in her mind. The pounds were melting away, and the loss of weight made her look older. The wrinkles on her face were more pronounced, her skin sagging under her eyes and chin.

And now he was going to have a child with a woman he seemed to know less and less. In fact, he didn't know her at all. He accelerated, overtaking two trucks in a row. A car coming in from the opposite direction made a panicked swerve to avoid him, furiously honking. He banged on the steering wheel again.

The rifle rattled in the trunk as he slammed on the brakes for a red light.

"Damn, damn, damn."

He scanned the other vehicles around him. If she was on her

way home, she could be sitting in one of the cars in front or behind him. She could be sitting in the bus. Segments of her profile reflected in car windscreens all around him. He was hooted at again. The lights had turned green and he fumbled with the gears before finally accelerating off again.

"Get a grip," he chided himself. "Everything can still be fixed. We can all sit down and figure this out. We're all adults, for Christ's sake. And with a child on the way . . . "

He ran a hand through his sweat-drenched hair and turned down the road of dingy houses in Holstebro, where he had been once before. There was no car in the drive in front of the low-roofed house; it was late in the afternoon and already dark outside, but the windows were black.

At the front door he found her name on an antiquated bronze plate. *Christi Pinholt Johansen.* Thin spider webs connected the door handle with the wall. The curtains were drawn. He banged on the front door, a stone lodged in his breast.

The silence was massive. No scraping or shuffling. No doors slamming. Only thick, dead silence. All around him the wind tore at the leafless crowns of the trees in the garden. He walked along the wall till he reached one of the dark windows, cupped his hands against the pane, and tried to peer inside. Nothing to be seen but dark shadows. Dead things. He walked round the house and into the back garden, panic rising from the pit of his stomach.

The neighbors' houses were hidden behind the shabby hedge and thorny brambles. The wet grass was so long that it had flattened out, turning yellow in a tangle of rotting autumn leaves and fallen apples, but he managed to kick free a well-laid, cobbled border of what he assumed had once been a flower bed. He worked one of the border stones free, testing its weight in his hand. On the road the headlights of a car swept through the hedge as it slowed down and parked against the curb with a thump of tires. He waited till the car doors slammed and the echo of voices had faded. Then he felt his way to the terrace door and shattered the pane. The smack of the stone against the glass was no more than a dull, lifeless thud, but an instant later, he held his breath as the shards fell from the frame with a crisp clang. Nothing but silence followed.

The house was deserted.

He could smell it the moment he stepped in the door. It hadn't been heated in months—if not years. The cold and damp clung to the walls. Even though he couldn't see the full extent of the decay in the semi-darkness, he could still make out the relatively pale patches on the carpet where furniture once had stood. Against the wall, a single bookcase and cabinet with open drawers remained, as well as a couple of collapsed, half-filled cardboard boxes. In the kitchen, the washing machine was disconnected carelessly. There was nothing of any value in the adjacent room. The house was stripped like a moped that had been deserted on the beach, and a single glance in the bedroom, at the darkly polished mahogany bed, was enough to conclude the house had been inhabited by an old woman. The floral bedding lay crumpled in a heap, a jewelry box gaped on the old-fashioned dresser. But there were also signs of more recent inhabitants. A pizza carton, the leftovers still identifiable. On the bedside table were several paper cups containing a rancid black-brown liquid, and a thin copy of the Bible was lying open on the bed. It had been purchased in a bookstore in Århus, still so new that the pages were stiff. He frowned as he swiftly paged through it. On several passages someone had underlined passages in pencil.

I am the way, the truth, and the light.

A caricature of cockeyed, dancing trolls rollicked in the margins, contrasting sharply with the industrious highlighting. He put the Bible down and went into the passageway again. Peeked inside some of the cupboards in the entrance at random. They were empty, apart from a few old blankets and a partly decomposed cardboard box containing a set of crockery. Something crunched under the sole of his boot as he stepped into the bathroom, and in the weak light from the window, he could see it. A hypodermic needle.

• • •

"**Christi Pinholt? She** died, let me see . . . hang on a minute." The man behind the door turned and called over his shoulder. "Pia? When did Christi die? Was it three years ago . . . ?"

The man's wife, a woman in her forties with a cascade of birthmarks on her face, appeared in the doorway beside her husband. He caught a glimpse of a half-grown boy in the brightly lit kitchen behind the couple in the doorway.

"Yes, it was the summer of ninety-one," the woman said helpfully as she dried her hands in her apron. "The house has been empty ever since."

Helgi cleared his throat. "Yes, well, please forgive the intrusion, but I'm looking for someone . . . and nobody has lived in the house since? No tenants or borders or . . . "

The woman shook her head. "The children can't decide what to do with it. The son is . . . he's a drug addict, and his sister doesn't want to sell the house so her brother can use the money for drugs. At least that's what she said the last time I saw her. So now the house is just going to ruin. The son—we don't know him personally—has been to the house a few times to get some things. And he stayed there once or twice with a girlfriend, but apart from that . . . "

"What was the name of the sister?"

"Charlotte Lundgård. She now lives with her husband near Viborg."

"And what does she look like?"

The woman stole an uneasy glance at her husband. He had gone too far. He looked down at his hands and realized that they were still stained with the blood of the buck, as were the knees of his overalls.

"She has short, dark hair, about fifty years old, I think, and is somewhat heavy-set . . . where did you say you were from . . . ?"

He recalled the needle crushed under the sole of his boot. The half-eaten pizza.

"I'm looking for my sister," he said quickly. "I haven't seen her for a long time, and I'm starting to worry. Sometimes she forgets to take her medication. She is thirty-three years old, and tall with blonde hair . . . pretty."

Husband and wife exchanged glances once more, but then apparently decided to take pity on a concerned brother. The woman even tilted her head to one side and nodded sympathetically. He guessed that they weren't very pleased with their neighbors.

"There has been a woman here matching your description. Quite recently, in fact. She used to come to the house with the son, but that was a long time ago, and she looks a lot better now. Nice. She has her own key, and she seems to come and go as she pleases. I don't know her name. But she scratched our car once, when it was parked on the sidewalk. Crashed right into it on her bicycle. Peter got her number so we could call our insurance and sort it out, but she never called back, and we haven't seen her since."

A grim line appeared around the corners of her husband's mouth.

"There was something wrong with that number . . . "

He took a deep breath. So he couldn't count on her showing up there again. *Fuck.* He didn't even know if Christi was her real name, it could have been a name she had taken from the nameplate on the door. She had never wanted him to find her. And she didn't want him to find her now, either. Especially not now. It had always been her who had contacted him, and it seemed she had no intention of changing the status quo.

"Thank you." He nodded at the elderly couple, politely wrote down the number they gave him on a business card in his wallet, said his goodbyes, and walked back down the garden path. He felt very old and heavy as a stone. Too old to run after girls and have children, and definitely too old for this—whatever this was.

THERE WERE LIGHTS on in the windows when he turned down the drive, but neither Anna nor Ella appeared to greet him when he dragged the dead buck into the garage, swearing under his breath as he began to partition the carcass. He cut out the lungs and the gullet and pulled the tongue through the slit neck.

But it was too late. Of course it was too late. The stomach was already swollen with digestive gases, the intestines and stomach lining punctured when he finally removed the internal organs, their reeking contents oozing into the abdominal cavity and spilling out over the dead animal's stiff coat. The meat was ruined. There was nothing to be saved.

He left the carcass lying prostrate on the garage floor, scrubbed his hands and forearms, and went indoors with a feeling of defeat.

"Anna!"

No answer. No answer from Ella either. He glanced at his watch. It was six-thirty, someone ought to have started dinner by now. If everything had been as usual, Anna would have been at the kitchen counter making carrot salad with Ella, chatting about seagull feathers and the wind blowing in over the sea, all the way from America. But the kitchen was cold and dark.

He went into the living room, and there she was, Anna. All the lights were on and she was lying on the sofa with her eyes closed. The television was running without sound, pictures of the war in Yugoslavia flooded into the room; children crying in make-shift refugee camps, ancient, toothless women wailing at the sky.

Seeing her, he was overwhelmed by an unexpected wave of tenderness. Not desire, not a need to penetrate and melt into her, but a glowing warmth; a stream of images and words they had said to each other over the years, trivialities that had become something else, something heartfelt. She looked haggard. Thin. Her wrists and hands were bony and frail, resting on her unevenly buttoned shirt front. She was not beautiful, not like Christi, but he knew her. Even when Anna was the darkest version of herself, he knew her, and he knew that she would never have toyed with him the way that Christi was toying with him now. Anna had no intrigues about her. She was herself.

He took a blanket from the foot of the sofa and carefully draped it over her. He wanted to grant her the rest she needed, but when he laid a hand on her forehead, it was damp and clammy with sweat.

"Anna!"

No response. Her motionlessness seemed unnatural. Even for someone who was sleeping deeply, she seemed unnaturally still, reminding him of a picture of Sleeping Beauty in a glass case in one of Ella's fairytale books. He shook her gently by the shoulder.

"Don't wake her up."

Ella was standing behind him with her wildly salt-and-wind-swept halo of hair.

"Where have you been?" He said, turning back to Anna, shaking her lightly again. Touched her cold lips.

"I went to play at Thomas's house. Mom said she wanted to lie down for an hour or two."

He felt a stab of cold in the ribs. A feeling of entering yet another uninhabited house.

"How long ago was that?" he asked gently, not once taking his eyes off Anna's face. He felt her wrist, counted her pulse. "How long have you been at Thomas's house?"

Ella shrugged and changed channels on the television with a tired look on her face. He shook Anna a little harder, then slapped her in the face, hard. Once, twice. After the second blow, she waved her arms weakly in front of her face, as if to protect herself. Ella stared at him with huge, frightened eyes.

"Ella, go up to your room."

She shook her head mutely, but he didn't have time to explain.

"Anna! Anna!" He pulled her up into a sitting position, threw her arms over his shoulder, picked her up, and carried her swiftly up the stairs. She hung over his shoulder like a dead weight, not moving once till he lowered her into the bathtub as gently as he could. He had to spray cold water directly into her face before she sputtered and lashed out at him.

"Let me go."

He slapped her again.

Ella, who had followed them into the bathroom, screamed at the top of her lungs and pounced onto his back, her small teeth digging into his neck. He winced and shrugged her off roughly, hearing her fall onto the bathroom tiles with a thud. Then he bent over Anna again.

"Dad, no . . . you're not allowed to hurt Mom. Don't hit her, Dad. She was just sleeping . . . " Ella was crying now.

"Anna! Have you taken something? What have you taken? How many pills have you taken?" Without waiting for an answer, he lifted her out of the tub and bent her head over the toilet bowl.

"Do you want to do it, or should I?"

Anna gasped. She sat drenched and shaking on the floor with her forehead resting on the toilet seat, the water running off her formed a pool around her.

"Again. Do you want to do it, or should I? Anna, help me out here ... say something ... "

"I'll do it."

Her eyes were blurred and half-closed, but she pulled herself into an upright position slowly, and he held her over the toilet bowl as she stuck two fingers down her throat and threw up. Two almost-dissolved tablets swam on the surface of the water for a few seconds before disappearing into the murky water. *Only two.* He felt a wave of relief.

"One more time."

She repeated the exercise, and this time, only a small cascade of clear fluid was deposited into the toilet.

"Good girl. Two pills. Is that it? Did you only take two of them?"

She shrugged, but then nodded. He let go of her shoulders and stroked a hand over her forehead instead, trying to regain control of his breathing.

"I just needed to get some sleep," she mumbled. "It was just a couple of sleeping pills. That's all. I thought you would be home sooner."

Behind him he could hear Ella hiccupping and crying hysterically.

LATER, MUCH LATER, he stood watching Anna as she slept in their bed. He brushed his fingers across her forehead before leaving her to sleep and going to check on Ella. The light was still on in her room, one of her legs jutted out over the edge of the bed, as if she'd fallen asleep in the throes of a wild kick, her cheeks were streaked with tears and dried snot. The cut over her eyebrow was gaping a little, but a trip to the Emergency Room would have to wait till tomorrow. There was no energy left. Not for him, not for her. He had tried to comfort her as best he could, tried to put some ice on the egg-sized bruise on her forehead from her fall in the bathroom, but she had fended him off with a manic fury. Kicks and blows with little fists that he had borne in silence. He turned off the light and quietly closed the door behind him.

He draped Anna's soaked clothing over the bathtub and emptied her pockets of coins and hair-clips and a couple of soggy bits of paper that he unfolded carefully.

Where will you be on judgment day?

There was also a photograph in the back pocket of her jeans. He stared at it, stupefied. It was a picture of him and Anna when they were very young. Someone had written WHORES END UP IN HELL in fat red letters across the picture. Anna's bikini bottom had been cut out. A disproportionately large and grotesque erection had been drawn onto his own bathing suit

He dropped the photo to the floor as if he'd been burnt. He hadn't seen the picture for a long time, but he knew where it came from: Anna's meticulously arranged photo albums in the living room. It was a picture from their first summer together. He went to the bookcase and ran a finger along the broad spines of Anna's albums. He found the first volume and began paging through it systematically. There were a few sharply-focused black-and-white photographs of the two of them doing homework together in his room. He recalled a friend of theirs taking the pictures; he'd been taking night classes in photography. There were also several shots with more classic motifs: He and Anna astride their bikes with a billowing cornfield in the background; the two of them at the prom together, Anna with a forbidden drink in her hand and a glowing smile next to his cheek.

Further.

There was a whole series of photos of the two of them on the beach together. They must have been about eighteen and nineteen years old, a year before they got married. Before the final exclusion from the church, before the harassment and the restraining order. At that time Anna had hoped that some kind of reconciliation with her family would be possible, that perhaps she would be given leave to live on the fringes of their congregation; this had happened before.

Anna is smiling into the camera, for once, stunningly beautiful.

Further. Pictures of them on the beach with a group of friends: Søren and Nils Peter, who had graduated and moved to Århus the following summer, another couple, Helle and Bjarne, were standing a little off to one side. They had moved to Hanstholm in the interim. He and Anna hadn't managed to keep contact with any of them.

The final series of pictures was missing from the album. A little row of trolls with horns had been drawn in the space instead, like an irrepressible running commentary of scorn.

Christi.

The break-in in spring when everything had been smashed onto the floor in the living room.

The telephone rang. He picked it up, knowing it was her. "Christi . . . "

Silence.

"Christi, we need to talk . . . " He took a deep breath. Tried to keep his voice steady, tried to control the wave of shock threatening to overwhelm his body. "Christi, of course we will be together. I'll leave Anna. My love . . . please don't . . . I will leave her. If you are pregnant, we will have the baby together. But we have to talk about it."

Silence.

"My love . . . ?"

"Do you love me?"

Christi's voice was a faint whisper in a rush of stormy rain in the background. A click from a coin being dropped into a call box.

"I . . . " He hesitated. He knew he had to weigh his words carefully. God forbid he scared her away before he knew where she was. "We need to talk about us. About the baby. Please don't disappear on me. I miss you."

A short laugh, bordering on a sob.

"I'll kill the child if you don't want me," she said. "I'll get an abortion, Helgi. I'll flush it down the toilet."

"Christi . . . Where are you?" He sank into the sofa.

Mumbled words, sniffing.

"Christi, I know it's late, but I want to see you. I miss you." He tried to inject his voice with the same depth of feeling they had shared before; only a couple of months previously their voices and words had entwined like two bodies making love.

"I'll come out to the dunes," she said finally. "The usual place. Now."

She put the phone down, and Helgi got up from the sofa slowly with some remnant of hope. Upstairs Anna and Ella were sleeping. Warm, living bodies. His family.

"Hallo?"

My grandmother's voice was clear and commanding on the line. It was her legs, not her head, that refused to work properly.

"It's Ella."

Pause.

"How are you?"

"Fine, thanks."

"Have you stopped drinking?"

"I don't drink."

She laughed hoarsely, triggering a memory from a thousand years ago. "You're more like your father than your mother. Helgi was also good at lying to himself. But the store owner says that the stream of alcohol to the house is thinning out, so unless your surrogate mother is buying your booze in Thisted now, it would seem you're on the mend."

I could see her sitting there rubbing her hands together in glee, ready to crawl into my head and take over—just like everybody else. I tightened my grip on the phone. Refused to bite. I hadn't called her to talk about myself.

"That house my father asked you to check out for him. Do you still have the address?"

"Yes. It's in a villa-district in Holstebro. The house was empty, but Bæk-Nielsen managed to get hold of a man that used to live there. The son of a previous owner. A drug addict. Coherent communication with the man had not been possible."

"What was his name?"

I could hear the rustle of paper as my grandmother riffled through her pile of documents. She kept them within reach and had probably done so for the last twenty years. She was an obsessed human being.

"Troels Pinholt. He lived in Århus back then. Across the road from the cathedral. He's probably still there, lying under a bench or a bush." The same dry laughter, followed by a string of Icelandic clicks that sounded like cussing.

"Thanks."

I ended the call and dialed up Information.

Troels Pinholt. There were three of them. Two in Jutland, one on Falster. I started with the two Jutlanders. The first one lived in Ringkøbing and had never been anywhere near Holstebro in his life. The other guy didn't pick up, so I left a message: if he had lived in Holstebro in the nineties, would he be prepared to tell me about it? I couldn't phrase it any better than that. I didn't know what I was looking for. Some connection to my parents in Klitmøller, perhaps, something that could help to explain the change in my father in the months leading up to my mother's death. I felt a sudden sense of urgency, but perhaps Barbara's hectic activity back home had rubbed off on me.

The entire house reeked of paint, and Barbara was no longer sleeping at night. We heard her working incessantly on her paintings instead; she only surfaced to refuel on red wine and rye bread. The heat had returned, and she roamed about barefooted clad in white robes splattered with paint. Her legs were dark brown and scarred, the two tattooed snakes that entwined her ankle ballooned, appearing almost three-dimensional in the heat. In the pits of her elbow joints was another cluster of tattoos, which I hadn't noticed before, dark red drops that looked like blood oozing from her veins.

Alex and I fled to the beach. I didn't dare nick a tube of sunscreen from the store—too many eyes were watching—so I went for a swim dressed in a T-shirt and otherwise kept close to the shade of the dunes to watch Alex and Lupo cavort in the waves that crashed to the shore.

Although the sun was shining, it wasn't crowded. There was more beach than one could ever need, but the German tourists, kitted out with sun-loungers, parasols, and plump towels, glared resentfully at Alex and Lupo when they whipped up sand in the wind.

A text from Magnus.

SEE YOU ON THE BEACH?

I didn't reply.

The blatant irritation in his eyes the last time I had dragged him away from the waves had pinched the last erotic nerve of our relationship. And I refused to be some kind of burden. Or feel like I owed him anything. Having sex with someone had always felt like an act bordering on humiliation anyway. I would rather find a new man. There were plenty of willing bodies to pick from.

I lay back in the sand and looked up at the sky as I ran a hand along the scars on my thighs. The sky was a series of veils borne in over the sea that dissolved up above me.

My telephone rang. Unidentified call.

"Ella Nygaard?"

The voice on the other end of the line was slurred, and rough.

"Yes." I sat up and brushed the sand off my legs. Some kind of manic impulse to please. A dumb habit I'd always had when talking to strangers. Lick your fur. Spruce up your feathers.

"You called asking about my time in Holstebro? What was it you wanted to know?"

I could hear a television running in the background. Live coverage of a game. The roar of a distant crowd, the voice of an excited sports commentator.

"I'm not sure, exactly," I said. "But if you're the man I'm looking for, then my father was interested in the house you were living in at that time."

"Your father? Uh-huh, well the house was sold years ago. My sister sold it. I've got nothing to do with it anymore."

He coughed away from the receiver for some time.

"I'd like to talk to you about it anyway. If that's okay?"

A long pause. More coughing.

"Can you come here?"

"Where do you live now?"

"In Aalborg. I have to be close to the hospital . . . it's the lungs. I have to stay close by in case of emergencies . . . "

"Fine, I'll come to Aalborg," I said.

I could already hear a laborious tale of pain and suffering unfolding. A record of misery. Troels Pinholt was among the living, but he was not a healthy man.

"Now. It has to be right now."

I looked at my watch. It was almost five-thirty in the afternoon. A trip by public transportation was not an option. Out here, the buses only ran till four.

"What about tomorrow? Around lunch time. Where exactly in Aalborg do you live?"

"No, that won't work. Eight o' clock tonight will suit me fine."

I bit my lip. Troels Pinholt was in all likelihood a pest. I recognized his attitude from my neighbors in Hvidovre; now ingratiating, now utterly obtrusive, and once they realized they had something to offer you, they knew how to pester you and draw out their advantage as long as possible. Attention was a rare commodity in Ghost Town.

"Okay . . . give me your address. I'll come to you. Tonight."

A renewed bout of coughing camouflaged by what sounded like self-satisfied laughter. I already hated him. Troels Pinholt, ex-drug addict from Århus, one-time social misfit and pusher from Holstebro. I had no idea how to get to Aalborg by eight o'clock.

Down by the water Alex and Lupo had been joined by Thomas. The boys were playing catch with Lupo. I got up, gathered my sandals in one hand, and called to Alex as I made my way down to the water.

"AALBORG. NOW? YOU may as well forget it, Ella. The buses aren't running anymore. You could catch a train from Thisted, but you'd have to get to the station first."

Thomas brushed a hand over his crew cut and smiled at Alex in the rear view mirror. He had insisted on driving us. He wouldn't hear of us hitchhiking to Aalborg as I would have preferred. It was awkward with him, Alex and me all squashed into his little Honda.

"We can stop and pick up a couple of burgers on the way, if you guys are hungry. Grub's on me."

Alex smiled happily from the back seat. The window was rolled down a couple of centimeters and was letting the wind rush between his fingers. His upper body was still bare and he had kicked his flip-flops off under the seat in front of him. A film of sand clung to his legs and ankles.

"Sure," I said, and lowered my gaze. "This is really kind of you." My debt to the world was increasing by the hour, and I hated it. The only thing I hated more was standing between Alex and a lousy burger.

"Who is this friend you want to visit in Aalborg?"

"Just an old friend. Alex doesn't know him. I thought maybe you guys could hang out while I go and talk to him. It shouldn't take more than an hour. Just a cup of coffee."

I had tried to persuade Alex to stay at home—without success. He didn't want to be alone with Barbara and I understood him perfectly.

"Sure. We can do that."

Thomas swung off the road when we got to a McDrive in Thisted and bought junk food for an indecent amount of money. Three big meals plus a few extra burgers, nuggets, and fries on the side. I cut a glance at him when he came back to the car and passed the brown paper bags through the window. I had never seen him so lightly dressed before, T-shirt and shorts. He was unbearably thin. His arms were very tan, sinewy, pocked with small, shiny scars. He gulped down his meal and extra burgers without batting an eye before putting the car in gear and swinging back onto the road again.

"What would you like to do in Aalborg once we've dropped off your mom?" he said to Alex. "Do you want to catch a movie?"

There was a *no* on the tip of my tongue, but I bit my lip. Alex was beaming on the back seat. I couldn't remember the last time he'd been to the movies, and I was pretty sure he couldn't remember either.

We drove on in silence for a while. Thomas tuned into a local radio station, drumming his fingers on the wheel to some semi-crap, over-synced Danish pop. Medina and her angel-blond ex-boyfriend, Christopher. Justin Bieber took over, but he only managed to coo through half a song before I pounced on the radio and shut him up. I couldn't help myself. It was an acute allergic reaction to anything that sounded like crying.

Alex sighed on the back seat, but Thomas just shot me a crooked smile.

"I don't blame you," he said. "Sometimes I feel the same. When I was having chemo, I couldn't bear hearing any kind of music at all. It was worse than torture. Even happy songs sounded like the soundtrack to *Texas Chainsaw Massacre 3*. For some reason, I used to think I would die with Jimi Hendrix strumming in my ears. Or Mendelssohn's Violin Concerto in E Minor. But even that sounds like shit when you're nauseous."

"What did you have?"

"Testicular cancer. The doctors gave me a clean bill of health this spring, but I still need some time to get back on my feet. I'm not working full time. Just doing a couple of jobs for my dad."

"I'm glad you're feeling better."

"Thanks."

He looked nice when he smiled, and the silence that followed was warm as water in a tub. I settled down into it, dozing off on the last stretch to Aalborg.

TROELS PINHOLT LIVED in a ramshackle red-brick apartment building on a busy road in Aalborg Vesterbro. When the trucks rolled by, the glass in the panes of the building shook. There was no intercom at the port, so I just let myself in and found his name on the sanitary, grey metallic row of postboxes in the entrance. I bounded up the first two flights of stairs, but paused briefly on the landing of the third to consider my approach, half-hoping that he had changed his mind. I had forgotten my phone back in the house when we left, so theoretically, he could have called and cancelled.

Fuck. I rang the doorbell and could hear him coughing long before he opened the door. A protracted shuffling behind the peephole, a fumbling with the door chain, but finally the door opened.

"Ella?"

The man standing in front of me was a bum. No doubt about it. He was one of those men who spent their lives on a bench in front of Netto or Fakta Discount Store. A life that made all bums look exactly the same. The jeans that were soft and smooth with grime and wear. The hair that could do with a cut, but was slicked back instead—so severely that the path of the comb remained like deep, oily ridges over the scalp. There were those characteristically deep furrows on the forehead and a network of shot blood vessels spread over a translucent grey skin. Troels Pinholt smiled, completing the picture with a flash of stubbed teeth and a look in his eyes that was at once embarrassed and triumphant. A pall of old man, smoke, and cheap aftershave flooded onto the stairwell.

I cleared my throat. "Shall we talk here or go out?"

"If you buy me a round, we can go to Friheden. It's just round the corner."

I swore under my breath, but I couldn't blame him. People like him—including myself—were apt to yank every one-armed bandit they got within twenty feet of. All I had on me was fifty kroner, but that ought to be enough for two pale ales at his local bar, and as far as I was concerned, he was welcome to drink them both, if this would spare me from going into his slum hole.

"Fine with me."

He backed up, scraping his feet in the confines of his entrance, hung his keys on a band around his neck like a seven-year-old boy, and came shuffling after me on his worn-out shoes. When we got to the bottom of the stairs, he was already out of breath, and we had to take a break twice before we finally reached the bar on the corner only fifty feet away.

"COPD," he said. "Smoker's lungs," he added with a cough. "A real bitch."

He greeted the clientele in Friheden by rote. Mogens, Peter, Jytte, Noller, and Mette. Clearly everybody knew everybody else. I guessed that they hung out together every afternoon from 1 P.M. onward. And yet—or perhaps precisely for this reason—there was scant evidence of joy in the reunion. Merely raised eyebrows and a couple of curious glances in my direction from the men. The atmosphere was dead.

We picked a table at the back of the establishment. Friheden looked like every other bar I'd had the pleasure of frequenting over the years. Dark yellow curtains, brown wainscoting, and cigarette smoke that billowed white in the poor lighting of marble-shaped lamps strung from the ceiling. On the walls, nicotine-stained beer advertisements from the '50s that paid homage to the refreshing qualities of cold beers on hot summer days that contrasted sharply with the decrepit guests hunched over their glasses at the counter.

"Nice place," I said.

"Yes. A sense of community—" he nodded, still doubled over to catch his breath. "—is heart-warming."

I MADE MY way to the bar and left Troels Pinholt to his own devices at our table, where he sat coughing up slime into a thick-bottomed ashtray. The two leather-skinned men on bar stools grunted over their glasses and stared at my ass as I sidled up next to them. The women, who were deep in their forties with hairdos sprayed stiffly into place and chipped nail polish, flatly ignored me.

When I got back to our corner I sat down opposite Troels and put a beer in front of him. "Tell me about Holstebro," I said, leaning forward and resting my elbows on the table.

He shot me a wounded look. "No small talk?"

I shrugged. "What would you like to talk about?"

"Tell me a little about you. Where you come from … And why you are so interested in my mother's house. It's kinda … private, you know. My childhood home."

It wasn't an unreasonable request. And I needed to give him a few hints, anyway, if I wanted to extract any useful information out of him. I decided to put him in the picture, regard him as kind of alcohol-pickled search engine. Feed him key words and see what popped up on the blurry screen.

"My mother was murdered twenty-one years ago. My father killed her."

"Oh..." He looked at me intently over the rim of his glass. "I'm really sorry to hear that."

"Yes." I felt an unexpected lump in my throat. It was the depth of sincerity in his tone that surprised me. Five seconds of shared unhappiness.

"I'm trying to find out what happened," I said. "My father was looking for something or someone who had seemed to have a connection to your mother's address in Holstebro in the autumn of ninety-four. Can you tell me who was living there at that time?"

Troels frowned, playing the palm of his hand over the mouth of his bottle. "I don't remember too good," he said apologetically. "I was pretty fucked up in the nineties. Narcotics."

He rested both forearms on the table and flipped them over to show me the scars on the insides of his elbow joints. It looked like an animal had clawed chunks of tissue and muscle out of his arms.

"Infections and the like," he said, shifting his gaze from his own forearms to mine. "You've got a couple of souvenirs of sin yourself, I see."

I shoved my arms under the table.

"But... 1994, you say. Nobody was living in the house at that time. My sister and I couldn't agree on what to do with the house. I wanted to sell. I needed the money, but she was against it. Irritating cow, my sister. So anyway, the house stood empty for a couple of years in the nineties, I think, except for when I stayed over."

"Alone?"

"Yes... that is, sometimes I had a girl with me."

A hint of a lewd smile crossed his bloodhound face. The memory of erstwhile greatness, I guessed, perhaps some satisfaction at being able to tell a young woman that he'd once been a man who could get the likes of me into bed.

"Okay. Were you pushing anything? Throwing parties?"

He shook his head. "We were doing heroin. It's a relatively unsociable drug, if you know what I mean. You basically sit around on your own and get stoned. Not like the party drugs—ecstasy, or whatever it is they're called nowadays..."

I pulled a home-rolled cigarette from my jacket pocket and

offered him one. "My parents lived in Klitmøller. My father was a carpenter, a big man. Well-built. I think he gave the impression of being a solid man, dependable. My mother worked at the fish factory near Hanstholm and was more . . . frail, very pale, a little shy. She had freckles on her face."

Troels shook his head again and took a few more slurps from his bottle of beer. "I might have seen them, but I doubt it. Not at the house, in any case. If we were pushing anything, we would have done it in town."

"And what about your girlfriends? What were they like?"

He grinned again. A toothless Casanova. "Crazy, all of them. When you're a junkie, like I was, that's all you can get. I think most of them are dead now. If you don't get onto methadone relatively soon, you die. I got treatment when I moved to Århus, and later, I got into rehab. I've stuck to alcohol ever since."

"Did any of your girlfriends come to the house more often than others? Can you tell me more about them?"

There had to be something. There had to be a reason why my father asked my grandmother to check out that house.

"They've probably all been locked up by now. They were crazy, I'm telling you. Completely nuts. But nice tits, a lot of them."

Hoarse laughter that tipped into an extended coughing fit that lasted for half my smoke.

"Tell me more about your mother," he said finally.

"I think she was very lonely," I said. "Her family didn't want anything to do with her. They were very religious and didn't approve of my father. She was completely alone out there by the North Sea."

"Inner Mission?"

"No. Jehovah's Witness. I met my aunt for the first time a couple of days ago. It was a . . . cold reception."

"Jehovah's Witness is a bitch," said Troels Pinholt, nodding significantly. "I had a girlfriend who was thrown out of their community. You can't be a drug addict *and* a Jehovah's Witness. You get kicked out on your ass if you try, like she did . . . "

He slammed his hand onto the table in indignation, blowing his pent-up breath through browned lips.

"It was pretty brutal on her. She had a husband and two children. Two boys. But she wasn't allowed to see them, the boys. She claimed it was because of the religion, but between you and me . . . she was a junkie, right? I wouldn't have entrusted any children to her either."

The words penetrated my mind like an echo. *A husband and two boys.*

"Was she one of the girlfriends who stayed with you in Holstebro?"

He looked up at the ceiling and drew even more smoke deep down into his smoking lungs. "Yes, goddammit. Lea. She was the most beautiful woman I'd ever had in the sack. Really beautiful. She got into treatment relatively quickly, pulled herself together, and then she dumped me, of course. To that extent, the drug scene operates the same way as the church. You can't be together, if you are on opposite sides of the fence. But beautiful, that she was, Lea. And very, very unhappy."

"Can you remember her surname?" *Lea.* The name sparked a rush of adrenalin.

"I could do with another beer."

I went up to the bar again and blew my last twenty-five kroner. When I got back to the table I put the beer down in front of him again, and waited.

"I would really like to help you," he said. "It sounds like your life has been pretty hard. But I can't remember her surname. That kind of thing isn't important when you're a junkie. She worked the streets for me a couple of times. I needed the money. We both did. So we could buy some stuff, but otherwise . . . I don't know her full name, all I know is that she wanted her family back. Or start a new one. She talked about that a lot. She was an angry woman. But they all are. Full of problems."

He pointed to his temple meaningfully. "Some people just can't tolerate life."

I nodded. The same could be said for all of Friheden's clientele that evening. It was a place for people allergic to their own pulse.

"Do you know where she is now?"

He shrugged. "I could bang the jungle drums for you, if you want. Find out if there's anyone who knows someone who knows someone, if you know what I mean." He smiled eagerly. "Give me a call, okay? Maybe I could find out something for you."

Troels Pinholt put one of his warm, dry hands over mine.

"I'm a lonely man, Ella. Do you know what it's like to be so terribly lonely? I hope you will come and see me again."

"Sure I will," I lied. I wasn't completely heartless.

Alex fell asleep as soon as we headed out of Aalborg.

The light of the street lamps played over his sleeping face in an uneven rhythm. It had cooled down, and I twisted round to the back seat and laid Thomas's thin jacket over him.

"So? Did you manage to talk to that friend of yours?"

Thomas shifted gears. The sky was black over the car, making the stars shine with a brilliance that could never be seen in the yellow-grey night skies of Hvidovre. I rested my forehead against the window and focused on the Big Dipper. Perhaps a teacher had pointed it out to me. Perhaps it had been my mother, or my father. It irked me that I couldn't remember which.

"Yes. Luckily he was home."

"You smell of smoke."

"We went to a bar."

"A guy? That surfer . . . ?"

I tried to hide my irritation. Was the whole fucking town keeping track of my sex life? Not even in the concrete blocks of Hvidovre did I have such a pervasive sense of constant supervision.

"I'm fucking the surfer," I said. "We don't go to bars. Not that it's any of your business."

"Okay."

Thomas sank a little deeper into his seat, keeping his eyes on the road. I felt like I ought to break the silence. It was his car, after all, and he had just spent an evening and a not insignificant amount of money on popcorn and seeing *Spider Man 2* with Alex.

"I'm looking for someone," I said. "A woman who could tell me a little more about my mother. She had a friend called Lea. It sounds like they met in a support group for former Jehovah's Witnesses. I know this from my . . . aunt."

He didn't say anything, but I could see he was listening.

"When my father was in jail, he asked my grandmother to find a woman at a particular address in Holstebro. He didn't know her name, but I might've figured it out. There was a woman who stayed in the house at that time. Her name was also Lea, and she had once been a Jehovah's Witness. I believe it's a relatively small sect, so it has to be more than just a coincidence, don't you think?"

"So your father was looking for your mother's girlfriend—without knowing that they were friends?"

"Maybe."

I bit into the inside of my cheek. Pain had always helped to keep me focused.

"Tell me what you can remember about my mother," I said.

"She was nice."

Thomas slowed, rolled down a window, and lit a smoke, offering me one as well. We smoked with a velvet soft wind in our faces.

"She was very pale. She had white-blonde hair and lots of freckles. She'd bring us sodas and ice cream in the yard when it was hot." He sighed and shrugged in resignation. "Hell, Ella, I don't know. I can't remember much more than that. Your father was also a nice guy. He used to hunt with my dad once in a while. They sat out in the yard polishing their guns in the sunshine before they set off to hunt. They let me hold the gun, I remember, and I still have my dad's . . ."

He trailed off. The subject was inappropriate.

"I mean, he seemed like a decent person. They both did."

"I don't want to talk about him." I stole a glance at him.

"All I can tell you about your mother is what I've heard from other people in town. Most people thought she was really sweet. Kind, and friendly. She worked at a fish factory in Hanstholm that has closed down now. But they had no friends, your parents. Mostly because your mother had some difficulty talking to other people, I think. She was kind of . . . shy. Apparently your father took really good care of her and people were very baffled by the fact that things could go so badly wrong for them. Maybe your father wanted to tell your mother's friend about her death. Maybe he just wanted to talk to her about what had happened."

"Yes."

I hesitated. In my mind's eye I could see my grandmother's bright, big eyes behind her glasses. My father hadn't been himself, she'd said. When I went back to our house I had remembered hearing him talk her, the other woman, on the phone. But till now, nobody had turned the stone this woman must be hiding under. Nobody had mentioned her. Just as nobody had mentioned my mother's friend, either.

"But . . . there was no mention of a Lea in the police reports, was there? Or in the court case. She hasn't existed—till now."

Thomas shook his head. "I've never heard a word about a friend of your mother's. According to local gossip, your mother was alone in this world."

The yellow rose popped up before my inner eye, a message attached to its stalk on a crumpled piece of paper. *Anna.*

THOMAS INSISTED ON driving us right to the front door. Alex stumbled, half-asleep, into the house and up the stairs, one arm slung over my shoulder. When I came back downstairs Thomas had taken two cups from the shelf and was pouring water into the kettle for coffee. Lupo had come to greet us briefly, but was now curled up asleep on a blanket in the corner.

There was no sign of Barbara. The house was dark and silent, but then it was after one o'clock in the morning. I thought of Barbara lying on the box mattress in her room, surrounded by paintbrushes and her ever more wildly wayward paintings on the walls and ceiling.

I hadn't told her where we were going. *That* we were going.

Thomas found some milk in the fridge and poured a few drops in his mug before sitting down and stretching his long legs under the kitchen table.

"Is she still here?" He nodded towards the dark living room and the door to Barbara's make-shift nave.

"Yes . . . she's just staying for a couple more weeks . . . just till we've settled in."

"Settled in," he repeated, raising an eyebrow and smiling

crookedly. "Nothing is going to change around here in the next two weeks. And that woman is stark raving mad, by the way. I know you like her, but you should know that she was kicked out of her place a week ago. I was out there yesterday to fix some pipes for the owner. She's left most of her shit behind. The owner is really pissed."

I looked at him in amazement. "She's been kicked out? But why?"

"I don't know. She probably didn't pay her rent. People laugh at her, Ella. Her drawings are a standing joke in town. She doesn't sell any of them, and the portraits she does . . . the children. It's always children, right? They all look the same. And she drinks—but you've probably noticed. You have to get rid of her, Ella. You know how people talk."

A window was banging in the dark of the living room and a cold wind filtered into the kitchen.

"She's helping me," I stammered. "You don't know what it's like."

"What *what* is like, Ella?"

I could feel his gaze on me, even though my eyes were fixed on my coffee cup. My grandmother's things, my grandmother's home. I owned nothing and I was surrounded by strangers. Nothing had changed.

"What it's like being a ghost."

He smiled. "No, I don't know what that's like," he said. "But maybe someday you will explain it to me. Over a hotdog at the grill-bar by the harbor—maybe even at a real restaurant in town."

There was something at once sarcastically flippant and deeply serious in his tone. He stood up without looking at me and tossed the last sip of his coffee into the sink in the washing room.

I felt the unease rising in my body. The thought of the two of us in a restaurant together. I could just see it. Me in my worn T-shirt and flip-flops. Thomas, stick thin, sitting at the other end of the table. I wouldn't know where to put myself. I had never had dinner at a restaurant, I had never had the money, I had never been asked. The thought made me sick. I didn't fit in a restaurant. I was someone who collected cans in the park, and I didn't have to talk to anyone when I did.

"That's sweet of you," I said. "But no thanks. I don't do that kind of thing."

"Date?"

"Among other things."

"What about that surfer guy?"

It was the second time he'd mentioned Magnus, and his attempt to sound flippant fell heavily to the ground. His voice was brittle.

"It has nothing to do with the surfer."

"Is it because of the cancer? Because I've been sick?" He had come back into the kitchen and was standing in the doorway with his hands buried deep in his pockets.

"I said no, okay?"

He smiled, and threw his arms wide to take in the kitchen like an estate agent showing a client the best deal he had on offer. "No, it is not okay, Ella. I invite you out for dinner, and you say no. I would like to know why."

I cringed. This idiot must be stone deaf. Where did he get off smiling at me like that, as if he knew what was best for me?

"Yes, it's because you're sick," I said. "I don't sleep with men out of pity."

He stepped back, as if I'd dealt him a physical blow. He even raised a hand to his jaw. His face was completely open and unguarded, and I knew I could destroy him completely if I said one more word.

I dropped my gaze instead, listened with a pounding heart to the sound of his steps in the entrance, the door being closed, the engine of the car roaring in the driveway. Then he was gone. Good riddance. Things were getting too weird. And besides, he was getting too close to Alex.

IT WAS ALMOST two in the morning, but I wasn't tired.

My phone vibrated on the kitchen table where I had left it. A message announcing missed calls. Not surprisingly, Troels from Aalborg had left three messages, all three of them listing what he'd had to drink at Friheden since I'd left, followed by a detailed description of some woman named Jytte's tits. Oh yes, and by the way, he missed me already.

Scrolling further down, there were four calls in a row from Rosa, who, for her part, hadn't left any messages. She never did. She was the only person I knew who telephoned from a landline only. It seemed she'd had an extended conversation with Barbara. The final call had lasted over twenty minutes.

I punched in the number and let the phone ring and ring in Hvidovre. No answer. I called again. After the fourth call, someone picked up, but it was Jens on the other end.

"Ella? Hi, pussycat," he slurred.

Jens was just as drunk as Troels in Aalborg. A wire snapped in my chest. I had only turned my back for a moment, for Christ's sake. I took a deep breath.

"I see Rosa called," I said. "Can I talk to her?"

"Of course you can, Ella-mouse." I could see him standing there, swaying on his feet in the dark, cramped bedroom. "There's just one itsy-bitsy problem. She's not here. She's . . . "

He grunted softly and the pause that followed was so long that I thought he'd put down the phone to go and look for her. Then he snorted down the line again.

"She left," he said. "She's gone. Finis, finito. Adios, Jens, you old bastard."

"Good for her," I said, gritting my teeth. "Jens, you're as pickled as a herring, for Christ's sake. What the hell are you doing?"

"Everything is just fine, Ella," he replied. "Everything is just the way it should be."

"Okay, if you say so." I took another deep, deep breath. "Where is she staying, Jens? Do you know? Do you have a number where I can reach her?"

He laughed. "Yes, but she'll be staying here when she gets back," he said in a tired voice. "She's just gone down to the store get a couple of beers. Just so there'll be something in the fridge when we wake up."

Something hard had lodged itself in my throat. I swallowed.

Bloody idiots. Both of them. Rosa had not gotten out of there in time.

"I'm going to wring your neck, Jens. I swear to God."

He laughed again. His voice was mild and gentle as always. "It isn't worth the trouble, little Ella. A complete waste of effort."

"Can you ask her to call back tomorrow?"

"Sure."

"Will you remember?"

I heard him fumbling for paper and a pen next to the bed, something falling to the floor as he repeated the crude message. "Call Ella."

"Thanks, Jens." I paused. "Look after yourself."

He mumbled something that sounded like the bars of a song. Then the connection was cut, and I sat staring at the dead phone for a long time before going into the living room. One of the bulbs in the ceiling had blown, and it was impossible to reach the switch of the orange lamp in the corner. It was cut off by a row of stacked furniture, rolls of tarpaulin, and half-filled buckets of paint. I carefully felt my way through the dark instead, and opened the door into Barbara's room.

There was no ceiling light either, but I could see the outline of the box mattress and the crumpled pile of bedding in the middle of the room.

"Barbara . . . " A couple more steps brought me to the wire at the end of her painting spotlight. "Barbara, are you awake? We need to talk."

The room reeked of paint and sour sweat. Even though it was hot, she hadn't opened a window. Condensation collected on the moonlit windowpanes.

"Barbara."

I crossed over to the bed, reached the duvet, and knew at once that she wasn't there. The blankets were cold and clammy.

When I looked out onto the yard, I realized that her car was gone as well.

"She's still out there. She exists."

It took a split second for me to recognize the voice on the line. Troels Pinholt. It was 11:30 in the morning and he was already so drunk that he was slobbering.

"Troels?"

"Yesh, for Christ's sake. We agreed I should call you, so I'm calling . . . " A lighter clicked, and there was a brief silence while Troels lit his cigarette. He had me on the line, and he was in no hurry.

I wedged the telephone between my shoulder and my ear and continued doing the dishes from the day before. I had fetched warm water from the bathroom and filled the sink in the washing room with a mountain of plates and dirty cutlery. Barbara had not returned.

"And? Have you found something?"

"Of course." He coughed. "It's so easy to find people nowadays. Everybody's got mobile phones and Facebook and all that. I took a trip down Memory Lane with a beer at the Internet café. Many of the old guys are dead, but the live are kicking—all you have to do is send a text! Anyway, I've spoken to one of the gang in Viborg. He used to live in Århus, but now he's in Viborg . . . smokes a little hash, and he shtill sells some shtuff. All kinds of stuff. He shtill sees Lea now and then. She comes to buy. In fact, he saw her a couple of weeks ago, and he'll try to dig out her number for you—if you're interested."

I took a deep breath. "Of course I am," I said. "How soon can he get the number?"

Troels faltered. "You'll need to give him some money first," he said, forcing out yet another murderous volley of coughs. "Ten thousand kroner. That's what he wants."

"Go fuck yourselves."

"Hey. I'm not the one asking for the money." Troels sounded mortally offended. "I'm just passing on what he said. And it's a reasonable request, for Christ's sake. He has a reputation for being discreet."

I heaved a sigh. There was a reason why former pushers, alcoholics, and other ghosts never changed. They had a chronic lack of judgment and no sense of reality. And they tended to exaggerate their own significance—even within the narrow, seedy confines of the cesspit they stewed in.

"I couldn't care a shit if it's a reasonable request or not. I don't have the money, and if I did, I would spend it on a new television. Tell him he can go to hell. I'll find her on my own. Like you said, it's easy to find people nowadays . . . "

"Not this girl." Troels lit his second smoke. "According to him, she changes her name as often as the rest of us change our underpants."

"Once every five years?"

He ignored my jibe. " . . . I'm just saying, it's not gonna be easy . . . "

"Go to hell."

"It's a fact. Well, I was just trying to help . . . " Troels sounded sincerely indignant. "How are you otherwise, Ella?"

"I'm fine, thank you, Troels. I'm going to put the phone down now, okay?"

"Oh, yes, I just thought maybe we could talk for a bit . . ."

"Maybe another time."

"Well then, farewell. Hey, do you know what it means, fare . . . well? Fare is an old word for traveling or driving. So fare plus well means to drive well, have a good trip, bon voyage . . ."

He was shitfaced. Another succession of coughs. This guy talked too much. I cut the connection and turned off my phone, bitterly regretting having given him my number. I should have simply called him up and remained anonymous. But I hadn't, and now I was saddled with him and his penetrating, drunken blabber, the same shit I'd had up to my ears back home in the ghetto.

I called to Alex and we went down to the beach together with
Lupo. The weather was grey, the motions of the sea heavy and lazy.
Far out on the horizon there was a glimpse of the black shapes of
container vessels. Alex followed my gaze.

"Do you think we could sail to England next year? I would really
like to see London."

"It's too far away."

"Everyone else goes on vacation." He was drawing in the sand
with his big toe, poked at a little pile of seaweed.

"We are not other people," I said. "We are us, and we can't travel
anywhere. If I go on holiday, I wouldn't be at the job market's disposal, and then I wouldn't get any money."

"We could collect more cans . . . "

"No."

"You could get a job. Then you would have a right to take a
vacation." He looked at me defiantly. "Why can't you just get a job,
Mom?"

I patted down my shorts. I had run out of smokes.

"What we are doing now is also fine," I said. "How many of your
friends in Hvidovre have a house by the sea?"

"If I'd stayed with Tom and Lisa, I could've gone on vacation to
Italy with them. They'd already booked the tickets and everything.
We were going stay in a hotel with a swimming pool."

I felt the wave of self-pity rising in my throat. "Tom and Lisa get
money from the state for letting you live with them and to take
you on vacations to Italy with them," I said. "I don't get shit. I can't
afford it, Alex. Okay? So quit pissing on me."

"Whatever."

He shrugged and walked down the beach on his own, kicked at
a few more piles of seaweed and finally sat down to study something more closely. Lupo had sprinted over to a little stream that
snaked through the dunes and was lapping up water with his big,
pink tongue.

"Hey!"

Alex looked up, when I called. His eyes were still darts.

"Do you want to come with me to Thisted?"

"Why?"

"We're going to visit your great-grandmother."

THE LONG CORRIDORS of the nursing home were cool and silent.

We had come during their midday nap, explained a nurse. All the residents were resting in their rooms to gather strength for their afternoon tea, but she'd be happy to show me to my grandmother's room; she might still be awake. She was young, the nurse, about my age, her step energetic in her sandal soles. If there had been no "family tragedy" and I had grown up in Klitmøller, we might even have been friends. Maybe even colleagues. I liked the way her ponytail swung cheerfully ahead of us and the fact that she had a black leather bracelet wrapped around her tan wrist. Some people were just nice to look at. Calm and at peace with themselves and the world. She would be hard not to like, I was sure.

The nurse stopped in front of my grandmother's door and knocked lightly. There was no answer, so she opened the door a crack and slipped inside, blinking conspiratorially at us over her shoulder.

"She's sleeping," the nurse whispered. "But why don't you take a seat inside. It would be okay to wake her now."

I remained standing in the doorway.

It seemed wrong to go into the room of a woman while she was sleeping. But Alex had already snuck into the stuffy room and was looking around curiously. The windows were closed, the curtains were drawn, and it stank of old person. An at once sweet and sour smell combined with the stench of urine from the adjoining bathroom.

We sat down at the narrow, dark-wooded table as the nurse opened the curtains. She sent us one last bright smile and then left us alone with the old woman.

Grandmother was lying in her high hospital bed, breathing evenly, calmly. Her mouth was open, her bald head buried deep into her pillows. This was a woman who had given birth to two boys; one had drowned at sea, the other was a murderer, and we were blood-related. We shared little genetic idiosyncrasies, this woman and I. Perhaps a particular movement of the hand, a characteristic curl of the lip when we smiled. Perhaps even a little chunk of Iceland had lodged itself in my brain. I came after her, she said. Like swallow chicks that seemed to have a map of Africa etched into their skeletons so they could find their way south, or eels hatched in the Sargasso Sea seemed to have an inborn homing device to their South Jutlandic stream in Varde.

Alex writhed on his seat. "Shouldn't we wait outside?" he whispered. "You can't just go into a person's room when they're sleeping."

I shrugged and remained sitting where I was. Alex could go if he wished, but I wanted to be there when she woke up. All at once I felt a sense of urgency. This woman was very old. She could die at any moment. I didn't want to risk missing the last of her waking hours, nor did I want to miss the chance of hearing what she knew about my parents.

"I'm going to get something to drink," mouthed Alex. "Coffee or some of that piss-colored juice I saw on the trolley outside. Maybe take a look around."

The door closed behind him with a dull thud. I checked my phone. Two messages from Magnus. I deleted without reading them. One message from Thomas. It was one of those idiotic sayings you can find on the back of toilet doors or citation sites on the Internet that were meant to enrich your life:

THE BEST WAY TO FIND OUT IF YOU CAN TRUST SOMEBODY IS TO TRUST THEM. ERNEST HEMINGWAY.

I deleted the message. It would have been easier if he'd stayed mad at me. And why the hell hadn't he just kept his mouth shut about the cancer? It was none of my business that he'd been sick, and I didn't need to know that he'd had his balls roasted in chemotherapy, and nearly died.

"He's a handsome boy, your son."

I shuddered. My grandmother was watching me with half-closed eyes, and she must have been doing so for some time.

"I can see both you and your mother in him. I was very close to your mother. Did you know that? Sometimes it felt as if she was the one I was related to, not Helgi. But then, I had also had her under my wing since she was sixteen years old. I still miss her. Could you give me a hand up?"

She lifted her arms to demonstrate the problem. She couldn't sit up on her own. Her gnarly fingers could reach a lever under the bed, but they weren't strong enough to pull it up.

I went over to her reluctantly, put an arm in behind her back, and lifted her into a sitting position so she could swivel her weak legs over the side of the bed.

"My wheelchair . . . " She pointed at the chrome-shiny vehicle at the foot of the bed.

I positioned the chair next to the bed and let her rest her arms around my neck, lifted the tiny body and deposited it on the lamb-skin cover of the chair. She weighed no more than a child. Perhaps she had read my thoughts, because once she had secured the oxygen tube over her nose, she cocked her head and smiled.

"I used to lug you around too when you were a little girl," she said. "You were such a crackerjack. Just like I used to be."

I shuddered again. "I'm not like anyone."

She lifted her frail shoulders ever so slightly and those dark eyes rested on my face.

"We did many things together, you and I. When your mom went shopping, or was too busy to play, you ran over to my place. We made vanilla pudding, drew pictures, or listened to the radio. Do you remember?"

"Nope."

"Your mom came over to my house when she needed to talk, just like you."

I had sat down on the edge of the chair again. I could have killed for a smoke, but there would be rules and regulations about smoking in an institution like hers. My hands twitched.

"What did she talk about? Was there something in particular she was afraid of?"

"Not your father, if that's what you're thinking. If she was afraid of anything, it would be the ghosts she had grown up with."

"So she was insane. Is that what you're saying?"

My grandmother laughed for the first time, revealing her slightly too perfect front teeth, which bounced a little against her tongue.

"She wasn't insane," she said. "Not at all. But her reality was a different one from ours. Her mind had been formed by the dread of doing something wrong, of losing her place in a millennial kingdom. When she was a child, she was told that the world would end soon, and there were so many things she could do wrong, things that were punishable by a painful death. Her heart was stained with these beliefs. Sometimes parents can do that to their children."

"But she left the church," I said. "She no longer believed what they preached."

"She left because she was in love, and sometimes a love can be so strong that you forget who you are. Ultimately, you can eradicate beliefs by thinking rationally, but you can't change who you are inside."

There was a picture of my father on the wall above my grandmother's bed. I knew it was him without being able to say why. It was a black-and-white photograph from when he was very young. Soft lips, big dark eyes, and a soldier's beret. He was very young in the picture, but it still struck a chord. A vibration radiated outwards from my breastbone—followed by the nausea, with only a moment's delay.

"Could I have something to drink?"

"You can get yourself a glass of water in the bathroom." The old woman nodded in the direction of the blue sliding door.

"I was thinking of a beer."

"There's vodka in the cupboard over there. I believe that's what you prefer, right?"

She followed me with her eyes as I helped myself to what proved to be a well-stocked bar. The old geezer had gin, vodka, whisky, and cognac in half-full bottles. Life in a nursing home seemed to require the same kind of medicine that I administered my own soul. Half a glass ought to be enough to get me through the conversation and the trip back home. No need to panic.

"Ever since that day, I knew that things would turn out badly for you."

I swung round, glass in hand, and met her gaze. Her face was calm.

"As I said before, you were a strong and happy child, but you could also whip yourself into a fury if the tide turned against you. I can still remember your eyes . . . It was quite frightening . . . "

"My life has not turned out badly. I'm alive, I have two legs, I have a son . . . "

She shook her head distractedly. "I remember one time Anna cut your hair too short. You must have been about four years old at the time, and when you saw yourself in the mirror, you lashed out at her, hitting her with both arms, demanding that she put the hair on your head back at once! You had absolutely no sense of restraint. Threw things against the wall, smashed your toys . . . Your heart never had room for either melancholy or grief, Ella. There was an abundance of wild joy and equally wild anger stored in there, and when they drove away that cold November day, I knew that the anger would force everything else out. Strangely enough, this is also something you have inherited from me."

I took another gulp from my glass. "Can I smoke in here?"

She nodded, mercifully, and I fished out my smokes and a lighter. My limbs began to relax after the first long drag.

"Can I borrow those notes of yours about . . . my father . . . about the case? Recordings, newspaper clippings—the whole damn thing."

She nodded, and pointed to the stack of papers lying on top of the bar cabinet. "Take those over there with you now. I know them by heart, anyway. Bæk-Nielsen can bring the rest over to the house, later. It's probably a bit too heavy to carry by yourself."

"Thanks . . . " I inhaled sharply. "That is very kind of you."

"Don't mention it. How have you been, Ella? How are you getting on? I've thought about you so much over the years. A small child, alone among all those strangers."

I didn't answer, allowed a kind of ceasefire of silence to settle in the room as I stuffed the papers into my rucksack.

Alex knocked on the door and came in with a tray of coffee, cake, and three cups that he put on the table.

"I scored the lot from the cafeteria," he said, glancing over at my grandmother. "A lady over there said it would be okay."

The look in his eyes surprised my grandmother. She withdrew into her chair, suddenly becoming acutely self-conscious in a way elderly people often do when confronted with a child. Perhaps you can get used to your own distorted reflection in the mirror over the years, but a child always sees the horror of your own physical decay.

"I look terrible," she said to Alex, covering her nearly bald scalp with her hand in obvious embarrassment. "I didn't always look like this, you know. I was pretty once."

"An Icelandic beauty," I said. "Fire and ash. We've got a picture on the wall back home. I can show it to you when we get back, Alex."

My grandmother smiled at me gratefully, and it felt as if we met for the first time. It was no more than a moment. And afterward, neither one of us knew what to say, so we drank our coffee in silence.

Alex shook my grandmother's hand before we left. It was a polite gesture that was unusual for him, and it made me happy, and proud. I don't know why. Children who shake hands and say thank you for the meal usually gave me creeps. It reminded me of schooled apes with their parents looking on like self-satisfied ringmasters.

There was a trembling at the corners of the old dame's mouth, and she pulled it into a narrow line as we made to get up and leave.

"Now I've also had a family visit," she finally said with a smile. "I'm so happy that you came to see me."

Bæk-Nielsen dumped a heavy black plastic bag in our driveway early the next morning and drove off again, lifting his hand to an imaginary cap. And that was just fine. Our relationship wasn't conducive to small talk, I gathered.

I dragged the bag into the dunes, sat myself down in the sand, and scanned through the piles of paper, beer in hand. It was the strongest beverage we had in the house. Barbara had called, saying that she'd be coming around midday and that she would buy some alcohol in Hanstholm on her way home.

She'd been gone two days, but hadn't explained her absence. I guessed it had something to do with that sleazy landlord of hers. Stacks of cardboard boxes, papers, and bills for paint and cleaning, including an extraordinary sanitation bill to replace the carpet in the living room that had been saturated in cat piss. People who leased their property to social scum knew perfectly well that subsequent tenants had no desire to live in the piles of shit inevitably left behind, not that this dampened their indignant outrage in the aftermath. I almost felt sorry for Barbara—not to mention the cats that no longer had a place to go. The landlord would probably feed them rat poison or have them shot, if he was more inclined to summary solutions.

She should have told me, and asked for help. I could carry a heavy load.

The pile of yellowed paper reeked of a bitter woman's desperation. After a transcript of my first interrogation, there was a record of my grandnother's own notes from the trial, written in an angular hand:

Court case, day 1: Helgi asked me not to come, but I did anyway. I want to be there for him. Even if he doesn't want to see me.

Court case, day 2: Helgi has lost weight. His pants are held up by a piece of rope, but he is not allowed to have the rope in his cell. They're afraid he might hang himself. He refuses to talk. Not just in court, but to anyone. He will not talk to his lawyer, doesn't talk to me. Has been denied access to Ella.

Court case, day 7: Guilty. Helgi has been sentenced to min. 12 years in prison. This seems to suit him fine. He called me finally when I got home. He sounds relieved. As if something had finally fallen into place. He has asked me to take care of Ella, but I don't know where they have taken her. They think my presence could be harmful. They say I'm too old. That my connection to my son is too strong. This could be difficult for Ella, they say.

Further.

A collection of newspaper clippings, meticulously organized. Most of them were from local papers, but there were also a few from the national papers that quoted the coroner's reports extensively: My mother had suffered a deep lesion in the lower abdomen, but the cause of death was attributed to a subsequent gunshot wound that had blown away part of the lower jaw and a significant part of the cranium. The shot had been fired by my father's hunting rifle, but a knife had never been found.

There were significant traces of prescription sleeping pills in her bloodstream; not enough to be fatal, but enough to impair her speech and faculty of movement. No prescription was found in the victim's possession, and there was no plausible explanation for their origin. However, the prosecution argued that the drugs in all probability had been procured by the accused, Helgi Nygaard; the accused held a position that allowed a large degree of flexibility, and Nygaard had had ample opportunity to acquire the pills in a larger metropolitan area. Furthermore, employees of the accused testified that Nygaard had been absent from the site for an extended period of time on several occasions over the preceding six months. The victim, Anna Nygaard, worked in shifts at the fish factory in Hanstholm, and, as such, it was highly improbable that she had either the initiative or the resources to seek out a supplier for this kind of medication.

Helgi was silent—and the journalists speculated ad infinitum. Had Anna Nygaard threatened to leave the accused? Perhaps she had refused to get a divorce? What was the nature of the relationship between Anna and Helgi Nygaard? And what was to become of their daughter, Ella, who had not been given an opportunity to testify?

It was reported that I had been found in a plantation nearly six miles inland. This tallied with what Thomas had said. By the time they found me, my body temperature was so low that death by exposure was imminent, and, it was sheer luck that a farmer and his dog had seen me hidden among the sapling Christmas trees. According to the farmer's particularly detailed description, he chanced upon me lying curled up in a shallow ditch in the forest floor: I had covered myself with a blanket of pine-needles; I was dressed in a bloody night-dress and a winter jacket, my bare legs stuck into a pair of blood-splattered galoshes; I had a deep gash over the right eyebrow, and two broken fingers.

Several people from the local community had called and volunteered to adopt me, but my welfare was a complicated question that deserved careful consideration. Everything humanly possible would be done to ensure the child's well-being, and for the time being she had been taken to a children's home beyond the reach of the media. She was doing as well as could be hoped under the circumstances.

I looked down at my right hand. The two broken fingers were news to me, but no surprise. The last digit of my ring-finger had always been a little askew, and, as a rule, this joint was the origin of the vibrations that spread throughout my body when I had one of my fits. A pulsing pain, severed nerve endings that had never been able to find peace, perhaps. Till now, I had always assumed that my crooked finger was a congenital deformity. I had no recollection of the pain of having them broken, nor did I remember anything about a lonely ditch in the plantation on an icy November night. It was like reading an account of the misfortunes of a someone else.

I opened beer number two, paged back a couple of articles, and reread the coroner's report: My mother had not only been shot, she had also been stabbed by a broad-bladed knife that had never been found. There had been a great deal of speculation over whether or not the child—me, that is—could have grabbed the knife, then dropped it in flight. The police had tried to find it. They combed the six-mile area with sniffer dogs. But the terrain covered both stubble fields and plowed meadows, and nobody could know for sure what route I had taken through the plantation. The search was abandoned. No explanation could be ruled out. In theory, either my father or my mother could have inflicted the knife wound, as the lesions on the victim's hands and stomach were equally compatible with assault and a self-inflicted injury.

There was no mention of my father's female friend.

I lit a smoke and squinted into the sky. How much had little Ella known about what was going on in the house that night? She had heard her father say that he was in love with another woman, that he was prepared to leave her mother for his lover. Perhaps she had even seen them together. I recalled the image of myself barefoot in the dunes, Thomas calling to me through the wind. *Did you see them? They were doing it. Did you see them, Ella?* A face turned towards me, distorted. My father's full beard.

Alex came walking towards me along the beach, his fishing rod slung over his shoulder, a silhouette cut against the sea. I wondered whether he could remember his father. Whether he thought about him at all. We never talked about him, and Amir had only seen Alex twice.

The first time was just after Alex was born. Amir had showed up—outside visiting hours, of course—and, with uncustomary gentleness, had lifted Alex out of the crib. The kiss Amir planted on his son's forehead was a farewell just as much as it was a welcome. I know that now. He had never intended to come back for us. Paradoxically, his parents only lived a couple of miles from where Alex and I lived in Hvidovre—but geography was hardly the decisive factor in such circumstances.

The second time he came was when Alex was about four years old. Amir had just been released on parole after yet another charge of assault. He was drunk, and when I opened the door, he threw his arms around my neck, and started to cry. For the first time it struck me how small he was. He, no further than the bridge of my nose. He was newly married, he said, to a girl from a good family. When he got to the living room, he picked up his son. Alex had been playing with some building blocks on the floor and immediately started to howl.

That was it. The moment was neither beautiful nor thought-provoking.

Parents can fuck up their children's lives whether they are there for them or not. So unbelievably effortlessly. The mind of a child is as fickle as a feather.

The telephone rang as Barbara and I were sitting in the sun eating tomatoes, boiled eggs, and rye bread. We had just finished unloading a pile of junk from Barbara's van: a couple of black plastic bags stuffed with clothes, half-done paintings, and four cardboard boxes filled with knickknacks, a lamp, files, tattered paperbacks, glasses, and plates. We dragged the lot into the garage without discussion. It was clear that Barbara's presence in my grandmother's house was fast becoming permanent, but neither one of us was in the mood to talk about it. Her van was parked in the middle of the yard, its doors wide open with the radio tuned into a local station that only occasionally managed to rise above the din of the ocean.

"Aren't you going to answer that?"

Barbara nodded towards my telephone that was vibrating insistently on the plastic tablecloth. I balked. Kirsten's name beamed on the display.

"Go on, take the call."

Finally, Barbara picked up the phone herself, punched the button, and held the phone over to me without a word. She was sober today. Her hair was wet and stiff with salt after a short dip in the waves. To wash the dust from her bones, she'd said, before wading into the sea wearing nothing but stretched underwear. Her stomach was scarred, as if she were veteran of war.

"Hello? Ella?"

The connection was distorted by static.

"I hope I'm not interrupting anything."

Kirsten sounded tired, impatient, as she sometimes could be. Not surprisingly, Kristen was a highly experienced social worker, whose desk was piled with hopeless cases, including the likes of me. The city of Copenhagen expected her to find solid employment on the job market for all of us. Once in a while, she exploded like the multicolored fireworks display on New Year's Eve.

"Nah . . . "

"You haven't found any employment over there?"

"And what kind of employment would that be?"

She sighed. "Stop being such a smart ass, Ella. Cut the crap. Get a job, like everybody else. I thought you wanted to make a fresh start."

The joy that had fluttered in my chest at the sound of Kirsten's voice evaporated. My voice flattened out. "There aren't enough jobs on the job market for the unemployed, Kirsten. It's a statistically proven fact that if the unemployed weren't around, there would be less competition for jobs and then the average wage would rise, and then all employers would start whining about having to pay their workers more. In fact, those of you who do have a job, ought to rejoice at the fact that the rest of us exist in order to maintain the balance for a bargain basement price. We have a vital role to play. Would you take it on for the lousy twelve thousand kroner a month we're getting paid?

"Ella, sweetheart. For once in your life, drop the socio-economic analyses and start fighting for yourself. No, not just for yourself. For Alex. Get a grip, Ella."

"Was there something in particular that you wanted?"

"Yes . . . no . . . yes." She fumbled with the receiver. "I wanted to give you a quick heads-up from our side. Lisa has decided to press charges after all, and this could have serious consequences for you as the charges are work-related. For her, I mean. I have tried to get her to drop them, but she has to report the incident if she wants to sue for compensation—and that she does. She sleeps badly at night. Post-traumatic stress and all that, you know . . . "

I stiffened. "I . . . I pulled her ponytail. Didn't the stupid cow ever go to school?"

"You pulled her ponytail till she fell to the ground . . . and then there's the incident with the diaper in her face, and no, Ella, she didn't go to the kind of school you've obviously been to. Stop being so stupid. You are lucky she didn't bring charges against you immediately.

That she has chosen to do so now is exactly what you could expect under the circumstances. I just thought you should know."

"Fuck it . . ." I looked at Barbara. "How bad can it get, Kirsten?"

"Bad enough. You'll probably be charged with assault, and then there will be a court case, perhaps prison, what do I know. If I were you, I would start behaving really, really well around Thisted Social Services. Drop the booze. Polish up your act. And those panic attacks of yours . . . Find a psychologist or a psychiatrist—and don't mouth off the moment you walk through the door. And arrange a backup plan for Alex. Find a good place for him to live if things go up shit creek. Otherwise you're going to lose him, Ella. You will. If Social Services doesn't take him, he's going to leave of his own accord—and he won't be coming back."

I had a "fuck you" on the tip of my tongue, but for some reason, it didn't get past my lips. In fact, I couldn't think of a single thing to say. I just sat there, glaring at Barbara.

"Ella? Are you still there? Are you listening?"

I said yes.

"And one more thing. I wasn't sure whether I should tell you this, but . . . it's your friend, Rosa . . . She was hit by a car late last night outside Pub48 in the city. She was drunk. Everybody in Hvidovre is talking about it. Or at least that part of Hvidovre we are responsible for. I don't know how serious it is, but, you know . . . It couldn't have done her any good."

"Where did they take her?"

"Hvidovre Hospital, I would imagine."

"Thanks."

I ended the call, feeling as if all oxygen had been sucked out of the atmosphere. *Rosa and Jens.* I had to get over there immediately. I thought of borrowing Barbara's van. I could drive okay, even though I'd never had the money for a driver's license.

"Problems?" Barbara was watching me with raised eyebrows; a few hairs remained, the bow drawn in thin black pencil, the stragglers helplessly sprawled in a thick cake of foundation.

"Can I borrow your van to drive to Copenhagen? You could come along. Visit your sons."

I got up and started collecting my things randomly. Scraped coins off the top of the garden table and put them in my pocket together with my packet of tobacco. I tried to call Jens, but nobody picked up. I called again. Still no luck.

"How are you intending on getting over the toll-bridge without any money?"

"Don't you have any? Can I borrow some?"

She shook her head. "There's also the question of gas, and who is going to look after Alex and Lupo while you're gone?"

"We could take them along. It's . . . there must be a way we can get over there. I have to go and see a friend."

"Ask that guy . . . Thomas."

I shook my head. Not Thomas. That was not an option. But I needed a plan for Alex. Barbara would have to take him for a couple of days, and then I'd have to take my chances with the train or hitchhike to Copenhagen—not a problem when you were traveling alone.

This was Rosa and Jens. But especially Rosa. They were the only family I had.

Barbara drove me to Thisted station. I bought a ticket for the first stretch of the five-hour trip to Copenhagen and used the last of my cash for a bag of rye-bread rolls and a bottle of water.

The weather was beautiful; the corn fields bellowed in yellow waves under blue skies that made me feel sad, like when you watch a beautiful love scene in a film, but have already seen the trailer and already know that the lovers part in a hailstorm of vicious words in the end. Soon I would be surrounded by a landscape of telephone wires, road work, and asphalt playgrounds, but for the moment, everything was filled with the beauty of what once was.

The train conductor was a friendly, dark-skinned man who merely glanced at my ticket and hurried on. This gave me some hope that he would overlook me on his next round, perhaps just remember me vaguely but forget where I was headed. I leaned my head against the window and closed my eyes. Made as if I was sleeping for half an hour, and then I actually did fall into a light, dreamless sleep with my legs tucked up against the edge of the table in front of me. The first time I woke, we were already in Southern Jutland and I ate two rolls with a little of my water at the stop at Fredericia. The next I knew, we were on the outskirts of Greater Copenhagen with a view of the concrete blocks of Høje Tåstrup, followed by the villa gardens in Valby, and finally, the filthy end of Vesterbro with its intricate network of railway tracks sprinkled with diesel-blackened stones and crossbeams. The electric lines loomed above, weaving in and out of each other under a pale night sky.

I called Jens again.

I still couldn't get a hold of him, but when I did, I would personally break his fingers so he couldn't open any more beer cans. I ducked into the S-train tunnel, hopped onto the train to Hvidovre, and jogged the last stretch of the way to Hvidovre Hospital along one of those anonymous highways leading into the city of Copenhagen.

ACTUALLY, SHE LOOKED okay, Rosa, as she lay there on the starched white sheets. You could see that she had bumped her head, but apart from that, she had come clean with a broken hip and some additional patchwork to her already patched pelvis. It was after nine in the evening and visiting hours were over, but the nurse let me in with a reminder to be absolutely quiet. Not that there was anything else I could do; Rosa had just been wheeled out of operation number two, and her consciousness was still hovering somewhere in the deep. Jens had been in to see her about lunchtime, the nurse kindly informed me, but they'd been obliged to throw him out because he was making such a racket, clearly under the influence of alcohol.

I sat down on a chair by the bed and watched Rosa's face of medicated calm; it was probably the best trip she'd ever had. At least that was something. How she was going to manage with a piss-drunk husband at home and a broken hip was another matter. But there was their son, of course.

I tiptoed out of the room and on down the corridor to the nurse's station, where I carefully rapped on the window.

"Yes?"

It was a different nurse to the one I had spoken to earlier. An elderly woman with a round face and a sharp gaze.

"Rosa Jensen," I said. "Do you know if her son has been informed?"

"Nobody but her husband has come to see her," said the nurse. "As I far as I know, she specifically stated that her son should not be informed."

"But you do have his number?"

She nodded. "Yes, we can find most things in the system."

"So I could give him a call?"

"Ye-es . . ." she began with a shrug. "I can't prevent you from doing so. The number isn't a secret, just hard to find when you happen to be one of several hundred Michael Jensens in Copenhagen."

She had already pulled the number up on the screen and briskly scribbled it down on a yellow Post-it.

"There you go." She handed me the note with a reserved smile. "I hope someone comes to take care of her. Else she won't be getting out of here anytime soon."

ROSA AND JENS'S son was twenty-three years old and still plagued by pubescent acne.

I had nodded a brief hello to him on the staircase in Hvidovre when he came on one of his rare visits, but Rosa had never let me come close or talk to him, terrified as she was that both her own misery and that of her neighbors would scare him off for good. He shook my hand like a polite teenager when he arrived at the hospital, although we were roughly the same age.

"It was nice of you to call. I had no idea Rosa was in the hospital. But I managed to get hold of Jens on the phone. Jesus Christ." He bobbed a little on his toes and avoided my gaze, and I could see an inkling of Rosa's awkwardness in her son.

"Is Jens okay?"

"I don't know, to be honest. He bawled the whole time, and it was hard to tell if he was sober or not. Jesus, I had no idea they had started drinking again."

He sat down next to me on the low wall bordering the hospital parking lot and offered me a smoke that I accepted gratefully. I had already bummed two smokes off arbitrary passersby, but it was starting to get dark, and soon there would be no one left to ask.

"So . . . can you take care of her?"

He was staring at his hands. They were nice-looking, clean. He was a computer nerd, and—according to Rosa—a really bright one at that. Welfare had found him a good foster family and his somewhat stunted size and lack of coordination seemed to be the only damage inherited from a childhood in a concrete block in Hvidovre, a prenatal development in Rosa's alcohol-stewed uterus before that.

"Can you take her in?"

He shook his head. "I live in a two-room apartment in Albertslund," he said. "On the fourth floor. It's not the ideal place to recover when you've got a broken hip, but I'll see what I can do. Maybe I can check in on them back in Hvidovre . . . talk to Jens. Although he sounds totally spaced out. He says Rosa was pushed in front of a car outside Pub48. That she'd gotten into a fight with some redhead bitch. Somebody saw them arguing. Jens has flipped out completely."

"Yes. Paranoia is one of alcohol's most prized effects." Suddenly I felt terribly tired.

"What about you?" He looked at me intently, all at once seeming a lot older than his twenty-three years. A wise old man in a young man's body. "Rosa was worried about you when you moved out. She said you had made a private pact with the alcohol devil."

"She doesn't know what she's talking about," I said. "I'm doing fine. Days can pass without me having a drink."

"Wow. Entire days!" He laughed, and stubbed his cigarette on the wall. "Did she get you those names I found in the social registry?"

A moment passed before I realized what he was talking about. Of course. Lea Poulsen. He'd found something.

"No," I said. "Rosa rang a couple of days ago and spoke to the woman who is staying with me, but I didn't talk to her myself. Did you find that woman, Lea?"

"Yes. It's not that easy to disappear in Denmark," he said. "Although I must say this lady gave it a good shot. Five names in a space of thirty years, and a long line of different addresses."

"But she's still around?"

He nodded. "Yes. I don't know all the details off the top of my head, but now I've got your number. I'll send you a message, okay? Have you got a place to sleep?"

I shrugged. "I'll figure something out. Probably take the first train back tomorrow morning. I'll be fine."

"Okay, I'll be getting back to my girlfriend, then. She's four months pregnant, and she doesn't like me going out at night. It makes her kind of . . . needy."

He smiled crookedly, and it struck me that Rosa had been wrong. They hadn't managed to fuck him up. He was solid. He had a stable core and a place in the world that couldn't be shaken by what he saw in Hvidovre. I made a mental note to call and tell her so when she sobered up. She would probably get mad at me, but it would make her happy.

I stuck my hands in my pockets and made my way to the train station. It had cooled down considerably, and I hugged my jacket up around my ears. At least I'd had the foresight to exchange my flip-flops for a pair of sneakers, and I congratulated myself accordingly. Barbara wasn't picking up her phone.

She didn't pick up either once I got to Copenhagen Central Station and learned that the first train to Thisted was at five o'clock the next morning. The battery of my phone was almost dead and I hadn't thought to bring a charger with me. I cursed. It was close to midnight and the night-life of Vesterbro was already crawling the streets. If I sat myself down in a bar on Istedgade and turned on the charm, I might be able to score a couple of beers to sleep on for the train home. Alcohol tends to soften the floor of the toilets on the train. It might even do something about the smell. I thought about Kirsten's advice and what Michael had said about my consumption of alcohol.

Yes, I had been drinking more since moving to Klitmøller. I had been drinking too much. A natural consequence of my surroundings. The dunes, the roses, the lyme grass, and daisy chains. And Barbara. I pictured those long nails of hers, tap-tapping on the glass of a bottle of vodka. It wasn't a crime to drink alcohol as long as you did it in the company of others, she liked to say. But it had to stop. Once I had finished my business in Klitmøller, once I had found what I was looking for, I would stop.

THE BAR I went into near Copenhagen Central Station was called Viggo. There was a dart board on the wall and a scratched pool table located at the back of the establishment. The kitchen was closed for the evening but the hint of roast pork and peas still lingered in the cloud of smoke and alcohol-sweat that bathed the guests at the bar counter. The clientele resembled the flock at Friheden so much that I experienced a brief, nauseating bout of déjà-vu, but there was nobody I knew, and nobody I had to talk to about anything other than the weather. I sat down next to a ruddy-faced guy in a checkered shirt, leaning my elbows on the counter. He was relatively old, an indecipherable age between fifty and seventy, and cast from a jovial mold. He was humming Aerosmith's "Crazy" above the din of corny nineties hits coming from the loud-speakers overhead.

"It's cold out there, isn't it?" He nodded at my light jacket that I still had buttoned up to the chin.

I smiled.

"Perhaps you could do with something to warm you up?"

I decided to be honest and spare myself any unpleasantries later. "I'm broke," I said. "I came here to visit a friend who's in the hospital, and I'll be on a train to Jutland first thing in the morning. If you'd like to buy me a drink, I'd be happy to accept, but there won't be any sex, and no pawing of my tits."

He laughed. "Good company can also be hard to come by. What can I get you?"

I ordered a beer and a chaser. Then I ordered the same again.

I noted that the message from Michael had come in at three in the morning when my phone slipped out of my pocket for the third time and landed on the floor under my barstool. My ruddy-faced new best friend, Morten from Vanløse, had bought me four shots and three beers and everything was coming at me in a delayed succession of waves. The light from the spots in the low ceiling unraveled into dashes and Morten's arm reached for the beer on the counter in clips of motion to his lips and back again. We had long since stopped talking, were just sitting there next to each other, enjoying our respective trips for ourselves. I sat submerged in the pulsing heat, lucky to have registered the fall of the phone from my pocket at all. It was a surprisingly arduous and complicated task to bend down and find the finicky little devil on the floor.

I squinted at the display.

HI ELLA, HERE'S WHAT I COULD FIND . . . PLEASE NOTE
THAT SOME OF THIS INFORMATION IS CONFIDENTIAL.
A FAVOR FOR MY MOTHER. OKAY?

Idiotically, I nodded in agreement before reading the list Michael had inserted below his message:

1961-1984 LEA FINNBOGADOTTIR LIVES IN
THORSHAVN, FAROE ISLES.
1984 MARRIES, TAKES ON THE NAME POULSEN AND
MOVES TO ÅRHUS.
1989 DIVORCES, MOVES TO HOLSTEBRO, THEN VIBORG,
THEN BACK TO ÅRHUS.
1994 CHANGES NAME TO CHRISTI JOHANSEN, NO FIXED ADDRESS.

1997 CHANGES NAME TO HELENA PETERSEN. LIVES IN HOLSTEBRO.
2009 CHANGES NAME TO BARBARA JENSEN AND MOVES TO HAGEVEJ 7, KLITMØLLER. THIS IS HER LAST-KNOWN ADDRESS. SOMETHING ELSE I THOUGHT MIGHT BE USEFUL: IN 1990 LEA POULSEN WAS CHARGED WITH KIDNAPPING AND GROSS NEGLIGENCE. SHE PICKED UP HER TWO BOYS, AGED 4 AND 5, FROM KINDERGARTEN AND TOOK THEM TO AN APARTMENT IN ÅRHUS. SHE WAS HIGH ON DRUGS, ONLY CHECKING ON THE BOYS SPORADICALLY. A FRIEND FOUND HER, TOOK THE BOYS TO HOSPITAL, WHERE THEY RECEIVED TREATMENT FOR DEHYDRATION ETC. THE BOYS WERE RETURNED TO THEIR FATHER. THE COURT DENIED LEA ANY FURTHER CONTACT WITH THE BOYS.

I leaned against the bar, reading the message again with great difficulty. I had to keep squinting to prevent the letters from flooding over the ends of the display.

The world was so incredibly small, everyone was connected; Barbara was on Michael's list. I downed the last of my beer, and read the list again with a creeping sense that I had missed something. Lea became Christi who became Helena who became Barbara, but it was only once I read the message out loud to Morten that I understood what it meant.

Lea was Barbara, and Barbara had been lying to me all along. That's what it meant. Barbara had known my mother. She'd been my mother's best friend. And now she had Alex.

The nausea that had been stalking me all evening swelled upwards as the realization dawned, quickly followed by images of the implications. Alex was alone with Barbara in my grandmother's claustrophobic little living room; those long nails in his hair, against his neck. I didn't know what she was capable of, but there must be a reason why she had wrapped herself in such an intricate tangle of lies.

I leaned on the bar and got to my feet, knocking my glass over on the counter in the process. I needed to get to the exit, but the door was a blurry quadrangle framed in matte-black panes on the other end of the room, and the air was an impenetrable barrier of smoke. I tripped over the leg of a barstool, banged my shin on the edge of an unexpected step, and chafed my chin on the grain of the pinewood floor as I hit the deck. Someone helped me back onto my feet and I managed to fight my way out onto the street in the hopes of finding a quiet corner.

The next implication took shape as I twisted my ankle on the cobblestones and landed on my ass on the sidewalk. Pain shot up from my coccyx. At best, there were six hours separating me from Alex and Barbara. More, if I waited for the next train to Thisted.

I needed to get a hold of someone to drive me home. But there was only one person I knew who would come and get me in the state I was.

The telephone rang and rang in Jens and Rosa's bedroom, and I let it ring till the beep at the end. Then I called again. And one more time. Mostly because I didn't know what else to do. My thoughts were slow, soft as cotton-wool in the midst of my panic. After the fifth try, Jens finally grunted something into the phone.

"Jens . . . can you come get me?" I could feel that I was on the edge of tears. He was a ship a long way off on a wildly whipping sea.

"Ella? Where are you?"

He sounded tired, but clear-headed. Sober. I closed my eyes and thanked heaven and a host of gods I didn't usually make a habit of calling upon.

"I'm on Istedgade," I said. "Jens. You need to help me get home. Now. There's something wrong with Alex, and I can't . . . "

My phone cut out. I was standing on the curb, alone with the noise of the road; drunkards calling after hookers on Helgolandsgade, the smash of bottles against the cobblestones, high-pitched laughter. I collapsed onto the stone steps in front of a darkened apartment building glaring at the dead screen on my phone. I rested my forehead against the cold of the wall, stuck a finger down my throat, and threw up on the steps.

Some time passed as the world revolved around me. A young couple touched my shoulder and asked me if I was okay. I was just fine, thank you. A man tripped over my feet, and swore loudly, as did two young girls who came out of the apartment building, swerving to avoid me and the pool of sour vomit on the steps.

Throwing up had helped to clear my head a little, and the cool evening air gradually made it easier to focus. At last I saw Jens's lemon yellow Volvo coming down Istedgade at a snail's pace, Jens's upper body hanging halfway out the rolled down window. Finally, he pulled up to the curb next to me and waved jovially.

"Hop in, Beautiful. You can fill me in on the way there."

"I AM VERY drunk, Jens," I said, leaning hard onto the glove compartment. "But she has got Alex."

I didn't hear whether he answered or not, I dropped out of time, but at one stage, I woke up and heard him talking next to me. About Rosa. That she had been far too drunk to be running around alone in the middle of the night.

"It's a dump," Jens was saying about Pub48. "It's just a pile of shit-faced people up to no good."

I tried to nod but my head kept lolling forward onto my chest. Rosa had been just as pickled as I was. And then an idea crossed my mind, slow as tumbleweed blowing in from the prairie.

"Rosa talked to Barbara, who is staying with me, didn't she? On the telephone. They were on the phone for more than twenty minutes. She told Barbara everything, didn't she? About the names Michael had found in the social registry."

Jens shrugged. "I wouldn't know, Ella. I can't remember shit from the last two weeks."

My brain protested against the strain of coherent thought. Through the window I watched the lights of the city trail like the tail of a meteor across the night sky. I resorted to help from my fingers. First came day one, day two, and finally day three. On the first day, Rosa talked to Barbara. On day two and three, Barbara was away without telling me where she was going. It was on the last day that Rosa ended up under a car in a drunken stupor outside Pub48 after an argument with a redhead. The fingers added up.

I threw up in a crumpled Netto bag lying on the floor in front of me.

ANNA. 1994

It was not the pain that woke her, but a warm sensation, some-thing flooding over her hand, dripping off her fingertips onto the floor. She rolled over onto her side. Her right hand found the source of the flood on her left wrist. Her fingers sank into the open wound, now a sear of pain, making her gasp.

She opened her eyes, but couldn't see anything in the dark. All she knew was that someone was in the room, and that it wasn't Helgi. The smell was strange and sweet, like peaches, the quick breathing was light as the beating of butterfly wings. Her eyes tried to penetrate the dark, finally fixing on the shadow of a figure about a yard's length from the bed. The posture hunched, the movements halting, hesitant, riddled with doubt.

"Helgi."

Anna whispered into the dark, hoping she'd been mistaken. Perhaps Helgi was there, after all; either that black shadow on the floor or lying next to her in their double bed, but her whispers dissolved unanswered.

"Helgi!"

This time she called a little louder, and the shadow lurched towards her. A rubber-gloved hand covered her mouth, but then let go, trying to grab hold of Anna's shoulders instead, but Anna had no difficulty in pulling herself free. Anna was strong. And she screamed as loud as she could. She screamed louder than she'd ever screamed in her life. If Helgi wasn't home, Ella was alone in her room at the end of the passageway. She had to warn her.

Anna rolled onto the floor and rammed into the legs of the dark shadow. He had a knife. The blade cut into her arm as they kicked free of each other. Anna threw herself at the door. The shadow had a hold on her hair from behind, but Anna kept moving forward, felt the sharp pain in her scalp as a large tuft of hair was ripped out at the roots. She stumbled down the stairs and into the living room.

The television was on. A chaotic succession of images, people and cars, the sound of gunshots from the screen, but the house was dead quiet. Helgi was not on the couch in the living room, and now she knew for sure that he wasn't anywhere else in the house either. None of this would be happening if Helgi had been there.

Anna turned to face the dark shadow behind her. The head was covered by a black mask, but it had to be a woman, Anna realized. It smelled like a woman, and if it had been a man, she would not have been strong enough to pull herself free in the scuffle in the bedroom.

The shadow held the knife in front of her, cutting the air in hypnotic curves, but she made no attempt to come any closer. Whatever her plan had been, she seemed to be having second thoughts now.

The intruder. The stalker.

Anna felt a moment of relief, for she was obviously just an intruder. The one who had smashed their vases and planted the bloody stake into the ground earlier that spring; the cross of Jehovah, she'd thought. But it was neither her sister nor the extended arm of God delivering a message just for her. It was just a common thief.

Her wrist was still bleeding, but the cut wasn't deep enough to be fatal.

"What is it that you want?" Anna asked carefully. "Do you want the television? We also have a camera somewhere."

The woman had started to circle around Anna, and did not answer. The knife was a mere blackened shadow in the dark.

"Please just go."

Strangely enough, Anna could no longer feel any pain in her wrist. In fact, she felt strong, invulnerable. Her senses were razor sharp, she could feel the intruder's uncertainty radiating into the room. Now she was the hunter, and the other a wild animal, its back to the wall. But this breed of animal would bite, if it could not flee.

Anna stepped aside so the thief could walk past her to the door, but she remained frozen to the spot, staring at her through the holes in the mask.

"Just go," Anna said, pointing at the door. "You can still get away. My husband will be here soon. He's just . . . gone out."

The other sniffed briefly, but took a step in the right direction after all, a moment where anything was possible, where something could still be saved; they could both walk away and never look back. Life could go on as before, and Anna sensed that both of them knew it. A bond, some common understanding that the situation had gotten out of hand, and yet could still be salvaged with a single move.

A sound from the first floor.

Perhaps it was only Anna who had heard it, but the sound was so distinctive and familiar to her, and it pierced her heart.

It was the tread of bare feet above.

She knew that sound, and she knew those feet. As a rule, she knew precisely where Ella was in the house at any given time, as if they were bound by invisible cords. But her sixth sense had failed her this time. Only now did she register her daughter's silent, unseen presence at the top the stairs.

Anna turned her head to her daughter, feeling the blow in her stomach in the same instant. *She hit me*, Anna thought in amazement. *Why did she hit me?* Then something burning hot and wet coming from the same place. She looked down, and saw a dark stain spread over her nightdress, just above the hip. Then the next blow fell, and she stumbled two steps back, colliding into the television. Anna put both hands against the wall to prevent herself from falling.

"Stop." Her voice was weak. "It hurts." She stared at the motionless, black mask in front of her, tried to catch those eyes, perhaps identify some feeling there that could help her make some sense of it. Anger or fear or pity. But Anna saw nothing. The woman lunged at her again, but this time, Anna moved. She staggered through the living room and into the kitchen. Away from Ella. She had to get the intruder away from her daughter.

The black shadow followed after, but stumbled over a chair in the dark. Anna reached the back door, opened it, and ran out into the night. Cold rain hit her face, her bare arms, the wind ripped at her hair and nightdress, as she half-ran, half-limped over the uneven lawn, onto the path between the naked hip bushes, and down to the sea.

Behind her, she could sense a presence, some hesitation radiating towards her.

But now there were no steps to be heard other than her own, no heavy breathing, only the ice-cold rain whipping into her. She was still bleeding: a warm stream flowing over her stomach and pelvis, and it hurt. Glowing hot, forging a path from within and out, as if working its way out of her body. She didn't dare look down, just pressed one hand firmly against her stomach, felt the warmth of her body seeping through her fingers.

Behind her, nothing but the massive darkness of the house. If Ella was still in there, she had not turned on the lights.

"Big girl," whispered Anna. "Go back to your room, crawl under your bed, or hide in the cupboard. Be absolutely still."

Anna took a couple more steps down the path towards the sea. A window in Agni's house shone through the storm, and she slowly made for the house. Agni would know what to do. Agni would find Helgi, and call for help.

The lyme grass pricked at her numb, naked feet, and it was difficult to see the bends in the path. Twice she fell down, but she managed to get up again, keeping one hand pressed hard against the rip in her nightdress. The third time she fell, she had to stay down, rest a little with her eyes closed. Grey dots, black dots flickered behind her eyelids, but still the panic didn't come. There was no room to feel it. She opened her eyes, and looked up into the colossal, starless sky. It was still raining, but the cold was coming from within.

She couldn't just lie there in the sand, she thought, so she got to her feet, stumbled onward, her legs reluctant to obey. Anna leaned on the wind and rain, and followed the light.

Klitmøller lay bathed in sunshine as we bumped along the main road into town.

It was nine in the morning and a group of tourists was already heading for the beach. The sky was clear and bright over the sea, and I was so scared my teeth were chattering.

I wasn't sure exactly what I was afraid of. All I knew was that this was a different kind of fear to the one that usually left me flat on the floor, arms and legs flailing.

This fear stemmed from something beyond my own person, from someone else, and it kept me awake on that madcap trip clean across country roads and bridges. Jens had been driving like a maniac, way too fast, not thinking to stop when I had to throw up once, twice, as we flew over the Great Belt Bridge—he simply leaned over and handed me a fresh Netto bag without a word. In fact, there were several plastic supermarket bags lying ready on the floor in front of me. Jens had taken just precautions before picking me up on Istedgade in Copenhagen.

For his own part, Jens was painfully sober, and he looked like hell. He had always been thin, but now he was skin and bone, his eye sockets sunk deeply, darkly into his skull after almost two weeks straight of hard drinking. But he hadn't had a drop to drink since the day before. He wanted to be sure that the hospital staff would let him see Rosa. It was a worthy project that he tackled with chewing gum, chips, cola, and a couple of joints from the glove compartment to take the edge off the worst of the jitters.

"I think she's mentally ill," I said. "When we met her on the beach . . . she knew who we were, but didn't say anything. She's lied to us all along. The drawings of Alex, everything . . . "

Jens didn't answer, just sat staring straight ahead, his jaws chewing on thin air; he had plenty of demons of his own to contend with just then. The cold surged from the pit of my stomach and spread to the extremities of my body, but the all too familiar shaking did not take over. My body remained mine. Nothing was shaking as I directed Jens onto the sandy road leading to my grandmother's house.

The first thing I saw was Lupo. He was squashed up against the front door. His coat was wet and rough, his head turned up at an awkward angle against the doorframe. Even when I got out of the car, he remained where he was instead of running up to me as usual.

The dread kneaded and keeled over my insides as I looked around me. All the windows were closed and dark. Alex's fishing rod as well as the spade he used to dig out worms lay on the ground in front of the garage. The weathervane whirred in the wind.

I strode over to Lupo. He tried to turn his head in my direction and growled deep in his throat, but didn't move. Someone had put a noose around his neck and tied it to the door handle on a leash so tight that he had to balance on his hind legs to avoid being strangled. The noose was locked round his neck and I couldn't pull it loose with my fingers.

"Barbara!" I called in through the window. Nothing but darkness behind the dusty reflections. I set off at a stumbling run to the garage where I found a rusty garden scissors and ran back to cut the noose. Lupo yowled, tumbled backwards, and sprawled, but finally stood up with a hesitant wag of the tail. His coat was bloody where the noose had chafed into the skin.

"Is everything okay?"

Jens had climbed out of the car and was standing next to me with his hands hanging down by his sides. An old man. He looked like something that could be carried away by the wind at any moment, but I was glad he was there. Sober, Jens was as gentle as a lamb. Actually, he was equally gentle as a drunk, but drunks—especially drunk alcoholics—thought only of themselves and their next drink. You can never rely on a drunk. I opened the door into the hallway and was met by a strong smell of methanol and gas.

"Alex!"

There wasn't a sound apart from the faint creak in the rafters when the wind lashed into the house. My heart fluttered in my throat.

"Alex, I'm home!"

Not a sound. If he were asleep, irrespective of how deeply, he should have heard me. Either Alex or Barbara. But the house was quiet as the grave.

When I got to the doorway of the kitchen I sensed the heat and the smell before I saw the glowing hot pot on the stove. A single flame had been lit below an unidentifiable, charred mass. The carpet was wet, soaked in petrol; my shoes left dark tracks on the thin grey piling as I cut the short distance to the stove and killed the flame. The air was thick and hazy with smoke. My eyes watered.

"Come out of there, Ella." Jens was standing in the kitchen doorway and nodded emphatically at the toaster that was placed on the soaked carpet on the floor. "This place is going to go up in flames any minute."

The wires of the toaster sparked, almost invisible blue flames hovered just above the piling. I spun on my heels.

Alex!

Jens stepped back as I rushed past him up and bounded up the stairs. In our bedroom, duvets and quilts were spread helter-skelter over the floor together with remnants of my files, papers, and reports. My grandmother's journals and notes were torn and scattered everywhere, arbitrary chunks of text loomed large . . .

. . . new foster family. Ella is uncooperative, she shuns physical contact and interaction with her foster parents. She says she wants to die, that she isn't a human being . . .

. . . in my opinion, Ella has a stunted emotional intelligence for her age . . .

. . . Ella is not suited to foster care . . . Ella requires

intensive professional care in a secure, institutionalized environment...

...Ella misses her mother...

The windows in the roof were wide open and the bits of paper were swept up in the draft. I searched all the rooms, opened all the cupboards, even though they were ridiculously small, but there was no sign of my son anywhere. Then I heard the flames take in the kitchen below; it sounded like a rushing river colliding with a cliff. I salvaged my rucksack from under a mattress and charged down the steps, darted out the back door of the washing room. I could feel the flames like a wall of heat in my back. My hair stank like pork roast.

JENS WAS STANDING outside on the yard with a smoke, watching the fire in resignation.

"He's not in there, Ella," he said. "I smashed a window at the back of the house to check that room as well... " He nodded over at Barbara's bedroom window. "Nobody is in there either."

The fire broke through the spine of the roof and a warm pillar of smoke rose up into the blue sky. I went around the back to Barbara's room in time to see the heat blacken the pictures of Judgement Day, peel them off the walls and ceiling. I felt Jens's hands on my shoulders, and briefly leaned back against his body, let him hold me for a moment. I fleetingly wished that someone were there for me. I was so utterly worn out by being alone. And this wasn't something I could handle on my own.

"Ella... you need to think," he whispered. "Where is she? Where could she be?"

People had started gathering round. Mr. and Mrs. Klitmøller in the front row, Mr. Klitmøller with a finger raised in the air to gauge the wind-direction in relation to his own thatched-roof house. He looked like an irate and aged schoolmaster, ready to give one of his favorite hobby horses a good kick in the ribs.

"One of the last surviving houses of the historic town of

Klitmøller," he said, as I walked past him. "I told you to be careful with fire out here. It's very dry, and the wind is always . . . I told you to . . ."

I left the burning house to the spectators and set off at a run, my rucksack bouncing on my back. As I turned down the road where we used to live, I could hear the sirens like a drawn-out, melancholy howl above the din of the wind. My childhood home stood naked and unprotected in the morning sunshine, but it was the house next door I was after. Here the hedge had grown thick and dense over the years so as to provide sufficient shelter to a garden that had become dark and lush as a jungle by comparison.

"Thomas!"

I called his name several yards before I reached the stone steps in front of his house, and I called it again as I hammered on the massive, oiled wooden door. I remembered the house fleetingly; screaming-yellow water pistols, tattered Donald Duck comics, and the taste of raspberries and golden gooseberries, absurd memories that muddled in rising panic. I couldn't shout anymore, so I settled for banging furiously on the door instead.

"Hey! What's going on?"

Thomas had popped up from behind the house and stood watching me with his arms crossed over his chest. He was wearing a sleeveless vest draped over his rod-thin torso. His shorts looped down from his waist like huge sails.

"Can I borrow your phone?"

"Okay," he came over to me and fumbled in his pockets. "What's the matter with yours?" he asked, finally handing me his.

"It's dead," I said, emptying the contents of my rucksack onto the ground. The pages were still intact, and the relief in my chest was so great I could have sobbed. There was the note from my grandmother, and there was the telephone number for Helgi Nygaard in Thailand.

I didn't allow myself to think, just punched in the digits. My father deserved no ceremony. This was for Alex. My core was hard and smooth and cold as stone on the shore.

The line crackled.

"What the hell is going on?"

Thomas had caught sight of the pillar of smoke over my grand-mother's house. The sirens moaned in the wind, then suddenly stopped.

My head lolled on my shoulders. A distant, metallic ringing tone went through, and then a voice answered in English.

"Hello? Hello?"

Hard and smooth and cold. I was granite and steel.

"Is this Helgi?" I said in Danish.

Scratching interference, alternating with dead air. The connection dulled out, as if a finger were pressed to my ear.

"Yes, this is Helgi. Who is this?" He switched to Danish.

I wanted to reply, but the words were stuck in my body. My throat closed painfully.

"Who is this . . . ? Ella? Is that you?"

The broad West-Jutlandic lilt made all the difference. It sliced into my flesh like a newly honed knife. It was him. My father. The feeling of his hand in my hair, a sharp, physical pain above my eye. My knees gave way, and I sank onto the steps.

"She's got Alex," was all I said.

Silence. Dead fucking air.

"Ella . . . I am glad that you called. Very glad. But I don't understand what you are saying? Who has . . . is Alex your son?"

"Barbara has my son. Barbara . . . or Lea . . . or Christi. You used to know someone called Christi," I said. "She has taken Alex, and I don't know where they are. Oh, God . . . " The sobs racked my throat. "Where are they, Helgi?"

"Christi! Has Christi taken your boy?!"

His voice was focused now, and a halting image of him took shape before my inner eye. The two of us on the garage floor, we are bent over his hunting rifle.

You put the cartridges in here. A brief smile, eyes narrowed, concentrated. *And you unlock the safety catch by pulling this lever back, here.*

Cool metal in my hands. I lean my entire weight against the lever.

*It's hard, but Dad says I should keep trying. That I can, if I want to.
Then, at long last, a satisfying* click.

"Where are they, Dad? Did you know her like that? Was it her
you were . . . ? Where do you think she would take him?"

"Jesus Christ, Ella. I don't know . . . but she liked churches,
and graveyards. Paintings—but it's such a long time ago. I don't
know . . . "

"Give me a church, Helgi. Name me just *one*, and send the rest
in a text later."

"Vestby Church . . . She liked Vestby Church. She went there to
think about her boys. Ella . . . I . . . "

I cut the connection, allowing myself a few precious seconds to
breathe deeply and wipe the tears away with the back of my hand.
Fucking bastard. He had been in love with Barbara. He'd been
screwing my mother's best friend, then he'd killed her and let
Barbara live. And now she'd taken Alex away from me.

He was nothing to me.

If I ever found Alex, and my life turned back to normal, I would
erase him from my mind. I would take my son someplace where
nobody knew us, and nobody would ever get close to us again. You
can collect cans anywhere in the world.

I got to my feet, fresh tears burning in my eyes. Jens was worn
out. He'd driven six hours straight, had chronic withdrawal symptoms, his hands shaking on the steering wheel on the last fifty miles
to Klitmøller. I looked at Thomas.

"Can you drive me to Vestby Church?"

He nodded.

"And Thomas . . . you hunt, right? Your gun. I need to borrow
your gun."

We could see the church clearly from a distance.

It was perched on a lonely hill surrounded by an otherwise flat landscape of farmlands. The narrow road we were driving along was deserted, the asphalt was light grey, burning hot, and riddled with cracks. I sat in the passenger seat with the rifle on my lap. Thomas had loaded his rifle for me and showed me how to use it. His hair was drenched in sweat.

"If something goes wrong, Ella . . . "

Things already had fucking gone wrong, but I bit my tongue. Barbara had my son, but that's not what he meant.

"If things go wrong, Thomas, I am the one with the gun. You could say I threatened to shoot you if you didn't come with me," I said. "Everyone will believe you."

Thomas pulled over at the foot of the long chestnut alley leading up the hill. If Barbara was in the church with Alex there was no reason to tip her off to our arrival.

The sun was sharp and white through a thin veil of clouds, but there were no larks swooping over the fields. No buzzing of insects. I imagined a farmer sowing chemical fodder in the soil and leaving the rest up to wind and solar powers. It felt as though Thomas and I were the only breathing beings left on earth as we set off at a jog up that endless alley.

Right in front of the graveyard entrance Barbara's green van was parked with the doors gaping wide. Music blared from the speakers, just like it had done on the yard at my grandmother's house. Glenn Miller. Alex's favorite CD. "Take the 'A' Train."

"You check out the grounds," I said. "I'll try the church."

The rifle lay comfortably in my hand, as if it had always been there. Thomas scanned the graveyard.

"What do you think she wants? Why do you think she came here?"

I shook my head. I didn't have the energy to ponder Barbara's motives, nor anything else she might have planned. If I allowed my mind to think of either, I would fall apart. There were certain scenarios I couldn't contemplate without going insane. I couldn't risk losing my mind. That would have to wait.

"You take the graveyard," I said.

I walked along the white-washed walls, found the entrance to the transept and tested the door carefully. It was locked, and I abandoned all attempts at being discreet.

"Alex!"

I yelled his name as loud as I could, but I wasn't at all sure that my voice could penetrate as far as the nave within. The solid walls gave the impression of a fortress, and the high, narrow windows were several yards over my head.

"Nothing." Thomas had appeared from the other side of the church and shrugged in resignation. "If they're here at all, they're in the church."

I kicked the door in front of me. It didn't budge a millimeter.

"The windows," said Thomas. "Windows can be smashed. You wait here."

He spun on his heels and disappeared behind the massive wall, Shortly after, I heard Barbara's van crunching over the gravel. Thomas parked the van parallel to the wall, just below one of the windows. The sun blinked through the glass mosaic Madonna above.

"After you," he said, bending down on one knee so he could give me a leg up onto the warm roof of the van. There was still a fair distance up to the window ledge, but I could just reach it, and pull myself up. The inner arches of the vault were visible through the red and yellow stained-glass window. Thomas passed up one of the stones he had nicked from the border of the nearest grave and I smashed it through the pane, hearing the rain of colorful splinters crashing to the floor below. Then I heard Barbara. She was singing. *Peace I leave with you . . .* It was the psalm the congregation sang at my mother's funeral. I remembered sitting between two strangers, the white coffin directly in front of me. This I could remember, and I remembered the voice of a beautiful, fair-haired woman ringing clear above all others. And just as I remember the voice was light and soft in the fractured acoustics of the church, the tones all wrong, tripping and tumbling over false scales.

Barbara did not react to the crash of glass behind her. She kept on singing. The rifle lay heavily against my shoulder. I could see her sitting in the first pew, she was facing the altar, but Alex was nowhere to be seen. A combination of relief and renewed fear pulsed through my body. I wondered whether he was in the church at all. He could have made a run for it, escaped down to the harbor. He was a strong boy, and she was an old woman. She could hardly do him any harm.

But still my heart froze. The stone floor was a good couple of meters below me, so I swung my legs over the window ledge, easing myself down the wall, the tips of my toes just reaching the back of the last pew. I had not been in a church since my confirmation, but as soon as my feet touched the nave floor, I recalled the smell of ancient masonry, candles, and charred electric radiators. The altar was small and sparsely decorated. The pews were carved in a dark, polished wood, the carvings dusted in a rust-colored pattern. I recognized some of the faded paintings on the walls from Barbara's murals. The Devil loomed large and fat and self-satisfied.

Barbara had not turned round, even though she must have heard me coming, but she had stopped singing, her shoulders twitching slightly instead. Her hair had not been gathered into her usual knot at the back of her head, it hung lifelessly down her back, exposing the curve of her cranium, the grey roots at the base of her scalp.

"You're back early," she said. "I didn't think you'd get back from Copenhagen before this afternoon. And I would never have expected to see you here. But that's just how you are, Ella. Out of sync. Always in the wrong place at the wrong time."

I approached her carefully from behind, as if approaching a wild animal. Let my hands trace along the back of the pews, the plastic ornamental roses displayed there, and caught my breath when I reached the front row. Alex was lying with his head in her lap. She was stroking his hair. His eyes were closed, his lips parted, slightly askew. A damp shimmer at the corners of his mouth.

Barbara didn't turn to look at me. She remained intent upon caressing Alex's forehead with one hand; in the other, she gripped a kitchen knife.

I had stopped dead in my tracks, one hand resting on the finely carved half-door of the front pew. The thought of dying had always terrified me, but the idea of losing Alex, from one moment to the next, was petrifying. Barbara could so easily stick the knife between his ribs and pierce his heart. Simply sever the pipes of his supple neck. I could see his soft pulse beating, just below the skin.

I lowered the rifle off my shoulder slowly and aimed it at her face, knowing I knew it was pointless. She had Alex, and she had a knife. And my hands were shaking so badly I was afraid I'd shoot Alex by mistake.

"Take a seat and look around you, Ella," she said. "This is my favorite church. It has been for many years. Even when I lived in Århus I would come out here sometimes. Nobody ever comes here. They want to tear it down."

I opened the little gate obediently and slid down onto the bench. I still had the rifle trained on her face, but it was an empty gesture, and she seemed to sense my desperate lack of alternatives.

I was so close I could've reached out and touched Alex's feet, but I didn't dare. I just wanted the world to stop turning, everything to slow down. I needed movements so slow they became imperceptible. I wanted time to stop, and wind slowly backwards. Back to when Alex and I stood on the yard in front of my grandmother's house in waves of lyme grass. Back to us walking in the park in Hvidovre, a plastic Netto bag filled with cans dangling between us, enough loot for cupcakes from the bakery. Further back. To the time I destroyed my foster mother's greenhouse and called her the fattest cow in the world. Further and still further back. To the dark, and the night the world went under.

"What have you done to him?"

She smiled, and all at once I could see the drug addict in the tired, unmade face of the woman before me. The teeth she had lost that had been replaced with a new set, white as chalk. The teardrop tattoos on the insides of her elbows that were meant to disguise the pitiful state of her lacerated veins.

"Angel dust for my angel," she whispered, turning to meet my gaze for the first time. She'd been crying. "A little for him, and a little for me. Just enough to blunt the edge. And a little to sleep on."

"Jesus fucking Christ, Barbara," I hissed. "He's eleven years old."

She nodded. "I never wanted to hurt you or Alex. When I saw you on the beach that day, I was just . . . happy . . . hopeful." She savored the words in her mouth, smacked her dry lips. "I had tried to find you before. I wanted to say I was sorry. I never meant things to end the way they did. That you should be left without a family. But you were such a slippery little devil, weren't you? I never found you. Every time I thought I knew where you were, you moved to a different place, and you left nothing behind but broken glass and beaten up kids. I lost track of you after foster family number four."

I could hear Thomas crawling through the broken window, yet another wave of shattered glass crashed to the floor, but I didn't see him. All I saw was Alex and Barbara's hands. The one gripping the knife, the other fondling his bangs.

"And then what, Barbara?" I said. "What happened?"

"I wanted to start over," said Barbara. "I thought we could be a family, just like Helgi and I had wanted. You had lost your mother, and I had lost my children. But you kept holding onto the past. Kept digging yourself deeper down. There was no need to do that, was there? We could have had a good life together, you and I, if only you had been able to let it go. But now I don't know if we can be saved anymore. I just don't know, Ella."

"Put down the knife, Barbara," I rasped. I was having great difficulty keeping my voice steady. I pointed the rifle in her face once more.

"Can you remember me from that night, Ella? I thought you saw me, but perhaps I was mistaken."

"What night?"

I couldn't take my eyes off Alex. His breathing was deep, peaceful. "The night your mother died. Did you see me?"

I looked at her and knew she was the kind of liar that lied not only to others but especially to herself. A woman who has lost her children on account of her own abuse must have formidable powers of self-deception to go on living with herself. Even so, I couldn't let it be.

"Were you there?"

She nodded. "Yes, I was there. I heard her die, Ella, and it didn't take long. It was painless, and for her, death was a salvation. In fact, I think it was the best thing that could have happened for Anna. But the circumstances were . . . unfortunate. You shouldn't have been there, Ella. It was supposed to be different. Anna was supposed to sleep, drift away from it all."

"You were friends, before you started seeing my father. Did he know? Did he know who you were?"

"No. I didn't think it was necessary for him to know. It had nothing to do with us, with Helgi and me—and you. And your mother . . . I thought we were friends, once. But because of her, I lost my boys. She betrayed me to social services, to my ex-husband, to Jehovah's fucking Witnesses, even though it had always been *us* against *them*. I asked her to come and help me with the boys—and she did come—but she took my boys away from me. I haven't seen them since. Only from a distance. And in pictures. You never become quite human again, once you've lost your children. Your mother deserved what happened to her."

It sounded like a story she'd told many times before. The words fell into place like the lines of a poem she was reciting. My mother's fault—not hers. I remembered the yellow rose I'd found in the dunes where my mother had died, and for the first time, I felt a stab of sympathy for Barbara, for no matter how many times she had come to the conclusion that my mother had deserved to die, there was still a part of her that succumbed to doubt. And doubt hurts.

Barbara smiled, leaned her head on the back of the pew, and gazed at the murals above.

"I was banished from the church because I was a drug addict," she said. "It all started with morphine. I had dislocated my shoulder and was prescribed morphine for the pain. I became fond of it. Dependent. And then there were so many other options at my disposal, pills available from the same supplier. I have always believed that life is like walking on a tightrope suspended between birth and Judgment Day. You have to be so terribly careful not to stumble and fall into the abyss, and the faster you come to the other side, the better. I was a very talented tightrope walker, Ella. Always in control. But then came the morphine, and afterward, there was heroin and cocaine. I let go long enough to look at the world around me, and I realized that I had been wrong. I wasn't balancing on a wire suspended over an abyss, I was walking along a line of chalk my parents had drawn in their backyard. It was . . ."

Barbara rotated her arms in the air above her head in a gesture of silent explosion.

"I tried to explain this to my husband. I wanted to get away, and I wanted to take my boys with me, of course. I was so completely, so vividly awake. My life was meant to be about passion and love, it was meant to be filled with beautiful things. I wanted to learn how to paint . . . And then I met your mother in that hopeless support group for people excluded from our church. The group itself was sickening, but your mother was wonderful. She became my first and only friend outside of the congregation. This is the part of her I miss once in a while."

I heard the dull echo of Thomas's steps coming down the aisle, the dust shimmered and danced in the tall pillars of light from the windows above the altar. A thought struck me, and it was so simple and so pure in its logic that I was amazed I hadn't thought it before.

"Did you kill my mother?"

Barbara's forefinger was resting on the edge of the knife, still without looking at me. "You really can't remember anything at all from that night, can you?" she said, shaking her head. "Amazing. But then again, we all have our way of warding off the dark."

She looked up and nodded at the Devil on the ceiling above, as if she were talking to him.

"I wasn't the one who killed your mother, Ella."

"You're so full of shit, Barbara."

She laughed drily. "I don't know anyone who isn't, but you, my girl, are right up there with the best of them in the bullshit-league. You just don't know it, and that's worse. Especially for you."

She raised the knife, her knuckles white, the thin hand shook ever so slightly. I didn't think. I cocked the barrel, leveled the gun, and pulled the trigger.

Rain. The rain is ice-cold, the smell of gun-powder is burning in my nostrils. My fingers hurt, my father is screaming into the dark like a wild animal. Like a wild animal gone mad.

The details flood in. A white glare, stark, and still.

My body remembers.

I remembered.

ELLA, 1994

Now it is completely quiet downstairs.

Mom has stopped screaming. The only thing I can hear is the television. Some music, someone singing. It sounds creepy, all those happy voices in the dark. Like a bunch of wicked trolls dancing and laughing in the living room. Gran knows all about trolls, and if they like to live in Iceland, then maybe they also like living here. I'll sit quietly and wait for something to happen. Wait for Mom to call me, like she always does, tell me it's just a game. That I don't understand, that I'm dreaming. But I don't usually dream with my eyes open, sitting on the steps. Nothing is happening. Where is she? Why doesn't she come back?

I sneak barefoot down the stairs to take a look. There are marks on the wooden floors, and on the carpet in front of the sofa. It's blood, it's sticky under my feet. I try not to step in the puddle, but it's so dark, and there's so much of it. The door to the kitchen and the one out to the hallway are open, the door in the hall keeps banging against the wall in the wind.

I see a glimpse of a shape disappearing down the path that splits down to the sea and Gran's house. *Mom!* Somebody has hurt Mom. It was Dad. He had a strange look on his face when he put her in the bathtub. His eyes looked weird. He was so angry, he kept yelling at her. I touch my throbbing face. My eyebrow hurts.

But I like Dad. He's nice to me. He's not usually like that.

Once Mom read me a story, *Ol' Yeller*, it was called. Ol' Yeller is a dog, he is kind and friendly—actually, he's really a very nice dog—but then one day, he gets bitten by a bear, and the bear gives him a sickness called rabies. People said Ol' Yeller would bite, if he got any sicker. So they put Ol' Yeller down, so he couldn't bite anyone anymore.

Maybe Dad also got sick like that.

I stand by the door for a long time. I can't decide what to wear. The rain is ice-cold against my face. I don't like going out when it's dark, but I don't like being home on my own, either. And Mom is out there in the storm. What if something happens to her, something that I can't fix again?

I stick my feet into my galoshes. It looks really dumb. Bare legs stuck into a pair of galoshes, my pink nightdress on top. Not the thing to wear in this weather. But I could zip my winter jacket over it. Yes, that ought to work. I step outside, carefully close the door behind me.

It is very, very dark, but I can see my galoshes, I can see my hands. And the tiles in the driveway. Dad's red car is standing in the drive. But nobody is in the car. I feel like I'm going to cry, I hate being alone, all on my own.

I bite into my cheek. I'm not going to cry. Once I start bawling, I won't be able to stop, I just know it. And if I'm bawling my head off, I'll scare whatever is out there away, it will hear me coming a mile off.

I go to the car. It's ice-cold and sopping wet. I open the door and crawl onto the back seat. I lean over the seat and reach into the trunk of the car, a black pit, but it's still there, the gun. I saw it when I got back from Thomas's place. It was zipped up in its bag, as always, but for some reason, Dad has forgotten to lock it into the big metal cupboard in the garage, as he usually does. I pull the gun-bag up onto the backseat and open it. The gun is heavy. It smells of iron and gunpowder, the barrel is all sticky with oil. I helped Dad oil the gun myself a couple of days ago. There's a little box of cartridges in the bag as well.

I kick the car door wide open with one leg, then the light goes on. So I can see what I'm doing. It's hard to cock the barrel, there's a knob you have to push down, hard, at the same time; you have to fold the gun AND squeeze it under your arm. It hurts a little, but the rest is easy. You put the cartridges in the barrel and click everything into place, just like Dad showed me. I get out of the car and close the door behind me. With the door shut it's absolutely black again, I'm a little scared now, but I feel better with the gun. A gun is not a stick or a knife or a stone. A little person with a gun can beat a big person with no gun.

I can take care of Mom.

I run down to the dunes; my bare knees are wet and so cold. The gun is banging against my shins. I fall down twice, I'm already so tired, and it's hard to run in the sand when it's so wet. But I keep going. I'm a big girl. Dad said so. I keep running. Looking out for Mom's white nightdress, listening for her voice. Trying to be quiet, creeping through the dunes like a little brown toad. My throat is thick and it's hard to breathe. The rain keeps getting in my eyes, I have to stop all the time and wipe them dry and my fingers are frozen stiff.

The light from Gran's house is coming closer. I must be going the right way. And then I see her. *Mom.* She's on her way up the dune just in front of me, her white nightdress shining pale in the dark, I'm so close now, I can see her blonde hair, and her shoulders. I try to run faster, but my legs don't want to run anymore. She hasn't seen me yet, but now I'm almost at the top of the dune, she's standing there at the bottom, looking at something in front of her. It looks like she's crying, but I can't hear anything in the wind. But then there is something.

It's a man, he's screaming like a wild animal.

"Ill kill you."

I hear the words quite clearly, I'm sure of it, even though the wind is howling. This is the dangerous part. I have to be really careful now. I sit on my knees and pull the lever back slowly. Now I'm ready to shoot.

I get up and start to run, the gun pointed at the bad guys just ahead. It's hard to keep the gun up, it's hard to keep running, even harder than it was before, but I'm a big girl.

And then I fall.

My fingers are stuck in the gun. It hurts when I try to pull them out. It sounds like an explosion, like a fat roll of thunder in my ears.

"ELLA!"

I was standing in front of the splintered pew with the rifle lying at my feet. There was a lot of blood and commotion on the bench and it took me a while to distinguish one body from another. Barbara's body was rocking back and forth over Alex's, and Thomas, who had jumped over a row of pews from behind, was holding Barbara under her arms, trying to lift her out of the pew without dragging Alex along with them. It looked like an awkward rendition of a dance macabre, everyone's clothes dotted in bright red blood. Especially Barbara was covered in the stuff. She had pearls splattered on her face and hair as if she'd been caught in a blood shower, and when Thomas finally did manage to pull her off Alex, there was almost as much blood on him. His face was bathed in red and black drops.

Barbara was grunting like a wounded animal, lashing out at Thomas, but at least her body was untangled from Alex's. His head lay dangling over the edge of the front pew.

"You take him, Ella! Get him onto the floor!" Thomas was yelling at me from his awkward position straddling the flailing Barbara on the floor. Fine droplets of blood sprayed over them every time she managed to fight an arm or a leg free. The kitchen knife stuck straight out of her left hand like a grotesque, modern body sculpture. Man and machine.

I bent over Alex, put an arm around his shoulders, and half-lifted, half-dragged him out of the narrow pew. Only a month ago, I had lifted his sprawling, living body into the air in the park in Hvidovre, but now it was limp and impossibly heavy. I battled to get him into a horizontal position.

My mind was blank, but for the first time in my life, I prayed to powers greater than myself—perhaps even to God, I couldn't tell to whom or to what. I just mouthed the solemn words soundlessly as I bent over my son. I prayed to be given a chance. Just *one* more chance to make it up to him. But it was not just Alex. I prayed for a chance to do justice to that little girl who—till now—I had deserted in the dunes by the sea.

Alex wasn't moving, but when I bent over his face I could feel his warm breath against my cheek, and the skin under his T-shirt was smooth, unbroken. I noted with relief that there was nothing amiss on his neck and head either. The blood was not his.

"THE BLOOD IS Barbara's, Ella," called Thomas, throwing his mobile phone over to me. "You'd better call an ambulance."

Afterward I sat with Alex's head in my lap, exactly as Barbara had done before, hoping that he would open his eyes and look at me. The two fingers I had broken that night were throbbing painfully. I could still feel the weight of the trigger, the finely polished wood of the rifle against my cheek. My body remembered it better than I had. It had been with me all along.

Alex moved under my hands. Shifted a little in his sleep and moaned softly. I realized that I had also been injured. The shot had hit neither Alex nor Barbara. I had inadvertently turned the barrel off to the side, and shot directly into the back of the pew instead, exploding splinters of wood in all directions. Two large splinters had bored themselves into my forearm and I had a number of cuts on my neck and face, where my skin stung and burned, making me feel alive in a way I had never experienced before.

The world was new and fresh, pronounced in brilliant color.

A little group had gathered around us. First Aid officers who had piled out of the ambulances were now pulling Alex out of my arms, lifting him onto a stretcher. Two police officers had picked up the rifle and a doctor in a neon yellow coat and rubber gloves was bandaging Barbara's hand. The knife was still stuck in her hand as she was rolled to a waiting ambulance. I registered this much, but apart from that, the scene didn't interest me very much. In fact, I couldn't have cared less about Barbara or what would happen to her. She did not belong to this bright new world of mine.

My father didn't murder my mother. He took the blame . . . for me.

I guess that's when curiosity begins to fade. When you have found what you were looking for.

The damp heat hit us like a wall as we walked through the battered sliding doors. The sun shone through a grey veil of clouds and a strong wind shook the palm trees that lined the cracked asphalt desert in front of the airport.

Alex took my hand and smiled. He had been very quiet on the trip over. At Frankfurt Airport he had eaten his fries in silence. He simply fiddled with my phone and read a few chapters of his first Stephen King book in English. *The Green Mile*. He had insisted on reading only English books ever since we got the plane tickets in the mail, and Rosa had bought him the novel before seeing us off at Copenhagen Airport.

She was still limping around with a metal screw in her hip after her altercation with Barbara outside Pub48. But she was sober. There was a grandchild on the way, as she said, and this time she wasn't going to fuck it up! Of course there was no guarantee that she wouldn't fall off the wagon again. By definition, alcoholics had shaky credentials, whether they were sober or not. But I believed in her—it was the least I could do after everything she had done for me. Before saying goodbye, she kissed Alex on the forehead, urging him to send her a picture of himself in his school uniform. The new school was American, and the uniform had already been ordered on the Internet. It was blue and white with a red tie to match.

"Are there any apes over here?" Alex squinted into the sky, his eyes following a flock of colorful birds across the grey skies.

"Sure there are," I said. "Otherwise we'll just have to make do with you."

"What about snakes?"

"Yep. And scorpions and lizards."

A couple of cab drivers called to me from their cars, fat Buddhas dangling from their rear-view mirrors, their windows rolled down, but I waved them off with a smile that I suspected was just as wide as Alex's. It was new to me, this abundance of joy. The sweat was already pouring off me, despite the fact that I'd changed into a T-shirt and sandals in the airport toilets in Bangkok. The warmth bubbled up from within. I didn't know what was in store for us, and my father was still a stranger to me.

I peered over the parking lot where the cars were sweltering in the heat. I wasn't sure I would recognize him.

But when I finally did catch sight of him, I was as sure as I could be. The years had worn him thin, and his beard was grey, but I recognized the slightly stooped posture of his walk, and when he came closer, his smile. I let go of the handle of my suitcase.

"There you are." My father stood at a safe distance. Embarrassed. "I've been looking forward to seeing you."

"Thank you. Did you recognize us?"

"Your grandmother wrote me. She said that you look like your mother. She's right. Remind me to call her tonight and tell her you've arrived safely."

"She was upset about the house."

"Not as much as you would think," he said. "In fact, I think it suits her quite well to quit this world without leaving any traces behind her. Fire and ash. Just like you, Ella."

I followed him with my eyes as he walked around the car with our suitcases and threw them into the trunk. We had spoken on the phone a couple of times, and he had told me the story—as he knew it. Together, we were able to tie the many strands of the tale into a coherent succession of events. All these years, he had thought that Barbara had given birth to a child. Their son. Even after all the masks had been peeled away, he still couldn't say how much of their relationship had been based on lies. She had never been pregnant.

"Traveling light?" he quipped in English.

He sent me a cautious smile. My father filled much less space than I remembered, and yet his actual and factual incarnation was overwhelming.

"And what about you, Alex? Are you ready?"

He clapped my son playfully on the shoulder and pointed at the waving palms on the other side of the barbed wire fence bordering the airport.

"Ready for what?"

"For everything."

My father laughed, and Alex lowered his gaze, smiling a smile that never left his face. Not once. Not when we climbed into the air-conditioned backseat, not once on our drive through the city's orchestra of honking horns and yelling street vendors.

"How long are you guys staying for?" My father eyed me in the rear view mirror. Just like he used to do when I was little.

I shrugged. I was watching the world go by beyond the toned car windows. Everywhere you could see small, cave-like shops; a chemist, snack-bars, bicycle shops, mechanics, T-shirts, and electronics. Wiring and advertisements strung haphazardly from the ramshackle façades.

"As long as it takes," I said, not knowing whether any further explanation was required. As long as it takes to make peace. It would have to be done here. Not so much by talking other than the fact of just being together.

By slogging our way through the days ahead, morning coffees and washing days, school-boy assignments at the kitchen table and hard work on frying-hot building sites below a merciless tropical sun in the afternoons. You grow to love the people you spend your time and energy on. And I would learn to love my father again.

He nodded. "And your friend? Is he coming to fix the kitchen sinks and toilets for me?"

I closed my eyes, saw Thomas before me, the look in his eyes when we said goodbye. Intense. It was hard to tell where we stood, Thomas and I. We had kissed and held hands, but I didn't know what that meant, if anything—apparently he didn't know either. Neither one of us had had much experience with serious relationships. We hadn't had the time.

"Yes, he's coming," I said. "He just needs to sort a few things out. Clear up. Sell the house. Get through the next check-up at the hospital."

"That's good to hear." He was drumming his fingers on the wheel. He glanced at Alex and me in the rear view mirror every time he had to break for pedestrians and mopeds and carts loaded with coconuts.

"We'll be there in fifteen minutes," he said. "It's a nice house. I live well. Plenty of blue sky. I missed that all those years . . . "

He dried the sweat off his forehead with the back of his hand, then suddenly pulled the car over. A couple of scooters hooted madly behind us, swerved wildly as he opened the car door and quietly asked us to get out of the car again.

We stood across from one another in silence, and this time, we gave each a little more time. I think he was crying, but perhaps it was just me. Details dissolve in memory. When you recall a scene, it could almost invariably have happened in any number of places. On a main road, a dark alley, in front of a store selling tires, a kiosk with a man-size stack of pink water containers. What you remember is the feeling, and all I remember is that I couldn't figure out if I should take a step towards him, or just stay standing where I was. I was so terribly afraid of him once.

He solved my dilemma by reaching out and crushing me on his chest. I remembered his smell, and I think this is what finally shattered something caught in my ribs. A final shudder leaving my body. It didn't hurt letting go of my anger. For so long, I thought I would die if I did.

But it opened the world.